Terry Marsh was born in a Lancashire coal mining town, into a family of several generations of coal miners and apart from two years in North Wales has lived all his life in the county. He worked for 30 years in local government before becoming a writer of travel and walking guidebooks. He holds a Master of Arts degree in Lake District Studies and a PhD in Historical Geography, both from the University of Lancaster.

Terry Marsh lives with his wife, Vivienne, in the market town of Chorley.

To my wife, Vivienne, for her constant support, encouragement and love.

Terry Marsh

THE GIRL IN THE PICTURE

A Genealogical Mystery

AUSTIN MACAULEY PUBLISHERS™

LONDON ∗ CAMBRIDGE ∗ NEW YORK ∗ SHARJAH

A CIP catalogue record for this title is available from the British Library.

ISBN 9781528993005 (Paperback)
ISBN 9781528993012 (ePub e-book)

www.austinmacauley.com

First Published (2021)
Austin Macauley Publishers Ltd
25 Canada Square
Canary Wharf
London
E14 5LQ

I have been helped in my research by several people, without whom I would have struggled to plug gaps in events: Stephen Knott of the Wigan Archive Service based in Leigh produced very helpful information and Geoff Parry, whom I met during my research for the book, was a serendipitous encounter of some significance, probably more than he may realise, albeit not quite as described in the story. Ron Cosens gave helpful advice on photographers operating in the area around 1870.

Information about Brindleford, a poor disguise for the ancient village of Brindle, is drawn from the website of the Brindle Historical Society, to whom I once gave a lecture on the "Guides to Morecambe Bay Sands".

Chronologically, I have tended to remain true to real events, although I changed the date of birth for Mary Ellen's first illegitimate child by a few months to better fit my storyline. And I've brought forward by twenty years the appearance of the kaftan worn by Lord Cavendish. The kaftan is believed to have been introduced to the west in the 1890s when Alix of Hesse wore the traditional Russian kaftan during her coronation.

For continuous encouragement, I have to thank my wife, Vivienne, who waited anxiously for me to finish the story so she could read it. I was also encouraged greatly by my fifth cousin, historical novelist Lizzie Jones, who gave me the benefit of her thoughts on my story and corrected several errors. Any that remain are entirely of my own making.

Author's Notes

The central historical character, Mary Ellen, is real. She was born on Christmas Eve 1855 and died, aged 83, in the spring of 1939. The cause of death was senile dementia. For the purposes of the storyline, I moved her birth date to October.

Mary Ellen lived all her life in and around Ashton-in-Makerfield and Billinge in Lancashire. She is my great-great-grandmother on my father's maternal side. She is buried in St Aidan's graveyard, Billinge, along with her husband, their son, James, and her illegitimate son, my great-grandfather. Like Alice, I did go with my father to visit the grave and returned many years later, unable to find it until persistence paid off, and a kind verger pointed me in the right direction.

Mary Ellen had several other siblings, all of whom are mentioned in the book, along with a second illegitimate child, Alice. She had five children by Joseph Cunliffe, who appears in the story as one of the footmen at Garston Hall, although in real life, by the time he married Mary Ellen, he was a coal miner.

The photograph of Mary Ellen and her son is real. I have it on my desk; it came to me, as it came to Alice in the story, from my father's possessions on his death.

Mary Ellen's elder sister, Jane, was a real person, my third great aunt, born in 1847. At the time of the story, in 1870, she would be 23 years of age. I have taken liberties with her dates and whereabouts. In 1862, aged just 15, in real life, she gave birth to an illegitimate child, William. Jane, in fact, at the age of 21, married Thomas Eden Mousdell in 1868 (two years before this story begins) and started a dynasty of eight children from which one of their descendants moved to live in America, where they settled and raised several families of distant relatives to the fictional Alice…and the real me.

All the events that happen to Mary Ellen and her family are entirely the product of my imagination, and nothing is intended to impugn the honour and integrity of a woman I could never have known; she died before I was born. I did, however, know her son, my great-grandfather, the illegitimate son, who died when I was fifteen and was a regular visitor to the house in which I was born and lived. There is no other record of the lives these people lived, so, much is invention on my part. All other storyline characters are fictitious and any similarity to real persons living or dead is unintentional.

Garston Hall is very, very loosely based on Garswood Hall, Ashton-in-Makerfield, the seat of the Gerrard family for many generations. I consulted census records to gain an indication of the extent of the household, especially the servants. But it is only the geographical context that is rooted in fact, and even that is distorted. All the characters living at the hall or on the estate are entirely the product of my imagination, as are descriptions of the interior of the hall. But if anyone wants to read more about the real hall, then *Garswood New Hall* by David A Fearnley is the place to look.

There is a copy in the Museum of Wigan Life (Ref: 942.736):

The "illness" experienced by the fictitious Clarissa is real. Depersonalisation Disorder is the experience of feeling unreal, detached, and often, unable to feel emotion. It is a phenomenon characterised by a disruption in self-awareness and emotional numbness, where many people feel that they are disconnected or estranged from one's self. Many people experience depersonalisation during a panic attack, and this is often characterised as the peak level of anxiety. It is one way that the mind copes during periods of high levels of stress. For some people the condition can feel as though the world around them is like a movie that they are watching rather than specifically being a part of it. (https://www.anxietyuk.org.uk/anxiety-type/depersonalisation).

All the locations used are real, although some are poorly disguised. The dates of any events I mention are correct, e.g. the freeing of the moors, which took place on the Darwen Moors as stated more than forty years before a similar but more widely publicised event in the Peak District. Lancashire folk play down this landmark event in opening up the countryside for recreational purposes; unlike the Peak District, the beautiful county of Lancashire doesn't have to work so hard to attract visitors!!!

Although I have generally used standardised speech for everyone, I've allowed Mary Ellen to drop her "h's" and to lapse into local dialect from time to time to add colour to her character. In fact, she speaks much as I did as a child. In reality, everyone would have spoken with distinctive local accents that if used phonetically would impede the flow of the story. So, I have used standard English. How distinct some of local dialects are in Lancashire was brought home to me several years ago when someone I met in Australia, but from my hometown, pinned me down very specifically to the very part of St Helens, then in Lancashire, where I was born and raised.

In the story, I have credited the young Mary Ellen with the ability to read and write. When she registered the birth of John in September 1873, this was not the case; she signed the certificate with her mark. Eight years later, when she married Joseph Cunliffe, she appears to have signed the marriage certificate, and while Joseph signs with his mark, Mary Ellen does not. That Mary Ellen could read and write was not uncommon for the time. Literacy increased significantly during the 17th century when grammar schools were established. The census records show that Mary Ellen and her siblings were "scholars". There is today a primary school in Garswood and a high school, formerly a grammar school, in Ashton-in-Makerfield, founded in 1588 as Ashton Grammar School by Robert Byrchall on land donated by wealthy local land-owner William Gerrard. The original building in Seneley Green is now Garswood Library.

The lives of the ordinary people of Lancashire are not well documented. The only time any of them become worthy of note are at births, deaths, and marriages or when they got in trouble with the authorities. But it would not have been out of place for Mary Ellen to have kept a diary. Social commentaries as they pertain to working people are few and far between, even for the Victorian period, but anyone interested in reading more on the subject will find *The Diary of Roger Lowe of Ashton-in-Makerfield* of particular interest. Written by an enterprising young man, the manager of a small shop in Ashton, it reflects a much earlier period than that of my story line, but is fascinating, nonetheless.[1]

---

[1] *Details of the diary and the means to download a copy can be seen at* *https://catalog.hathitrust.org/Record/000112672*

It is difficult to get a valid description of the hierarchical status of a gamekeeper on a Lancashire estate, but I have taken the line that he would have been a valued and respected member of the community, both that of the estate and of the surrounding villages. For this reason, I have inferred that he might have been treated a little more favourably, in terms of the standard of his living accommodation, than the ordinary working people of the time.[2].

Equally difficult to portray with satisfaction is the nature of the clothing Mary Ellen and her family might have worn. Poor families had a few everyday outfits and a "Sunday Best" worn when going to church and on special occasions. Many outfits would have been bought second-hand and passed down through the family, mended and patched for as long as possible. Clothing had to be practical – there were no "Fashion Statements" for Victorian working-class people. You had to be able to work in clothing made from wool or cotton, invariably in dark colours. Women wore caps or bonnets not just to keep hair tidy, but to be seen as respectable. I have portrayed Mary Ellen's family, rightly or wrongly, as a little above the poorest working-class folk, based on her father's employment, although her brothers were all coal miners. Their mother, Alice, was a capable dressmaker, able to make the sort of dress I depict Mary Ellen wearing a dress, although the working classes invariably wore skirts and blouses, over which they had a shapeless woollen coat.

---

[2] *I have no real evidence for this, and for reference have drawn on* Life in a Victorian gamekeepers Cottage *by historian H J Brown.*
http://www.hjbrownhistorian.co.uk/Life%20asvicGK.html

Chapter 1

Friday, 7 January 1870

Mary Ellen stood naked in front of the mirror, frustration mounting as she struggled to pull a hairbrush through her thick auburn hair, already grown long enough to conceal her pubescent breasts.

Just three months past her fifteenth birthday, she was preparing to go to Garston Hall – where her father held the position of estate gamekeeper – hoping to be taken into employment as a housemaid. Such an opportunity was rare, and in spite of her tender years, she knew she was fortunate just to be considered, there being so little work for young girls and many candidates for what did become available. So many of her age came from hard, impoverished and often cruel backgrounds in which they found themselves by circumstance and neglect. For a blessed few, domestic service, tiring routines and limited freedom aside, was a better life than the cold, hunger and poverty facing many of Mary Ellen's contemporaries. Thanks to her mother's careful ways and her father's employment, their combined frugality, and the far from lucrative, but no less welcome irregular earnings of her sister, family life in the Liptrot household, while never free of worry, was nonetheless a better experience than that endured by many friends of her childhood years.

Mary Ellen's earnings as a housemaid would make life less challenging, less unremittingly hand-to-mouth. For her, life in the aristocratic world of Garston Hall would be a major step up in the world. There was just the small matter of the interview with the housekeeper, Mrs Bonnivale, to survive first. She was the one Mary Ellen had to impress.

'Bugger!' she swore aloud, rubbing a hole in the steamed-up mirror, pulling wayward strands of hair from her face and mouth, regretting swearing the moment the word passed her lips.

'Mary Ellen!' a strident voice scolded from the adjacent room. 'Language. Please.'

Mary Ellen sighed heavily. 'It's my bloody hair,' she continued, too pre-occupied to take in the admonition. 'It's flitting all over the place.'

She leaned forward to the mirror and pulled her cheeks downwards, emphasising her hazel eyes and a dark mole high on her cheek bone. 'And my face is a mess.'

'It's the one God gave you.'

'Well, 'e must have used up all the decent ones by the time 'e got round to me. I'll be lucky to get a job mucking out stables, never mind 'ousemaid. Even then, chances are I'd fritten th'orses. An' who'd to want to see this mush in the parlour, gawking at 'em?'

'You won't be seen by anyone,' her older sister Jane's soothing voice insisted as she entered the veranda-cum-washroom built onto the rear of the house in which a low fire was already heating the washtub, bringing welcome warmth to the room. 'Well, not anyone important. You're supposed to do your jobs then vanish, like magic, without any of the household seeing you. That's why they have back stairs. So the lords and ladies' sensibilities are not offended by the sight of servants.'

'So we don't see what they get up to, more like.'

'You may be right, but that's the way of it, and it's not your place to question it. You'll be a "Maid of the Back Passage".' Jane giggled softly at the innuendo and playfully patted her sister's bottom.

'Sounds disgusting if you ask me,' Mary Ellen whined, gathering the tresses of her wayward hair and tucking them behind her ears to cascade down her back. Arms raised she took her time securing her hair neatly with a slender black ribbon.

With reason no more justified than adolescent angst, Mary Ellen disliked her appearance. She was, in fact, shapely and slender and into blossoming womanhood since the middle of the previous year, yet in her mind she was neither child nor woman, and that irked her. In her teenage impatience she saw herself perpetually waiting to metamorphose from the ugly duckling of Hans Christian Anderson's fairy tale her sister had read to her, into the serene and beautiful swan she longed to be.

I'm going to be an ugly duck. Forever.

Coming to a decision, Mary Ellen massaged her cheeks vigorously, bringing colour to them, then casually ran her hands over her breasts and stomach down to her pubic growth.

'This will have to do,' she grumbled irritably, glaring at herself in the mirror, and turned to leave and pulling a clean shift from the washing line.

Playfully, Jane gave Mary Ellen's bare bottom a slap again as she passed. 'Get some clothes on. Henry's still upstairs. You wouldn't want him to see you like that.'

Mary Ellen placed an arm across her breasts and a hand over her public growth and giggled but knew that Henry had already seen her naked. Often, in fact, having spied on her as she undressed for bed, or, more usually, as she took a bath in the metal tub that stood against the washroom wall when not in use. Nor, in one of the impish moments for which she had become renowned, was she beyond intentionally affording titillating glimpses of her body to the far-from-covert Henry. And it would be only a matter of time before her youngest brother, George, shared in the voyeurism.

Neither was she beyond turning the tables, having several times watched Henry from her bedroom window, masturbating in the garden shed. Indifferently she supposed, it's just the way of male adolescence. Boys being boys.

Stupid tossers the lot of 'em.

And, anyway,' Jane continued pleasantly as they returned to their shared bedroom, 'there's nowt wrong with you, Mary Ellen. You're just fine.'

'I don't want to be just *fine*! I want to be…special…beautiful…' She twirled around suddenly and threw her arms into the air, '…*wonderful*.'

Jane helped her, smiling to herself, as she pulled the shift over her head, and tied the laces at the neck. 'Just wait. Twelve months from now, you'll have them queuing up for your hand in marriage. You'll have the pick o' the crop. Mark my words. Sod it, you're only just fifteen. You've still some growing up to do. And it starts with getting a job.'

'I know, and I want to 'elp,' she protested with a sigh, trying not to succumb to cheerlessness. Life for the family had taken a downturn when their mother, Alice, employed as a washerwoman by the estate three days a week had died a year earlier from consumption, leaving Mary Ellen and Jane to raise themselves and two young brothers. Their mother, a kind and gentle soul given for the most part to quiet and sometimes firm Christian persuasion rather than harsh discipline, was someone who had made all of them feel safe and loved, and nurtured them into what they were, imbued in them a sense of legitimacy and fashioned for them a warm and loving home. Thankfully, their elder brothers, Thomas and Edward, had left the family home, found employment in the Garston coal mines and wives and homes of their own nearby. To make matters worse, it was only a matter of time before her father, now sixty-eight years old, must retire. He probably should have retired already, and when that did finally happen the family would have to quit the tied cottage and find someplace else to live.

The immediate future would be a worrying time for all of them.

Mary Ellen adored her older sister, as envious of her looks as she was oblivious to her own. Jane had developed a perfect figure, a natural beauty with light brown hair and deep brown eyes, and never seemed to need to fiddle constantly with her hair or do anything to enhance her complexion. And yet she was still unmarried, at an age when several of her friends had long since married and had children. Often it seemed to Mary Ellen that Jane had no desire to have a husband or a home of her own. From her rosy-eyed viewpoint, Mary Ellen had long hoped that her sister would find an honest, hardworking man and settle down. She deserved greater happiness and security than she presently had, and a man to care for her in the way she had helped their mother to care for the family over the years, and then their ailing mother herself.

What Mary Ellen could not know was that her sister had a secret, a dark and sad secret.

Jane helped Mary Ellen into a simple, handed-down calico blouse and woollen skirt she'd worn herself at Mary Ellen's age, and gave her shoes a quick rub on the hem of her skirt. As Mary Ellen pulled a dark woollen coat around her shoulders, her sister handed her a neat, brimmed felt hat.

'Are you ready?' she asked gently, placing a comforting hand on her sister's shoulder, catching her eyes and smiling encouragement. 'It's time to go.'

Mary Ellen didn't need a chaperone, but on such an important occasion Jane wasn't going to let her wander across the vast Garston estate and through the dank woodlands on her own on this of all days. She knew that wandering the woodlands was something Mary Ellen had done many times over the years since, unnoticed by anyone, as a baby not yet able to walk, she had crawled out of the safety of their home and across the lane and into the park. So, today, in a gesture of sisterly solidarity she would accompany her to the hall and wait until she was ready to leave.

Jane doted on her sister, a lovable and incorrigible paradox: a young woman forever diverted by the power of mysterious and sudden enthusiasms, switching in an instant from childish wonder to a maturity beyond her age; the innocence of youth melded with the wisdom of age. Growing up far too rapidly, yet in some respects not grown up at all. In truth Jane marvelled at her sister's boundless resilience and determination, but was less enthralled by her often quarrelsome nature, thankfully these days confined to a fundamentally friendly love-hate relationship with the boys of the Welsh family that lived at neighbouring Torpen Lodge.

Mary Ellen was remarkably at odds with her years. She had learned to read, write and, as, she described it, "do sums", at an early age, initially at one of the few state board schools in Lancashire, and, since she reached the age of ten, at another rarity in this part of the country, a voluntary parish school. In spite of her evident eagerness to learn, a quality that made her unique among the children of the neighbourhood, she had never found enthusiasm for school disciplines, which she suffered with ill grace. Since leaving school at fourteen and turning her hand to helping her sister with household routines, she had developed a restless appetite to be somewhere else, doing something else, in which quest she was invariably disappointed. Their mother more than once had joked that Mary Ellen charged about so restlessly, she would one day meet herself coming back from somewhere she hadn't been to yet.

Not surprisingly, Jane had cause to wonder how she might fare when tasked with the strictures of domestic service.

Chapter 2
1870

The family lived in a lodge, Penny Hall, at the boundary of Garston Estate, an ancient medieval holding that had belonged to the Garston family in direct male succession from the time of Edward the Confessor. The estate was one of four great manors that came together only two years earlier to form the municipal borough of Saint Helen. Coal mining and glassmaking had long been the most affluent economic activities in the former townships and manors, along with cotton and linen industry. But gone were the unprofitable sailmakers, the lime and alkali pits and copper smelting.

The Garston Estate was a thousand acres and more of rich agricultural land, a deer park, opencast coal mines and dense woodland dells, all managed by an army of work and tradespeople from blacksmiths, ostlers, foresters and wheelwrights to in-house domestic employees whose ranks Mary Ellen hoped soon to join.

Access, for those of rank and privilege, was past an ancient and ornate lodge its Tuscan columns and straight-headed broad windows with round arched lights, a curious combination of French Revolution and Tudor thinking at variance with the design of the hall itself, a substantial and rambling building more than one hundred years old, and one of the first classical buildings to be built as the ideals of Italian architect Andreas Palladio became more widespread across England during the eighteenth century.

Beyond the woodland, on the periphery of the estate, Penny Hall Lodge, a markedly different standard from the main estate entrance, was sufficiently distant, almost four miles, from Garston Hall to require Mary Ellen to live in servants' quarters at the hall. And so, a light dusting of snow on the ground and a keen wind whistling through the trees, whipping up tendrils of freezing crystals that stung their cheeks, Jane and Mary Ellen set off to take the path that led into the estate, through the woodland and, near the hall, around a large walled garden and potager.

'Bloody hell,' Mary Ellen exclaimed, pulling her coat collar tighter around her neck. 'Brass monkey weather.'

Jane giggled at Mary Ellen's capacity to invent bizarre metaphors and moved to put her arm around her shoulder, pulling their bodies closer together. Silently for the moment, they walked on into the woodland, their shoes crunching as they crossed the virgin snow though it lay less thickly within the confines of the trees. From time to time, the smell of woodsmoke drifted through the branches emanating, Jane knew, from clearing the estate's charcoal burners used at the heart of the woodland.

'Bloody wind,' Mary Ellen snapped, pulling tangles of hair from her face. 'I'll look like I've been dragged back'ards through an 'edge when I get there.'

'Stopping bothering so much,' Jane said impatiently, tucking strands of her own hair into her bonnet. 'You're going for a housemaid's job not a stage actress. And a second housemaid's job at that.'

Her remarks carried irritation she hadn't intended, and Jane regretted the sharpness of her tone the moment she had spoken. Mary Ellen felt her cheeks rouge in uneasy embarrassment. 'I just want to look my best. I need this job. We all do.'

'I'm sorry, Mary Ellen,' Jane apologised, giving her a sisterly hug and a peck on the cheek. 'That came out all wrong. You look great. You'll get the job, no bother, lassie.'

Mary Ellen smiled and wished her sister's confidence would flow through her veins, too.

'Did you remember to put your drawers on?'

'They're not interviewing my arse,' she quipped, 'so they won't be interested in my drawers.' With a smile on her face she sighed theatrically, '*Yes*, I'm wearing them.'

'Well, that makes a change. You're a bugger for not wearing 'em. You'll catch a chill in this weather.'

Silently, the two walked on, heads bowed against the cold, their breath forming clouds in front of their faces. The only sounds a gentle soughing of the wind punctuated by the staccato crack of a falling branch from somewhere deep among the trees. Wordlessly they emerged from the woodland like rabbits tentatively appearing from a burrow and scanned the way ahead. They gasped as the bitter wind from which they'd been sheltered caught their breath, carrying with it flurries of icy snow and adding to the chill the sisters already felt.

Through the gloom Mary Ellen's gaze fell on the imposing façade and walls of the slowly approaching Garston Hall, and, feeling her teeth starting to chatter, she hoped for a warmer atmosphere inside.

At length, the two young women paused momentarily at the gates giving into the enclosed quadrangle to which the massive Palladian hall was central. Few gazed on the splendour of Garston Hall without a sense of awe. Mary Ellen's heart raced at the prospect that soon she could be working in that daunting place; more than that, living there, too. She said nothing, but in her mind the voice of doubt gnawed at her confidence.

This is not for you. You're just a silly little girl.

As instructed, they passed around the hall, veering away from the impressive front door, a grand entrance where snow had freshly settled on the broad stone steps.

One day, Mary Ellen thought on a whim of fantasy, ignoring her nagging doubts, *I want to walk in through those doors. Make my own grand entrance.*
And, I will.

Wordlessly, they made their way to a concealed side entrance, a humble, plain wooden door. With a brief enquiring glance at her sister, as if to ask if she was ready, Jane stepped forward and seized the Classical Lion-head brass door knocker, rapping twice, and stepped back, to wait.

A warm draught of fresh-bread-and-cinnamon-scented air washed across their faces as the door opened. In front of them, in the starchily pressed uniform of the housekeeper was the fubsy form – small, rounded, squat and bountifully bosomed – of Mrs Bonnivale, with whom the sisters were familiar from around the village. She beamed at them benevolently from a friendly, jovial face, her jet-black hair pulled severely back into a neat bun at the back of her head.

'Come in, girls,' she invited, stepping aside to allow them to pass.

Jane and Mary Ellen were instantly enveloped in the heated embrace of the bustling kitchen, replete with domestic servants of one station or another busily going about their duties in what seemed like a well-choreographed routine. The cook, who might have been a doppelgänger of Mrs Bonnivale, was heftily prodding the nearest of three kitchen maids with a rolling pin, while remonstrating with all three of them as they scuttled around the kitchen, a look of fearful dread in their eyes.

An involuntary smile lit up Mary Ellen's face as she faced her destiny. Here, in this grand hall, she decided, was where she belonged, where she wanted to be – an as yet small, *but important* (she thought), part of the managed domesticity of Garston Hall. As if welling from springs long dormant, her mind gushed with impossible plans that saw her rising from the certain drudgery of second housemaid to the position of housekeeper and, in time, intimate confidante of Lady Garston and ultimately, by a misplaced surfeit of ingenuity and artifice yet to be devised, to the wife of her only son in readiness for the time when he would inevitably inherit the hall, the estate and all the wealth and circumstance that went with it.

Oh, yes, the task would be arduous, demanding long hours with little time to herself. But she had never been afraid of hard work, and her efforts meanwhile would be rewarded with the handsome wage of twenty pounds per year, more than she could imagine, and, as she saw it, the beginning of a journey to great personal wealth and independence.

'Jane,' Mrs Bonnivale began, 'take your sister's coat and go and wait in the chair by the door.' Jane did as she was bid, and Mrs Bonnivale beckoned to Mary Ellen: 'Come with me, Miss Liptrot. Are you ready?'

Mary Ellen, savouring her new name – *Miss Liptrot* – followed Mrs Bonnivale. No one has ever called her *Miss* Liptrot before.

'I've never been more ready.'

Chapter 3
Thursday, 28 March 2018

On the edge of the Lancashire Pennine Moors, the White Crow Inn was a sometime coaching inn and cosy, country pub with a pedigree reaching backwards as far as the sixteenth century. A firm favourite, locals and others living farther afield came here for its cosy, welcoming atmosphere, regularly changing supply of real ales, and well-prepared pub grub.

Duncan Cooper had just finished one of the landlady's popular steak and ale pies with twice-cooked chips and Lancashire caviar – mushy peas to the uninitiated, they joked – and was nursing a Bundaberg ginger beer while chatting amiably to people at the next table. With a blast of cool air, NotonyourNellie walked in, a whirlwind of a woman, casting noise and jollity across the room in equal measure. She spotted Duncan instantly, huddled in the corner by the roaring log fire like a cowering dog, shying away from attention. She waggled her fingers at him in a sketchy wave.

It was the monthly get-together of the North West Geocachers, one of the few social events Duncan made the effort to attend since his wife died two years earlier. It took him out of the house; made him socialise in a way he knew he needed to, but rarely did. Geocaching, that GPS-based game of treasure hunting introduced in the USA in 2000, was something he and Isabel had done for years. Something they enjoyed, something that took them to places, many close to their home, they never knew existed. And it also let them indulge their passion for walking and birdwatching.

Geocachers use a pseudonym. His was DunanCo, not the most imaginative and, sadly, no longer appropriate. NotonyourNellie was the handle for Nellie Norton, another feeble play on words, but better than some – Low Flying Chicken Shed was overmuch to be writing in logbooks. But the owner, Jack Davies, someone Duncan had introduced into geocaching several years earlier, didn't seem to mind that what at the time had seemed suitable for a teenager, as he then was, was probably now juvenile in his late twenties. Jack was well on his way to finding 30,000 caches, compared to Duncan's 6,000.

Waving greetings and launching long-range air kisses to others in the crowded, oak-beamed room as she passed, Nellie worked her way to where Duncan was sitting and settled in beside him.

'Eh, up, chuck,' she leaned over and gave him a peck on the cheek, 'budge up,' As she sat beside him, Duncan saw that Nellie was not alone. Another woman sat down. Nellie introduced her: 'This is Alice, found her wandering on the moors like a lost soul the other day trying to find a cache buried in heather. So, I offered to bring her along tonight. She's a newbie. An event virgin.'

She was petite. Her pleasant, rounded face glowed in the warm atmosphere after coming in from the bitter chill that had settled for the past few days. Her slim and shapely figure was noticeable as she removed a windproof jacket to reveal an open-necked T-shirt, ladies' waistcoat and faded blue jeans. Hazel-green eyes, sparkling brightly with bewilderment and delight at encountering so many new faces, were set beneath the fringe of curvy shoulder length deep red hair that fell around her face, softening her features and emphasising high cheekbones further nuanced by deft traces of makeup. Her nose was fine and pointed, above shapely lips and a philtrum free from the etched lines of a heavy smoker. Some men home in on breasts, others on bottoms. With Duncan it was the medial cleft. He would have no explanation had anyone asked about his fixation; it was…weird, at best.

For her part she saw an uncertain man probably in his early sixties, broad and sturdy shouldered with a cleanshaven, agreeable-if-not-conventionally-handsome face and an emergent double chin mirrored in the modest dome of an incipient paunch. His hair was fair and may have been strawberry blonde in his youth, cropped around the ears and full at the back, not quite reaching his collar. He was wearing a dark blue Weird Fish shirt and beige padded gilet. His complexion was pale, as if he needed to be outdoors more. He wore gold-rimmed bifocal spectacles that drew attention to his piercingly blue eyes with a steady gaze that held Alice's attention, radiating, at odds with his evident desire to stay out of the limelight, a self-assurance and poise in equal measure that seemed to conflict with his Pic'n'Mix approach to dress sense.

Duncan smiled and said hello. Welcome. 'Can I get you both a drink?' he offered, getting up and easing past the newcomer. As he passed Alice, he picked up the scent of something pleasant, not perfume as such, a more enveloping quality, scented soap, perhaps. Lavender, maybe. A clean, outdoorsy fragrance.

'Just a Chardonnay for me, Duncan, please,' Nellie prompted.

He turned to Alice, who smiled uncertainly and said, 'That's kind of you. I'll have the same.' Duncan shimmied through the crowd to the bar, nodding and smiling greetings to newcomers, Nellie's 'Make 'em large, Dunky' in his wake.

She turned to Alice and quipped: 'Got to keep 'em house trained.'

Alice smiled openly, not sure what to say, but happy, for now, to let the evening run its course. But the equable familiarity between her companion and the man had not escaped her notice.

When Duncan returned, Nellie saw that he'd bought another ginger beer. 'What is it with you and this cat's piss?' she asked, pointing at the bottle.

'I'm driving that's all. Don't drink and drive these days. Just not worth the trouble.'

Alice looked at him meaningfully: 'You mean you used to? Drink and drive?'

'Sadly, yes,' he confessed, wondering if he'd detected a note of disapproval in her voice. 'When I was much younger and infinitely more stupid.'

Nellie picked up his bottle and read the label. 'Bundaberg. What's special about that?'

'Nothing that I can think of. Other ginger beers are available,' he said dramatically, mimicking a familiar television quip, 'but this one caught my eye. It rang a distant bell.'

Alice smiled at him, and asked, 'What kind of bell?'

'When I started work, back in prehistoric times, I worked for the council. One day a letter arrived at the office from a schoolgirl in Australia asking to be put in touch with anyone who wanted to be a penfriend. It was in the days when people still wrote letters; some sort of outreach project they were doing at school. For some reason, the boss gave it to me to answer, which I did. It turned out she lived in Bundaberg, on the east coast, close to Brisbane. Well, close by Australian standards, about 250 miles north. So, when I saw Bundaberg ginger beer, I bought it on impulse. Nothing more deep-rooted than that. They don't even make ginger beer in Bundaberg. Apparently, it's famous for producing rum. Lots of it. I Googled it.'

'Did you get in touch with the girl?' Alice asked pleasantly.

'Yes, I wrote back, and we exchanged letters a couple of times or so. Then she stopped responding. Maybe a junior clerk in a Town Clerk's office just wasn't intriguing enough to maintain her interest. I suppose she would have written to more than just one council and was probably inundated with replies; mine being among the least interesting, I shouldn't think.'

Nellie chuckled softly. 'Blimey, mate, you might have taken off and lived down under, caching with the roos, and we'd never have met you. How sad would that have been?'

'Oh, I'm sure you'd have found someone else to keep you in Chardonnay,' he said, smiling. 'How is Jim, anyway?'

'A pain in the proverbial, as ever. He doesn't understand geocaching. Just looks at me with exquisite disdain on his face and shakes his head whenever I tell him I'm going out caching. I've given up trying to get him interested. But, to be fair, he did drive us both here, and he'll come when I call him to take us back, bless him.'

Duncan turned to Alice: 'So, what's your caching name?'

'Just my name: Alice Marsh. Not very imaginative when you see some of them. Actually, it's my maiden name. My married name is Brewster.'

Nellie butted in: 'So, is your husband a lost cause, too?'

Alice laughed lightly. 'You could say. He's long gone from my life. Divorced years ago. I don't know why I never reverted to my maiden name. But it still wouldn't produce a better geocaching name.'

'You can change it if you want. Conceal your identity. Most of this lot...' Duncan jerked a thumb at the still filling room, 'are known only by their aliases. It's taken me ages to get to know them. Figuring out who they really are is a feat of memory, I can tell you. And I fail. Dismally.'

Alice sipped her wine. 'Oh, I'm not very imaginative. I wouldn't know what to change it to.'

'Use an anagram,' Nellie suggested and pointed across the room. 'That man in the green jacket over there is Herr Smarty. You can work that out, if you like. But it's an anagram of his name.' She took a mouthful of wine and chewed it thoughtfully before swallowing. 'Mind you, he's regretting it now.'

'How so?' asks Alice.

'Well, he's a writer of sorts, walking and travel guides. That sort of thing. Quite successful apparently, in a small-town way. Never be a millionaire. But I don't think he's bothered. He's one of the most contented little souls you can find. Got a lovely wife. But he went on to write a guidebook about geocaching,

25

and now he feels that being called Herr Smarty makes him sound like an arrogant prat.'

'And is he?'

'No, not at all. He's just a regular guy. Just a bit away-with-the-fairies, like the rest of us.'

'Well,' Alice continued, 'it would take me an age to figure out an anagram of my name that wouldn't be too embarrassing.'

'Far from it,' interjected Duncan helpfully, taking out his mobile phone. 'There's a program that does it for you.' He punched a few keys. 'Here it is.' He typed in Alice's name, and ran the program. 'There you are,' turning the phone towards Alice to see a long list of complex re-arrangements of her name. 'Mind you, most are stupid.'

Alice laughed out loud and held her hand to her mouth. 'I'll have to think about that.'

Duncan handed Alice his phone. 'Put your number in there, and I'll send you the program link.'

Momentarily Alice looked concerned and glanced at Nellie, who picked up on her thoughts.

'Don't worry. I can vouch for him. Any of this lot, too. We're all family. A slightly dysfunctional, random, often incoherent, usually boozy, moderately silly family, but family, nonetheless. And Duncan's no stalker, although he could stalk me anytime he felt the urge.' They all laughed. 'Mind you, I'd have to slow down a bit to let him catch up.'

Alice took the proffered phone and entered her details. Handing it back she asked, 'What would you change your name to, if you wanted something else?'

'Had you asked me that a couple of months ago, I'm not sure I'd have an answer. But I was in Lisbon, in Portugal, recently and found a restaurant with an intriguing name that looks odd when you see it written down.' He fished in his pocket for a notebook, and wrote down "JNCQuoi", turning the book around so they both can see.

Nellie said, 'Jernk-oi?'

Alice smiled widely. 'I get it. It's a play on a French expression. *Je ne sais quoi*. I don't know what. Clever.'

Nellie leant back against the seat, appraising Alice. 'Speak French, do you?'

'Well, passable French,' she admitted, but then added with a smile, 'If you pass quickly, and don't take too much notice. I used to have a French boyfriend,' she explained, 'so I spent a lot of time in France.'

'Me, too,' added Duncan. 'Not a boyfriend, I mean. Love the place, went every year with my wife…but…' he paused, gripped for an instant in sudden and tragic recall, then changed tack… '…as I get older, I'm not so keen on the long drive south to the ferry ports, plus whatever comes afterwards driving across France.'

Nellie sensed the change of tack in what her friend had said. She tilted her head in a sideways nod towards Duncan and said to Alice, 'He won't tell you himself. But his wife died a few years ago. The big "C". We all know. We're all a bit protective of our Dunky.'

Alice said, 'I'm sorry to hear that.'

Duncan sighed heavily. 'Mostly, these days, I've come to terms with what happened. It's just when something triggers a recollection, I get a bit maudlin.'

Alice apologised, but Duncan raised his hands in a gesture of appeasement. 'There's no need to apologise. You weren't to know. And, anyway, it helps in a perverse kind of way for it to be out in the open. Everyone can say how sorry they are, and we can then move on.'

He realised, however, that for the past two or more years he hadn't moved on, not significantly, anyway. Nor yet felt the willingness needed to…what? …compartmentalise the tragedy? …write it off as one a life's sick jokes? …forget about it? That was never going to happen; could never happen. But it was a brutal truth that he either moved on or remained forever at the mercy of gloom and self-pity.

'And that's where you should be,' Nellie threw in. 'Out in the open a bit more often. Get some vitamin D. I've seen pasta with a better complexion. You spend far too much time barking up bloody stupid family trees in front of that computer of yours.'

Alice looked puzzled.

'Duncan's one of those genie-wotsits. Does family history and coats of arms and stuff.'

'Genealogist,' responded Alice brightly, her interest aroused.

'I'm hardly that,' added Duncan. 'It took me an age to get started. I didn't get many well-paid assignments, and I undercharged for most of those given the amount of work that was involved. Things are better now, but I doubt I'll ever be rich.'

'It sounds fascinating,' Alice said. 'But isn't it all a lot of dead ends and brick walls? There's someone at work who's doing their family tree. She's always moaning about not being able to find records. It must be frustrating.'

'It can be. Most of the time it's tedious methodical work, following promising leads only to find them spurious, and trying to make sense of half-remembered snippets of someone's family history. I did a degree in genealogy and heraldic studies, but I reckon I scraped through by the skin of my teeth.'

'Is that what you do now? As a job, I mean,' asked Alice.

'I suppose so. I took early retirement and had a lump sum that let me pay off the mortgage. And I can manage on my pension. Plus I'll get the state pension before too long.'

'If they don't move it further away,' Nellie added gloomily and drinking her wine, thinking about her own pension prospects.

'Well, there is that. But I get by. And I'm not sure I want anything more than I have. You can get bogged down chasing money you don't need.' He sipped his ginger beer. 'What about you, Alice?' he asked pleasantly. 'What do you do?' He smiled at her, 'You're obviously far too young to be of pensionable age.'

'I'm a librarian. Local history librarian, actually. With Chorley Council. And closer to a pension than you might imagine.'

Before Duncan could question her further, another geocacher sauntered to their table, one half of Dum'n'Dummer, and excused the interruption, amiably slapping Duncan on the back. 'Duncan, you'll know this. What's Archimedes Principle?'

'Archimedes Principle?'

'Yeah, there's a cache on the moors we're trying to figure out how to get to. There's a pond, an island and a boat involved. I won't bore you with the details, but someone thought that Archimedes might be relevant. I said they should wait for a dry spell and just walk out, but you know what they're like.'

It was genial of them to ask; it was a way of ensuring Duncan knew that he had family, of sorts. There was, after all, good Wi-Fi at the White Crow, and they could just as easily have googled it in seconds. Duncan thought for a moment, then intoned what he could remember of it. 'Or something like that. Does that help?'

'Well, not me,' he admitted, 'but then I'm "Dum", aren't I? Or am I "Dummer"? I can never remember, and I just can't get my head round puzzles. Don't have the patience. But thanks, anyway.' And with that, reciting aloud what Duncan had said so not to forget it, he returned to the huddle on the other side of the room.

Alice turned towards him, 'That was impressive. I'm sure I couldn't have told them.'

Duncan smiled, but before he could respond, Nellie butted in. 'Hides his light under a bushel, does our Duncan. He's got degrees in history and geography, but you'd never know it from just talking to him.'

'Well, that's a bit of an exaggeration,' replied Duncan. 'I suppose you could say that I know a bit about a lot of things, and a lot about nothing. I just remember things.'

'Eidetic memory?' Alice suggested.

'Not really. That's more to do with having a photographic memory, I think. I just remember things, although less so, as I'm getting older.' He turned to Nellie with a puzzled look on his face and said jokingly, 'Who are you? Do I know you? Are you stalking me?'

She laughed and nudged him in the ribs with her elbow. 'I'm your guardian angel.'

'More like a fairy godmother,' Duncan jibed. 'I'd love to see you with a Christmas tree stuck up your…'

'Duncan!'

'I was going to say nether regions.'

They all laughed, and Duncan stood up. 'Another round?'

'Let me get these,' Alice offered, getting up and walking with him to the bar. As they threaded their way through the animated excitement of geocachers, Alice was aware of several pairs of eyes appraising her and her evident association with Duncan. *What are they thinking?* she wondered. *And why?*

As they stood side by side at the bar, she noticed that Duncan was head-and-shoulders and more taller than her barely five feet three inches frame. To her surprise she felt at ease standing there with him, a sensation of comfort she had not known for years. He was, after all, a virtual stranger. Yet he made her feel…what exactly? Protected? Maybe. Comfortable? Well, unthreatened, certainly…as if she'd known him for a long time. And that took her pleasantly by surprise.

While they waited to be served, she asked: 'I've never been here before. Why is it called the *white* crow? I didn't know there were white crows.'

'Well, I didn't know myself until a few months ago,' Duncan admitted. 'Then one of this lot put out a circular series of caches based around the pub. They researched the name, so far as anyone can. It seems it should have been called the White Cross. Apparently, a white cross is part of the coat of arms of the local gentry. But an eighteenth-century sign writer, a little the worse for too much ale it seems, mistakenly wrote the name as "White Crow", and the name stuck ever since. I think it's unique. I did a bit of research myself but couldn't find another White Crow anywhere.'

'It's a lovely pub,' Alice said admiring the large Inglenook fireplace, oak beams, part-panelled walls, the ubiquitous wall-mounted stag's heads, a barn owl in a glass case, a fox head with a lop-sided snarl, and the large arched doorway.'

'Yes, it is. The original inn is sixteenth century, and that arched doorway must have been built to accommodate stagecoaches, or mail coaches. But I'm not sure there were any stagecoach routes through this part of Lancashire in the sixteenth century. So, maybe it's just a sixteenth century inn that later became a coaching inn, and then a hotel. There's certainly been bits added on to it over the years to make it into a much larger building. And I remember seeing a picture somewhere of the building described as the White Crow *Hotel*.'

Alice said, 'I read something the other day by chance. It was about a film that's being made about Rudolf Nureyev and his defection. It's going to be called *The White Crow*, apparently.'

Duncan smiled at her. 'That would make interesting viewing.' Alice nodded her agreement, 'I'd like to see that when it comes out.'

As they walked back to the table, Nellie detected the pleasant frisson between the two. They were certainly chatty and seemed comfortable together. *Maybe our Dunky has finally met his match*, she thought. But then dismissed the thought as readily as it sprang up; wishful thinking for her, on the part of her friend.

Back at their table, Alice asked Nellie if she knew anything about the place.

'Only rumour about highwaymen and ghosts. I've not heard anything else. I don't know of anyone who's seen a ghost, and the only highwaymen round here are the traffic wardens in the town centre.'

As they chatted and joined forces to become a team for the ritual quiz, which they lost dismally, Duncan found his attention increasingly focused on the newcomer, and felt flustered when she caught him staring at her. But, he thought, it's just the fascination of someone new in the group and dwelt no further on it. It was one of the oddities of these gatherings that you can instantly be drawn into social conversation with a stranger, sometimes revealing more than you might otherwise. No qualms; no prejudices on display; no hidden agenda. Just easygoing superficiality.

Chapter 4

Later that evening, as he poured himself a generous Highland Park malt whisky to settle the ginger beer sloshing around his stomach, his thoughts returned to Alice Brewster née Marsh, aka "Alimar" as, by the end of the evening, she had become.

To his mild consternation, what stirred him most was that he realised his thoughts were persistent and not disagreeable. Yet they unsettled him. He tried to shrug them off, persuading himself that the chances of meeting Alice again were minimal, even though he knew he could take matters into his own hands.

If he had the courage.

So, quite what it was that prompted him to send her a text message, he couldn't say.

Lovely to meet u this evening. Hope to see u next time.
Duncan xxx

The "kisses" were a default setting. A conclusion he added to text messages to female acquaintances without thinking. He'd pressed "Send" before realising what he'd done. At least now, he reflected, they both have each other's number.

Back at her cottage, Alice, wrapped in a dressing gown and sipping a camomile tea, received the text with a mixture of surprise and, if she was being honest, pleasure, too. Do people normally send text messages after such a brief encounter? And add digital kisses? Short and to the point. No subtext to read into it, apart from the expression of his hope there would be a next time.

It wasn't an altogether unpalatable prospect, she thought. Something had happened between them that evening, of that she was certain; there was no denying it. But she wasn't in the market for the emotional attrition that went with relationships that didn't work.

She'd had enough of that.

If this was to go further, it would have to be slowly.

Chapter 5

Sunday, 9 January 1870

Two days after her interview at Garston Hall, Mary Ellen put in a rare appearance for Evensong with Jane and her brothers at St Aidan's church in Billinge, which was still brightly decorated for the festive period. Tomorrow, she would return to Garston Hall as second housemaid.

In the event, the interview with the jovial Mrs Bonnivale, seemingly still in festive spirit amid the extravagantly decorated hall, was a formality. No doubt the fact of her father having been long and reliably employed by the estate helped in no small measure. Having confirmed and been agreeably surprised by the fact that Mary Ellen could read *and* write, Mrs Bonnivale had handed her a sheet of paper on which was set out the duties she was to perform and the routine to be followed.

'These are your duties and responsibilities, your daily routine. It seems a lot, but you'll soon get used to it, I'm sure. You will have to live in the servants' quarters, but you'll be free from duties from lunch on Sunday until Monday morning. But if you mean to stay over at home with your sister on Sunday evening, you must let me know; otherwise you could find yourself locked out.' She paused to let that sink in. 'You may also be given additional days off at my discretion, but that...' and here she regarded Mary Ellen sternly, '...will be entirely dependent on good behaviour and attention to your duties.' She looked directly at Mary Ellen, 'Do I make myself clear?'

'Yes, Mrs Bonnivale,' Mary Ellen replied, taking the proffered sheet of paper.

On reading it later she realised that domestic service at Garston Hall was going to be a far more taxing experience than she could possibly have imagined.

SECOND HOUSEMAID
DUTIES AND RESPONSIBILITIES

6.30am: Rise

Clean grate and lay fire in Dining Room, Sweep carpet and dust.

Clean grate and lay fire in Library. Sweep and dust.

Clean grate and lay first in Billiard Room. Sweep and dust.

Polish staircase.

Clean grate and lay fire in Drawing Room. Polish floor.

Clean grate and lay fire in Morning Room.

Sweep and dust vestibule.

Sweep and dust blue staircase.

8am: Breakfast in Servants' Hall.

9am: Start bedrooms. Help First housemaid with bedmaking and slops and fill ewers and carafes.

Clean grate and lay fires. Fill up coal boxes and wood baskets.

Sweep and dust bedrooms.

Clean bathrooms.

Change into afternoon uniform.

1pm: Lunch in Servants' Hall.

Afternoons, clean silver, brass, water cans, trim lamps, needlework.

4pm: Tea in Servants' Hall.

5pm: Light fires in bedrooms.

6pm: Cans of hot water to bedrooms.

7.30pm: Turn down beds, make up fires and empty slops. Fill up coal and wood containers.

Leave morning trays set in housemaid's pantry.

In the unflattering light of reality, Mary Ellen's illusions started to evaporate like morning dew under a rising sun. But she knew that if she failed, she would not only be failing herself, but failing Jane, and, more to the point, her father who as gamekeeper held a key position with the estate and relied on that employment to secure a roof over the family's heads. Her failure would reflect badly on her father, a situation made all the more uncertain by his impending retirement, and the need to find elsewhere to live…unless, against all probability, his lordship allowed them to remain at the lodge. That, she knew, was unlikely. Penny Hall

Lodge was tied to the position of gamekeeper. Matters had not been improved when Mrs Bonnivale had imparted the news that much of her first few months' salary would be taken up paying for her uniform, and Mary Ellen rued the fact that had she been more of a Godly person, the parish might have subsidised that particular cost.

With the burden of misgiving resting on her shoulders Mary Ellen walked with Jane back to their home, a watery sun trying to pierce a layer of low cloud did nothing to lighten her mood.

'I'll never manage this,' she complained, waving the sheet of paper at her. 'Look at it; it goes on forever. And what's *slops*?'

'Piss pots,' Jane explained. 'Only sometimes there's more than just piss in them. Good luck with that, sister, dear. You'll just have to grin and bear it,' adding unconvincingly, 'I'm sure it won't be too bad.' And then, adopting a more placatory tone and putting her arm round her shoulder, said, 'I know it seems difficult, but remember that if you spend too much time worrying about what might be, you risk losing what is. You're young and you're going to live and work in one of the grandest mansions in the county. In the whole country, probably. Be proud of that. You should live for now; for what is, not what waits in the future. Get started, get stuck in. See how it goes. I'm sure you'll be fine. I'm proud of you, and I'm sure Father will be, too. It won't be forever.'

Mary Ellen was less persuaded and dispiritedly now saw her pathway through life strewn with the dead leaves of childhood's aspirations. For Jane it was sad to see her sister's optimism drain away, but she vowed to raise her spirits again before she needed to return to Garston Hall.

Chapter 6

Having started Sunday with renewed hopes and a restored sense of impending adventure, bolstered by Jane's comforting reassurance, and having exhorted God to bless the Garston household to which she was bound, Mary Ellen went to bed in a less fretful frame of mind.

In the morning, hours before sunrise, she awoke to a cold room with ice on the insides of the windows and felt unhappily weighed down by a renewed sense of foreboding. The fire, well fuelled the night before, was long since dead, a grey relic of ash and partially burned wood. She swung her legs over the side of the bed and wrapped a blanket around her as she parted the curtains. By the light of a gibbous moon she saw that more snow had fallen, lying heavily on the garden yews. Even for the walk to Garston Hall she would have to wrap up warm, but having been told to be there by six-thirty she needed to pack what she required for living in.

She gazed at a wraithlike self, reflected as a blur in the frosted window, and shivered as she turned to see Jane still buried under a mound of blankets.

Bugger. Time to grow up, Mary Ellen. You've got a good job; just make everyone proud.

Bracing herself against the cold, Mary Ellen scurried into the bathroom to use the toilet and splash water on her face. Trying not to disturb her sister, she started to dress, adding more layers of clothing until she finally stopped shivering. Stepping carefully to avoid floorboards she knew would creak, she began packing a small, battered carpetbag, wishing she'd thought to do so the night before. With one last glance at her sleeping sister, she made her way out of the bedroom and into the cold embrace of the downstairs rooms. Leaving what little bread and cheese remained in the larder for her siblings, Mary Ellen pulled back the bolts on the front door as quietly as she could, confident that a hot and warming breakfast awaited her at Garston Hall.

It seemed impenetrably dark outside. The snow had stopped, but black clouds hung low, turning the dull monochrome world even darker. Sound seemed to have gone, too, absorbed into the blanket of whiteness, leaving a brooding silence. Feeling more gloom than optimism, Mary Ellen set off towards the track that led across the Great Meadow and on towards Crow Orchard Plantation, her footprints the only blemish on the pristine landscape. In summer the hedge-rowed lane was heady with the scent of pineapple mayweed crushed underfoot, honeysuckle and blackthorn, the berries of which they habitually gathered and turned into a fake port wine or a tart sloe chutney, which Jane sold at the market in nearby Ashton.

Today, the way was bleak.

Through a hole rubbed in the ice on the inside of the bedroom window, Jane watched her sister go, hair flowing wildly in her wake. Silently she wished her well, and just as mutely she feared for her. She would pray for her, even though, if she was being honest, she no longer embraced the power of prayer. Nor, she reflected less than piously but with a measure of confidence, was Mary Ellen ever one to find herself seeking Divine intervention. Her self-sufficient young sister was made of stern stuff, a proverbial rough diamond.

She'd come good.

When, finally, Mary Ellen was lost from view, consumed by the snow-laden beeches and birches of the woodland, Jane returned to the rapidly cooling warmth of her bed, making the most of the time before she had to rise to prepare breakfast for the boys.

Chapter 7

Another month went by before Duncan and Alice met again; a month in which Duncan had necessarily pitched himself into research among wills and probates for a new client. When assignments came in, he had to deal with them promptly and efficiently.

In spite of that, if he'd said he'd given Alice no thought at all since their first meeting he would have been lying. She had wormed her way into his consciousness at the most improbable moments: in the restless, small hours when his mind ached from a day of research, but his body refused to sleep; as he was preparing a meal, or as he vacantly trawled supermarket aisles half in the hope that meals would throw themselves onto his trolley.

When he did call her to mind, or when she entered it uninvited, he realised that he had only the one image of her to reflect upon, that of her on the night she'd come to the White Crow. Without particularly knowing why, he realised that he wanted a *second* image of her, *any* other vision of her, to sit alongside the first. Maybe yet more, so that when he tried to *see* her, he had a mental camera roll of pictures to choose from. As much as memories and things shared, it was this tapestry of images that fashioned recollections and thoughts, especially of loved ones with whom life was shared. Duncan was as prone to it as the next person. What he didn't openly acknowledge was that what he *wanted* was to see Alice again. To his surprise, he came to realise that he was unwittingly fashioning a blueprint for his life to come. His thoughts, he found were not abstract, but of a future shared. And even more surprised at the persistence of those thoughts, when they slipped into his head.

As before it was the North West Geocachers who were the catalyst in re-uniting them, when someone organised an event to commemorate a significant moment in gaining access to the Lancashire moors.

During the nineteenth century, a great saga took place over oppressed common rights of access onto the moors. It was a long-drawn-out process during which several protagonists were sent to prison in the manner adopted by other agitators who did likewise in the Peak District forty years later. With success in their grasp, on one memorable day in 1896, the leaders of the protest organised a great demonstration to celebrate the ultimate freeing of the moors; it was an event today's geocachers wanted to commemorate, as close to the original date as possible consistent with encouraging a good attendance. It was to take the form of a walk to the great tower central to the moors, not far from which Pennine Way pioneer, Tom Stephenson, had been born. The outdoor gene was ingrained in the blood of folk from this part of the county.

Everyone gathered in the Barn House car park and set off on a circuitous trail that led round a couple of reservoirs and then up steeply to the top of the moor, known as Toppat Hill, a minor summit that had acquired its name when a government surveyor in days gone by had asked a farmer what the prominent hill was called. 'Why its top o' t' 'ill,' he'd replied, the local dialect getting the better of the surveyor who had journeyed from Southampton to compile a list of geographical features in readiness for the impending building of triangulation pillars. And so, Toppat Hill it became.

Alice spotted Duncan immediately and made her way to him, for a moment wondering whether a light peck on cheek in the manner of the French *bisou sur la joue* was too familiar, too soon, although many of her erstwhile friends in Liverpool would have thought nothing of it. She decided it was, and simply said, 'Nice to see you again. Lovely day for a walk,' hunching her shoulders and clasping mittened hands in front of her against a chilling breeze.

She was sporting a knitted bobble hat in kaleidoscopic colours, and a padded jacket over pale walking trousers that had clearly seen better days. A pair of Merrells Gore-Tex boots clad her feet, and a battered rucksack hung from her shoulder.

'It's lovely to see you again,' he said, realising how much he meant it. 'Is Nellie here?'

'I don't think she's coming today. She's not logged an intention to attend.'

'That's a shame; she's always good for a laugh. Just don't expect to see any wildlife if Nellie's in the group. She's not the quietest of folk when you get her going.'

'Maybe, but from what I hear, she's got a heart of gold.'

That morning, Alice had risen to the sight of long-tailed tits and a male bullfinch on the feeder in her cottage garden. She lived in the hamlet of White

Coppice – which boasted its own cotton mill at the start of the Industrial Revolution – owned by a fearsome supporter of the Temperance Movement, a fact that explained why the hamlet had never had its own pub. But in spite of its small size and arguably the smallest cricket field in the county still regularly in use, White Coppice could boast being the birthplace both of the sugar merchant and philanthropist, Sir William Tate, founder of the Tate Gallery in London, and Walter Haworth, who in 1883 won a Nobel Prize for chemistry.

Alice had bought her tiny retreat after her husband decided to "seek pastures anew", as he grandiosely and unfeelingly put it, without much in the way of explanation. Over the final years of her marriage, Alice had come to suspect someone else was part of the equation. Three into two never would go, and the split, when it came, had been laden more with relief than immediate concern about her future.

For the past five years, life had revolved around her work as a senior librarian, one Saturday a week working in a charity shop, and her loves of reading, music and walking. She had been emphatically and speedily positive in coming to terms with her husband's departure and realised that for some time it had been a mutually loveless relationship that had borne no children – not that either partner had wanted any – and suffered ever-decreasing companionship as her husband's interests kept him away from their home in a Liverpool suburb. In exchange for Alice not petitioning for maintenance payments, he had given her his share in their Liverpool home, which she later sold for a hefty profit, sufficient to pay off the mortgage and buy outright her nineteenth-century white-walled cottage. Since then, while money had never been tight, it wasn't overly relaxed either. So, when Alice applied successfully for a librarianship in the nearby market town of Chorley, her salary and her few savings were all she had to live on.

But Alice was completely at ease with herself and had taken to living alone with ease and a sense of relieved happiness, not until then fully realising what a burden her married life had been.

For a moment, as they walked, Duncan was thrown back to his teenage years when, on his bicycle, a Gresham Flyer bought for thirty-five guineas from his earnings delivering newspapers, he had cycled from his home across the urban heartlands of industrial Lancashire out to the moors where, he was told, he would find a ruined castle where knights on great, armour-clad white horses once lived, and a tangled garden of mysteries and magic where elfin princesses drifted among the trees. It would have been a journey of twenty miles or so, and yet he had no recollection of the route he'd taken, or even whether he did so on his own or with others. In those days, he recalled, it had been possible to cycle all the way across moorland tracks to the rocket-like Victorian tower that stood starkly above the urban valleys. Now it was a protected area, owned by United Utilities who provided water to the surrounding towns and villages. Then as now, the cerulean sky was filled with the fleecy furniture of clouds that once he could have named – cumulonimbus, cirrostratus, cumulus congestus, but which were now simply "clouds".

By the time the walk was completed, both Alice and Duncan had relaxed into a comfortable. easy-going bonhomie. It was that which prompted Alice to suggest a drink at the nearby Farmers' Arms. There was something, she said enigmatically, she wanted to show him; something on which he may be able to shed light.

Settled in a corner in the pub, Alice opened her rucksack and produced an old photograph. She flipped it over, and Duncan read: Great-grandmother and son. Taken in 1873.

'That's my father's handwriting,' Alice said. 'But I know nothing about who she is, or who the child is. I've wondered, of course, but I'm not very adept with computers and so I've never managed to do any research. If truth be known, I wouldn't know where to start. So, I wondered if you could find anything out about them. If you don't mind, that is.'

Duncan studied the picture. Not a well-produced print, he noticed, showing signs of having been developed incorrectly, as if the chemicals used to develop it had been applied unevenly.

'I'd be disappointed if I couldn't discover something.'

The edges of the photograph were flared and stained, and it was evident that light had seeped onto the film during processing. But the central part of the picture was clear and sharp. It showed a woman wearing a dark, broad-skirted dress with long sleeves, drawn close at the neck but revealing a white chemise fastened with a dark ribbon. Her full skirt embroidered with ribbons of black lace, lay draped across the chair on which she was posing. The fabric seemed soft and flowing and dark in colour, decorated with light-coloured ribbons at the waist and hem. She was wearing a hat garlanded by a wide ribbon running around the hat and hanging over her right ear; on top there was what appeared to be a feather. Draped around her neck was a substantial fine chain hanging as low as her bosom. Another fine chain circles her neck on which there appeared to be a silver locket.

In this patently posed image, she was not smiling, but she was an attractive woman in an understated way…a young woman, probably not yet in her twentieth year. She had a straight and narrow nose, slightly down-turned mouth, pale eyes and eyebrows that appeared to have been plucked. A dark mole, that many would describe as a beauty spot, was prominent on her upper cheek. Her right hand was concealed, but her left hand, holding the child, had slender fingers and manicured nails. She was not wearing a wedding ring.

The unsmiling child on her knee was broodily looking downward and wore a white hat and bib over a hooped dress decorated at the hem with three bands of differently hued trims.

In all, it was a picture of elegance and refinement, seemingly that of a serene woman of substance and a young child.

He placed the photograph on the table.

What did it tell him? Simply that here was a young woman to outward appearances of some wealth, with a child of maybe twelve to eighteen months of age. She appeared to be unmarried, in an era when a stigma would have attached to such a condition, but without a name to the photograph, it wasn't possible to know whether the girl was from the paternal or maternal branch of the family.

'I'm happy to pay you,' Alice cut into his thoughts. 'I wouldn't want you wasting your time on tracing my family tree.'

Duncan smiled at her. 'There's no question of payment. I'm happy to do this for you. It should be straightforward family tree research, depending on how deeply you want to go.'

'I just want to find out who the girl in the picture is. How we're related. If she's my father's great-grandmother, then she must be my great-great-grandmother. Yet I have no idea who she is. And if she had brothers and sisters, then I would have other great-great-grandparents.'

Duncan looked again at the picture. 'I'm sure I can find something, but first I need a starting point. Just basic information about you and your family as far as you know it. That would be the best place to begin.'

With that, he opened his own rucksack and produced a notebook and pen. 'Since the note says that it's your *father's* great-grandmother, what I need to do is go back up his paternal and maternal trees and out along the branches to find a child born around 1873. That should then give us the mother.'

Alice regarded him for a moment, pondering. Then came to a decision. 'Look,' she said firmly, 'if you're not going to let me pay you, at least let me cook you dinner.'

Duncan smiled, and leant back against the chair. 'That sounds delightful. When do you have in mind?'

'What are you doing this evening? I'm okay with that if you are.'

'Well, er, yes, if you're sure. That would be lovely. Where do you live?'

She smiled again, it's a feature he was coming to like. 'I'll send you the coordinates. If you're handy with a GPS, you won't have any trouble finding me. Is seven, okay? And is there anything you don't eat? Mind you, it will only be whatever's in the fridge, catch-as-catch-can as my mother used to say, but I do a mean stir fry.'

'Sounds delicious. Seven is fine, and I eat just about anything, although I've never quite understood the fascination my grandfather had for tripe and pig's trotters.' He shuddered involuntarily. 'Yeuk.'

Alice laughed. 'You have my number in case you can't find me. Just call.'

Chapter 8
Monday, 10 January 1870

Arriving at the servants' entrance to Garston Hall, Mary Ellen was anticipating the warm and welcoming smile of Mrs Bonnivale. Instead, as she once more swept back her tangled hair, the studded wooden door yawned open and she found herself gazing at a young woman wearing the black and white uniform of a domestic servant.

'You must be Mary Ellen,' she said, a welcoming smile on her face. 'I'm Elizabeth, you can call me Beth. Mrs Bonnivale asked me to settle you in and show you what to do. Come in. I'll be helping you for the first week. But then…' pausing to give Mary Ellen a telling look, '…you'll be on your own.' Then, noticing Mary Ellen's frown of consternation, Elizabeth smiled, 'Don't worry; it's not that bad once you figure out everything.'

'Nice to meet you,' Mary Ellen managed, still shivering from the cold walk from the Lodge. 'When do we get breakfast? I'm freezing. My nips are bigger than bloody acorns.'

'We don't get anything until eight. Come on, I'll show you to your room. You'll be sharing with Martha, one of the kitchen maids. She's a bit dozy, and a bit clueless when it comes to personal hygiene but might make a good cook one day, if she ever gets rid of the butterflies in her brain…and washes more often.'

Sharing? A bedroom?

Mary Ellen was soon to be enveloped in dismay. Worse was to come.

Elizabeth led her along a narrow, green-walled passageway hung with copper pots and pans. Beckoning Mary Ellen to follow, she turned through a concealed doorway and set off up a flight of well-worn, bare-wood stairs that seemed never-ending, its length punctuated at intervals by small landings onto which doors opened. Only when she noticed a sloping ceiling above them did she realise they were in the attic, having vertically bypassed the entire main part of the hall.

'Most of the domestic staff sleep up here,' Elizabeth explained. 'Well, not Mrs Bonnivale, cook and Mr Grimes the butler, although we see very little of him, except at mealtimes; he's always with his lordship. He has rooms on the same floor as the family. Cook – Mrs Croft – has her own room near the kitchen, and Mrs Bonnivale you know about. The rest of us are up here in the rafters with the rats. The men's rooms are along the corridor,' she said, waving a hand in the direction of a narrow passageway. 'It's the wrong road round if you ask me.'

'What do you mean?' Mary Ellen wondered aloud but couldn't help noticing that Elizabeth suddenly seemed to tense, her shoulders rising into her neck, her face clouding over.

'Well, they have to pass *our* rooms to get to their own. And they're not beyond gawping round the door, trying to catch us undressed.'

'Are they all like that?'

Elizabeth didn't reply immediately, as if thoughts passed across her mind. 'No, not really,' she exhaled, softening her tone, retreating from whatever dark thoughts had occupied her mind. 'Some are okay. You'll soon figure out who's who. Just don't give any of 'em any encouragement. Give 'em an inch and they'll take a mile.' She laughed, as if willing to move on from the moment.

Opening a nearby door, Elizabeth waved her in, 'This one's yours. It's not bad. Could be worse. Some rooms are grim. But this is okay, not that you'll get to spend much time in 'ere, sleeping or awake.'

As Mary Ellen walked into the room she was taken agreeably by surprise. She'd been expecting something not much larger than a broom cupboard. Instead, while not large, she found a pleasant room with double windows and curtains in front of which stood a chest of drawers topped by a mirror on a pivoting stand, and a pair of candlesticks. A small washbasin sat on a tile-backed washstand beside a low towel rail. A red-hued, patterned carpet that had seen better days, covered most of the floor and supported two well-worn armchairs with cushions. Just one iron-framed bed was pushed up against the wall, and beside it a bedside table and a narrow wardrobe the doors of which she saw were hanging precariously by their hinges. The walls were unadorned save for a small wooden cross, and a framed embroidery sampler spelling out the Lord's Prayer. A patch of wall darker in colour showed where a picture had once hung. A tidy pile of clothing that she took to be her uniform sat on the bed.

Not what I had in mind, she thought less dolefully than she'd anticipated. *But I'll manage, as long as Martha doesn't snore.*

Elizabeth smiled sheepishly at her. 'I know it's not much. Mine isn't much better, but I do get the bed to myself.'

'It's better than I was expecting,' she said, 'but I wasn't expecting to 'ave to share a bed.'

'Yes, not ideal, but I think they're trying to get her a room downstairs, near the kitchen. It may not be for long.'

At least, Mary Ellen thought, *I get to sleep under the same roof as the Garstons. Not many could say that.*

'Shall I unpack?' she asked, starting to unbutton her coat.

'No time, I'm afraid,' Elizabeth replied apologetically. 'We need to be downstairs and ready for six-thirty. You've just got time to get your uniform on. Be sharp. I'll let you do that and come back in a few minutes.'

'There's no need to go,' Mary Ellen protested affably. 'I don't mind getting changed in front of you. It's not like I've anything different from you, although your tits are bigger than mine.'

Elizabeth laughed lightly; she was already getting to like this young girl who seemed more self-assured than her age suggested. 'Always keep your back to the door if you think there's someone outside. If they get off on ogling your arse, that's their problem.'

Already, Mary Ellen was certain she would get on with Elizabeth; she was confident and seemed wise to the ways of the world beyond Garston. Removing what clothes she'd arrived in, she changed quickly into an ankle-length, long-sleeved black dress of French twill with white collar and cuffs. Over this she fastened a lace-trimmed white bib apron, which she pinned to her bodice, topping the uniform off with a small white bonnet. She felt ridiculous, constrained by more buttons and heavy fabric than she thought possible. *How can I work in all this?* she thought, but soundlessly followed Elizabeth, leaving her day clothes in an untidy heap on the bed.

'Come on, we'll get into trouble if we're late.'

In spite of her youthful years, Mary Ellen was paradoxically mature in many ways; confident and resourceful, sometimes alarmingly so – helping to raise two young brothers had seen to that, that and waiting on an ageing father on the increasingly rare occasions that he came home rather than spending the night patrolling the woodlands and riverbank on watch for poachers. Yet she was in equal measure childishly naïve, and disappointed when Elizabeth took her once more through concealed doorways and down hidden stairs to the kitchen in the basement. Even though Jane had told her otherwise, Mary Ellen had mistakenly assumed she would be free to move freely around the house using the great central staircase, a magnificent construction carved by English craftsmen from intensely dark wood from the other side of the world.

How mistaken could she be?

And with that in mind, she began to wonder what else might be different from what she was coming to realise had been misplaced notions about life at Garston Hall.

Once more on the ground floor, as they passed along a dimly lit corridor leading to the kitchen, Elizabeth stopped outside a door bearing a plaque that read "Housekeeper". She knocked twice and waited. Moments later Mrs Bonnivale opened the door, appraising them both. 'Come in, girls. Welcome to Garston, Mary Ellen.'

They entered the sanctum of the housekeeper's sitting room, a private retreat at once cosy and functional. A cast iron fireplace stood at one end of the room, a mahogany grandfather clock beside it, ticking loudly in the heavy silence. Beside the fire, a comfy armchair covered in a cream-coloured floral fabric was festooned with plump cushions, and in front of it, a low footstool dressed in matching material. A small desk and chair stood at one wall, while a larger table, on which stood a vase of fresh flowers and a porcelain candlestick, took up the centre of the room. The opulence of the room took Mary Ellen by surprise. Framed artworks ranged across the walls and above the fireplace, the mantle itself supported large brass candlesticks and several small trinket boxes. Most surprisingly, much of the floor was covered by a rich and intricately designed carpet on the luxurious edge of which she now stood.

Hands clasped behind their backs, Elizabeth and Mary Ellen halted before the housekeeper, who reached out to tuck a strand of Mary Ellen's hair beneath her bonnet before circling around the pair assessing the neatness of their uniforms, like soldiers on parade.

'You'll do,' she said in a tone both officious and friendly. 'Now, off with you and, Elizabeth, be sure you teach Mary Ellen to be thorough. We want no shortcuts or shoddy workmanship here. Do we?'

'No, Mrs Bonnivale,' the girls intoned in unison.

'Now, shoo,' she said, wafting her hands in front of her.

As they left, Elizabeth said, 'She's good with us girls, but you wouldn't want to get across her.'

Five minutes later, they were in the dining room, a vast and sumptuous room to which a massive mahogany table was central, surrounded by plump, ornately carved chairs. Paintings of people with stern faces hung on the walls and heavy, embroidered curtains framed floor-to-ceiling windows that looked out onto a wide lake on which two white swans were patrolling. At each end of the room, stood large Robert Adam fireplaces, each adorned with floral tiles, chains of bellflowers, urns and pateraes and fronted by massive brass fire dogs, and here Elizabeth showed Mary Ellen the Garston way of removing the ashes without raising too much dust, cleaning the grate and setting the fire in readiness.

'The footmen bring up the wood and coals in a scuttle, and then come back when we're done to take away the ashes,' Elizabeth explained. 'We don't have to do that.'

Next, it was the turn of the ornaments and candlesticks, the furniture and dark-oak panelling, the top of which Elizabeth reached with a large feather duster on the end of a broom handle. Finally, taking care not to cause more dust in doing so, she swept the floors before looking back into the room to check that nothing had been overlooked.

'Do we get a break now?' Mary Ellen asked, more in hope than expectation. She was right.

'Now we move on and do the same in the other rooms, as quickly as we can, so we don't get in the way of the footmen. And all this has to be done before breakfast. Or you'll get no breakfast. Come on, get a move on.'

Chapter 9

Find her he did, and just a few minutes before seven parked his Volvo exactly on the spot where the GPS resolved to zero, right by a Chili Red Mini Cooper Classic hatchback. He was outside a small, white-walled and oak window-framed cottage with a modest garden protected by a cherry laurel hedge that seemed to run down to a stream. Even in the fast-fading light he could see a garden flowing with penstemon, hydrangea, phlox and stonecrop.

Not for a moment had he expected to find that Alice lived in one of the most sought-after locations in the county. White Coppice was a delight, a mock-Tudor hamlet that had experienced turmoil in the nineteenth century when the surrounding area was filled with the cacophony of mining and blasting from the rock quarries that provided the slab-stones with which many of the county's towns were paved.

As he approached the door, the shadow of a figure appeared behind a stained-glass panel depicting butterflies set in the doorway. Alice looked radiant, a welcoming smile on her lips, her eyes bright, reflecting the doorway light. She was sporting a black kitchen apron on which are printed the words "Bah humbug", worn over an attractive flower-print dress unbuttoned below the neck to reveal a silver locket.

'*Bienvenue*, welcome to my humble abode,' she said, holding the door ajar. 'You found me. Obviously! Come in. You're very punctual.'

'To be honest,' he confessed, 'I'm normally well ahead of time. I hate not being on time. Personally, I'd rather wait outside in the car for half an hour than be late. I think it's just plain bad manners. Unless you're French, of course, in which case seven generally means eight fifteen.'

'Yes, I learned that to my embarrassment a few years ago when I was invited to dinner by friends living in Toulouse. Turned up for seven, as requested, and the hosts were still in bed making babies, well, making a lot of noise, anyway.

To make matters worse, they'd left their bedroom window open, much to the amusement of the people enjoying a pastis on the café *terrasse* below.'

She ushered him into a neat living room, plush with baggy armchairs, a two-person sofa and a small coffee table on which stood a peace lily and a large Dell XPS laptop. Artful watercolours of country scenes formed an asymmetric pattern on sea green walls along with a small mirror and a framed print of what he recognised as an old map of the county. In an Art Deco fireplace with tiled inserts and oak surround a small fire burned, and an alcove beside it was filled floor to ceiling with books. The balancing alcove held a small flat-screen television, Sky Q box, DVD player and Technics stack of CD player, turntable and amplifier from which emanated the floating harmonies of Vaughan Williams' *Serenade to Music*, a piece he recognised but couldn't immediately identify. But he could see nothing of any DVDs, CDs, vinyl records, or speakers come to that. The whole effect was, what? Not tidy, but not untidy either; lived in, certainly, clearly reflecting eclectic tastes that ranged from the early twentieth century to present day.'

'This is very...' he began, then paused momentarily, searching for an opposite word.

'Homely?' Alice prompted. 'At least that's what it's supposed to be. My personal cocoon. My refuge from the daily terrors of the Reading Room,' she quipped. 'A place for everything, and everything in its place, but with the edges knocked off. I suppose these days they'd call it shabby chic, but that would imply that I'd designed it this way, when in fact it's more the result of mismanaged chaos.'

'Not *feng shui*, then?'

'If it is, it's wholly unintentional. I don't do balderdash.'

Duncan smiled at that and peered more closely at the wall-mounted map. 'Well, it looks neither shabby nor chaotic to me. It's a lovely room. Is that the John Speed map of Lancashire?' he asked, moving closer to inspect a framed print on the wall.

'Yes, it is. I got it in an online auction. Someone in Portugal had come by it and put it on eBay.'

'Is it original?'

She chuckled. 'It would be nice if it did date from 1610; in which case I'd have bought a rare map for several thousand pounds less than it was worth. But no, while it's an old copy, probably around 1920, the original I believe is contained in a book about the county now held in Merton College, Oxford. I'd like to see that sometime, but I think the college are reluctant to let non-academics anywhere near their incunabula. So, if you ever find yourself heading for Oxford and fancy taking along someone to carry your briefcase, do let me know, although,' she said pointedly, looking at the briefcase he clutched to his chest, 'you do seem reluctant to part with it.'

Duncan relaxed and placed the briefcase on the sofa, then stepped back and inspected the room. 'What a lovely touch you have,' he said approvingly.

'Well, it's hardly *Good Housekeeping*, but 'tis mine own. Come through into the kitchen. Would you like a glass of wine?'

'Why not. One glass isn't going to take me over the limit…hopefully.'

'Red, okay? It's only a cheap Malbec from the supermarket.'

'Red's fine,' he said as she filled a glass standing next to her own.

Alice was preparing a chicken stir fry. 'Park your bum,' she said, gesturing at the kitchen table. 'This won't be long. I hope you like it as I do, hot and spicy.'

'I'm sure I will. Stir fries are what I do to avoid eating cold beans out of a tin, which, primitive as it sounds, is sometimes all too tempting at the end of a tiring day.'

Chapter 10

The meal passed in amiable companionship, during which they chatted idly about music, books, food and wine, striking numerous notes of accord. Duncan declined a second glass of wine, although Alice filled her glass again and led him back into the sitting room, poking life back into the embering fire.

'So, where do we start?' she asked, keen now to get down to the business for which she'd invited him.

'I just need to make a note of basics at this stage, so I can make a start and be confident that I'm not wasting time by barking up the wrong family tree. Sadly, I'm quite good at that. It's so easy to get misled, even going back just a few generations. So many members of the same family lived cheek by jowl and stuck to a very limited range of family first names. You'd think they'd no imagination. Everyone seemed to have been named after a favourite aunt or uncle or parent, even someone who'd died in infancy. It's not uncommon to get two or more people in the same family generation all with the same name. It confuses Ancestry no end. And me. A hundred years from now, family historians will have it so easy. What with all the Zaks, Beyoncé's, Rocky's, and Megans to work with.'

He sighed theatrically, as from his briefcase produced a spiral-bound notebook and pen. 'Let's start with you.' He drew a rectangle on one of the pages and wrote her name in it. And then drew more rectangles for the names of her parents.

'Do you have any middle names?'

'Margaret. I'm Alice Margaret.'

'And when were you born? Don't worry, I won't tell anyone!'

She laughed openly and gave him a date that put her about five years younger than himself.

'And where were you born?'

'Well, I was brought up in Ormskirk, but I was born in St Helens, in a place called Thatto Heath, part of Ravenhead parish, I think. There were a lot of Marsh's about, but I don't know where any of them are buried. The parish church, St John's, doesn't have a graveyard. My dad's mother's family were called Liptrot, and I think they came from Billinge, and I can remember several of them being around in Thatto Heath. And I have a vague recollection of my father taking me as a child to the churchyard at the top of Billinge. St Aidan's, I think it was. He told me that his grandfather was buried there. In my head I had an idea where the grave was. But when I went back years later, I couldn't find it.'

'Memory displacement, I call it. You have a clear image in your head of something, but when you return to it, the reality is completely different. In my case, I see things in reverse. If my memory tells me something is on the right, it invariably turns out to be on the left. It's the same when I read a book. As I read, I visualise whether something is on the right or left, but in the next paragraph it turns out to be the opposite of what I've been thinking. Not sure what a psychiatrist would make of that. But anyway…let's start with your parents and work back as far as you know.'

Alice gives him her parents' names, and their details, but can't go back much farther. Although she knew the names of her maternal and paternal grandparents, that is all she knew; there was nothing she could recall about earlier generations, for which she apologised.

'There's no need to apologise,' Duncan said. 'Few people know more than a generation back. We're not often called on to say when or where our grandparents were born, so there's no reason to think about it. It's not stuff we carry around in our heads. And if you go even farther back, it's a complete blank with most folk. Almost as if their ancestors never existed. In most instances it's the archetypal tale of there being an "Uncle Tommy", who isn't really an uncle, and who was the black sheep in the family. Funny how people always remember the black sheep, but no one else.'

'So, I'm not a complete numpty, then?'

'I'm sure you're not any kind of a numpty, complete or otherwise.' He snapped his notebook shut. 'But this will be a start from which I can start building your tree.' Then added as an afterthought, 'Do you have any brothers or sisters.'

She smiled at him, 'Not that I'm aware of. If I have, Mum and Dad never told me, and I never saw anyone unfamiliar wandering around the house. Mind you, Dad always was one for chatting up the ladies. But no, as far as I know I'm your archetypal spoiled-brat-of-an-only-child.'

She was sat next to him, her hands resting in her lap. Unthinkingly, he reached across and placed his hand on hers. 'I doubt very much you're any kind of a brat.'

Only once back at his own cottage, as he allowed himself a small glass of cognac before going to bed did he realise that she'd made no move to withdraw her hands from his. But by then, the fresh air from earlier in the day and the soporific warmth of Alice's sitting room had left him too tired to dwell on the moment.

Chapter 11

By the time the breakfast bell rang, Mary Ellen was already feeling jaded. She had never shied away from hard work and always pulled her weight at home, but this was so much more than she'd anticipated.

This was ridiculous.

The two of them trooped into the servants' hall, Mary Ellen wearily, and Elizabeth directed to a seat at the end of a massive table. It was, she couldn't help noticing, the furthest from the fire, reflecting her lowly position in the domestic hierarchy. Higher up the table sat the Lady's Maid, senior housemaids and the male servants – the valets, the footmen in order of rank and a couple of nondescript individuals not in uniform. All unfamiliar faces. The head of the table was reserved for Cook and Mr Grimes. Several curious faces peered briefly down the table at Mary Ellen, registering the presence of a newcomer, and then turning their attention away, chatting among themselves in hushed tones. She noticed there were still several empty chairs, suggesting that their usual occupants were busy elsewhere. Mary Ellen wondered what would happen if they missed breakfast altogether.

Thankfully, Elizabeth sat close by, next to the kitchen maid she introduced as Martha – her bedfellow come night-time – and several kitchen maids along with a timid, fearful-faced maid, who, Elizabeth told her was a maid-of-all-work, a slave, the very bottom of the pile of servants, and because of that she slept in a chair in a cupboard in the kitchen. Ironically, Elizabeth told her, she was quite content with that; it was the warmest room in the house, even though no larger than a small larder.

Mary Ellen glanced around her, and said to Elizabeth, 'Where's the food? I could murder a cup of tea, I'm spitting feathers.'

'You have to wait,' she said in a low voice. 'Be quiet. Sit up straight. Ruth, the senior housemaid, will serve us with tea or coffee, and then Mr Grimes serves whatever is on today's menu, such as it is. Probably sausages; bacon, too, if we're lucky.

'Why are you whispering?

'It's the way it is. If we all talked loudly, all at the same time, it may disturb the family, and we wouldn't want that.'

Once tea or coffee had been served, Mr Grimes struggled to his feet. For all his status a scruffy, unkempt man whose ascetic appearance – pinched nose, eyes too close together set beneath beetling eyebrows reminiscent of startled caterpillars – was corralled in jowls of fat that extended to a double chin that quivered like not-quite-set blancmange as he moved his head. Greying mutton-chop whiskers and thin lank hair combed optimistically across a balding pate gave him a mildly hysterical mien. He was wearing a stained, black suit and waistcoat both much in need of pressing. With some unsteadiness he retrieved a dish of sausages and bacon from the serving table and walked slowly behind the servants, forking out two sausages and a rasher of bacon to each plate. As he passed down the table, he sent a smile in Mary Ellen's direction that he might have thought was meant to be warm and welcoming, but which, she thought, would make a cat scream.

Elizabeth leaned over to Mary Ellen and whispered darkly, 'He's a lecherous bastard. Don't turn your back on him if you can help it. He's got WHD.'

'He's got what?'

'Wandering Hands Disease. He's a groper, and he'll have you if he can. He goes for your arse. By accident, of course. Slimy bastard!'

As Mr Grimes passed behind Elizabeth, placing food on her plate, he leaned forward and said pointedly, 'Not speaking out of turn, are we, Miss Bampton?'

'No, Mr Grimes, just explaining the breakfast arrangements to Miss Liptrot here. This is her first day.'

On reaching Mary Ellen's place, he moved closer, surreptitiously pressing himself against her as he leaned over her shoulder. She could feel the unwelcome nudge of his manhood. 'Well, welcome to Garston Hall, my dear. If there's anything – *anything* – I can do for you, Miss Liptrot, my door is always open. Don't be afraid…to ask.'

Mary Ellen swallowed audibly and shot a glance at Elizabeth, who lowered her head, her face a warning. *Don't say anything, Mary Ellen. Keep quiet.* Further up the table, two of the older footmen sniggered mutedly, but a third, younger, footman, sitting opposite them caught Mary Ellen's eye and shrugged, pulling an apologetic face.

Throughout breakfast, Mary Ellen tried in vain to engage Martha in conversation; after all, they were going to be sleeping together, the least she could do was be civil. But her monosyllabic replies to even the simplest of questions and permanently glum face served only to generate exasperation, and Mary Ellen was relieved, if still hungry, when breakfast was formally concluded.

'What now?' she asked Elizabeth.

'Now we start on the bedrooms; make the beds, see to the candles, set the fires, dust and sweep as we did earlier. We usually work in twos for the bedrooms. The work has to be done pretty sharp. Thankfully, we only have to do the junior family rooms. The senior housemaids do those of Lord and Lady Garston and their mother. We also do those of Mrs Bonnivale. We'd be horsewhipped if we were found alone in any of the bedrooms.'

'Why, what are we going to see? Do they think we're going to steal something?'

'If they thought we were likely to steal anything, we wouldn't be here in the first place, and you could be certain you wouldn't get no job anywhere else, neither.' She stopped and regarded Mary Ellen sternly. 'Think about it. It's safer for us if we work as a pair. Can't be accused of filching stuff if you have a witness working alongside you.'

''S'pose not.'

'Oh, and, whatever we see, is not to be spoken of, whatever it is.'

'But they're only bedrooms.'

'Yes, they are, but Master Cavendish – he's an earl, by the way – is not beyond inviting…er, guests…into his room. And his guests, especially the female ones, don't usually leave before breakfast. And he seems to spend a lot of time in his sister's rooms. An awful lot of time.'

'I thought we weren't supposed to talk about things like that,' Mary Ellen smiled at her new friend.

'Like what? I didn't say anything. Did I? You must have bad hearing. Hush now, we must get on.'

They both laughed companionably and started out along the labyrinthine corridors that led to the bedrooms.

Chapter 12

By the time the two girls returned to the servants' hall a few minutes before one o'clock, Mary Ellen was more exhausted than she could have imagined possible and only half of one day done. Her gaze took in the faces at the table; not one seemed even remotely as fatigued as she. Once more her eyes were caught by those of the youngest of the three footmen. He smiled as if sensing how overawed and distressed she must feel faced with the reality of domestic service. For a fleeting instant, she wondered if the gesture was anything more than empathy.

What if he has designs on her?

What if he's tarred with the same brush as the others?

Well, he'd get a swift kicking if he tries anything, she thought with more conviction than she felt.

Suddenly, a hand rested on her shoulder and she turned to see the smirking face of Mr Grimes, his black eyes roving her body, as if mentally peeling away her uniform. 'How are you getting on, my dear? Miss Bampton showing you the ropes, is she?'

'Yes, she is, thank you, sir. It's all just a bit confusing.'

'Well, should you need me to explain anything to you, any time day or…night, just come and find me.' Mary Ellen detected the slight pause before he said "night" and she instantly resolved that at no time, especially at night, would she be seeking advice from Mr Grimes. She had already decided to give him as wide a birth as possibly and shuddered involuntarily as he gave her shoulder a squeeze before continuing his travels around the table. Even in such a short time, Mary Ellen was repulsed by the man and wondered at his capacity to make her feel so ill at ease. Elizabeth reached out and touched her arm as if to erase the unpleasantness she sensed in the new second housemaid, and gave her a sympathetic smile of encouragement, mouthing wordlessly, 'It's not all bad.' But try as she might, Mary Ellen couldn't get her mind around what she was coming to realise was a destiny laden with mischief and risk.

The idea that this...this...*slimy arsehole*, she could think of no other description, might use his position to impose himself on her sickened her, so much so that she managed to eat very little of the beef stew, potatoes and bread cook had placed in front of her. She was annoyed at foregoing healthy sustenance by the man's lecherous innuendos when she knew her brothers would walk a mile for a plate of stew so heart-warming. But the man had robbed her of her appetite; she just wanted to get away. Even so, she needed her strength to cope with her duties, and knew she must eat. With an effort, she spooned up a few mouthfuls and sipped at a mug of weak ale, praying that lunchtime would soon be over even if it meant returning to what she even now thought of as drudgery.

An afternoon of more cleaning, filling water cans and trimming candles followed, there seeming no end to the tasks she must carry out. And tomorrow would be just the same, and the next day, and the next, and on...forever. Thankfully, there was no needlework on the day's agenda; Mary Ellen was not the most adept with needles and she dreaded being required to sew for the Garston household. Unevenly darning socks for her brothers was one thing, but precise needlepoint was quite an altogether different proposition.

The short break for supper in the servants' hall, during which Mr Grimes was conspicuous by his absence, eventually arrived. As a result, Mary Ellen was able to manage two cups of tea and a slice of cold ham, by now ravenous. But the evening break was over all too soon. Silently, she followed Elizabeth to light the fires in the bedrooms and check that the coal and wood boxes were full.

In the first bedroom, a large four-poster bed hung with curtains and crisp cotton sheets faced across the room to a window giving on to a view of the woodland. An ornate dressing table stood against one wall, close by a chest of drawers and writing desk against the facing wall. She had been there earlier in the day but had taken in none of it. As if seeing it for the first time, she asked, 'Whose room is this?'

'It's Lord Cavendish's. But he's often not 'ere, as now. He stays with friends in London and...' she looked around to ensure she was not being overheard speaking out of turn, '...spends a lot of his time spending his father's money down there from what I've heard.'

Mary Ellen walked across to the bed and ran her hand across the white sheets, to the touch like nothing she had ever felt before. For a moment she drifted away into reverie.

This will be my room; it is perfect.
I will sleep here, with the man of my dreams.

When, finally, all her chores complete, she climbed the unending back stairs to her bedroom where Martha, the kitchen maid was already asleep, Mary Ellen reflected on her first day in service. Her aspirations had petered out within hours. She had certainly not expected to work with little respite from early morning until late evening, leaving her so exhausted that what time she did have to herself she needed to recover in readiness for the following day's toil.

Nor did she imagine she would have to share a room, even though it was something she was accustomed to. In her Master Plan, she had a sumptuous, well-appointed room, like the master's room, with a view across the estate grounds to the eastern hills of Lancashire. To make matters worse, she was expected also to share a bed with a kitchen maid to whom a good wash seemed anathema and whose preparation for bed comprised only of removing her shoes. As a result she spent her first night at Garston Hall clinging to the edge of the bed trying through a sleepless night to avoid physical contact with the flaying arms of her restless companion.

For the first time since her mother had died, she cried.

She cried for the pain she was feeling in every bone of her body; she cried for the service to which she had committed herself; she cried for the life she wanted, so close yet impossibly out of reach.

And she cried for futures lost.

Chapter 13

In the years following the end of Alice's marriage, she languished in emotional limbo. Because she'd seen the writing on the wall, the end when it came had less destructive impact than it might have done. So, she was able to absorb the changes in her life more readily. Once the house transfer was finalised, she felt a need to leave Liverpool. And that dismayed her, because she'd made many friends in the city, people who were unfailingly jovial, friendly and idiosyncratic as only a Liverpudlian can be. And for someone who so enthusiastically enjoyed entertainment, music and socialising the heritage and culture of the city, was on a par with the best in Britain.

She resented that the consequence of her husband's actions pressured her to leave all that behind. Remaining in Liverpool, which for a time she managed, served only as a constant and unappetising reminder of circumstances and people she wanted to forget, especially those erstwhile friends among them who in the end turned out to be shallow and false. She wanted, too, to remove herself from the years of what she now saw had been fabricated goodwill, and the social gatherings at which she came to identify the ever-present and unattached common denominator with her daunting bust, curvy figure, short skirts, revealing tops and a pitying glint in her eyes, circling like some rapacious beast.

The immediate aftermath, in spite of her preparedness, had been traumatic, a time when Alice found herself not knowing who she could trust. Tom had made several clandestine visits to the house to remove his belongings, and Alice found herself wondering if anyone she was working with was calling him to tell him the house was empty, that Alice was at her desk. Two months after his departure she returned home and realised everything that had been his had gone; nothing of him remained save a lingering smell of aftershave. Not one she'd bought him, she realised poignantly. His keys he'd left on the kitchen table. She almost cried with laughable disbelief when she noticed that along with a good vintage bottle of Chateau Mouton Rothschild intended for her birthday, he'd also taken an ornate Laguiole bottle opener she'd bought for him as a birthday present. It was rightfully his, of course, but taking it – and the wine – just seemed pathetically puerile. Thanks to Amazon, she had a replacement bottle opener the very next day. At least he hadn't divided the cutlery, and with any luck his new bed mate would choke on the wine.

Jennifer Bounty, a research fellow at Liverpool University, had been the only one of her circle of friends Alice was confident with and trusted. In the first few weeks of adjustment she'd found her a stalwart support, ever ready to listen, not once judgemental. She had been chopping onions, allowing her emotive tears to blend with those induced by the onions and easing some of her inner turmoil and fragility, when Jennifer first came to call. She had a look of consternation when she saw Alice's reddened eyes, until she explained about the onions.

For months disorientated and demotivated Alice became self-admonishing, blaming herself for her predicament. Jennifer was the catalyst who built in her the belief that she had in no part been responsible. If she was guilty of anything it was that she'd been too trusting and not observant enough to pick up on the nuances that in the end betrayed a man having an affair. *He's just an outright bastard*, she'd said. Alice had sighed heavily, willing to submit to Jennifer's view of reality, but sensing that disruptive times lay ahead. She hoped she'd be ready for a difficult passage but had no expectation of finding it easy. Jennifer, for her part, had brought comfort and friendship, and in time that resurrected Alice's inherent self-confidence. At times it was a calming, rejuvenating relief simply to let tears course freely and not feel the need to hold them in check, as if the tears washed away her self-pity.

Alice was again peeling onions when the doorbell rang. She swept her face with her sleeve and went to answer the door. It was Jennifer. Come to call.

'Onions. Again,' she sniffled, through a welcoming smile in answer to Jennifer's look of concern and stepped back to let her in.

Jennifer slipped off her coat and draped it over the back of a chair. 'How you diddling?' she asked, giving Alice a hug, and kissing her cheek.

'In spite of the tears, I'm actually diddling better than I've felt for some time. Come on through.' She headed back into the kitchen and grabbed a bottle of Malbec and two glasses from a worktop.

'Fancy a glass?'

'What? Just one?' She smiled at Alice. 'Have I come all this way for just *one* glass of wine?' Jennifer plonked herself at the kitchen table and placed her handbag on it. 'I never had you down as a penny-pincher.'

'You only live round the corner,' Alice joked.

'Yes…but…' she pressed a button on her Nokia Smartwatch, reading the output '…it's one thousand, five hundred and seventy-two steps. I'm parched, and my feet urgently need wine.'

They both chuckled, and Alice handed her a glass.

'Cheers!' They touched glasses. 'So, what's new?'

Alice sat down and regarded Jennifer with an expression of excitement on her face. 'I'm moving. Leaving Liverpool.'

'No!'

'Well, I had intended to stay. Make the best of things. Not be seen to be giving in. But then I started to see through the hollowness of some of the so-called friends around me when push came to shove. So, I thought I'd make a new start. Pastures anew, and all that. Maybe finally get my MA done. Tom gave me the house, so I should be okay for cash. I could sell the Jag, get something smaller, more eco-friendly.'

Jennifer sipped her wine and nodded sagely. 'You know, I think you're right. But won't you miss everything? Theatre, restaurants, pubs? Me?'

'Of course, and I hate Tom for bringing me to this. But I'm still young…ish. I can start again. And anyway, they have theatres, well, one theatre, restaurants and pubs in Chorley, and Manchester isn't that far away. And you can always come to visit.' She leaned forward and touched Jennifer's arm affectionately. 'I really wouldn't want to lose you. You've been a brick. The only solid foundation I've had, since…'

Jennifer smiled and nodded and patted the back of Alice's hand reassuringly.

'Chorley! she said, belatedly picking up on Alice's remark. 'Why Chorley? A bit backwoods country, isn't it?'

Alice pulled herself up in her chair, bridling theatrically and peering down her nose at her friend, 'Chorley is a very pleasant market town with a great history and lots of lovely people. Forty thousand of them, in fact.'

'But. Chorley? What's there for you?'

'Senior librarian in charge of the local history department.'

'You're applying for a senior librarian's job in a small market town?'

'No. I already applied. I've got the job. I start in two weeks' time, which is why I wanted you to come round. So, I could tell you in person, rather than send an email.'

'What about somewhere to live? And what about this place? You'll have to sell this house before you can buy another.'

'Well, you wouldn't believe.'

Jennifer regarded her quizzically.

'I put this house on the market three weeks ago, and it's sold already. First time buyer. Some stockbroker from London, looking to move to the Northern Powerhouse, or whatever. The deal goes through next week. I couldn't believe my luck.'

'Bloody hell. You don't hang around once you've made a decision, do you?'

Alice laughed. 'I suppose not. It did all happen rather quickly. The elements must have aligned.'

They sipped their wine in silence for a moment.

'And have you found somewhere to live?'

'Well, that's another serendipitous bit of the equation.' She refilled their glasses with wine and took a gulp.

'I was driving around one day, looking for suitable places, and I ended up in a lovely little hamlet. White Coppice. Right on the edge of the West Lancashire moors. Anyway, I got chatting over a garden fence with an elderly lady who noticed me wandering about. Turns out her husband had died the previous year, and she was looking to go and live with her daughter and son-in-law and grandchildren in the Lake District. But she'd backed herself into an emotional corner, worrying about estate agent fees, legal fees, etcetera. Said they were all sharks. Only interested in ripping her off. I asked her how much she wanted for her cottage – it was such a lovely place, with a neat garden that she'd obviously spent a lot of time on. She said she didn't know, but she showed me around. It was perfect. Well, for me, at least. So, I told her to get a valuation. Just that, not listing it in some agent's portfolio. And I said that if I could afford it, I'd pay whatever the valuation came to.'

'And?'

'Well, she rang me back a few days later. I'd almost forgotten about her. She gave me a figure that would eat into what I make from this place, but it was just such an ideal cottage in a stunning location. So, I offered her what she was asking. It didn't feel right to haggle. And as soon as the deal on this place is completed, I dash over to Chorley to complete the sale there.'

'And all this has happened…in…what…a matter of two to three weeks?'

'Something like that.'

Jennifer drank more of her wine and looked at Alice thoughtfully.

'That must be a world record. You know what? It was meant to be. It's all just fallen neatly into place for you. That's brilliant. All you need now is a man you can trust.'

'Uh, oh! No thanks. I'll do without.'

'Well, you deserve to be happy. I don't know of anyone who deserves it more than you. You're such a kind and generous person.'

'Shut up,' Alice playfully remonstrated. 'You'll have me in tears again.'

'And you've always had a great wine cellar!' Jennifer said, waving an empty wine glass in the air.

Chapter 14

As soon as she started her new job in Chorley, the ground beneath Alice's feet found a firmness she felt she could trust. In the years that followed, there had been no new relationships beyond a tipsy and inelegant fumble-up-the-jumper at a Christmas party, of which the Chardonnay had been the more memorable ingredient. Try as they might, others who sought to gain ground with her were doomed to ruin on the rocks of her defence. Once, she had been outgoing, affable, unceasingly equable. Now, while outwardly cheerful and friendly, she found she had regressed behind an unyielding façade, damaged by mistrust and deceit from which she sought to shield herself. She hadn't quite expected that but was disinclined to do anything about it; marking time felt reassuringly prudent. Serendipity had come to her aid twice before; it could come again.

Over time, she settled into a domestic routine punctuating the work she enjoyed with weekends away walking in the Lake District or the Yorkshire Dales, and once getting as far as the Isle of Mull to look for otters and eagles and ended up stranded by the tide for six hours on the island of Erraid, which she'd visited for its literary association with Robert Louis Stevenson's novel *Kidnapped*. One of her work colleagues was a member of the local rambling group and for a time she considered joining them, only to realise that there would inevitably be questions she preferred not to answer, and chattering, garrulous treks that despatched for cover any wildlife they may have seen.

Alice had long been a capable map reader and navigator and had her father to thank for an upbringing surrounded by maps and guidebooks wherein lay places to be visited, mysteries to be resolved. But these days, with the advent of GPS technology, she ventured farther afield confident in her ability to retrace her steps, to find her way back to her car, and home. She was fit and healthy and had a metabolism that allowed her to eat almost anything without gaining weight. As a result, she had retained a youthful figure, perhaps now rounding a little, but she was never going to be Michelin Woman.

Life in White Coppice was peacefully sedentary, and that suited her. At weekends the hamlet was inundated with walkers heading for the high moors, and most summer Sundays saw cricketers playing on the sloping field backed by a row of white cottages, the air filled with the sound of leather on willow and calls of "Run, you dozy bastard".

On weekdays, she and her neighbours – who, while remaining communally watchful, for the most part left her to herself – had the place to themselves. On summer evenings, she would sit in the garden with a chilled glass of wine reading a book or just listening to birdsong. In winter, she metaphorically hunkered down into a cosy, comforting hibernation, listened to her eclectic collection of music or watched recorded or Catch-Up TV to evade all the advertising, warm and secure in her cottage cocoon. She was contented now. She was happy, and finally at ease with herself.

And then she had been introduced to a man who had rippled the walls of her bubble. It had been no earth-shattering moment, but increasingly he persisted in invading her thoughts in the quiet hours, and she questioned whether inviting him to help with family history had been a wise decision. It would only serve to bring them closer together.

And was that what she wanted?

Chapter 15

Garston Hall, the seat of the family for many generations stood central to an estate of over 1,000 acres originally fashioned by Humphry Repton, the last great English landscape designer of the eighteenth century and regarded by many as the natural successor to Capability Brown. Historically, the land on which the hall stood was part of the manor of Ashton, acquired by marriage by the Garston family in the fourteenth century. Not until the mid-eighteenth century was the original hall extended to its present form, an enormous and needlessly large building, home and central to the lives of more than sixty servants, and just five surviving members of the Garston family. Excluding the servants' quarters, the hall had in all no fewer than forty rooms including a great hall, a grand foyer, a dining hall, a music room, a billiard room, fifteen bathrooms, fourteen bedrooms and an extensive but largely unread library that includes several hundred first editions of little-known works by equally little-known authors. Most of the bedrooms were opulently furnished yet remained unoccupied for the greater part of each year. Only occasional visiting guests used these rooms, whenever Lord Garston's business meetings ran late, or Lady Garston, as she was wont to do at impromptu moments throughout the year, arranged a spurious celebration of events the significance of which only she knew. Some would say, indeed had said, that it was to relieve the boredom of a loveless marriage; others that it was a means of bringing desirably young men into her orbit. But none had said that in her hearing; nor would they dare.

Lord Mansfield Garston, the eighth Marquis of Windleshaw, and his trophy but increasingly estranged wife, the extravagantly beautiful Lady Arabella, daughter of a wealthy shipping magnate, occupied separate suites of luxurious rooms in the south wing of the hall, while the marquess's octogenarian mother, a haughty and bitter woman who – with no provenance to support it – styled herself "Lady Makerfield", lived a semi-hermitic existence in a suite of rooms that faced east to the rising sun. She was attended by just one Lady-in-Waiting, a faithful retainer of many decades, who in spite of her loyalty, was probably destined to a life of penury and loneliness when her ladyship died...if Lord Garston's son had any say in the matter.

The north wing was where the two children of the marriage, Cavendish and Clarissa had opulent suites, removed as far as possible, intentionally or otherwise, from their parents, an arrangement that pleased everyone.

Although not himself a peer, twenty-eight-year-old Cavendish Garston, in common with the practice of the time held his father's title of "Earl of Windleshaw" by courtesy. It was a privilege he was not beyond exploiting, especially among the ribald Victorian contemporaries of his acquaintance who frequented his London apartment. His twenty-three-year-old sister was known simply in the household as Lady Clarissa, and seldom seen outside her rooms, wherein she continued with stubborn determination to resist any and all attempts by her father to match her to a suitor appropriate to a titled lady of her wealth and distinction.

Chapter 16
Saturday, 15 January 1870

Lady Clarissa awakened slowly, her head a hazy muddle of half-formed images and kaleidoscopic colours that flared and faded in rapid and dazzling succession. The room revolved slowly. Her head fizzed with an irrepressible dizziness; her ears filled with a constant hissing sound nothing seemed to ease.

As if disembodied and hovering above the ornate, curtained four-posted bed, she saw herself brooding in many colours, separated from her living self by a pane of glass she somehow knew was there but could not see. Uncaring and without compassion, she gazed down at the young woman's body now balanced tentatively at the edge of the bed.

Her breathing comes rapidly, gasping as if she can gain no purchase on the air, she so urgently needs to sustain her. Beads of perspiration form on her brow, gather force and, diverted by her dense, dark eyebrows, form rivulets down her cheeks.

Then, without warning, she was once more in the body of the confused woman on the bed, convulsed by a panic she feared and did not comprehend, wiping sweat from her eyes and clutching desperately at her throat as hazy images of people she thought were familiar swirled before her eyes in striated hues of red, blue and green. As she strove to gain purchase on reality, the room continued to spin, its dark, oak-panelled walls spiralling in on her. The air, stale and laden with the lingering smell of fireplace ashes and burned-out candles. She was ill, but she knew not why. She did not understand the illness. No one understood the illness, and several minutes passed before her tremors subsided sufficiently for her to lower her feet tentatively to the polished floorboards and trust her weight to them.

A richly patterned carpet covered the centre of the room. A large circular table stood on it, a mahogany wardrobe against the wall with a toilet table, towels and washstand close by. The heavy, embroidered curtains at the two wide window frames were closed, a large mercury plate pier glass and over-mantle mirror standing between them. A chiffonier occupied the wall by the door, beside a chaise-longue embellished with the family crest. Behind a concealed doorway, a small anteroom housed a lavatory washbasin and toilet. Another door led into a sitting room where Clarissa spent most of her day languidly ebbing and flowing between intolerant awareness and unfeeling misty impassiveness.

Since dawn the housemaids had returned at intervals to replenish the water jug with hot water, each time taking care not to disturb their sleeping mistress. The tiresome routine was something they had had to become accustomed to, for their mistress was not one to rise voluntarily before midday and only then when the sounds of industry in the gardens punctured the depths of her slumber. But on those rare occasions in the past when she did surface at an earlier time, her anger on finding only cold water in her jug had unjustifiably been laden with a level of fury and vitriol that had reduced more than one housemaid to tears. Although her parents were unaware or uncaring of her condition, the household had long suspected there were uncontainable things at work in their mistress they should be wary of...should fear, even.

Things no one understood.

For a moment she stood, swaying, a sapling in a breeze; uncertain. She urgently needed to piss and spun anxiously in search of the doorway to the toilet, where she relieved herself. Back in the bedroom she unfastened the buttons of her embroidered white cotton nightdress, letting it fall to the floor, and stood in front of the pier glass, seeing a body she didn't know, a face that glared at her malevolently without recognition. With an effort greater in the mind than in the doing, she drew the curtains aside and stood before the window peering out at a pale blue sky streaked with wispy clouds. In the garden below, two gardeners were pruning bushes. They noticed the drawing of the curtains. They knew she was there. She was always there. They knew, too, that she was naked. They longed to gaze up at her, to pamper to a lust she aroused daily, to take in her luxurious figure, but they feared to let their gaze be noticed, and so kept their heads bowed and observed through upturned eyes and continued their work.

Clarissa's wakefulness was confined to the sensation of cool air on her body. She looked on the men with the same cold indifference with which she regarded the trees and flowers. She was uncaring and had feeling for nothing of what she saw.

She longed only for the return of the man she loved.

Behind her, silently, the more elderly of the maids had entered and having replenished the water jug, went to Clarissa and with gentle persuasion guided her back to the middle of the room. In a reverential, caring silence and with gentle hands she helped her to wash and dress. Moments later a second maid entered, and placed a tray of food on the table, before leaving.

When they had gone, she ate desultorily, barely touching the food. Later, more assured and lucid, she stood again in front of the mirror. She was attractive rather than beautiful; slim and shapely. Long dark hair tumbled around her face, reaching in natural curves to below her breasts. Dark eyes, an aquiline nose and full lips were marred only by a smooth white scar on her forehead, shaped like a star. It was too low on her forehead for her hair to conceal it, and so it usually remained visible. She had no recollection of how she gained the scar, but in healing it became taut enough to leave one eyebrow raised in a frown of permanent enquiry.

She was wearing a heavy full skirt of deep claret velvet with an embroidered band of white silk at the hem that matched the long-sleeved blouse with a large lace collar and cuffs. A simple brooch of diamonds around a large oval stone of jet pinned to her breast was the family's token acknowledgement of the mourning experienced by their monarch. Unlike her mother and her contemporaries, she chose not to wear constraining fashionable undergarments, preferring to be as Nature intended in a way that would have scandalised her mother had she known. Only the maids who dress her, have seen her naked body.

And one other.

Suddenly, Clarissa was ravenous and irritable. With renewed vigour she attacked the food the maid had left, all the while feeling as though time had slowed down, that her movements were mechanical and leaden, uncontrolled, unbidden.

On the table stood a carafe of red wine. She filled a wine glass and pressed a hidden button to unlock a concealed drawer in her desk. From it, she retrieved a leather pouch and, opening it, pinched a small quantity of its dark green contents between finger and thumb and sprinkled it onto the wine, which she then stirred with her forefinger before sucking her finger absently and returning the pouch to the drawer, checking that it was locked. She took a deep draught of the wine, closed her eyes and breathed deeply before turning to a second, much larger compartment from which she extracted an ornate coromandel writing box with a golden mount. From within the satinwood interior she pulled a Celtic leatherbound notebook, opened it at the last entry and unscrewed the cap of a silver fountain pen that had been a birthday gift from her brother. After a moment's thought, she started to write in a neat legible floral hand, as she had done every day since her fifteenth birthday. This was her Book of Days for the year 1870, an incoherent assemblage of imaginings, ramblings, irrationalities and less frequent lucid thoughts. She had many such diaries concealed in her suite of rooms. Diaries to which no one was privy.

Chapter 17

During a lull in his research, while waiting for a client to return from an extended trip to Australia, of which he had felt envious, Duncan relaxed in the spare bedroom he used as an office, sipping from a large mug of black coffee, and studying with a professional eye the picture Alice gave him. He knew from the inscription that he was looking for Alice's great-great-grandmother and a child, who presumably was either her great-grandfather or great-grandmother; the Victorian practice of clothing both sexes of young children in dresses in their early years served only to cloud the issue.

He needed to draft a basic chart to enable him to regress into the genealogical comfort zone of pre-1911 census records, and to 1873, the date on the reverse of the picture. He needed to follow both the Marsh lineage and the Liptrot, too, looking for connections and a correlation between the date on the photograph and the approximate date of birth of the child, who he guessed to be less than a year old.

The first puzzle to present itself was how Alice's father could have known that the picture was taken in 1873. Her father, Alice had told him, lived into his nineties, and would have been born shortly after the First World War. *His* father, therefore, was probably born at the end of the nineteenth century, and assuming it was him who had passed the photograph down, he could only have known from his own parents who the mother and child were. Luckily, the information and the photograph had safely travelled down the generations; it wasn't conclusive, but for the purposes of this exercise it was more than adequate. It was not always the case; it was a myth that family photographs gravitated into shoes boxes under beds or at the top of wardrobes. Usually they went missing. Lost without trace.

Duncan googled information about photography in the Victorian era and was surprised to read that commercial photography was not only increasingly widespread but becoming a favoured profession of women. So, improbable as it seemed, it was not beyond the bounds of possibility that this photograph was one of the earliest by a female practitioner. But intriguing though that avenue was, it got him no closer to identifying the mother and child. He needed to be methodical, but he liked to cover as many bases as possible. So, he sent a speculative query via the contact form on the Photographers of Great Britain and Ireland 1840–1940 website, not anticipating a helpful reply, but he knew that once you started unravelling family history, nuggets of vital information arrived from the most unlikely directions.

He then logged on to the Ancestry website and using data Alice had given him, soon confirmed the date of birth for her father, and found the General Register Office reference. That didn't immediately help because the GRO online index stopped at 1918. But the information was listed in the England and Wales Civil Registration Birth Index, and from there he was able to order a copy of the birth certificate. Standard practice dictated the necessity to gather all the documentary proof-positive that was available, whatever the source. Duncan knew that many a child had discovered an altogether different "father" from the one they had known, when the evidence of a birth certificate was revealed.

From that date of birth, which was a Boxing Day, he could search back, widening the date parameters to embrace likely dates in order to find a parental date of marriage, which turned out to have been on Christmas Day the year previous, the Banns having been read in October, which also confirmed that the marriage was a church wedding. John Marsh, Alice's grandfather, married Alice Liptrot. Duncan was pleased to note that unlike so many marriages of the time, this one had not been dictated by a pregnancy. He ordered that certificate, too, and had now corroborated the information from Alice, but, more importantly, the record gave him the name both of Alice's great-grandfathers, the paternal Joseph Charles Marsh and the maternal John Liptrot. Duncan recorded the details and turned to tracing their birth dates.

From the Bishop's Transcripts for St John's church, Ravenhead, he found that Joseph Charles Marsh was born in 1864, and for John Liptrot the year 1873. From that it was a reasonable deduction that John Liptrot was the child in the picture. The transcript also identified the mother, Mary Ellen Liptrot. Duncan was aware that he was being temptingly drawn into the Liptrot family tree and knew that he must also plot the Marsh tree to be sure of his conclusions.

In researching this far, however, he'd made an intriguing discovery that he opted to pursue for the moment.

He leant back and took another sip of the now lukewarm coffee and decided to make fresh. There was a new element to dwell on: Alice's maternal great grandfather was illegitimate. That would make it difficult, if not impossible, to trace the father. But Duncan hadn't finished yet. Mary Ellen may have had other children. If they were legitimate, it could give him a possible lead to the missing father. It was not unheard of for a man not to marry a woman until she could prove that she could produce children. There was as yet no evidence to imply that was the case here, but Duncan's synapses were brilliantly adept at keeping tabs on stray snippets on information. For now, he needed to check whether Mary Ellen had siblings; it would have been odd had she not. So, Duncan turned to the census records, beginning with that for 1881, the next census taken after John Liptrot's birth.

The census was taken on Sunday, 3rd April. A few Ancestry keystrokes and the relevant page from the census appears on screen. It shows Mary Ellen, aged twenty-four, and "Head" of the household, then living in Arch Lane, Ashton. Her occupation was given as "Washerwoman", but there was nothing to tell where her place of work might have been. Duncan identified John Liptrot, then aged seven, and another child, Alice, aged just one year old, and made a note to trace her in the records; it was possible that her father was the parent of her illegitimate older brother. Mary Ellen also had two younger brothers, Henry, aged twenty-one, and George, aged nineteen; both employed as coal miners. Duncan made a note to check which coal mines were operating in the Ashton area in the 1880s, but he rather suspected there were several. He also now knew that if Mary Ellen was twenty-four in 1881, she would have been born around the mid-1850s, but also knew not to place too heavy a reliance on the accuracy of ages. Most people living at this time rarely came into contact with officialdom – births, marriages and deaths, and that was about it for most of them. In reality, few truly knew *when* they were born, or *where*. And when women were giving birth almost annually, and managing families of up to ten children, it was not surprising for memories to be less precise than latter-day genealogists would have liked.

Duncan saved the census record to his computer and copied it to an external hard drive. Then he decided to trace Mary Ellen Liptrot starting with the 1851 census, taken on Sunday, 30th March. He found her quite quickly, living with her parents at Penny Hall Lodge, Ashton. Or so it seemed. This Mary Ellen, in 1851, was just one year old, daughter of John Liptrot, a gamekeeper, aged forty-nine, and his wife Alice, who was nineteen years younger than him. Again,

Duncan progressed cautiously; dates and ages were an untrustworthy commodity. This *could* be the same Mary Ellen, but Duncan knew that if a child died at an early age, its parents having used a name that had close familial meaning for them were not beyond giving the same name to a later child. It was a genealogist's nightmare. So, for the moment, he kept an open mind, but noted two other children of John and Alice: Thomas, aged five, and Jane, aged three. John Liptrot's brother-in-law, William Berry also lived at the Penny Lodge, along with his wife, Ellen and their daughter, Anne. The presence also of a fifty-two-year-old mother-in-law, Elizabeth Berry, went a long way to identifying John Liptrot's wife's maiden name, Berry.

The 1861 census presented Duncan with an altogether different picture. The parents were still living at Penny Hall Lodge with Thomas and Jane, but Mary Ellen, who would have been eleven years old was missing. In her place was Edward, aged seven, Ellen Mary, aged five, and Henry, aged two. All of which suggested to Duncan that the young Mary Ellen had died before Edward was born in 1854. This was something else Duncan made a note to check.

Turning to the 1871 census, Duncan saw that Ellen Mary, aged five, had become Mary Ellen, aged fifteen, and so, born in or about 1856. He added another note to his list. He should now be able to order all the birth certificates for the family, including another child, George, aged nine. Typically, the census page was inconsistent, and no longer specified where the family was living, other than in Arch Lane.

So now Duncan had a fuller family tree from John Liptrot, born around 1801, and his wife Alice Liptrot née Berry, born around 1821, through seven children from Thomas to George. He had not identified the father or fathers of Mary Ellen's children, John and Alice, nor the father of John Liptrot senior, the gamekeeper.

And something, his intuition told him, was missing.

He pulled out an A3 sheet of paper and drew the family tree downwards from John and Alice, adding in their approximate birth dates. Then he saw it. Between the birth of Mary Ellen in 1849 or thereabouts, there was a gap of four years before the tree reached Edward born in 1853. Possible; certainly not impossible for any number of reasons. But given the pattern of births on either side of the gap, it was unlikely. One or more children might fill that gap.

It was time to switch to another data system, one for which genealogists in the county rejoiced – the Online Parish Clerks records. Duncan knew this to be a vast compendium of data from the earliest records that can be found up to the end of the nineteenth century, when there were almost 400 parishes within the pre-1974 county boundaries. Data was compiled from parish registers, census records, cemetery records, churchwarden's accounts, overseer's accounts, land tax records, wills, business directories, postal directories, church and village histories. For anyone researching family history in the county it was a Godsend, and doubly acceptable because it was entirely free. He would have happily paid for access.

Half an hour later, Duncan had filled the gap. The first Mary Ellen was born on the 19th August 1849 but survived only two-and-a-half years, and died in March 1852, and lay buried in the graveyard of Billinge parish church. Before she died, her mother gave birth to another daughter, Catherine, who fared less well than Mary Ellen. She was born on the 12th October 1851, and died in January 1853, aged just fourteen months.

Convinced that he had followed the correct line, Duncan nevertheless must repeat the exercise, tracking back up the paternal line, looking for someone, male or female, born around 1855, with a child born around 1872. Thanks to the census records, and the confirming evidence of the Online Parish Clerks records, it was a relatively easy matter. Alice's paternal great-grandfather was Joseph Charles Marsh, born in 1864, the last of a long line of children born to Joseph Marsh and Jane Forest. Of those siblings of Joseph Charles born between 1850 and 1860, one had five children, but none born in the early 1870s. Another died aged just fifteen, a daughter, who died as a child, and another son, born in 1858, but whose first child was not born until 1887.

Duncan was as certain as he could be, that the girl in the picture came from the Liptrot branch, by way of her paternal grandmother. It had taken him just a morning, but he had done what Alice had asked.

He had identified the girl and child in the picture.

But there were several interesting aspects that he knew would serve only to ensnare him further into the family's history, and which professional curiosity compelled him to pursue.

Having saved everything, to two locations, he uploaded the entire file to iCloud, which meant he could access it from Alice's laptop and save everything to that. Mug in hand he crossed to the window and gazed out to the moors where bruised purple rain clouds were gathering, the wind freshening. Rain or shine it was a stunning view, and one of the reasons he and Isabel chose the cottage –

that and the fact that it had recently been fully renovated and had modern features, like central heating, floorboards that didn't creak, and double glazing, unlike the pokey terraced cottage in a dismal town centre they had lived in when first married.

He picked up his mobile phone and dialled Alice's number. After three rings she answered.

'I've got to the bottom of the girl in the picture,' he said.

He heard Alice laughing aloud. 'Would you like to rephrase that comment? It's a bit robust for my delicate ears.' He chortled himself: 'You know what I mean. I know who she is...or, well, was.'

'Certainly was, at any rate; she must have been dead for the best part of a hundred years. When can I see?'

'Whenever you like. I could come there again. You could come here. Or we can drive out to a pub. Your choice.'

'I'll come there, this evening, about eight, after dinner. Is that okay?'

'You think I can't cook?'

'Can you?'

'Yes, of course, though it tends to be more Cordon brown than Cordon bleu.'

'You've persuaded me! I'll stay here and come later.' She laughed. 'Actually, I've something already cooking in the oven. It's not big enough for two and won't keep.'

'In that case, I'll see you later. Oh, and bring your laptop so I can transfer information to it.'

'Right-o. But it will help things along if you tell me how to get there.'

'Ah, yes. Time for more coordinates, I think. Stand by.'

And with that he sent the coordinates for his cottage to her mobile and set off in search of a bottle of red wine that might need time to breathe.

Chapter 18
Friday, 21 January 1870

Mary Ellen and Elizabeth had finished their day's work and were climbing to their rooms in a state of honest fatigue when the door onto one of the intermediate landings burst open. The two footmen Elizabeth had warned Mary Ellen about appeared, laughing loudly. Seeing the girls, their faces lit up as they stood shoulder to shoulder, barring the way upwards, hands on hips.

'Look what we got 'ere, 'enry. One each.' He leered at Mary Ellen and moved to stand in front of her, blocking her as she tried to manoeuvre around him. 'Or maybe we could do 'em both, and then swap. How would you like that, girls? Fancy a man, do you?'

With a rapidity that took all of them by surprise, Elizabeth stepped between them and thrust her hand forcefully against his chest, forcing him backwards against the door, its handle jabbing painfully at his spine. Years of hard domestic toil had clearly given Elizabeth a strength that belied her size. 'I'm always up for it...' she snapped, '...with a *real* man.' Continuing to pin him against the door, the second footman looking on speechless, she continued, 'If I find any, I'll let you know. There's sure as Hell none round here. Now, fuck off, you slimy tossers!'

And with that Elizabeth elbowed him out of the way, forcing him to collide with his colleague, who stumbled and fell to his knees. For good measure, as she squeezed past, Elizabeth scraped the edge of her leather shoe down the length of his shin, which set him howling with pain. 'Bitch. You'll fucking pay for this. Who'd want a slapper like you, anyway?'

Elizabeth turned and eyed them both squarely, 'Well, not you pair of cock-sucking weirdos. That's for sure.'

Mary Ellen was astonished by Elizabeth's foul language yet impressed with the way she dealt with the two men. When they reached the bedroom floor, she followed Elizabeth into her room still buzzing from the encounter. 'What did you mean, weirdos?'

'Oh, believe me, the only ones they love are themselves. They just make a play for women to cover up the fact they'd never get it up, even if a woman offered it on a plate. They are seriously disturbed, if you ask me. There's something not right about them,' she tapped the side of her head with her forefinger, 'but I don't care, and I don't want to know. They're just a pair of gobby little shites.'

'What about the other one?'

'Joseph? Oh, Joseph is okay, I guess. Actually I quite fancy him myself, but I think he's a lot to learn. He'll make someone a decent husband. Maybe. If he lives long enough and figures out what to do with his todger.'

Elizabeth started to undress and ready herself for bed, and Mary Ellen saw that she had a firm, graceful and shapely figure, a little cushiony around the rear end, but still something that would make her the object of many a man's desire.

And yet there seemed to be no one.

'Don't you have a fella, yourself, Beth?' she asked.

Elizabeth shook her head, smiled and took hold of Mary Ellen's hand, holding it between both her own. 'Don't get me wrong. I'm not all sweetness and light, Mary Ellen. Well, you've just witnessed that first-hand. I've had plenty of men, but I decided to give 'em a rest for a while. I just got fed up with backstreet sex, tumbles in the hay, hairy arses and stale beer breath.'

Mary Ellen held her hands over her mouth in surprise, and blurted 'Bloody hell, and here's me thinking you're all prim and proper.'

'That's never going to happen, Mary Ellen. I like sex. Probably too much for my own good, but these days only on my terms. I want something with more than lust and thrust in it. A bit of love wouldn't go amiss. I've had sex with hundreds of blokes. Some stayed around for a few months. Some managed two minutes. Just.' She laughed loudly. 'Well, not literally hundreds. But certainly quite a few.'

They both found that amusing and laughed companionably. Mary Ellen nonplussed by her misjudgement of her friend rooted in her own naivety, which led her to take everything at face value.

But, she found herself thinking, *safer to take everything at face value 'til you know different. For now at least.*

'Do you have kids?' she asked, realising that if Elizabeth did have sex as often as she said, the chances of getting pregnant somewhere down the line must be high.

'No,' Elizabeth said. 'And I'll let you into a secret my grandma told me. She said that if you only have sex just before or just after your time of the month, there's less risk of you having a baby. She said it was summat to do with women being more fertile at some times than at others. Don't understand it myself, and it didn't seem to have worked too well for her because she had nine children. But I've always done what she told me, and I haven't been caught yet. It may be an old wives' tale, but it's worked for me. No way do I want a brat until I'm good and ready.'

Mary Ellen grinned at her. 'Not for the want of trying, eh?'

'Nope, and I'm starting to feel I'm ready to come out of retirement.'

She pulled a nightshirt over her head and ran her hands downwards, caressing her body. 'Very ready, in fact.'

Chapter 19

Sunday, 13 February 1870

More than a month had elapsed since Mary Ellen started her employment at Garston Hall, and her first half day off had arrived. At last, she was free from the repetitive routine, free as a bird, if only for a few hours. She didn't need to return until after nightfall and intended to make the most of her liberty by catching up with her sister and family news.

Just as the other servants were gathering for lunch, she eagerly yanked open the rear door and launched herself into the fresh air, its sudden chill sharpness filling her with elation, like a prisoner released from long and dismal confinement. A blackbird sang stridently from a nearby bush, and the air was pleasingly punctuated by the loud *thwack, thwack, thwack* of heavy wings as a pair of mute swans lifted from the large ornamental pond where each year they'd taken to breeding. Impatient to be away, she skirted the walled garden, almost colliding with the footman who had smiled at her on her first day. She now knew him to be Joseph Cunliffe, and she liked him; or, probably more accurately, didn't *dislike* him as much as she positively disliked the other footmen, although she barely knew him. 'He's a gentle soul,' Elizabeth had said, 'and I think he likes you.' But putting that to the test within the time-demanding routines of domestic service was far from easy.

He dodged deftly out of her way, and called laughingly after her, 'Don't let me get in your way.'

'Never,' she yelled over her shoulder, setting course for the oak woodland and across the meadow to the gate lodge where her sister Jane would be waiting for her news.

The snow that had lain across the estate when she'd entered Garston Hall had now completely melted, leaving no more than patches of moistness where deeper drifts of snow had lain. The sun shone from an unseasonably clear sky, tacking shadows to the trees and highlighting drab winter hues in the manicured lawns and flower beds. She felt happy, eager to see her sister, and raced across the meadows and through the woodland scattering woodcock and pigeons into startled flight. But her happiness was short-lived, as if the world was conspiring to deprive her of even the smallest measure of elation. As she ran towards Penny Hall Lodge, she noticed the absence of smoke rising from the chimney, no flickering candlelight dancing within, and the door, usually wide open when it was warm outside to encourage fresh air to flow through, was closed. But it was not locked, it never was, and she let herself in only to find the cottage deserted and silent. Jane was nowhere to be seen, and her young brothers, normally engaged in loud and querulous disagreement, were nowhere to be heard. She called out, but only echoes answered her call.

Mary Ellen ran upstairs and checked the bedrooms, thinking they'd spotted her coming and decided to play a prank on her. But there was no one. The beds had all been made, and no clothes lay strewn about, even in the boys' room, which, she thought, was not natural. Something was amiss. It's like that ghost ship: The *Mary Celeste*, found abandoned in the Atlantic Ocean only eight years earlier, about which her father had told them much at the time because it was laden with coal mined in the Lancashire coalfields, owned by a consortium in which Lord Garston was an investor. Financially, it had been a damaging blow, and for several months fuelled talk of the family being compelled to leave Garston and retreat to their smaller, less costly estate in Somerset.

Returning to the kitchen she noticed that the tea pot on the table was warm to the touch and half a loaf of brown bread, a crucial part of the family's diet, had been left beside a handful of poor potatoes half of which had been peeled and then left for no obvious reason to turn brown and rot. The family couldn't afford to waste food, and instinctively Mary Ellen wrapped the bread in a sheet of newspaper and finished peeling the potatoes before putting them in a pan of cold water.

Reluctantly, Mary Ellen faced the disappointment of returning to Garston Hall sooner than she'd expected, much earlier than she needed to. Something, she realised, must have called Jane away unexpectedly; something urgent for her to have had to take the boys with her.

Aware that she had the entire afternoon and evening to herself, she wanted to remain free for as long as she could. Yet instead of counselling her to wait a while, her sudden loss of purpose was drawing her back to the hall, plodding the field paths, unthinking, at a loss for somewhere else to go. As she retraced her steps, she glanced repeatedly over her shoulder hoping in vain to see her family returning, willing them to do so. To no avail.

Heading back into the woodland so recently left, she paused. *This was ridiculous*, she muttered to herself. How could she not have somewhere else to go? Why on earth was she going back to the hall, where she'd only mope around for the rest of the day? Only months ago, she would happily have wandered off unaccompanied around the estate, across the fields to Billinge, even further afield, into the grimy, smoky streets of Wigan.

On an impulse she took a branching path from the one she was following, one that took her around the beech-bordered lake to a lichen-covered rock outcrop perched directly above the water. If nothing else, she could enjoy the solitude, the heady sound of silence, and what warmth the weak sun provided. Anything was better than returning to her room where the entrapped, lingering body odour of the maid she and Elizabeth had come to nickname 'Mouldy Martha' never quite made it out of the window. *It was a wonder,* she thought, *that the girl had managed to keep her position in the kitchen when the cook was such a stickler for cleanliness.*

Cleanliness is next to Godliness.

Rousing a family of dozing teal she clambered onto a lakeside rock and sat down, fingering its lichenous crust. Uncaring of the fact that, as had become her way, she was not wearing drawers – itchy and irritating things – she hitched her skirt almost to the top of her slender legs. Gazing out across the lake to the distant brick icehouse beside which a grey heron stood motionless, she drew her legs up and sat, elbows on knees, chin cupped in her hands. A pair of squirrels scurried into the branches of a nearby tree. The rock and its encircling arm of trees was a sun trap she'd known since her early years exploring the estate with her father and was warm even at this time of year. She was born here, and anchored in this place, as permanent, she hoped, as the rocks. The details changed with the seasons – the broad-leaved woodland shedding its leaves in multi-coloured hues; the bruising skies and snowstorms of winter; the spring lambs bounding playfully, oblivious of their fate; sun-burnished crops swaying in the distant fields. And warm summer days when she'd wandered the woodlands with her father and noting her interest in the birds, he'd told her in an oblique way she didn't understand at the time how to distinguish crows and rooks. 'If there's one rook,' he'd said, 'it's a crow. But if there's lots o' crows, then 'em's rooks. A *parliament* of rooks.'

A parliament of rooks.

A murder of crows.

The distinction had remained in her mind ever since, reminding her of what her father had taught her. Always take pleasure in Nature and the small details in life.

The sun-heated rock caressing her bare bottom with its warmth, she sighed heavily, reluctant to give in to her unplanned predicament, a weary melancholy nonetheless settling over her like a heavy mist. No use fretting; fretting would get her nowhere. If Jane wasn't at home, there had to be a reason. Irritably, she snapped a twig into pieces and threw them into the lake watching ripples flow away, jewelled by the low winter sun, as a sob forced its way up, persistent, sending tears trickling down her cheeks.

She raised her hands and untied the ribbon that held her hair, letting it cascade over her shoulders, shaking her head and running fingers through the flowing locks. How stupid of her. *Stupid* girl. She could have stayed at the house. Her sister would have come home, sooner or later. She hadn't needed to leave. But she'd come to think of Garston Hall as her home, and it had called her back. Only an access of determination had turned her away, to sit by the lake. Brooding.

She longed to smile again and wondered gloomily if she ever would. Wistfully she dwelt on how quickly she had lost a carefree, innocent life with her sister and brothers and succumbed to one of tedious constraint and discipline. It was not what she'd envisaged when first she and Jane had spoken about working at Garston Hall. Fuelled by juvenile imaginings of grandeur and elegance, she had what were, had she but realised it, farfetched and much-mistaken ideas of a luxurious lifestyle and comfortable living. Now, growing rapidly more mature by the day, she was coming to understand that it had been a silly and ambitious fantasy that would never…*could* never, translate into real life for her. Yet, in a spirit of dogged and youthful optimism, a glimmer of hope clung on, a hope that one day things might be otherwise. She must have something, she reasoned, to hold on to, some future in which all this…no longer mattered. When she would be free. There had to be a future to look forward to. The thought that the life she lived now would rumble on inexorably until she died was too forbidding to contemplate. So, as she leaned on her rock, in the tapestry of her mind she returned to fashioning a better future, one filled with love, a home, a husband, a family of her own. Briefly, she was peeved that Jane had not done more to dissuade her from this domestic service route, or at least brought her down to earth and forewarned her of the realities that lay ahead. But the harsh reality was that for a young woman, little more than a child, of her low standing there were so few career opportunities, and of those most were repulsive and demeaning.

Don't think about that anymore. *You've* got a job; *be thankful. Silly child,* she silently chided herself.

She lay back and stared at the leafless branches swaying idly above her, feeling she'd never felt so…alone. No, not *alone*. Lost, maybe. No longer with a hold on her life. No, not even that, not exactly. More a sense of not yet having *found* a direction. Things have changed, and for the better; it was to be expected it would take time to adapt. But the thin warmth of the here and now consoling her, gradually feeling her body relax, she resolved to make the most of her free time. Listening to her heart pulsing rhythmically through the veins in her head, she watched the sunlight catching the tiny waves rippling at the edge of the lake. Silently, she inhaled chill air and exhaled a degree of tranquillity.

As her mood lightened, from the corner of her eye she noticed a weak shadow appear on the water at the edge of the lake. She turned her head and saw the silhouette of a man standing over her. For a moment she felt the tang of fear, then recognised Joseph, who she recalled also had the afternoon off, but unlike Mary Ellen seemed to have nowhere to go, no parents, no family, no home beyond the confines of Garston Hall. He was out of uniform, dressed in rough-cloth breeches, a collarless shirt and clogs. *All a little grubby,* she thought.

'Mary Ellen, what are you doing here?'

She sat upright and faced him, a cross expression on her face.

'Are you looking up my skirt? Pervert,' she spat, tugging her skirt down below her knees.

'*No,* Mary Ellen. I wasn't looking up your skirt. Anyway, it couldn't have been any more *up* if you'd pulled it over your head, you silly mare. Nice legs, though.'

That brought a half smile to her face, and he moved out of the pale sunlight to crouch beside her.

'Why didn't you go home?' he asked. 'It's your afternoon off.'

She told him what had happened, and he said, sitting beside her, 'but you can still go back. They may have come back by now; they may be expecting you. Did you tell them you had a day off?'

'I never thought to. I s'pose I could 'ave told Papa, and he could 'ave passed a message on. But I never thought on it.'

'You should have written a note. I could have delivered it; I go past the Lodge most days on my way to Ashton.'

She turned to face him. This was the closest they'd been together, and she saw he had vibrant grey-not-quite-blue eyes and a dark mole below his right ear. He was not handsome. But nor was he unattractive, and she recalled Elizabeth's comment that he was a good man at heart, who meant no harm. *He seemed kind enough,* she thought, lending veracity to the belief her sister often expressed that there was more that was appealing and worthy in a man than mere good looks. Leaning forward, she regarded him obliquely, noticing his covert glance at her breasts as her top gaped open, and realised that in more ways than one he may become an ally in the Garston household. Someone, given the opportunity, she might use to enliven the burden of daily routine. Allies were in short supply at Garston for those as lowly as a second housemaid.

Time would tell.

For now they spoke of trivial things – birds, flowers, trees and distant lands – and the darker undercurrents of the Garston household she was already coming to experience.

'Be wary of Grimes,' Joseph warned. 'He looks on the doms as a perk of his job. Does his best to…you know…'

'Beth's already warned me. If he tries it on with me, 'e'll get a swift kick in the nuts.'

'Maybe, but he's bigger and stronger than you, and you have a routine to follow. You can be sure he'll always know where you are, and when you're likely to be on your own. And he's not alone in thinking that way; those fucking weirdos, John and Henry, are not to be trusted either.'

She regarded him sideways. 'We've already had a run-in with 'em. Beth put 'em in their place, right enough. Anyway, how do I know I can trust you?'

He shrugged dismissively and looked thoughtful for a minute. 'You don't, I suppose. But I'm not like them. I'm Chapel, we don't tolerate that sort of thing. And anyway…I like you. I wouldn't do anything to harm you,' adding as caveat afterthought, '…or do anything you didn't want me to.'

Mary Ellen eyed him suspiciously, his words unclear of meaning. *He wouldn't do anything she didn't want him to.* Was he putting out a feeler? Testing the water?

'Have you been following me?' she asked. 'Is that why you're here?'

'No, no,' he protested, holding his hands palms facing towards her. 'I was looking for beech mast, and I saw you coming my way. Look, there's my basket over there.' He pointed to where a wicker basket was lying on the ground. 'Most of the nuts have rotted away over the winter. I really just wanted an excuse to get some fresh air. It's a nice day.'

She regarded him pensively, and saw eyes edged with concern. 'I believe you,' she said finally. 'We can be friends.'

'I'd like that.'

'Really?'

'Very much.'

She studied his anxious face for a moment, then said: 'Is it true?'

'Is what true? That I like you?'

'No. That you don't 'ave a family. That you're an orphan?'

His face became a mask of tragedy, a passing shadow, the change of direction taking him by surprise, and he fell despondently silent, chewing his bottom lip as if framing a response that didn't expose him to ridicule.

'I was taken in…adopted, I suppose, by an aunt at Chapel End when Mam died. Da had been killed in an accident down one o' t' mines a while back. Then when mother died, I were at risk of ending up in t' workhouse. Being taken in spared me that.'

'So, why don't you visit them. Chapel End's only over th' 'ill.' She nodded in the direction of the slight rise of Billinge Hill.

'Too crowded now. It were alright when we were young, and boys and girls could share a bed. Top to toe, like. But when t' girls started…you know… turning into women, they needed their own rooms, and there just weren't enough; it were only a small cottage on t' Main Street. So, they farmed me out. One less mouth to feed, as well. And I ended up 'ere. Started by mucking out stables until Mrs Bonnivale took a shine to me and found me work in th'ouse.'

'You must have been pissed off.'

'Yeah,' he grimaced, his head falling forward. 'It felt weird, frightening in a way. They'd taken me in, fed and clothed me like one of their own. Then just tossed me aside when I became inconvenient. Not one of the family anymore.'

'So, you never go back?'

'No point. There's nothing there for me. Garston's my home now.'

'But would you go back if they asked?'

'I dunno. S'pose. Maybe. Oh, I dunno.'

She giggled loudly. 'Are you always this certain about things?'

Joseph laughed with her, an experience he realised he rather enjoyed. Laughter, like friends, was hard come by at Garston. 'Always. I think. Usually.'

The swans were back, and for a moment they watched their graceful ways in silence.

'How old are you?' Joseph asked.

'Fifteen, last December.'

'Bloody 'ell. I thought you were eighteen at least. Maybe older. You'd pass, you know.'

'Do I need to? Pass, I mean. Does it matter?' Suddenly she had a thought. 'Do I get more wages if I'm older.'

'I don't think so. The only way you'd get more wages would be to move out into a classier place. Like wi' them Bradshaws at Haigh Hall in Wigan, maybe. Them's not short o' a bob or two.'

She moaned. 'Like that's going to 'appen. I'll just 'ave to marry a rich man, an' 'ope he dies soon.'

'So, that's your plan is it?'

Mary Ellen shrugged dismissively. 'Not really. I 'aven't got no plan. I'll 'ave to see what 'appens.'

For a moment she let her eyes roam over him and then, reaching a decision about her new-gained friend, she said unexpectedly, 'You can kiss me, if you want.'

'What?'

'Kiss me. On the lips.' She was being playful, teasing; it was a strange and, she realised as she said it, a new thrill for her, and found that she liked the sensation...of being able to tease.

'I... I...' his voice trailed off, but hesitantly he leaned towards her, uncertain, half expecting to be pushed away and mocked for falling for her jest.

But, no.

Breathing in the smell of...what, exactly? Leather? Soap? Polish? She was acutely aware of his warm, moist lips on hers, cautious, and then for longer, pressing more firmly.

They broke apart, but said nothing, foreheads touching, and she gazed into his deep-set eyes, a wayward lock of hair falling across his forehead. For a moment, neither moved, each balanced on the crest of uncertainty. *Was that what kissing was all about?* she asked herself. Perhaps it got better with practice, though that first kiss had taken her by surprise. Tentative, she leaned towards him and they kissed again.

The second kiss was better; more gentle, more assured, both drawing confidence from it, she parting her lips instinctively, her tongue tasting his lips.

Slowly easing apart, they leant back against the rock and on an impulse, he dared to put his arm around her shoulders. A small flock of greylag geese landed on the lake, close by the wooded island at its centre, putting the swans to flight again.

And then…silence.

She daren't confide that it was the first time she'd been kissed; she'd be embarrassed if he thought of her as a novice in such matters. And while she had no idea what had prompted her to invite his kiss, she realised it had left her shimmering with a strange eagerness for it to be repeated. She nestled into him, her thoughts suddenly invaded by a half-forgotten memory of her sister explaining… *the Birds and the Bees* she'd called it …the way attraction could arouse you, and what it was men did to women that ended in babies being born. In spite of a worldliness in many ways, Mary Ellen had yet to grasp the process of childbirth, and had been disgusted by her sister's explanation of what was involved. Yet, embraced as she was in this young man's arms, she was sure she felt an excitement that, in no small way, made her feel less resistant to the idea. More curious, maybe, to discover. Until this moment she had not known how it could be possible to feel anything other than revulsion at the intimacy Jane had described, still less that pleasure could flow from it.

And, if it was such a pleasant experience, why was it not part of Jane's life?

Maybe it was. Maybe her sister just didn't talk about it.

Maybe *she* shouldn't talk about it.

Joseph, for his part, was baffled, less by the experience than his response to it. He hoped Mary Ellen hadn't realised he'd never kissed a girl before. He was sure it wasn't a new experience for her, she'd been so confident and assured, parting her lips a little as they gently met his in a way that excited him. Now, with her cradled in his arms, the scent of her flowing hair in his nose, her body pressing against him, he was aware of being aroused, a growing sensation in his groin that he did not associate with kissing a girl, but with other...self-indulgent...activities learned in his teenage years. Easing up onto an elbow, he tried to change position to conceal the growth, and hoped she hadn't noticed. Above all else, what shook him most was a sudden urge to masturbate. Idle self-pleasuring in the privacy of his room was one thing, but this was so pressingly, urgently different.

When, finally, they returned to the hall, they bumped into Elizabeth, who raised a questioning eyebrow at the sight of the two of them together but greeted her with the news that Martha had been moved to a room in the scullery. Mary Ellen beamed with pleasure. Now she had a room of her own.

To no avail, Elizabeth pumped her for an explanation of her encounter with the footman, but Mary Ellen protested innocence and a chance encounter Elizabeth was not convinced told the truth. But she was happy for Mary Ellen, who found herself revisiting every moment of her time with Joseph.

Later, spread across her bed, blankets pulled tightly, sleep eluded her. The mattress was lumpy away from the two depressions she and Martha had made, and the blanket for all its warmth was harsh against her skin when her nightshirt rose above her waist as she tossed and turned restlessly in and out of dreams of wealth and luxury, happiness, lots of children and a strong and reliable husband ...like Joseph.

Maybe.

When she breathed deeply, she was sure she could smell his lingering earthy manliness. In her mind, she re-affirmed her liking for him, but was convinced he would not, *could not*, be the pathway to the life she dreamed of.

But, for the moment...

Chapter 20

Alice arrived promptly, pulling her mini onto his driveway as Duncan appeared at the doorway. She was wearing a light grey skirt and long-sleeved shirt with flared cuffs, open at the neck. Around her shoulders she had draped a red shawl which she held clasped at her neck. To his surprise and delight, she kissed him briefly on the cheek, her hand giving his shoulder an affectionate squeeze as she did so, 'Lovely to see you again.'

He stepped back to let her enter, and then led her through to the large open-plan kitchen where two glasses of red wine, which he'd poured as he'd heard her arriving, stood waiting.

'Cheers,' Alice said merrily. 'I do like a wine-infused reception.'

'You're welcome,' raising his glass in a mock salute. 'Cheers. And may I say how beautiful you're looking.'

Fearing he may have committed a *faux pas*; he regretted the remark instantly. There had been so much in the news in recent years about sexual harassment in the workplace, so much so it became impossible to know whether it was acceptable to compliment someone on their appearance, or whether it would be deemed improper. Ridiculous, he thought. If that was the way the world was going, he didn't want to know.

But he had no need to worry. 'Thank you, kind sir, 'Alice said, smiling at him, her eyes sparkling in the light of a candle standing on the kitchen table. 'Pure Marks and Spencer, through and through. I'm not one for wasting what remains of my life traipsing round fashion stores when I know what's comfortable for me and where to get it.'

Alice had always prided herself on her appearance, without being a slave to contemporary fashions. Comfortable and smart with understated flair hit the mark. If some saw the way she dressed as borderline sexy...well, that was their problem, not hers. She didn't dress to be provocative, although in times past she had like many women dressed to excite. These days, she dressed for herself and no one else, and would luxuriate in preparing herself for the day ahead, even on the days she planned to remain at home. Being a quinquagenarian didn't equate with the demise of elegance and self-esteem.

Yet, she now realised, it had been with a frisson of pleasure that she'd responded favourably to Duncan's appraisal. A man who noticed and let her know without innuendo; now there was a rarity.

'Well, it suits you,' Duncan said hesitantly, relieved not to be digging himself from an embarrassing hole.

Drink in hand, Alice commented, 'I couldn't help noticing what a fantastic view you have from here; it's beautiful.'

'Yes, it was what finally decided it for us…my wife, Isabel, and me. Sorry.'

'What are you apologising for? There's really no need. I know about your wife, and I feel for you. But I'm certainly not going to take umbrage if you mention her name. For a start, I've already seen three photographs of the two of you happily together, and all I've done is walk through to the kitchen. From what Nellie tells me you and Isabel were together from school days; that's most of your life spent with the same woman.' She smiled warmly at him, 'I'd be surprised if a man of your, er, senescent years…' and here she playfully brushed aside a lock of hair that had fallen onto his forehead, '…didn't have an endless store of memories. You can share them with me anytime. I'm not the jealous type. You clearly loved Isabel. Probably still do. I'm not going to usurp her place in your life. We're just good friends. Right? Family history geeks.'

In that, she felt sure, she was not being wholly truthful.

But the whole truth could wait.

'I'm sorry…'

'There you go again. Stop apologising, it's unsettling.'

He took her through to the living room where the chart he had drawn lay open on a small table.

'This is a beautiful room, Duncan,' she said, keen to change the subject. 'You must be very happy here.'

'I am. Very happy. As much as I can be. I've barely changed anything since Isabel passed. So, I can't take credit for anything other than the mess.'

'Well, *I* like it,' she said, and pointed to a sizeable collection of albums on a shelf built into a corner of the room. 'I'm guessing those are photo albums. Lots of memories, I'll bet.'

Duncan turned to see what she was looking at. 'Actually, no. In fact, they should be better protected, not left out like that. It's a stamp collection. Isabel collected stamps. Mainly British stamps, and she invested a fair amount of money in buying them. Some are quite rare, she told me. I know a bit about the collection, but philately isn't my thing. Isabel found it very therapeutic after a difficult day trying to knock sense into her students.'

'Ah, I see,' Alice said, sitting down and settling herself. 'Now, tell me, what you've found about my motley family?' suddenly purposeful, again sensing the need to move on.

'Well, only the bare foundations at this stage. What you asked me to look for. But it has piqued my curiosity, I must say.'

'Really? In what way?'

'Look, I'll show you.'

As they got down to studying the chart, she leaned nonchalantly close to him, and he felt the warmth of her body and could again smell a familiar perfume that, from a visit to her bathroom a few weeks earlier, he now knew was lavender-scented shampoo.

He took her through the chart, from herself up through her parents to her grandparents and then to John Liptrot, her great-grandfather. Against each name he'd written a number.

'What do these numbers signify?' Alice asked, pointing at the chart.

'It's just a genealogical numbering system for listing a person's direct ancestors in a fixed sequence of ascent. Ahnentafel, it's called. It's German for "ancestor table". The number sequence becomes unwieldy if you stray from the main line, but it helps link people together when you're trying to match a tree with a document that provides additional information.' He laughed, 'It looks complicated, but surely it can't be as bad as the Dewey Decimal system you librarians work with. I don't think I've ever understood that.'

'Me, neither,' she replied. 'Thankfully, I don't have to understand it. I leave that to others.'

'Well, this...' he said, indicating the chart, is much easier to follow...as I say, up to a point. See...' he pointed to Alice's name. '...you're number 001, because this is your tree. Your father is 002, your grandfather is 004, and your great-grandfather 008.'

'I see, each doubles the one below. What about the female line?'

'They are their male partner's number plus one. So, your mother is 003, your grandmother 005, and so on. It's fine for a while and it makes clear which family line you're following. If you were going up your mother's tree, then since she is 003, her father would be 006, and her mother 007.'

'I'm not sure what my great grandmother might have made of being described as Double-oh-Seven. But I never knew her, so I guess we'll never know.'

Duncan turned again to the chart. 'I've looked at your father's male bloodline, and then the female line. I'm confident that our mysterious lady lies up the Liptrot tree, so to speak. Anyway…along that line things start to get interesting with your great-great-grandfather, John, zero-one-zero. It took me a while to find it, but it turns out he was illegitimate. I took the liberty of getting a copy of his birth certificate.' He laid the certificate on top of the chart. 'You'll see that there is no entry under "Name and Surname of Father".

He also showed Alice a printout from one of the Parish Clerk records he had found:

Baptism: 1 May 1873 St Aidan, Billinge, Lancashire, England
John Liptrot – Illegitimate son of Mary Ellen Liptrot, Single Woman
Born: 23 April 1873
Abode: Garston, Ashton
Birth registered: 25 April 1873

'Likewise, when he later married, his father's name is omitted from the marriage certificate. I was able to download that from the internet.'

'Presumably illegitimacy would be frowned on?'

'To an extent, but between around 1850 and 1950 as many as seven percent of children were illegitimate. So, not altogether uncommon. But there are a couple of things about this record that make it intriguing. For a start, it was quite common for a couple to marry only after a girl became pregnant, or even after she gave birth. In those circumstances, the child is regarded as legitimate and takes the name of the father. But that doesn't appear to have happened. Equally, the parish may not recognise the father if he and the mother are not married. Yet in this instance, the child was baptised, and that of itself was not uncommon.'

'It sounds like it's getting complicated.'

'Well, it could be worse. At least your great-great-grandfather was only described as illegitimate. Some records use emotive terms like *baseborn*, *whoreson*, *misbegotten* or simply *bastard*, I've come across them all.'

'And can you trace the family line back any further?'

'I've gone a little further, but I spent some time trying to locate this John Liptrot in the records, not least because I can't find Mary Ellen having married anyone…yet. But I can look further, if you want me to. I tried checking the records of the parish overseers, because they like to identify fathers so that they could be made liable for a child's maintenance. So far, I haven't found any helpful records. But what I did find was that Mary Ellen had a second illegitimate child…as it happens also called Alice…and born seven years after John. And, for me, that opens a whole new can of worms, because I can't trace that father either. And what was Mary Ellen doing in those seven years? Apart from being a mother to a growing child. How was she managing? What did she have to live on? All fascinating stuff.'

'Do you think it could be the same father?'

'It could be, but I don't think there's an easy way of finding out…at least, not without a touch of forensic genealogy. Digging deeper, searching more widely. There could be a trace somewhere that gives us a clue. A slice of good luck would be helpful, too.'

'But basically,' said Alice leaning back into the sofa, 'you've done what I asked. You've identified the child in the picture as my great-grandfather, if I've understood your correctly, and his mother, Mary Ellen, my great-great-grandmother.'

'Exactly. I should have explained that earlier. But now I'm intrigued, and want to find out more, if it's possible. And there's almost always more.'

Alice sighed and patted his arm lightly. 'I can't ask you to do that. It could take an age, and I can't really afford to pay you.'

'You don't need to. I'm happy to do it, just pay me in wine. And, anyway, we can work together. There's a reasonable chance your library connections may provide access to archival records from around this time or can locate them. John's birth certificate shows the family to be living in Arch Lane, which is on the outskirts of Ashton, and by the time he married, he's living in the main street in Billinge and was married at Billinge parish church. That's somewhere we can start.'

'Well, if you're sure.'

'Of course. It's interesting that the Liptrots appear to be centred around Billinge, but the Marshes are from St Helens. Perhaps we could find out why John Liptrot moved from Billinge, where he was born, to St Helens. I know it's not far, only about four or five miles by crow, black or white, but it's quite a shift of family base. Why did he leave Billinge? When did he leave? What was happening at that time? A lot of people moved around, and there were scores of coal mines dotted about south Lancashire. Maybe he moved because where he was working was closing down. Unlikely, but it's possible. On the other hand, there would have been new mines opening up. I'm no geologist, but Billinge is a hill, I used to cycle there as a kid, and I don't think you find coal mines on hills. I could be wrong, of course, but maybe it was as simple as that. He went where there was work for him.'

'You sound as though you're getting very involved with this.'

'I can't help it. Once I get a scent, I like to track it down. Just let me do some more basic digging, and we can meet up again.' He started putting the paperwork away then had a thought. 'What did I do with that photograph; the one you showed me?' He found it among the papers.

'Is there something else?'

He studied the image for a few moments. 'Possibly. Take a look at the picture. This is an elegant woman, well dressed, wearing fine clothes. And look at her hands. If you look closely, you can see she has elegant fingernails.'

'Is that important?'

'Well, it's certainly puzzling. In the 1881 census records, Mary Ellen is a washerwoman. Do those look to you like the hands of a washerwoman? And would a washerwoman be able to afford such finery? They were the lowest of the low. Admittedly, the picture was taken in 1873, and she was recorded as a washerwoman in 1881, eight years later. But she could have already *been* a washerwoman at the time of the picture. We've no way of knowing...' he paused, hand on chin, '...or, maybe there's something we can trace in the newspapers of the time. So far I've only looked at the census records.'

'Either way, you think there's something we're missing?'

'I do. Or this *isn't* Mary Ellen, and the child *isn't* your great-grandfather. But if the 1873 date is correct, then it has to be who we think it is. Unless I've gone up completely the wrong tree.'

He pondered that for a moment. 'In which case, how did *your* father come by the photograph?'

'Curiouser and curiouser…'

Duncan smiled at her literary reference to Lewis Carroll. 'Oh, very good, Alice. Now we are in *Wonderland*.'

Before Alice leaves, Duncan suggested, 'Just a thought, but why don't you take a DNA test? If nothing else, it could tap us into research done by other family researchers.'

'How do I do that?'

'You can buy a kit from Ancestry. I'll order you one; I get a professional's discount. All it takes is a bit of spit, and we should get the results in around three weeks. Just don't spit after eating a curry.'

'Why?'

'We could find you're related to half of India.'

Chapter 21

July 1870

Mary Ellen had been working at Garston Hall for six months. To her joyous relief, the aches and pains she'd felt during those first weeks were long a thing of the past, replaced by strong arms and firm muscles. At last her arms once more felt as though they belonged to her, no longer weary appendages hanging leadenly by her side. What in the beginning had seemed an insuperable list of chores, she now disposed of efficiently, trilling through the days with ease. Where once she had felt ragged and haggard, she now felt strong and self-assured, confident in what she was doing. She was maturing as a woman, too, her figure, benefitting from the daily exercise housework imposed, was shapely and lithe. She felt robust and fit and had regained her energy and with it a renewed zest for life.

In the evening, when not so long ago she barely had the energy to undress before collapsing into bed and crying herself into a restless sleep, she now found time to socialise with Elizabeth for an hour or so, chatting idly, amusing themselves by recounting the day, poking fun at the lecherous Mr Grimes who during her first weeks at Garston had succeeded more than once in catching Mary Ellen unawares, grabbing and squeezing her arse as if testing the ripeness of a melon. To his irritation, Mary Ellen quickly became adept at dodging his nail-bitten paws and picking up on the slightest sound of his approach. To her relief, after three months of his unwelcome attentions a new third housemaid, younger than Mary Ellen, had started at Garston, and Mr Grimes' focus had turned to more compliant game.

One evening, at the golden end of a warm summer's day, Mary Ellen was in Elizabeth's room lying snugly beside her on the bed babbling about nothing in particular when Elizabeth eased herself up, leaned forward and kissed her fully on the lips. She pulled back in an instant and beamed at Mary Ellen.

'Just wondered what it would be like to kiss a woman. Well,' she added playfully, '…you. Not just *any* woman. I wouldn't want to kiss Mrs Bonnivale, or Cook, and certainly not Mouldy Martha.' She grimaced at the thought, pulling a face and miming being sick. The effect disarmed Mary Ellen and forestalled any unease that may otherwise have flowered.

For her part, Mary Ellen was bemused. The kiss had been brief and spontaneous, and not something she had had time to take in. To her surprise she reached up and touched Elizabeth's cheek, a spontaneous acknowledgement that the kiss, although unexpected, had not sent her scurrying away in horror. Elizabeth's lips on hers had felt soft and moist and tender. Warm. Inviting.

Gazing into Elizabeth's eyes, Mary Ellen giggled and lying fully on her back said mischievously, 'Do it again. To be certain. No one's ever kissed me like that before.'

This time, Elizabeth slipped one arm around Mary Ellen's shoulders and with the other pulled their bodies into closer union. Then, not leaving her gaze, she placed her lips once more on Mary Ellen's, pressing gently and teasing her lips apart with her tongue. Mary Ellen kept her eyes open, and saw that Elizabeth had closed hers, as if tasting her, intent, focused on the moment. Then she, too, felt her eyes closing as she absorbed the new sensations rippling through her body. Warm fingers teased open the ties on her shift and slipped beneath to caress her breasts. Then, with equal gentleness, Elizabeth lifted the hem of Mary Ellen's shift and slipped her hand between her legs, arousing Mary Ellen in a way she had not known possible…until that moment. Hesitantly, she tried to mirror Elizabeth's actions, exploring, caressing, teasing fingers through silky hair, feeling dampness and finding a warmth and pleasure that excited her and set her heart thumping in her chest.

Then, as abruptly as she had begun, Elizabeth sat up, tracing a serpentine line on Mary Ellen's face with her fingers and gently brushing a strand of hair from her face. She pecked her quickly on the lips and smiled warmly at her.

'You're a gorgeous bitch, Mary Ellen. But I think I'll stick with men.'

They both laughed at that and leaned back onto the bed still embraced in one another's warmth.

'Me, too,' Mary Ellen murmured, halfway to sleep, but knowing that she had yet to discover that for herself.

The harsh bark of a fox roused Mary Ellen from her slumber. Releasing herself from Elizabeth's encircling arms, she slipped silently away to her own

101

room, enveloped in a warm inner glow that countered the first chill contact of the cold blanket on her skin.

In the days that followed, her mind revisited the intimacy with Elizabeth, which, several opportunities notwithstanding, had not been repeated, not even on one dark and scary night when they had spent the late evening hours huddled in front of a small fire listening to thunder crack savagely overhead and jumping in fright every time lightning lit up the bedroom. It was as if the kiss, the intimacy, had never happened, and yet Mary Ellen still puzzled over it. She had enjoyed what they'd done. A part of her wanted to repeat the experience, but the Bible said that God created Man and Woman, and all Mary Ellen's experience of life confirmed that as the norm. Elizabeth had touched her private place and caressed her in a way that had pleasured and stimulated her.

Surely that was a sin? Was she destined for Hell's fires? If so, it didn't seem to bother Elizabeth, and she was the one who went to church.

And so, in time, the episode slipped to the back of her mind. Maybe in her fatigued imagination she had invented the whole thing; maybe it had been a dream.

An unanticipated consequence of kissing Elizabeth was that it served to rekindle thoughts of Joseph. Against the promise and possibilities of their first liaison beside the lake, there friendship, constrained by the routines of service, had withered to a level that was unremittingly platonic. And there it remained, firmly planted in indecision, going no further. From time to time, they met on Sundays, walked in the woodlands, sat chatting by the lake, but physical contact was minimal, almost passive as if doubt wracked Joseph's every thought.

As if he was afraid.
As if he didn't know what he wanted.
As if he was wrestling with the Devil himself.

In silent moments, she wondered whether Joseph could ever arouse the feelings Elizabeth had done. His kisses had been tense, bristly affairs, hard, when she thought of it now, in comparison with the serene tenderness Elizabeth had shown.

Drifting lazily into sleep, she determined to find out. Her next meeting with the shy, bumbling Joseph was going to mark a new step in her life...and his, too.

102

Following that first encounter, anticipating an escalation of her relationship with Joseph and remembering what Elizabeth had said about timing sex to her monthly flowering, she had decided to keep a diary. Using sewn-together sheets of paper stolen from cook's supply of menu sheets and a pencil that Jane had given her, she painstakingly wrote out the days of the month, marking the start and end of her periods. Over time she saw a pattern emerge and she felt sure she could plot it ahead. After two months, she was sure.

In time, from simply inscribing her projected time of the month, she began writing longer notes; of the weather; of happenings in the household, repetitive though they often were. She wrote about anything she found interesting and surprised herself with her command of her limited vocabulary and her ability to note her observations with paradoxical maturity and thoughtfulness.

Chapter 22

Spring 2019

Duncan Cooper pulled slowly into the car park of the Brindleford Arms. Like the White Crow, it dated from the sixteenth century, with leaded windows, some of them bayed, ancient gritstone walls and a sagging moss-covered roof pressing down companionably on ageing timbers. Unlike many neighbouring buildings, the gritstone had been cleaned to reveal its natural golden sandy colour, not unlike in colour the Jurassic limestone of the Cotswolds. Climbing red roses festooned the arched doorway and ivy had long since colonised the stonework. The pub reminded him of one on the outskirts of Blackpool in which he'd had his first alcoholic drink at the age of seventeen: lager and lime, a once-only experience that had made him feel queasy. Until the recent upsurge in micro-breweries and artisan ales he'd never touched beer or lager since. Now he had a taste for them.

Some of them.

The pleasantly warm day carried a hint of a breeze, the blue sky dotted with wispy clouds. In the beer garden – a modern concomitant of any pub wanting to attract customers – several rustic tables and chairs were arranged on a flagged terrace. It was a sun trap, and popular with smokers banished from the interior. The pub sign had recently been re-painted in gold, and the front of the building was bright with colour, early summer flowers overflowing from hanging baskets and window boxes, with yet more in recycled chimney pots and old beer barrels.

Brindleford, though formerly much larger than today, was one of those places set amid farmland that you had difficulty finding on a map. In addition to several privately owned farms, five more were still actively working as part of the estate that until recent times was owned by the Cavendish – Dukes of Devonshire – family for almost 400 years. Until the late sixteenth century, the manor and estate of Brindleford was held by the Gerards of Bryn. Sir Thomas

Gerard unwisely supported the cause of Mary Queen of Scots and was imprisoned in the Tower of London. In consequence, he forfeited his lands to the Cavendish family, beginning their long relationship with the area.

The whole place thrived on its in antiquity, although few today bothered to notice. At the heart of the village was the parish church of St Joseph, in pre-Reformation days known as St Helen's. That the village was ancient was attested to by the fact that the first rector was recorded in 1190 as Uhtred, a Norse name, although the village itself was absent from the Domesday Book. The present church tower was raised in 1497 and one of the original bells still regularly rung. Many of the family names that could be found in the parish registers as far back as the sixteenth century were still imprinted on farm gates. As the name of the village suggested, there was a ford here, though no longer in use other than by farm vehicles, and the name was thought to mean "the hill by the stream". A short distance down the main street, still cobbled in parts, past a row of seventeenth-century white-painted cottages, was the village school established in 1623 as "Brindleford Free Grammar School". It was relocated from its place in the churchyard to its present location in the early nineteenth century. There were fewer than twenty other buildings, all made from stone garnered from nearby quarries: several were listed by Historic England as being of architectural and historical significance.

There were many parallels with Garston, the locus of Duncan's research. During the nineteenth century and earlier, village life reflected agricultural and industrial changes. Handloom weaving in most of the farm cottages was a necessary extra to the earnings of a basic agricultural livelihood. Not until the construction of a cotton mill in 1853 was local employment placed on a stronger foundation; the opening of a paper mill at nearby Withnell Bank also provided much-needed regular work. Both villages had a workhouse, bleak places for the destitute and what were indecorously called the pauper lunatics of the Poor Law Unions.

Duncan had arranged to meet Alice for lunch on the pretext of discussing what little more he'd uncovered about her family. There was not much to report, but in calling to invite her to have lunch with him, he realised he was in a sense crossing a personal Rubicon, moving himself on from the bereavement that had left him stranded, and engineering the possibility of a pattern of social encounter – away from the chaperone of the ever-jovial Nellie, enchanting though she was – that they could both, if they wanted to, take further. For him it was a challenging moment, a first positive step towards releasing the anchors of the past yet confounded as much by an intrinsic shyness as by his inability to re-awaken the mechanics of social interaction with a woman he knew little about.

Since their last meeting, Christmas had come and gone, and Duncan had been busy for a client, with little time for "Alice's Project" as he'd dubbed it. Even so, giving in to nagging about "down time" from Nellie Norton, the three of them had managed several days out on the moors together, ostensibly searching for geocaches, but mainly just walking and talking, he forever fretful that he should be at his desk but delighted to be in this company; she happy to let things take their course. It did Duncan good to get out, and Nellie knew that. Tempted to suggest meeting up with Alice over Christmas or the New year, Duncan had instead taken the non-confrontational option, and headed for the hills, specifically a woodland cabin in a Lake District forest he had visited for several years with Isabel.

It the event, it had been a miserable time, during which he was confined to the cabin by days of unrelenting bad weather. There were memories of Isabel everywhere: in the cabin where they'd often made sensitive and deeply caring love; along the soggy footpaths that led around Loughrigg Tarn and up onto Loughrigg Fell; in the restaurants in Ambleside, and in the pubs in the Langdale valley.

Increasingly, whether in the Lake District or back at his home, Duncan could never side-track himself from thoughts about Alice for more than a brief time. The longer he spent out of her orbit, the more he felt a rising need to see her again. In vain, he tried to divert his mind by persuading himself it was puerile fantasy that, at his age, he should have long since outgrown. Yet in all too frequent moments, he realised too, it was growing from a need to do more with his life; more, at least, than spending his life burrowing into the often-mundane lives of others long dead. Now he was more certain than ever that he *wanted* to move on and felt he had found someone he might move on with.

Someone who could be a cathartic gateway to a new period in his life.

Yet, as if determined to cast gloom on his every plan, he worried that such a prospect was overly ambitious? Was it, in any case, a reciprocal feeling? Had he completely misread what signs there had been? He was so long out of practice when it came to embryonic relationships; in fact, given that he had been exclusively with Isabel since their teens, he'd had no "courtship" practice to speak of at all. As a result, for much of the last year, when he could have been emerging from self-imposed, grief-laden emotional hibernation, it had always proven easier not to bother. The thought of *chatting up* someone terrified him.

For her part, Alice, apart from the days out geocaching with Duncan and Nellie, had spent Christmas and New Year at White Coppice, cocooned in warmth and music and books and wine, with the television decidedly off in silent protest at the repetitive garbage that flooded the channels at this time.

At odds with the way each was starting to feel about the other, it never occurred to either of them to commit to some time together over the festive and New Year period.

They just furrowed their separate ways.

Chapter 23

Once back in the confines of her work office, Alice spent the days cataloguing a substantial intake of documents donated by the family of a deceased and once-prominent councillor. Alice had outstanding professional skills in indexing and cross-referencing, and that meant more than simply adding documents to an inventory but adding theme and topic reference tags and then linking the documents to other related documents already in the system. In this she was meticulously thorough, and by chance that brought to light a collection of files in the county archive relating to the Garston estate and its colliery. They included over 750 documents from letters giving accounts of deer hunting and timber sales to property terriers, steward's records and even a few marriage licences. Some she noted, while having a reference number and title, also had a note that they were "Missing" – the antiquarian's *bête noire*.

This was work she could relax into, but the association with Garston brought Duncan Cooper back to mind, setting in motion a train of thought that led her to pondering what she felt about the man.

Why she even felt anything.

Her DNA results had shown that she was emphatically of Western European origin, mainly from the North West of England, but with a small percentage of Irish descent. That DNA was worth investigating, but the arrival of the results served only to re-focus her mind on the man, and her five years of … what … *avoidance* of regular male company during which she had built a system of defences that rendered her impervious to unwanted attentions. She was perfectly happy as she was, and any kind of relationship, even a platonic one, would involve compromise and a change from the secure bubble of the status quo. An unaccompanied way of life was a status she had come to be happy with, and the fact that it meant she was forging ahead into a solitary and possibly lonely old age had not unduly waylaid her thinking.

Until now.

Now there seemed to be the...*prospect*...of an alternative future she may be able to mould to her liking. In any case, she thought after a moment's hesitation, platonic was good, wasn't it? Platonic with a likeminded intellectual was even better. And while she had not also thought that platonic *with benefits* was even better, the idea was there, simmering below the surface of her consciousness. That was far too soon an expectation, wasn't it? Again that moment's hesitation.

She was coming to realise that there was something about Duncan Cooper that was starting to rekindle a long-dormant flame. She was far from sure how brightly she wanted the flame to burn and she hadn't forgotten that those who played with fire often get burned. But there was something about the man, a reticence, a shyness, maybe – she couldn't believe it was lack of confidence – that had her wondering how deeply his waters ran, and how far he would need to be nurtured. She was still uncertain of her own feelings, but they would never resolve into anything positive if she didn't move forward a little on her own account.

So, when he rang to ask her out for lunch in nearby Brindleford, Alice accepted instantly.

Chapter 24

Sunday, 18 September 1870

For several Sundays throughout the spring and summer months, Elizabeth Bampton had left Garston secretively. Since her run-in with John and Henry, the footmen, some months earlier, and a second encounter when she had whacked Henry between the legs with a hot poker, doubling him up in agony, she had become the focus of their growing hatred. That they nurtured a hatred of women, and Elizabeth in particular, was increasingly obvious, and threats of beatings, rape or worse continued to circulate the walls of Garston Hall.

While in the hall, and never far from help, Elizabeth enjoyed a modicum of security. Once she left the sanctuary of the hall, she was exposed and vulnerable. Increasingly, she was afraid, and right to be so, but she could not afford to leave her employment at Garston; not while she needed to save her earnings in the hope of one day setting up a home, possibly with the apprentice blacksmith working in Billinge who had been courting her. Only once his apprenticeship was complete would he be free to marry, and with two years yet to run Elizabeth needed to make the most of her time at Garston. *If it was not the blacksmith,* she thought philosophically, *it would be someone else.* Her plans for the future she did not confide to her lover, it was too soon for that; Elizabeth had not yet finished playing the field, but her – *issues* – with the footmen he had dragged from her when she had turned up with angry purple bruising on her arms. Not without reason, Elizabeth feared what he might do; everyone knew that a hammer-wielding blacksmith was the last person to cross, even an apprentice blacksmith.

Mary Ellen had occasionally noticed Elizabeth glancing furtively about her as she headed in the direction of Arch Lane but knew that from there paths radiated in several directions: Ashton to the east, Billinge to the west, Chadwick Green to the southwest and Winstanley to the north. She thought of asking her sister Jane if she could discover where Elizabeth disappeared to, but Jane, too, had taken to spending time away from home and the unattended boys left to their own devices were as useful as a candle in a storm. Mary Ellen assumed that in Jane's case it had been to spend time with the Mousdale man she had spoken of, and with whom she seemed to be developing a happy relationship. And because Mary Ellen wished for nothing more than her sister's happiness, asking her to spy on Elizabeth was a needless and intrusive request.

Today, having changed into a simple linen dress that once belonged to Jane, and untangled the knots in her hair, Mary Ellen fled the hall shortly after one o'clock. The sun shone brightly from a clear sky, but a chill wind was blowing from the east, and within minutes she wished she'd brought more than a woollen shawl to keep her warm. Because of Jane's increasing absence from the family home, Mary Ellen had almost given up using her precious time off to tramp the miles to Penny Hall. The time would come during the wet Winter months when what she had planned for today would not be possible, and a visit to her home a warmer and drier prospect. For now, she was seeing Joseph, and today, having calculated her days with care, she vowed, she was finally going to *see* him. She was approaching her sixteenth birthday and under Elizabeth's guidance had matured rapidly since joining the Garston household. Now more than ever she longed to leave childish ways and thoughts behind her and to experience womanhood. She hoped Joseph can get away.

Today, he was integral to her plans.

Chapter 25

On the far north-western boundary of the woodland, Mary Ellen had re-discovered a childhood haunt, an old woodman's hut, unused but dry and intact even if it did smell of mould and rat droppings. A rusting iron-framed bed stood in one corner of the single room, its mattress long since passed its best, but dry. Summer swallows had been nesting in the eaves, such as they were. Here she came cautiously to wait for him, hoping he could follow her directions. He was late, and Mary Ellen wondered if he might not come. Shielded by the woodland trees from the rays of the sun, it was cool in the hut, and she sat shivering on the edge of the bed for fifteen minutes before she finally heard the sound of a twig snapping and then the door creaking slowly open.

He was not the man of her dreams, and certainly no musclebound woodsman, but he would do.

For now.

Well, for today, at least.

'It's freezing in here,' she snapped, more sharply than intended. 'I hope you remembered to bring that blanket.'

'All here,' Joseph said meekly, holding up a bulky hessian sack, which he opened and pulled out a thick tartan blanket, spreading it over the mattress, straightening the edges. His gaze took in the hut, 'This is not bad. For an old hut in a wood.' He turned back to adjusting the blanket.

'Don't fuss so much,' Mary Ellen playfully scolded. 'It's not some swanky hotel, in case you hadn't noticed. Now come here and keep me warm.' She held her arms out towards him.

Joseph, forever tentative in Mary Ellen's company, put his arms around her and pulled her close, pressing their bodies together and kissing her neck before leading her to the bed. 'Did you think I wasn't coming?' he asked, sitting beside her and resting his arm around her shoulders.

She remained quiet for a moment. 'Naw,' she finally lied. 'I know you can't resist me.'

She was right, and Joseph knew it. Since that first kiss he had thought of her constantly, frustrated in his plans to meet her by the demands of the hall and its chaotic routines that kept them apart and afforded only fleeting moments together too risk-laden to do more than speak briefly. Now, with her in his arms, he turned towards her and rested his forehead against hers, pausing before finally pressing his lips to hers. She ignored the itchy stubble and accepted the sensation of his tongue between her lips, touching her own tongue, their lips moist and warm with saliva. Briefly she thought of Elizabeth, but to her delight Joseph's probing tongue aroused an urgency within her quite unlike that she'd felt with Elizabeth. Had she not been preoccupied, she might have wondered why two kisses, one with a man, the other with a woman, could excite differing emotions.

He pulled away and gazed into her eyes. 'You taste salty.'

'You're not 'ere to eat me,' she retaliated lightly, punching him good-humouredly in his chest. 'And anyway, you've been eating cheese. I can taste it.' And with that, she pulled his lips back to hers, allowing a sudden and unfamiliar passion to arise, aware that she was trembling with pent up expectation.

'You're shaking. Are you cold?'

Without answering she spun him round and using her body weight rolled him back onto the bed. 'No, far from it. I'm hot,' she replied as she turned round to straddle him, her legs drawn apart, touching the outside of his thighs.

When the time comes, Jane had told her during one of their sisterly tête-à-têtes, *do what comes naturally.*

So she tugged at the hem of her dress pulling it free from beneath her and briefly exposing to his startled gaze a thick growth of dark hair. With the challenge of uncertainty hovering above him like storm clouds on a winter's day, Joseph averted his eyes.

This was wrong.
This was sinful.

But by the time she had dragged the dress over her head and discarded it onto the floor, tousling her hair and exposing firm breasts with large, dark nipples that had responded to the chill air, such thoughts evaporated. Reaching out to touch

113

her breasts, Joseph watched compliantly as she shimmied backwards and untied his breaches, easing herself up so that she could pull them down to his knees. His manhood long since risen to the occasion, Mary Ellen was seeing it for the first time and took its hard warmth into her hands, moving forward astride him and, guided as much by instinct as sisterly advice, eased him inside her until he was wholly consumed.

Do what comes naturally. And enjoy it. It isn't all about making babies.

Jane had told her to expect pain when first she had sex; *deflowering* Jane had poetically called it. Searing pain, distress, blood and sticky mess. But there had been no pain. Just the solidity of Joseph inside her. Unfamiliar, but…thrilling. Lacking guidance, she began rocking, inexpertly, experimentally, backwards and forwards, hoping it was the right thing to do, rising and falling uncertainly and then more confidently as the exotic sense of testosterone-fuelled Joseph inside her, inexpertly thrusting against her, incited emotions, wild, reckless and with uncontrolled, quickening urgency, her hormones rampant. Suddenly, cupping her breasts like prize trophies, Joseph arched his back and gasped loudly as he thrust deeper, and then in one surge she felt the moment she had longed for, a powerful throbbing release, an explosion of ecstatic sensations rippling through her young body, leaving her gasping for air, her heart hammering in her ears and beating at her chest. Her skin prickled with excitement, pulsing blood sending a warm flush to her cheeks. Her whole body trembled in the joyous grip of her climax.

Hot, perspiring and gulping air, she fell forward on top of him, feeling his cock shrinking inside her. With a smile on her lips, she kissed him passionately, then sat up and ran her hands upward over her breasts before theatrically flinging her arms into the air.

'I think that means we're not virgins anymore.'

Joseph, struggling for words that might match the circumstance, just smiled, the wide languorous grin of a young man who, for a fleeting instant at least, had the world at his feet, and then found his voice and croaked, 'Fuck me.'

'I just did,' was Mary Ellen's giggled reply. 'So much for Chapel, then.'

Wrapping themselves in the blanket, they lay in each other's arms, their bodies warm and slick with sweat. Joseph's mind a confusion of emotions. Mary Ellen's thoughts more mundane…of mission accomplished.

In her diary that night she wrote: *Fucked Joseph. No longer a virgin.*

She was a woman now.

Chapter 26

Duncan kept turning his attention to the car park, anticipating the arrival of Alice. But he ought to have realised that since Brindleford was linked to White Coppice by a path alongside the River Goyt, she would come that way. Moreover, it was such a warm and pleasant spring day, it would have been silly not to.

He saw her before she saw him, as he was cleaning his spectacles, a blurred image in consequence, but he'd know that figure anywhere. She had paused to peer up into a tree where something had caught her eye. He wondered what she'd seen; what she saw in the wider wooded and peaty moorland landscape in this part of the county. He felt a keen and unaccountable urge to find out. When she did finally catch sight of him, she waved; he waved back in acknowledgement. He had no qualms now about anyone noticing an evident connection between the man and the attractive woman, of realising that she was arriving to be with *him*. She was, he recognised as if for the first time, beautiful, wearing a simple front-buttoned sleeveless floral midi dress in pale blue cotton, cut low and with a buckled belt and pockets. On her feet, like the dress completely inappropriate to a walk in the countryside, she was wearing heelless ladies' canvas pumps. To Duncan's eye, she looked radiant, the sunlight obliquely catching her deep red hair, pulled back and tied in a small ponytail that swished rhythmically from side to side as she walked.

They air-kissed briefly, on both cheeks in the manner of northern France, Duncan placing both hands on her shoulders, feeling her warmth and breathing in that familiar scent. He went inside to order drinks and returned with menus; glad the weather was so favourable. When Alice ordered chicken, ham hock and leek pie, Duncan realised that having been up early to visit Isabel's grave, he hadn't eaten for hours and decided to go with her choice. The food was always good here and the pub had recently been awarded a Michelin Bib Gourmand for its restaurant food, while the bar food was more plebeian but no less well prepared. He wasn't snobby about food; he just wanted honest cooking at a sensible price. Much as he liked the theatre of a Michelin-starred experience, good pub grub was hard to come by, especially food cooked *Fait Maison*, as the French say, homemade, fresh, not precooked and packaged God knows where. He'd found this pub long before the Michelin people got there, and recalled visiting with Isabel, eating slow-cooked wild boar from a small herd raised on the Cavendish Estate and drinking a Fuzzy Duck Golden Cascade not long after the Fylde microbrewery had started making blond ales in 2006. But today he was driving and nursed an alcohol-free Fentiman's ginger beer from Northumberland.

'I was expecting you to come by car,' he said in a surprised tone. 'I'd forgotten about the path from White Coppice.'

'Well, it's a lovely day for walking,' Alice responded. 'So, why not? Got to keep my figure in shape.'

He suppressed the urge to say there was nothing wrong with the shape of her figure. Instead, as she sat beside him, he said, 'It seems an age since I last saw you. I was thinking only the other day that it was silly not to have arranged to have met up over Christmas. It's never a good time for people living on their own.'

'I suppose we just got embedded in the domestic and forgot about other things. It would have been nice, but I'm a curmudgeon at Christmas, and not good company. In fact, I positively hate Christmas. I suppose I must have liked it at some time, when I was a child, but I can't remember much except disappointment. I don't think I ever got the present I wanted. So, in the end, I stopped wanting. Thankfully, around our home there was plenty of countryside. So, even on the gloomiest of days, I would go out, walking muddy paths rather than endure the mindless torture of repeated Christmas Specials; they were bad even then. No one seemed bothered about where I was, or what I was doing. Of course, in those days it was never an issue for a child to wander off on their own. Even at Christmas. And the older I've become, the less tolerant I am. It just seems never-ending. It starts in October and drags on unbearably into January. And then it's Easter.'

'I know what you mean. In recent times, I've just turned the television off. Or logged in to Netflix or Amazon Prime. But you're right, altogether too much insincere jollity and stupid spending sprees. And unless you turn yourself into a hermit, there's little or no escape.'

'Too true. And folk used to say, *"Oh, you'll change your mind when you're grown up and have kids of your own."* Well, that didn't happen, did it?'

She sighed and her shoulders sank. Then she laughed lightly, 'We make a right pair. Thankfully, that's all behind us for the next few months.'

Trying to lighten the moment, Duncan changed tack. 'Anyway. Family stuff. I can't remember if you've told me, but you're not from round here, are you?'

'Well, I was born in St Helens, but mostly I'm from Ormskirk, hence no Liverpool twang, much as I love it and in spite of having lived there for years. Mind you, I have picked up quite a repertoire of Scouse expressions in my time.'

Duncan smiled at her. 'I can imagine. I remember the first time I met a Scouser. I hadn't a clue what he was saying, and his sister was worse because every other word began with "F", and quite a few began with "C", although, as I learned later, she did have a particularly bad case of Tourette's Syndrome. So, maybe that wasn't surprising. She was such a sweet thing otherwise.'

Alice laughed, her eyes catching the sun. 'That must have made for interesting conversations.'

He liked the way she laughed so readily. It was a warm, soft laugh, and it brought out the smile in him, too.

'I lived most of my young life in Ormskirk. Went to the venerable Ormskirk Grammar School at the same time as a bright young kid called John Forshaw, who went on to become the chief architect at the Ministry of Housing and Local Government as it then was. John Rankin Christie, the deputy master of the Royal Mint also went there, too, and Helen Hayes who became, I think, MP for Dulwich, but that was much later.'

'So, you've been in some select company.'

'I have.'

'And now you're slumming it with the hoi polloi.'

She laughed again. It was infectious. 'I'd hardly call you hoi polloi. Nellie said you had a raft of degrees.'

'Well, not a raft you'd want to sail on. I did all my studying at Lancaster University, starting there not long after it was founded and got myself a BA in History. I hated it at first, but by the time I got to the end of the course and got a 2:1, I realised that I'd quite enjoyed the experience. So, I persuaded my parents, bless 'em, to stump up for more research and went on to do a Master's degree in of all things the history of the royal guides to Morecambe Bay sands. That was fun. I got to know the present guide very well and did several bay crossings with him.'

'That sounds like a lot of studying.'

'It was. I really enjoyed it; it was great. But needing to earn a living brought me down to earth with an unhealthy bump. What about you?'

'I managed a BA, too, at Liverpool Uni – that's where I met my husband, Tom. He went on to be an architect, and I got a job working for Liverpool library service. I wanted to do an MA in Librarianship, but that didn't work out until after I'd started in Chorley. Money was always an issue and, as I don't doubt you know, these courses are not cheap. So, I've only recently been awarded the MA.'

'You sound a bit disappointed.'

'Well, not really. I suppose it was having to be careful with my money that irritated me. But it was the right decision, at the time. Once I was on my own, and my finances under control, I was able to enrol and get my Masters. But Nellie said something about you doing a degree in genealogy. What was that?'

'Well, that was quite recent. Before then my professor at Lancaster persuaded me to do a PhD in historical geography. One of the twentieth-century writers about the Lake District had commented in an article how no one had researched the evolution of tourist accommodation in the national park, and the Prof suggested that would be something I could look into on a part-time basis.'

'What exactly is historical geography? she asked.

Duncan laughed. 'To be honest, I'm not sure. I did ask the Prof, and he just gave me a five-hundred-page book on the subject, which I never did read. So, I just distilled it into history being about the passage of time and geography about landscapes and such like, so historical geography is about the impact of history on landscapes. How things changed. It's my definition, and it's all mine, in spite of its imperfections.'

'But that didn't involve genealogy?'

'No, but it did involve a lot of research among census records, rate and tax records, wills and probate and a shedload of other stuff that overlapped quite a lot with a course they do at Clyde University on genealogy and heraldic studies. So, I did that, and ended up getting another MA by studying the incidence of the influx of landed gentry of the Lake District. It wasn't quite as simple as that, of course. But I won't bore you with the details. Most of them were wealthy industrialists who made their money on the backs of poor people in the

Lancashire and Yorkshire mills, and used it to build mansions in the Lake District, every one of which has since been turned into a hotel.'

'So, let me get this right, *Doctor* Cooper. You have a first degree, two Master's and a doctorate?'

'Yes, and you can throw in a postgraduate certificate and then a diploma which were an unavoidable part of the genealogy course.'

'So, what next?'

'Well,' he said, spotting a young man heading their way with plates piled high, 'what's next appears to be grub.'

Hot chicken, ham and leek pies and mash in front of them Alice tucked in enthusiastically. She seemed so unselfconscious and completely at ease, as if she'd known him all her life. For a moment, as Duncan speared a large chunk of ham, he wondered if she *did* know him. Whether, perhaps, their paths had crossed at some other time, and he'd forgotten. But he dismissed the thought with the certainty that Alice was the sort of woman he was unlikely to forget.

They ate in a relaxed silence that Duncan found comforting. Was it possible to enjoy being with someone so much, especially someone he had known for such a short time? Well, it was if you were never any good at forming relationships of any kind, let alone a new one with a beautiful woman.

Lunch over, they ordered more drinks, which Duncan brought from the bar. As he emerged, pausing to let someone else pass, he stood for a moment surreptitiously watching Alice and suddenly felt not so much a relaxation of the past as a glimmer of something new for the future. An attraction he had not felt for many years, nor wanted to. Now it was there. Again. So, he wondered, how did you determine where the line was between being good, platonic, friends, and…something more? And, assuming you wanted to, how did you move on from one to the other?

Placing their drinks on the table he diverted his thoughts by saying, 'I've hit a bit of a wall.'

'Nothing to do with your driving, I hope.'

She was quick-witted, too, he thought. 'No, I'm saving that for some other time. I'll try not to involve you.' He smiled pleasantly. 'It's not an unusual occurrence in family research.'

'Something you can work round? Rather than drive through, so to speak?'

He took a mouthful of ginger beer. 'Usually, but not always. If the principal records are missing, there are other ways. Newspapers, for example, but they usually aren't indexed in a way that lets you pick out individuals. But, it's something I *will* try.'

'Who's the problem?'

He laughed lightly. 'Me, probably. You get so close to the research you sometimes don't see the wood, etcetera. I've expanded on Mary Ellen's family.'

He rummaged in the briefcase at his feet and pulled out a sheet of paper on which he'd drawn a rough family tree.

'Mary Ellen had an older brother, James, who lived only until he was twenty-three. He may have married, but I've not found a marriage record yet. If he did marry, there may be descendants down to the present day. If I can find the cause of death, I may get an indication of whether he could have been married.'

'What do you mean?'

'Well, if he's recorded as an imbecile, or has a cause of death that indicates a long-term or terminal illness, he probably didn't marry. Then again, if he did marry, it could have been his wife who registered the death.'

'Ah, quite, I see what you mean.'

'Then there's Jane, also older than Mary Ellen. I think I've nailed her down, and I *think* I've found that she married, but there's a muddle in the records – two marriages in the same place on the same day, both involving a Jane Liptrot, but with two different men. I need to untangle that one before I can find out what happened to Jane.'

'Well, if nothing else, it sounds like there's a few miles of winding trails for you to follow.'

'It gets even more interesting. I found another Mary Ellen, but she survived only two-and-a-half years, and then a Catherine, who did less well, and lived for only fifteen months. They were both baptised at St Aidan's, and buried there, although I can't trace a grave section.'

'Infant mortality must have been a real heartache for the parents.'

'I'm sure it was, but you never get to discover anything that tells you exactly what they thought and felt. History is seldom written by ordinary people. You don't always get to find a death certificate either, which as I say can sometimes tell you more than the mere fact of death.'

'Are things always this difficult?'

Duncan smiled, 'This isn't *difficult,* this is just low-level frustrating. It's what I call "Missing Record Malaise". One minute you're doing great and then suddenly you grind to a halt…'

'I know that feeling,' Alice interjected, referencing her past.

'Quite. Me, too. To highjack John Lennon, it puts a Spaniard in the works. But in cases like your tree, there's nearly always a work-around. Sometimes it's a question of transcription error. I did find one "Liptrot" in the records as "Lephthrot". Just a case of someone at the end of a tiring day, not reading the original correctly. It happens a lot, annoyingly. But quite often the issue is simply that the record hasn't been digitised yet. I get emails almost every week telling me about new records that have been entered in the database of Ancestry or, more usually, Findmypast. There are more records coming online all the time. In the case of the young Mary Ellen and Catherine, it doesn't matter too much. Cause of death just gives those particular records some closure.'

'So, Mary Ellen had an older brother and sister and two sisters, deceased? Is that it?'

'Nope. She had another elder brother, Edward…he'd be your third great uncle. I wasn't looking for information about him specifically, but I did find that he married a Welsh woman, Ellen Williams, from what is now Gwynedd. They had four children, one of whom was born in Haydock and they daringly gave him the name Owen Glyndwr. I don't think I need to tell you what the name of Owain Glyndwr means in Wales, the last native Prince of Wales.'

'It's very patriotic, though.'

'Quite so. He *was* patriotic, too. He joined the Royal Field Artillery and served in France and Flanders, and was then killed in action in 1917, and buried in Ypres, where my own grandfather fought, having lied about his age.'

'And you discovered all that, what, just like that.'

'Oh, it doesn't always tumble out of the woodwork quite so readily. And it helps if someone else in a family has done research; maybe a marital offshoot of your own tree. Ancestry picks up on that, and all you have to do is confirm it to be correct and reliable. I don't know who wrote the Ancestry algorithms, but he was a genius. But then, what do I know about computer programming?'

Alice sipped her drink thoughtfully. *Clever man*, she's thinking. *I like a clever man.* She smiled at him encouragingly, 'So, someone else is researching my tree?'

'Well, someone is researching a branch of it, but it could be a distant branch, and they just wandered into your tree. You'll need DNA and a lot of detective work to find out who. Well, not so much who, because the DNA profile tells you who they are, albeit it anonymously. But making the connection *on paper* can involve barking up a lot of wrong trees before you get the right one.'

'Oh, I meant to say,' she said suddenly. 'I've got my DNA results. Apparently, I'm mostly *here*, but a bit Irish, too.'

'Most people born in west Lancashire are the same. You can trace it back to the time of the Potato Famine in Ireland in the 1840s, when a lot of Irish came into Liverpool, mostly, hoping to get away from mass starvation and disease. Of course, it can go back much earlier than that. The Irish have been coming to England for centuries. And before them the Vikings were never far away during the so-called Dark Ages. Many of those stayed on when they were finally defeated and married into the local population.'

'Still, it's nice to think that some bit of me comes from the Emerald Isle.'

Duncan laughed. 'I thought there was a bit of the leprechaun in you,' adding, 'not that I've anything against leprechauns…or fairies…or any form of upwardly challenged people.'

Alice sits up in mock indignation, 'I should hope not. You don't get diamonds as big as bricks.'

Duncan was amused, 'No, but it would be nice to find just one, though. A diamond as big as a brick, that is.'

Turning back to his notes, Duncan showed Alice the details of two brothers younger than Mary Ellen, Henry and George. He had found little information so far about Henry, except the fact that his father, like George's was a gamekeeper, and that pointed him in the direction of the only sizeable estate in the area that might require a gamekeeper, Garston.

'So, does that mean looking into what we can find about the Garston Estate?'

Duncan noticed the "*we*" and the future promise it seemed to hold.

'I want to pin down what I've found so far with certainty, and back it up with documents… I'll get those from the General Register Office…then we're moving forward on a solid foundation.'

'So, I'm guessing it would help to see my DNA results.'

'Absolutely. I can create an Ancestry tree for you, and let the algorithms do their work.'

'Well, there's no time like the present. Assuming you're free for the rest of the day.'

Duncan might have had an engagement with the Queen that afternoon, but he would have changed it for spending more time with Alice.

'I am, if you am,' he said playfully.

Chapter 27

Having driven back from Brindleford to White Coppice they stood for a moment outside Alice's cottage looking across to the greening bracken-clad moors. Rather than squeeze his car into the small space near Alice's cottage, Duncan left it at the entrance to the hamlet, and they walked up the lane, and cut through a small copse of trees, along pathways full of celandine, daffodils and the last of the snowdrops. Beyond the cricket field the landscape was strangely undulant, dotted with elongated humps and bumps now mostly overgrown with grass and moss.

'When I first came here,' Alice said, 'I wondered what all those humps were. It seems they're rabbit warrens, built by the then lord of the manor. I've seen them in Yorkshire, where they call them conygers, but I don't know if there's a Lancashire name for them. I always assumed they were for keeping rabbits for food, but apparently there used to be a trade in rabbit fur for London clothing makers. It doesn't seem to have lasted long, but the rabbits stayed on and made a mess of the landscape until there was an outbreak of myxomatosis, which I've heard suggested was introduced intentionally.'

By early evening, Duncan had studied Alice's DNA, and pronounced it *interesting*, and then created an Ancestry tree with Alice as the root. After a few entries, the tree seemed to take on a life of its own, as the system hit them with rapid-fire "Hints" about possible relationships and data.

After a generous lunch, neither wanted much to eat, and so Alice prepared a plate of sandwiches, which they consumed absentmindedly as they added new records to the database. Once it was established, Duncan shared Alice's tree with himself, and gave himself editing authority, which meant that once back home he could access Alice's tree, and add new information as he found it.

Having moved forward as far as they reasonably could without running the risk of inadvertently setting up false trails, Duncan started putting away his notes, and prepared to leave.

Alice excused herself on the pretext of visiting the bathroom. She found herself poised in a situation she had anticipated several times in recent months and knew the moment would present itself sooner or later; the moment when she was certain she would invite the man to stay, the moment it was timely to do so.

Was this the moment?

Chapter 28

October 1870

Summer had come and gone. Life at Garston had simpered through the warm months with barely a whisper to disturb the routines of the household. Until, that was, not long before Mary Ellen's birthday, two of the footmen returned shiftily from a visit to the Stork pub in Billinge, John sporting a loose tooth, a black eye and a bloodied nose, Henry with a bloody cut on his face and nursing an arm lividly scarred as if seared by hot iron. They had become involved in a bar room scuffle over a silly wager, they said, during which Henry had fallen against a hot fire dog that stood in front of the log fire. For fighting in a public place, they were docked a week's wages and left the butler's office with the threat of dismissal hanging over their heads. It was common knowledge that the two footmen were distant relatives of Mr Grimes, and that saved them from the instant removal from office they deserved, but Mary Ellen sensed there was more to it than they would admit.

For months Elizabeth had done her best to avoid the pair and would have succeeded had they not finally orchestrated a trap to catch her alone. Cornering her in one of the basement corridors, they savagely beat her to the ground, tearing at her uniform and dragging her skirt above her waist. Henry stood over her, his manhood exposed, his intentions more explicit than Elizabeth cared to imagine. Only the sound of heavy footsteps along the corridor intervened to save Elizabeth.

Henry leered at her as they scuttled away. 'Next time, bitch. We'll have you,' he spat at her. 'Next time.'

But two events happened to ensure that there was no "next" time. The first when Elizabeth confessed the assault to her lover apprentice blacksmith, adding insult to injury in his mind. The second when on a market day shortly afterwards John and Henry unknowingly ventured into the apprentice's domain. When officers of the local constabulary made enquiries into a disturbance at the Stork, no one could remember a thing. Everyone swore that the two footmen had never set foot in the inn, and none could explain how they might have sustained their injuries.

Transient global amnesia to a man.

Elizabeth was never troubled again, and quickly regained her customary poise and confidence.

Mary Ellen and Joseph meanwhile repeated their visit to the woodman's hut several times, each time turning their hideaway into a more comfortable nest for their lovemaking. On Mary Ellen's birthday, Joseph surprised her by producing a bottle of wine from a leather satchel he'd taken to carrying. She read the label: Chateauneuf du Pape, and a date, 1865.

Joseph hadn't brought glasses, but he had a corkscrew on the pocketknife he carried. Mary Ellen was wide-eyed with concern.

'Joseph, you'll get sacked. You can't steal wine, and you'll get me sacked too, you dozy bugger.'

'No one will miss it. For a start, I hardly ever go down to the cellar, so no one has reason to suspect me, even if they do miss it. I just saw an opportunity and took it. The opportunity, I mean. Well, and the wine, too. I overheard Grimes saying it was a new wine from somewhere in France. I just wrapped it in some towels I'd been carrying and hid it in my room.'

'So, what do we drink it from?'

'The bottle, stupid.' With that he inserted the corkscrew and removed the cork.

Mary Ellen sniffed at the bottle and wrinkled her nose. 'It smells disgusting.'

'If it wasn't a good wine, they wouldn't have it in the cellar, would they? And anyway, what do we know about wine?' And with that he put the bottle to his lips and took a long gulp, trying manfully not to pull a sour face. The third swig had him licking his lips. 'It's actually nice, once you get over the first taste. Try it.' He handed the bottle to Mary Ellen who sipped at the wine, tasted it, rolled her eyes, then tasted it again.

From his satchel, Joseph produced a hunk of cheese and some bread. 'Happy birthday, Mary Ellen,' he said.

She smiled and kissed him. 'You remembered.'

'Did you think I wouldn't?' he asked, pushing her onto her back.

Their lovemaking took Mary Ellen by surprise. Joseph was tempestuous and, for the first time, aggressive and rough, leaving her feeling bruised and sore inside. The wine had stimulated a passion within her, and she responded to his fervour like with like until, exhausted, they collapsed, arms and legs entwined, into an inebriated and sweaty daze, pulling the blanket over them.

Chapter 29

The sound that awakened Mary Ellen was not a familiar one, not so early in the day: an axe biting into a tree close by. She opened bleary eyes to find not the attic bedroom she woke up in every day but that she was still lying on the bed in the woodman's hut.

'Joseph!' she yelled frantically, pushing aside the blanket that had covered them. She leapt out of bed, the morning chill biting into her nakedness as she struggled to dress. She slowly pulled open the door and peered out. It was still dark, the night sky just yielding to dawn's light. There, not more than twenty paces away, a forester was cutting a fallen tree into logs by the light of storm lanterns. It was not normal for the gardeners to be about in darkness, but equally it was not unknown if they wanted to earn time off. If *they* were up and about, the rest of the servants wouldn't be far behind.

'Joseph, for fuck's sake,' she said, shaking the still sleeping form of her lover. 'We need to get back to the hall.'

Finally, hearing the urgency in Mary Ellen's voice, Joseph opened his eyes, the realisation of what had happened settling heavily on his face like the shadow of doom. He ran a hand over his face, knuckled his eyes to clear them of sleep, and quickly pulled on his breaches. Before leaving, he hid the empty wine bottle under a floorboard, along with the blankets from the bed, doing what they could to leave the place looking as though no one had recently been there.

They checked where the woodsman was, and whether he'd been alone. Urgently, they set off in the opposite direction, taking care to keep within the shelter of the trees. Cautiously, ever alert, they made their way through the trees and into the copse that surrounded the icehouse. Only chance would reveal them thus far, but beyond the copse they faced half a mile of open ground to the servants' entrance; there they would be exposed. They could offer no explanation other than a lie, or the truth – which was unthinkable – had anyone seen them, so they set off walking as quickly as they could, trusting that the hall and everyone in it was still asleep.

But that was not the case.

Chapter 30

A year after the death of his wife, Duncan had started to feel more grounded, finally beginning to accept that there was life after the death of a loved one. For months he'd found it depressingly distressful to come home to an empty house where once music, laughter and love had prevailed, or to work within it, absorbed in a vicarious world, delving into other people's lives when his own was in such distress.

On an impulse he bought a kitten and called it Mij after the otter in Gavin Maxwell's *Ring of Bright Water* and in memory of a visit to the sanctuary at Sandaig overlooking the Isle of Skye he'd visited several times with Isabel. The cat was no substitute for the woman – *obviously*. But it was displacement therapy, a distraction, and in that, it worked. Given a choice, he preferred dogs, but felt that the way he had to work, a cat would be less demanding on his time. Cats came and went as they pleased; dogs needed daily exercise.

Mij soon settled in. Duncan had a cat flap installed in the rear door, which Mij used with the proprietorial air of one who'd been doing it all her life. Given that Mij, a tortoiseshell with beautiful markings and white paws like socks, had been only recently weaned when Duncan brought her home, she had indeed been coming and going most of her life. To his amusement, she'd cultivated a habit of poking her head through the flap, as though to check the coast was clear, retreating and letting the flap clatter with a noise she seemed to enjoy, before fully entering. It was an announcement that she was back, and ready for food or love depending on the time of day…usually it was food. It was a habit that, for reasons only known to her, she did not repeat when leaving the house, which often left Duncan wondering whether she was in or out.

The cat's evident pleasure with her new home had a reassuring, confidence-restoring impact on Duncan, and that had prompted him to stroll down to the local pub, the Black Horse, from time to time, and enjoy a pint of risquély named Fuzzy Duck Cunning Stunt from the Fylde, or a Ribble Red from the Crankshaft microbrewery in Leyland. Like many pubs in rural Lancashire, the Black Horse was steeped in history, a beautiful redbrick, two-storey building first licensed by Leyland magistrates during Elizabeth I's reign, in 1577, but some records suggested it had been selling ale since 997. Even with a date of 1577, the Black Horse was one of the oldest pubs in England and may have played host to Oliver Cromwell during the Battle of Preston. As was his wont, Duncan researched the history of the pub, but the earliest record he could confirm with satisfaction was that of William Hargreaves who was shown as occupying the pub in the Leyland Hundred Poll Books of 1835. Born in 1806, this young man in the 1841 census was recorded as a farmer, publican and pattern drawer.

The name of the village, Limbrick, in the area known as Heath Charnock, was thought to derive from an Old English personal name, Landbeorht, which to Duncan suggested Norse origins dating from the sixth or seventh century. Others suggested that its name meant simply the "Land of the lime trees". For months as he and Isabel drove back and forth looking for somewhere to live, he laughingly referred to the village as Limp Prick, which made him think there may be something unsavoury in the water. Only when they finally found and moved into Brimstone Cottage, appropriately named after a butterfly, did he make the effort to pronounce the village name correctly. In fact, Limbrick was a hamlet rather than a village, there being no church, the nearest being St Paul's at Adlington.

When Duncan and Isabel first saw Brimstone Cottage they knew instantly it was the place for them, considerably beyond their budgeted price range, but once seen, nothing was going to stop them. Duncan was in gainful, well-paid employment in local government, and Isabel earned double his salary as a senior lecturer in the history department in the University of Central Lancashire in Preston. She specialised in early modern history.

Brimstone Cottage was more than two hundred years old, probably an original part of either Bibby's Farm to the north, Fish Barn Farm to the east or Brindles Farm to the south; it had proven impossible to determine which farm it had belonged to. Built for agricultural labourers, like most cottages of that era, the cottage was built to last for generations. Along the gables and below the windows, the gritstone walls were more than two feet thick, no wattle and daub that you were afraid to lean on or could put your fist through with little effort. The modern M61 motorway was less than a mile away, but with the doors and windows closed you heard nothing of it. Even on warm summer's evening when they sat in the garden with a chilled white wine, the hum from the motorway settled back in their consciousness so much so that when visitors asked what the noise was, they didn't at first realise what they were referring to; it had become something their minds absorbed and lost.

The cottage almost certainly had history: the wear on the steps leading to the front and rear doors, worn smooth by its previous occupants, testified to that. But beyond its entry in the various census records, Duncan could find nothing, not even in the rating and valuation books in the county archive, to reveal more of its history. Looking east over the Anglezarke and Rivington reservoirs to mast-topped Winter Hill, the cottage was tucked into a verdant hollow above the River Yarrow. So melded was it into the landscape that it seemed to have grown organically from it, or to be sinking organically back into it, free of competition for space and light save for a copse of mixed woodland that backed onto it and wherein woodcock were known to breed. It was as much a part of the landscape as the trees, the fields and the time-weathered drystone walls, blending in, it seemed to them, with the countryside in a synergy of harmonious relationships.

On summer evenings, he and Isabel would sit on a small-paved terrace at the side of the cottage, open a bottle of sauvignon blanc, and relax as they took in the view across to the moors stretching eastwards to Holcombe Tower above Ramsbottom and the Irwell valley. As much as the beauty of the cottage, it was that view that had determined them to buy the cottage. When he looked out across the view now, glass of beer to hand, Mij curled up and purring deeply on his lap in a rare moment a feline acceptance, the sun casting cloud-shaped shadows across the heathery slopes in the distance, painting and repainting the landscape in violet hues as it went, catching the windows of farmhouses, he felt once more contented.

The outline of drystone walls lay like a network across the scene, holding the landscape together. Some said that ancient ley lines ran across to the summit of Winter Hill, holding a mystery beyond his understanding, but imbuing the countryside with an intrigue and fascination. He was accustomed now to tracing lines through history for those who came for his help. Perhaps one day he would trace some less fathomable lines to see what history they held.

He rarely saw his neighbours. The country lane that accessed the cottage was fifty metres away, but he would occasionally get a friendly wave as folk passed. And he caught up with several of them at the Black Horse. He felt even more connected once high-speed broadband reached the cottage, remote as it was. The cottage was cool in summer, cosy in winter, and with Mij as a companion, he began to feel a measure of contentment for the first time in a long time.

A huge part of his life was missing now, but at least he had a life. Sadly, a year after her arrival at Brimstone Cottage, Mij disappeared. Duncan assumed she'd been run over or taken by a fox.

But he would never know.

Chapter 31

October 1870

Lady Makerfield watched the young couple as they returned furtively to the hall, a sour expression on her face. She found little need for sleep, invariably the last to retire, seldom before the witching hours, and wide awake again a few hours later. Her habit on rising was to envelop herself in a heavily embroidered gown, a gift from an eastern potentate with whom her husband had business and stand at the window watching the arrival of the dawn. In the warmer summer months, when dawn came early, she would open one of the tall windows that gave out onto a small balcony and listen to the dawn chorus. To her there was no better part of the day, a time when the world was at peace; a time when only the nefarious were about; a time before the daily tribulations of her existence surfaced in her waking mind.

The morning was gloomy and cold, so she narrowed her failing eyes and pressed her face to the window, bringing their faces into focus. *A footman and a second housemaid*, she silently mouthed, her breath misting the window. Then, murmured aloud, 'What have we here? What *do* we have here?'

She continued to watch as the pair scuttled from view, heading no doubt for the servants' entrance. Her face, etched with lines of age, betrayed a lifetime of disappointments, so many that she had long since forgotten how to smile. It was not smiling now, any more than a thin-lipped grimace might be considered a smile, her face a mask of exaggerated disdain.

But there was a wicked smile shaping in her mind.

Life at Garston Hall had been an irksome ordeal since Lady Makerfield had been widowed at the age of sixty. Now it was her son, Mansfield, who was Marquess of Windleshaw, a miserable, inadequate, pompous businessman, unworthy to hold a candle to the renown of his illustrious father, a man whose acumen and sound business sense had built the Garston estate and fortune and brought great esteem to the family name. Now, not only was his son investing that fortune unwisely into the dirty work of coal mining, but, to Lady Makerfield's disquiet, his morality was at some remove from the standards he applied to the unfortunates that appeared before him as a Justice of the Peace in the Magistrates' Court in Wigan. Not as careful in covering his activities as he imagined, Mansfield Garston thought his mother knew nothing of his philandering during his frequent visits to London, ostensibly to attend meetings with his bankers. *Thieves and charlatans, the lot of them!* But she did, and she despised him for his weakness and shame.

Nor to her chagrin was his wife a paragon of virtue. No stranger was she to brazen flirtation when the opportunity presented itself, disporting herself in obscenely low-cut dresses that several of her guests construed as an invitation. She was not, it was widely rumoured, unaccustomed to welcoming those she favoured into her bed. And there had been several of those. It was a disgrace. She was behaving like a common...*housemaid*...a strumpit.

To compound Lady Makerfield's desolation, her wastrel of a grandson, was styling himself the Earl of Garston, heir to the estate and its fortune. The very thought that this...*irresponsible*...*scoundrel* was frittering away the family fortune on drugs, potions and a new-fangled contraption that made pictures of people was abhorrent. Why on earth would people want flimsy, insubstantial photographs? What was wrong with an honest portrait by a reputable artist, Tissot or Watts, like those of her husband and his illustrious father in the great hall?

That he might one day become the head of the Garston lineage sickened her, a condition not in the slightest relieved when her mind turned to his sister, the Lady Clarissa, sorely demented child, tormented by demons beyond redemption, deprived of love and affection her entire life, abandoned at birth to a wet nurse and nannies, only to sequester herself in her boudoir consuming Heaven knew what potions of evil her cavalier brother brought her.

Lady Makerfield turned a sour face from the window and rang for her maid.

Chapter 32

It has been a trying few days, and Duncan was becoming exasperated. Whichever trick he tried to move forward, he was meeting with frustration heaped upon confusion as he tried to break through or find a way around a seemingly impenetrable wall in research he was doing for an important family in Southport. His most highly paid task to date, he needed to impress, but was getting nowhere. There had to be another way; there always was. It was just a matter of looking in the right place.

And in the right frame of mind.

He just wasn't finding the way through today. It happened; it was nothing unusual. He knew it was a temporary thing, and that he was missing something obvious. He was tired, and in need of a break. To walk away from the problem.

By lunchtime, he'd had enough. He needed to refresh his head, to escape if only for a short while.

He sat briefly in the garden, but that wasn't doing it for him.

So, changing into walking gear, making a flask of coffee and grabbing a fistful of energy bars, he jumped into his Volvo. He drove north through Chorley, relieved to get away from the cottage. The sun shining from a cloud-studded sky, shadows scudding across the slopes of Winter Hill to the east. He joined the M61 at Hartwood Hall, near the Mormon temple. Many locals saw the towering steeple as a blot on the landscape; Duncan was ambivalent but knew that he'd often had cause to be thankful to the Church of Latter-Day Saints for the family history database they compiled.

Sticking to the speed limit, not least because his dashcam recorded his driving speed, he travelled up to the M61, leaving it at Walton Summit, a place known locally as the Bermuda Triangle, a largely industrial rash of offices, warehouses and delivery hubs enclosed by the M6, and M65 and the M61. He followed the M65 eastwards until finally able to leave it at Guide and head onto Haslingden Road for the stunning drive down Haslingden Grane, and then south on B-roads to Holcombe. There was a shorter route to his destination that used the Bolton bypass, a far less attractive option, and invariably slower.

Once past the ancient Shoulder of Mutton inn, formerly called Lower House to distinguish it from Higher House, which used to be known as the White Hart inn – a conundrum he'd never understood – he parked in the Peel Tower car park. Breathing the refreshing air deeply, he put his boots on. Minutes later he was striding a charming section of ancient cobbles, Holcombe Old Road, a lane of widely spaced setts flanked by the pink displays of rosebay willowherb, herb Robert, ragged robin and an occasional silver birch. He loved this short stretch of exposed cobbles; they provided an instant fix of nostalgia for a time almost gone from living memory, but ever-present to local history researchers.

A light breeze wafted lazily down the valley, and on it a pair of buzzards mewed and circled, as anything that might be on their menu scurried from view. This was a part of the county that spoke loudly of William Blake's 'dark Satanic mills', of the Industrial Revolution, of river power and of rough-edged, characterful settlements like Haslingden, Ramsbottom and Tottington peopled by hardworking and determined parochially patriotic individuals. Above, their waters feeding the River Irwell, moors loomed, topped by the huge monolith of Peel Tower. A distinctive monument on the West Pennine Moors, the tower was built in 1852, to commemorate the repeal of the corn laws by Robert Peel, the founder of the modern police force. Duncan had a vague idea about the corn laws, but "vague", in this instance, was the operative word.

From the car park, most walkers headed directly for the tower, on the edge of Holcombe Moor, using a steep zigzag pathway. Keen to revitalise his brain, Duncan had a long circuitous approach in mind, one that rose gently along the base of Holcombe Moor, and then ran die-straight to the cluster of farm buildings at Chatterton Close. He smiled inwardly at the memory of the first time he'd come this way, just before Easter in 1987, following one of the weekly walking routes published in the *Lancashire Evening Post*. As he'd approached the farm, he'd seen what appeared to be a top hat floating along the top of the boundary wall. Closer inspection, as he'd peered over the wall, revealed a group of children in costume putting on a show for the farmer and his wife. It was a performance of pace egging, an ancient Lancashire tradition, on this occasion given by the Holcombe Pace Eggers, as they called themselves, a group of children who toured the local hill farms bringing the Easter tradition to them. He wondered how many of today's children were as connected with their local history. Or had the past thirty-odd years changed all that? Were those traditions still passed on? He rather hoped so. He didn't want to be one of the last generations to see top hats floating above walls.

Beyond the farm, Duncan pulled up through a wide, walled break onto Bull Hill, deeply breathing in the invigorating afternoon air, and doing his best to avoid less pleasantly aromatic, fly-ridden cowpats that warned of cattle ahead. On a whim, having spotted the cattle, he decided to deviate briefly from his intended route and seek out another Lancashire landmark, the Ellen Strange monument. The monument is not marked on maps, so trying to find it needed a clear day. Not of itself ancient, the monument commemorates Ellen Broadley, whose maiden name had been Strange. An itinerant worker, who lived at Ash Farm in Hawkshaw, she was murdered here in 1761. Her husband was charged and tried for her murder at Lancaster Assizes, but acquitted for lack of evidence. A different version of events claimed that Ellen was murdered by her lover, a packman, a wandering pedlar who confessed to killing her, was tried and found guilty and hung. But the truth would never be known. Such folk tales, Duncan knew, were to be taken with a pinch of salt, not because the fundamental facts were not true, but because over time they became embellished and distorted, and much detail lost in translation. That they continued to hold a place in the communal history of the adult population of these remote settlements was demonstrated in 2015 when forty people, including Duncan and Isabel, then quite poorly and deteriorating visibly day by day, gathered at the Ellen Strange memorial to commemorate what had happened on that blustery night so long ago. It was the last time Duncan and Isabel ventured out onto the moors together, and the recollection pained him.

Leaving Ellen Strange's monument, Duncan strode across the peaty banks of Bull Hill, a landscape fashioned by quarrying, and on to the so-called Pilgrim's Cross, believed to have been a marker for monks travelling to Whalley abbey. Here, he sat on a rock and poured himself a coffee. Relaxing against the stump cross he let his gaze roam across the undulating moors. It was hard to image that less than a hundred years ago, this whole area, on the high moors and in the river valley, had been a hive of industrial activity.

As he crunched his energy bar, he spotted a rock at his feet that looked alien among the dark gritstone blocks. Picking it up, he saw that it was a piece of limestone, and could only have been brought here by a walker. This is gritstone country, not limestone. That the rock was limestone was evidenced by the presence of very clear fossils – crinoids and brachiopods – embedded within it. It was a weighty chunk of rock; someone had gone to a deal of trouble – *Why? To confuse future generations of geologists?* It had to be a prank.

Suddenly, as if revived by a good night's sleep and only now awakening to a new dawn, his forensic mind pinged chaotically and illogically from fossils and Jurassic Park to DNA, and to what was really an obvious way around his problems of the last few days, had he but thought of it. And if he could get the family to agree.

The stumbling block he'd been tussling with, if he was being honest with himself, had been no more than a pathetic excuse not to work. Some days a mental inertia settled on him. But, as was so often the case, the walk on the moors had cast its rejuvenating spell.

With his mind on a DNA and other solutions to his problem, his thoughts also turned, warmly, to Alice, and he felt a longing to be back in her company. Her DNA, too, was going to be a way by which he could dig deeper into her family's past. But he didn't know if DNA could survive from the nineteenth century in a form that would prove useful.

But he knew someone who would.

Chapter 33

April 1871

Spring had been slow coming, languishing on the heels of a bleak and miserable winter when it seemed the rain and wind would never stop. Such few lambs as were about in the Home Farm fields were thin and undernourished and would bring a poor price at market. Tom Smallwood, a tall, gaunt man, the sixth generation of farmers at Garston, had confided in Mary Ellen's father that Lord Garston was planning to sell all the farm stock and invest in a large-scale expansion of his mining operations, in spite of sustaining heavy losses when one of the company's coal-carrying ships was lost in the Atlantic. The news of the plans came as a blow. Game rearing, mostly pheasants, on the estate was now almost entirely confined to the deer park and the land surrounding the Carr Mill reservoirs that belonged to Liverpool Waterworks to the west. If the planned changes occurred, instead of the relatively limited infrastructure and buildings associated with drift mining, the countryside would be lost beneath pithead winding equipment, underground haulage and steam-operated engines. From a gamekeeper's point of view, it meant disaster, and foreshadowed the worst possible future.

With little or no game left to manage, John Liptrot would be out of work, and that inevitably meant out of a home, too. That was going to happen soon enough anyway; Mary Ellen's father was due to retire, and they could only hope the plans might not come to fruition. The changes would serve only to bring his era to an end. For the family, it meant disruption, the need to find a new home, and goodness knows what unforeseen difficulties. In his most dour moments, John Liptrot thanked God that he wouldn't live to see it, although he had long since lost his faith. As he saw it, faith was a slender notion; the only thing that separated the conviction that the Lord will provide from leaving everything to chance. He could no longer believe. He wanted to, but so many years of tragedy and unanswered prayers had brought him to this. Now, in this sixty-eighth year he faced a new beginning he had never contemplated, a prospect laden with foreboding, and one he would have to face without the love of the wife, his second wife, who had died barely more than a year ago. His will to live, he knew, was leaving him; he was weary, tired of a life that in spite of his contented employment as a gamekeeper had been compressed with grief.

At the age of twenty-two, a time when he was working in his father's trade as a weaver, he married Mary Berry. A year later, Mary gave birth to a daughter, Elizabeth, who survived one of the harshest winters on record for just two months before succumbing to neo-natal infection and malnourishment. Within five years, Mary also had died, and plunged John into years of heartache, during which time, no longer able to cope with the confined space and unrelenting noise of the weaving shed, he gave up his employment as a weaver and found a new role at Garston, as its gamekeeper. Instead of a fusty, unhealthy indoor workshop, John was now out in the countryside he loved and understood. With the passage of time he rejoiced in it, and came to find love again with, of all people, Mary's sister, Alice, eighteen years his junior. By the time Alice in turn had died she had given birth to eight children, three of whom were already dead, two barely surviving beyond two years.

On the Garston Estate, Gamekeeper Liptrot was an important man, though he earned little more than one pound a week. There were recompenses in kind, of course, and his pay was fortified by tips from visiting sportsmen to whom he ministered, breeding what for him was an unnatural obsequiousness founded on the recognition that for anything more than his meagre wage he was dependent on the charity of others. It was a condition that settled uncomfortably on his shoulders.

He dispensed charity, too. Woodpigeons were among the perquisites of his job, and apart from responding to requests for the birds from the household kitchen, any woodpigeons, rabbits, too, that he shot he was allowed to keep. When there were too many, there were always neighbours happy to accept a bird or "bunny" destined for a pudden pie. But he dealt honourably with game birds and hares and would not think of trespassing on his lordship's domain in spite of the temptations and opportunities: honour and integrity had always formed the backbone of his life.

Chapter 34

Arch Lane zigzagged from the outskirts of Ashton, past Tithe Barn Hillock and continues, made up with grassy banks and hedgerows on either side, to the lane end at Charity Farm from where ancient packhorse trails, long since without such trading purpose, ran on to Carr Mill and the great Laffak Moss. Several smaller cottages flanked the lane, all of them originally lived in by farm labourers, but increasingly the need for farm hands was diminishing, prompting some to transfer to work in the estate's coal mines.

The middle of the lane was cleared by the passage of people and horse-drawn vehicles, so there was no need for a footpath. In summer it was idyllic with the hawthorn, elderberry and blackthorn hedgerows and their shiny black sloes in bloom, the banks bright with cowslip, bluebells and the poisonous and, some would say, erotic Lords-and-Ladies plant, which the children laughingly called "Naked Boys", all untouched by the scythe. Winter was an altogether different matter, with deep furrows cut by cartwheels, often full of freezing water making it difficult to walk. A few of the women then wore belts with clips to lift their skits clear of the mud but that did nothing for the clogs or rough-made leather shoes they wore on their feet.

Penny Hall Lodge halfway along Arch Lane was a tied cottage reserved for the gamekeeper and his family. The Lodge was one of the largest and newest on the Garston Estate, built within the last five years of Ravenhead Brick and with a roof tiled with slates from North Wales, and gas lighting. John Liptrot and his family moved into it as soon as it was built. The front garden was small with a white picket fence and a gate, but the back garden was large and mostly used for growing potatoes, swedes and carrots that were stored in clamps in the garden, and onions they could store in a small outhouse along with various animal traps of different sizes. Like their neighbours, the family kept chickens in a run, feeding them on food scraps and ground-up chicken feed, and over the years the children had given them all names. Eggs were always to hand and as the hens grew old there was an occasional roast that filled the cottage with mouth-watering smells. From time to time their father came home with a rabbit for the stew pot that was a permanent fixture on the stove. Woodpigeons were a treat for the family, and many a bird found its way into the family pot.

The cottage had the luxury of three bedrooms upstairs, with large beds and thick feather mattresses, and floors covered in rag rugs made from old clothes. There was a bathroom with a freestanding large tin bath, and a toilet that flushed into an underground tank out in one of the fields, as did the brick-built toilet outside at the rear of the cottage. One bedroom was used by their father, while Mary Ellen and Jane shared another, and the young boys the third. It had not been so convenient when the older Thomas and Edward had also lived at home, and it had come as a blessing when they married and were granted the tenancies of adjacent semidetached cottages farther down the lane. Unlike Penny Hall Lodge, these older cottages had no water supply, and their young children had to trail down the lane in all weathers to the well bearing a rough-hewn yoke that enabled them to carry two buckets at a time.

The back-room downstairs was the kitchen and held a small range for cooking and a large strong kitchen table with chairs. Pride of place was the solid wooden Windsor chair for the head of the family. A meat safe stood on the wall, alongside a simple wooden cupboard with sides and door of perforated zinc that keep the contents cool and the insects out. It left the large larder free for less perishable foods. In one corner was a simple flat stone sink, which emptied into a large bucket underneath. Hung from the ceiling a six-lath laundry dryer, operated by a rope pulley was invariably festooned with drying clothes. A small mainly glass veranda had been built on to the kitchen with a washbasin and plenty of room in which to do the weekly wash.

The front room downstairs was the parlour, repository of the best bits of furniture the family could muster and whatever prized possessions they had, few as they were. The parlour was seldom used. They mostly lived in the kitchen. On the mantelpiece there stood an old marble clock, two brass candlesticks and several polished brass containers of uncertain origin from which rose long pheasant feathers. The mantelpiece cover, their late mother's most treasured possession, a hand-down from her own mother, was of chenille velvet with macramé work and bobbles hanging from it. On the chest of drawers stood a glass dome with a stuffed barn owl and owlets, together with an oil lamp. The wall held a picture frame containing old sepia prints of adverts for guns, showing smiling gunmen standing proudly over braces of pheasants and empty cartridge cases in the long grass. The most important item was a large glass cabinet containing two shotguns, one double barrelled and the other a single bore. They were under lock and key, and the key always hung on the belt of John Liptrot, gamekeeper.

Chapter 35

In the months that followed her mother's death, Mary Ellen often found herself looking up sharply thinking she'd heard her voice, snatches of conversation, a quick rebuke the venom of which invariably dissipated faster than it came. Not from her childhood, but more recently, when her mother was ailing. In her final months, her body had been despairingly frail, yet her eyes continued to yearn for life and burned with love and a zest for a more fulfilling life than the one she'd been handed. She'd never been any other way, full of energy, overcoming one obstacle after another as the hardships of domesticity and motherhood raised their heads, day after day. Mary Ellen's father, older than his wife by fifteen years, by comparison had been taciturn, given to an introspective moodiness that Jane had once said she thought was rooted in the constant struggle to make ends meet and to provide for his family.

There had been times, many times, when her parents had argued in a gentle almost apologetic way, mostly about her mother's plans to redecorate the rooms of the house, to make new curtains, to cultivate a corner of the garden in which she wanted to grow flowers. Hollyhocks, montbretia, marigolds, red-hot pokers and roses, lots of roses, and huge bushes to provide habitats for the blackbirds, dunnocks, robins and tits that were plentiful in the surrounding countryside. But to a gamekeeper, land was for growing crops, raising cattle, breeding game birds…not for flowers. Flowers, he said, were plentiful in the hedgerows. Why not be content with God's gift?

Yet in spite of his objections, her father always gave in to his wife, for whom his love was plain for all to see. In the months after she passed, he would make the time to go into her garden, to sit on a log he'd fashioned into a low bench and smoke his pipe, watching the birds come and go as the dying sun sucked the light from the sky, and with it the light from the world that had been his life.

It was a disappointment for him, for all of them, that she had not lived long enough to enjoy her garden and the joy it brought her more than she had done.

Mary Ellen was still not free of the memory of that dreadful day, the day when her mother's body was brought home from the estate washhouse where she had died. She would probably never be free of the sight of the oak coffin laid out in the parlour as a stream of visitors came to offer condolences and pay their respects by dutifully placing a hand on its lid. Mary Ellen was put to helping Jane in the kitchen provide nourishment for the visitors, while their father did his utmost to affect dignity, sadness and gratitude combined, his sorrow-filled eyes permanently on the brink of tears as the light of his life left him, just as her sister had done so many years before.

Two sisters; one man, and he had married and outlived them both.

The two young boys, too young to fully take in what had happened – except that their mother had died – were sent up and down Arch Lane and to neighbouring Garston village with messages, as much to get them out of the way as anything else; news travelled fast in small communities where everyone knew everyone else.

During a lull in the stream of visitors Mary Ellen went into the garden, glad to be out of the house for that love-filled place had suddenly become cold and unfamiliar, no longer the focus of her universe but a dark and sombre void of sadness, her mother's dead body filling every room with dread.

That night full of unhappiness, no longer able to cry, Mary Ellen lay awake listening to the light breathing of her sister exhausted by her day. Sitting up, Mary Ellen started to throw the blankets aside thinking to slip downstairs, into the parlour intent on being with her mother for one last time. At that moment, a moonbeam, breaking free of scudding clouds, shone briefly into the room and she realised that there was no need to visit her mother; her mother had come to her. She no longer inhabited the body in the wooden box downstairs; that was not her mother, for she was with the angels now in a garden full of colourful flowers where birds sang, and the sun shone unendingly from a cloud-free sky.

The funeral was held on a market day, and as they left the churchyard Mary Ellen could not understand why the village, their neighbours, could appear so untouched by the tragedy of her mother's passing, everyone about their business: street haberdashers selling buttons and threads; costermongers with carts of fruit and vegetables; Irish tinkers who had moved to Lancashire in the years following the potato famine in their own country; nail makers from Chowbent and Shakerely over Atherton way, nicknamed "Sparrowbills" after the nails they fashioned; housemaids spinning out their errands to trawl the throngs for would-be suitors; housewives, some who had turned to the market directly from the church service, back in their weekly routines haggling over prices; apprentices tormenting street urchins by throwing stones at them, and a Punch and Judy show bringing merriment to the children.

Mary Ellen, incensed, was moved to stand in the middle of the street and scream at them that her mother had died, that life would never be the same. Why did they not care? Only the arm of her sister round her shoulder and the reassuring smiles of her older brothers and their wives brought her comfort in her distress as they led her home, their head-bowed father walking in their wake.

Chapter 36

Duncan was weary after the train journey to London, followed by tube connections across the city to Brentford. As he walked from the tube station to his hotel, taking in the unsightly clutter of shops, office and second floor flats, he wondered why everyone insisted on saying that you went *up* to London? Compared to his beloved Lancashire it was decidedly *down*.

He checked in at the Premier Inn at Kew Bridge he regularly used, then strolled the short distance to a favourite Thai restaurant where he took a table with a view over the Thames. An unfamiliar, unsmiling face wearing garishly red lipstick took his order of a Thai Dim Sum, a delicious blend of minced pork and prawns, and a hot and spicy Pla Nung Ma Naow that turned out to be the hottest sea bass he'd ever tasted. He washed it all down with several Chang beers and returned to the hotel where he slept deeply through hours of dreary television and awoke in the morning to find the television still on – news readers and political pundits blethering on about whatever was topical.

After a Continental breakfast he wandered, briefcase in hand, beside the Thames, feeling better for a decent night's sleep. He strolled through Waterman's Park on a short stretch of the Thames Path, the air pierced by the shrill cries of ring-necked parakeets, an alien species to Britain that has colonised this part of London and spread further afield, even reaching as far as Anglesey in North Wales. He crossed Kew Bridge, and then took to a riverside path that led past Oliver's Island to the National Archives. It was a warm and sunny morning, and when he reached the building, he headed for the toilets where he changed out of his now sweaty T-shirt into a clean one carried for just this purpose. Then he stashed all but the essentials in a locker and prepared to face the dragon who guarded the inner sanctum. He had never understood what he had done to incur the displeasure of the security officer at the entrance to the reading rooms. Even though she must know him as a regular from his numerous visits in the past, she still treated him as a stranger, making him switch on his laptop – presumably to demonstrate that it wasn't a bomb, the true reasoning eluding him – and checked his reader's ticket against his picture on her monitor before admitting him.

Some people! he thought. Yes, there had to be protocols. Some of the documents in this archive were priceless. He just wished for something a little more pleasant, more human, less humanoid.

'Thank you, Candida,' he said with forced politeness, delighting in noting her squirm when he addressed her by her first name.

'It's Mrs Holland to you, as I've told you before, *Doctor* Cooper,' she snarled, seeking to recover the upper hand.

'Ah, you *do* remember me then,' a note of sarcasm barely restrained. 'Have a lovely day, won't you.' He made to enter the reading room, but turned back, 'Oh, by the way, it says "Candida" on your name badge, not "Mrs Holland". Perhaps you could keep that in mind before you snap people's heads off.'

It was an untypical reaction, but he felt better for having said something.

Candida Holland sneered at his retreating back and turned away to admit a plaintive-looking man who, having witnessed the exchange, was meekly waiting to enter. Duncan rationalised that she must have a cheerless private existence. By any standards, it was saddening to think that this might be the apotheosis of her day, cooped up in a cool, dry, air-conditioned environment that was good for documents, but not so good for the health of those who worked there.

To his delight, the documents he'd requested before leaving home were already waiting for him, and he was surprised by how speedily he completed his research. He'd been lucky; it wasn't always like this. He double checked everything he'd found, then ordered copies of the pages he needed for his client, which would be ready in an hour or so. He checked the time and thought about leaving early and heading home as soon as the copies were to hand. But his rail ticket permitted him to travel only on off-peak trains and it would be early evening before he could catch the first of these. So, he decided to take the opportunity to scan the catalogue for records that might relate to Garston Hall, where he knew Mary Ellen's father was employed.

But first coffee.

He smiled awkwardly at Candida as he passed through the barrier. She studiously ignored him, affecting preoccupation with sheets of paper on her desk. Outside he headed through the National Archive garden across to Kew railway station where he knew there was a small café selling excellent coffee. A young waitress made her way around the tables to his window seat to take his order. Unlike her contemporary in last evening's Thai restaurant, she smiled pleasantly. When she returned, she placed a coffee mug in front of him, and set a small jug of milk beside it.

'Americano, with milk on the side.'

He sighed silently. Why can you no longer get a simple, uncomplicated mug of white coffee? What was it with mochas, macchiatos, lattes? And the only difference he could see between an espresso and an Americano, was that the latter had very little coffee and a lot of hot water added to let it down.

'Will there be anything else, sir?'

At least she was polite, and pretty too. Perhaps he was being boorish, his mood irrationally influenced by the accumulating trivia of the day, though little of it had been unpleasant.

'Not at the moment, thank you,' he said smiling at her. 'But I'll probably be back for lunch.' He wondered whether she cared, and whether a Sandeman's steak pie and chips was enough of an incentive to return.

Probably not, he concluded.

He took out his mobile, and in an effort to raise his mood, sent a text to Alice.

In London at the National Archive. Going to look for anything about Garston Hall, while I have time to kill. Fancy meeting up for lunch tomorrow? 12 noon. Nova, Chorley?

Duncan xxx

Two digital kisses this time, consciously added. Then, in the hope of a positive reply, called Nova and booked a table.

Returning to the archive, he endured Candida's rite of passage a second time, collected his waiting documents and sat down at a terminal to search through the online catalogue for anything listed against Garston that didn't relate to the estate's development into deep coal mining. What he found wasn't much, but it intrigued him. The hall had been sold in the late 1880s, not long after the dateline he was researching, and subsequently demolished in the 1920s. The news shouldn't have surprised him, after all, Garston Hall was no longer there. All he had to do was drive to where it had once stood to learn that first-hand.

Maybe he would do that anyway. Taking a cue from Isabel, he'd long since learned that just being in the place that had an association with the past seemed to infuse a connection that few would acknowledge – and psychiatrists have a field day with. He'd even joined her in hugging ancient standing stones in Orkney...but only if he thought no one was watching.

For now, he noted what he'd found on his laptop for future reference, and decided to call it a day, collecting his things from the locker and ambling across to the station again where he caught the Overground back into central London and the tube up to Euston.

Wishing he'd eaten earlier; he headed up onto the balcony at the station and went into Gino d'Acampo's Italian restaurant where he ordered lasagne and a large glass of Valpolicella. With time on his hands, he asked for a coffee, and made it last as long as he reasonably could before heading down onto the concourse and into *Paperchase*. Here he purchased several greetings cards in ornate styles, blank for him to insert his own message. It was something he always did when passing through Euston, and the cards subsequently carried loving messages to Isabel on birthdays and anniversaries or just simply to say how much he loved her.

Chapter 37
Sunday, 9 April 1871

In the morning's early light, the brightening sky still graced by a waning gibbous moon and a panoply of the brilliant stars, she left her sleeping brothers – one snoring basso profundo, the other emitting a high-pitched whistle – and set off down the lane that led into the Garston estate, treading warily to avoid the worst of the waterfilled holes. At odds with the yellowing sky, a mantle of low mist hung in the air, placing dewdrops on her cloak, and lending the beech woodland she soon reached a dank, unnerving sheen. At its edge, wild daffodils were growing, bright sentinels against the woodland's dark, and she stooped to gather an armful of those not yet fully opened before pressing on into the shelter of the leafy trees. At a cross-path she paused for a moment, listening as the woodland slowly stirred into a new day's life. Over the years of her childhood, her father had taught her to identify the song of the birds presenting in the dawn chorus: the blackbird, the robin, the wren flitting about the shrubbery around the streams, and then the song thrush. Soon the great tits and coal tits would join the chorus, and in another month or so the sound of warblers, too, would resonate around the woods.

For the past six years, on this same day, she had made this pilgrimage. Deep in reverie, she turned at the cross-path and a few strides farther, at the very heart of the woodland, quit the branching path, her feet now stepping a way she could follow blindfold. By an ancient towering beech she stopped, reached out with her hands and placed her palms against its smooth, grey bark, as if affecting a connection, to earth herself with it by some process of osmosis she would never comprehend. In her mind, she was simply saying 'Hello' as if to a friend; she was saying "Thank you" too. It would make no sense to anyone but herself. Nor was it meant to. Many would think her strange, in league with the Devil, witchcraft still lingering in the folk memory of these parts. But she was at ease.

This was a simple communion between the woman and the tree that no one would ever understand. At the tree's base, the letter "W" and a date had been carved with care and artistic precision; someone had been at pains to make it sharp-edged. Breathing slowly, as if to compose herself, she knelt, sat back on her heels mindless of the woodland damp seeping through her skirt, and gently placed the flowers on the ground where last year's flowers had long since withered and died. When she stood, she bowed her head. To an onlooker, she might be praying. Yet she was not praying, she no longer saw the point. In moments of introspection, she wondered whether she ever had. Today, in the growing light of day, she was merely standing there…the pain of loss once more cascading down the years, remembering, with a singular sadness only someone who had borne the pain of childbirth and loss could truly understand.

Chapter 38

Unsettled by the impending uncertainties of the family's future, Jane sat in their lodge home peeling potatoes in front of a fire that gave out little heat, and onto which she threw a small log. She was awaiting the arrival of Mary Ellen, eager for her news, but keen, too, to impart news of her own – uncertain how it would be received.

Mary Ellen visited when she could, but of late left early to spend the evening hours with the man she had taken to. Only on that first Sunday off had Jane not seen her sister, and that because of an urgent need to assist a neighbour in premature childbirth.

With a sound like a bull crashing through a fence, Mary Ellen gushed into the lodge dragging a blast of chill air in her wake and throwing her arms around her sister.

'I've missed you,' she cried excitedly, throwing off her cloak and hat.

'And we've missed you, too, although it is a hell of a lot quieter without you.' They both laughed and hugged one another closely.

''Ow are the boys?'

'Oh, the same noisy, troublesome, argumentative, snotty little brats they were last week.'

'No change, then.'

'Not a lot, and thankfully they're outside most of the time. I only see them when their stomachs bring them home.'

'And 'ave you seen anything of Papa?'

'He came home midweek, but I've not seen him since Thursday. He seemed okay, but he's feeling his age. Said there were poachers about, so he's gone off to give them something they won't be expecting. Took the double barrel and that heavy overcoat he wears when he stays out all night.'

Jane placed a large black kettle on the stove and swilled out the cold teapot. 'So, what's new at Garston? Still in love?'

She protested, 'I'm not in love. I just like being with 'im. 'E's just a friend.'

'Him being Joseph Cunliffe?'

Mary Ellen nodded and pulled out a dining chair to sit on.

'Has he tupped you yet?' Jane asked playfully.

Mary Ellen flushed, her voice rising too stridently to ring true. 'No, 'e's Chapel; 'e's not like that.'

She knew she was lying; Jane saw it in her sister's colouring cheeks but smiled to ease her evident embarrassment. 'Well, that only means he's non-conformist, not Protestant, like us. It doesn't mean he won't pass a chance to get up your skirt any more than the Proddie bastards would, believe me.'

Mary Ellen sat more upright, eager to change the subject. 'Well,' she began, pouting petulantly, ''e's had plenty of chances, and 'asn't done nothing except fondle my tits.'

Jane snorted loudly. 'That could be useful if you ever get a cow, and it won't make babies,' adding, 'it's alright. I'm teasing you. I'm very happy for you. He sounds like a nice man. Just be careful. The last thing you need right now is a baby to look after.'

''E is. A nice man. And anyway, I don't want babies; shitty little things.'

'You were one yourself once, and shitty with it.'

'Maybe,' she mused, momentarily turning to look out of the window, as if calling something to mind. When she turned to face her sister again, she shook her head: 'I don't know what goes on inside a baby, but it's 'orrible, and it comes out o' both ends.'

Jane burst out laughing at that, and turned her attention to the kettle, pouring hot water into the teapot to warm it, before tipping it out and spooning in dark tea leaves from a battered caddy. Refilling the teapot she covered it with a knitted cover and left the tea to mash.

A few minutes later, chipped tea mugs in hand, as they settled at the kitchen table in a companionable silence, Jane casually said, 'Actually, I've got a man myself, now.'

Mary Ellen spluttered into her tea. 'What!'

Jane nodded, and smiled, hoping her sister would feel pleased for her.

'A man? Who? Where? I thought you didn't like men.'

'I never said that I didn't like men. I just had other…*more important*…things to deal with, like bringing up you lot for a start. And since mother died there's not really been much time.'

'But now you've found time,' Mary Ellen said, a little more tartly than she intended. For her part, Jane was always uneasy when Mary Ellen suddenly matured like this. She could cope with a wayward sixteen-year-old, just, but in this mood, Mary Ellen was sixteen going on forty and wise with it.

'Well, it just sort of happened. I wasn't looking for anyone.'

'So, who is 'e?'

'One of the Mousdell's, from Billinge. I was over there on market day, getting some cheese and more eggs because the chucks had been a bit lazy, and I knocked him over.'

'What do you mean, knocked him over?'

'He was on one o' them bike things, and as he passed behind me, I stepped back. I didn't know he was there, and I just…knocked him over.'

'Was 'e 'urt?'

'Well, his pride certainly was, and when I saw him again later, he had a bump on his head the size of an egg. That's what made me say I was sorry; it was huge. And he joked about me having come for eggs but probably not expecting to find the one he had.'

'And then what? It doesn't sound like you just walked away.'

'No. Well, I mean, he's good looking, fit and strong, and he offered to buy me a mug of ale in the Stork to show that he'd forgiven me…he said…and I did feel sorry for him. So, I said yes.'

'So when did all this 'appen?'

Jane looks sheepishly at her sister. 'Before Christmas, at one of the Christmas markets.'

Mary Ellen felt her jaw drop, and she theatrically placed her hands on her hips. 'You go on at me about … about … *doing things* with Joseph, and all this time you've been at it like bloody rabbits.'

'No, no,' Jane protested feebly. 'No, we haven't done anything. He seems to have gotten it into his head that I'm still a virgin…'

'…as if! Is 'e real?'

'…and he wanted to wait…until we were *better* acquainted.'

Mary Ellen clasped both hands in front of her mouth, as if in mock horror, but her eyes betrayed a smile that beamed at Jane when she removed them.

'Is there a better way of getting acquainted than a quick rut in the hay barn? Five months…nearly…and you've still not…' and then, suddenly concerned, 'he *can* manage it, can't he? 'E's not *important*, is 'e? 'E 'as got a cock?'

Jane's eyes widened, and a smile lit up her face. 'Oh, no,' she said emphatically, 'he's not *impotent*. 'And he's most definitely got a cock. I've felt it often enough when he holds me.' A gleam came to her eyes, and she flicked her eyebrows upwards. 'Like a stick of dynamite, it is.'

'So, why doesn't 'e use it? Why don't you do something about it? Are you afraid he might blow your head off?'

'Oh, I'm about to,' Jane answered mysteriously, turning her head away to gaze out of the window, regarding her sister obliquely.

'What do you mean?' Suddenly Mary Ellen looked around her and turned her head up to the ceiling, trying to catch any sounds there might be. 'Bloody 'ell. 'E's not 'ere, is 'e? Do you want me to go?'

Janes placed her hands over her sister's and smiled tenderly at her. 'No, he's not here. I'll be seeing him on Wednesday. It's his birthday, and he's going to get a birthday present he's not expecting.'

'Bugger me. And after all this time. Jane, that's wonderful. Fuck me.'

'*Mary Ellen*! I don't know what manners they teach you at that hall, but your language is shameful. You're getting worse.'

'Sorry. I'm just excited for you.' And then, as an afterthought she added, 'You're *not* a virgin, are you? Surely you must 'ave...'

Jane didn't answer immediately. Instead she gave her sister an appraising look, and started to refill their mugs, then put the teapot down, and, as if coming to a decision, stood up and said, 'I've been meaning to do this for a long time. Put your cloak back on. We're going for a walk.'

Mary Ellen looked puzzled but didn't question her sister. Apprehensively, she did as she was bid, and followed Jane out of the lodge and down the Garston lane. They barely spoke as Jane led Mary Ellen along the pathways, she'd taken only that morning, back all the way to the beech tree, where she pointed out the letter "W" and the date 1863.'

Mary Ellen, noticing the daffodils, said, 'Someone's been 'ere.'

'Yes, me. This morning, before the boys were up.'

'But why? What's this?'

'*This*,' she gestured to where the daffodils were already wilting, 'is a child's grave. William, he was called. He lived just long enough to be baptised.'

A tear came to Jane's eye. Mary Ellen noticed, but sensing that silence would bring out the rest of the tale, said nothing. Instinctively she put an arm around her sister's shoulder and pulled her into her arms.

'He was mine. My child. And when he died, they said that because he was a bastard, we couldn't put him in the churchyard, even though they'd baptised him. And that hurt me. So, we came here one night, and buried him by this tree.'

'We?'

'Papa, and me. He's now the only other person who knows. And I made him swear not to say a word, as you must swear. Mam helped me to give birth and had a hard time keeping the nosey Jones's from Torpen Lodge at bay. But she couldn't face coming with us while we buried him.'

'What about the father? Who's 'e?'

'I don't know,' she said almost inaudibly, stepping back from her sister. 'It was market day. I was sixteen, the same age you are now, and I'd had too much ale – I was with the lasses from Charity farm, and I'd just sold a pig. I was happy because the money was going to be a big help. So I felt I deserved a mug of ale, which turned into three or four. I went outside for a piss, and suddenly this man appeared out of the shadows, and shoved me up against the pub wall, lifted my skirt, and…'

'And forced you?'

'Yes. It was over before I knew it had happened, and I've never been able to remember much about it. I was so drunk; I might even have agreed to it. I can't remember. He never spoke a word. And then the bastard just ran off. It's as well he didn't know about the pig money, or that would have gone, too.'

'What did you do?'

'There wasn't much I could do. It was going dark, and I never saw much of his face, just long dark hair, a ragged beard and thick eyebrows, and a scar across his nose. And, if I'm honest, I was too addled to know whether it had happened or not. At least until my periods stopped and my stomach began to swell. And by then it was too late. I didn't even say anything to my friends. Just acted like I'd been out for a pee.'

Mary Ellen put both arms round her sister again and pulled her close, feeling tears course down her cheeks. 'Fuck me,' she whispered, feeling for her sister in a way no child of sixteen should ever need to. It certainly explained the lack of interest in men, and for Mary Ellen, young as she was, it was hard not to feel that the events of that day had contrived to rob her sister of a different future.

Chapter 39

When she had opened the text from Duncan inviting her to lunch Alice hadn't intended to accept. She wasn't quite sure why or knew what hesitant was clouding her mind.

That morning, instead of the usual quick shower, she had luxuriated in a warm bath scented with lavender, all the better to ponder her feelings. Since Duncan had come into her life, something, certainly, had changed, but what it was she was unclear about. That she even had to think about it, was a change in itself. Like a stone dropped in a mill pond, you never quite knew what the ripples would encounter.

When last they had been together at her cottage, two months earlier, she'd been on the verge of inviting him to her bed. By then they'd known each other for more than a year, and it seemed bizarre, given the obvious mutual attraction, that their relationship hadn't progressed. She'd accepted some time ago that – for her – theirs was more than a platonic friendship. Whether Duncan was ready for more than that, she couldn't be sure. There were times when he seemed so…lacking in confidence…directionless…cast adrift without the support of a safety net. That had gone when his wife had died. So, at the last moment, something – febrile speculation; uncertainty; fear of where it might lead; the probability that it was for him still too early in their relationship – had prevented her from doing anything about it. In any case, she'd later persuaded herself, admittedly with lack of conviction, that certain things were all the better for keeping. On life's trajectory, such connection as she had with Duncan was still closer to a beginning than an endgame voyage into contented old age. Loving sexual intercourse was a threshold beyond which lay a world of changed futures, and, as yet, she wasn't sure she wanted to surrender her solitary way of life; not that she would need to. The problem was that she'd become comfortably set in her ways, had her own routines, her own disciplines. Inviting someone into her personal world would alter it irrevocably. So, much as she'd come to acknowledge that she did want to sleep with the man and once more to feel a warmth and intense passion that has been missing for so long, she opted for playing a slightly longer game, and seeing what cards life dealt her.

For the moment.

She took her time getting dressed, undecided what to wear, standing in front of her wardrobe in her underwear before taking out a pair of wide leg cropped trousers and a button front printed blouse that she left unbuttoned as low as her cleavage.

Duncan hadn't mentioned that he had more news about her family. He'd just invited her for lunch.

So, was this a proper date?
Did she want it to be a proper date?

Yet here she was, sitting at a reserved table in a corner of a small restaurant in Chorley owned by a chef trained in Michelin-starred restaurants around the world but who'd chosen to abandon all the kudos – and constant pressure – of that to set up his own much less-demanding enterprise for discerning clients in a medium-sized market town in the middle of Lancashire. *Nova*, as he'd called it, was not widely known among the pie and chips fraternity but had become the province of dedicated foodies from across the county of whom there was a growing number.

Alice had arrived in town early and taken her time to saunter through the terraced streets from which a narrow alleyway branched to the restaurant.

She sighed and picked up the untouched Cuckoo Spiced Gin and Fever Tree tonic in front of her, one of her favourite tipples, from the Brindle Distillery not far from where she was now. From the corner of her eye, saving her from further contemplation of what she hoped were temporary uncertainties and reluctances, she saw Duncan walk in, catching sight of her immediately and waggling his hand in a cross between a wave and a salute. She smiled inwardly: awkwardness and indecision seemed to pursue him everywhere. He was wearing a shirt and tie beneath a Tweed jacket, a lightweight briefcase over his shoulder.

He slipped into the chair opposite her and started polishing his spectacles on a napkin. 'I'm not late, am I?' He glanced at his watch, knowing that he wasn't.

'No, I've only just arrived myself. Just time to get a G and T.' A lie but just a white one.

A young waitress brought menus, smiling a welcome, and Duncan ordered a martini. 'I decided to leave the car at home,' he said. 'I've come in on the bus.'

'Well, they say great minds think alike. That's just what I've done. It was a bit of a trek out from the village to the bus stop, but it's a lovely day and I don't mind the exercise.'

Duncan scanned the room, taking in the gleaming mirror bar and the subdued conversation from other tables.

'I didn't know this place existed until I read about it in *Lancashire Life*. Interesting name. *Nova*. A transient astronomical event, something that flairs up and then dies. Not sure that would be what they had in mind when they were starting out.'

'You'd hope not,' Alice agreed. 'There's a restaurant in Copenhagen called *Nova*. It was once ranked the best in the world.'

'Have you been?'

'Tom and I went for an anniversary.' She smiled sheepishly, and shrugged, her shoulders hunching. 'In the proverbial good old days. The meal cost as much as the return flight from Manchester.'

'I can well imagine. You never know, you may go again.'

The waitress returned with the martini, and they ordered from the "Daily Specials" board: sea bass for Alice, seafood risotto for Duncan and an award-winning Sancerre red.

'I'm not sure I'd go back to Copenhagen,' Alice said pensively.

'Too many memories?'

'Oh, gosh, no. It's not that. If we never returned to anywhere, we'd been with someone else, we'd probably never go anywhere, or end up visiting places that weren't as good as the places we *did* visit – did that make sense? A bit like cutting off your nose to spite your face. If I went back to *Nova*, I wouldn't be thinking of being there with Tom; I'd be there for the food and the company of whoever I was with. No, it's just that there are other places I want to visit; loads of places in France, for a start, and I've always wanted to go to Australia and New Zealand. Then again, I *may* go back. As I get older, I'm more comfortable with familiarity and less drawn into new adventures. Know what I mean?'

'I do. I know exactly what you mean. I've been to Australia several times, and you'd think I'd had enough. But I'd go again, at the drop of a hat. Knowing where I was going, and what to expect has become more comforting as I've got older, too. If I ever suddenly disappear, you'll find me in Alice Springs.

162

Assuming I could afford it, of course. My recent visits knocked my credit cards for six, and it's taken years to clear a debt I've no wish to re-create.'

'You'll have to get a wealthy, ageing client and persuade them to leave you a fortune in their will.'

'Well, that probably offers better odds than waiting to win the lottery. But I guess neither are going to happen.'

Further conversation was halted by the arrival of the food, and for a while they ate in silence. Then Alice said, 'I was thinking the other day how you had the edge over me.'

'How so?'

'Well, with all your research into my family, you know a lot about me, and I know precious little about you. I know you're well qualified, but very little else.'

And so he told her. The start in local government; straight from school. Moving later from job to job as he climbed the ladder ultimately to become a deputy town clerk. Then an unavoidable change of horses when local government reorganisation muddied the waters in 1974 to being a Chief Administrator in an umbrella department combining all aspects of leisure and tourism. The department was even responsible for cemetery management, and he'd joked about how a leisure department was the perfect place for that, given that it dealt with the ultimate in relaxation.

Before long, the joy and satisfaction that came with setting up procedures and policies for a new department, something he did with skill, had gradually perished in the face of petty office politics, corruption and what turned out to be a resource wasting curse – compulsory competitive tendering brought in by Margaret Thatcher's government. Under this system, many of the council's services had to be put out to tender, thrown onto the open market, against which the department had to compete on a so-called level playing field. In a way it was no bad thing, ensuring better value for money. He'd once heard a university professor giving a lecture on local government, in which he spoke of being asked the question 'How many people work in the town hall?' The answer he gave was "half of them". Sadly that was true, it summed up a reality Mrs Thatcher was trying to get at: there was a lot of 'fat' built into the office management structures that needed to be exorcised. What it meant for Duncan was that since his job as a departmental administrator was an on-cost across all budget heads, he was moved sideways and given responsibility for parks and open spaces, to keep the admin overhead costs down. In truth, he'd always known that all good administrators eventually do themselves out of a job. Once everything was operating perfectly, there was nothing left for them to do.

Parks and Open Spaces was a change he wasn't expecting, but a responsibility he was happy enough to take on board, not least because it meant more time could be spent out and about rather than in an overheated, unhealthy office. But it had been a slap in the face. The beginning of the end so far as his local government career was concerned. When, after thirty years, ironically to the day, the end did finally come – in the form of voluntary redundancy, he told her – it wasn't a moment too soon.

Duncan looked pensive for a moment. Then said, 'Actually, that's a lie I've been living for some time.'

Alice looked up enquiringly. 'What is?'

'That last bit. The voluntary redundancy.'

'Oh?'

'I was sacked. For gross misconduct.'

Chapter 40

'Look,' Duncan began once another round of drinks had appeared, 'I did something silly, unprofessional, and I was dismissed after a three-day hearing. The general consensus was that I just deserved a hearty bollocking, final written warning, that sort of thing. Not dismissal. But a new chief executive had started with the council only a couple of months earlier, and he'd opted to chair the hearing. He didn't know anything about me or all the developmental work I'd done as a senior officer for the council, and decided he needed to make an example, to flex his muscles. You could say he was all the more objective for that.'

Some did.

'Anyway, he clearly couldn't make his mind up because he delayed making his decision for three weeks. And then he sacked me. I'd already been suspended for five months while they tried to make the case against me, which from what I was told they were having difficulty doing. Even the solicitor presenting the case against me apologised openly for doing so. He was only doing his job, he said.'

Alice sighed sympathetically. 'Well, I don't want to know the details, but you must have been devasted. And your wife, too.'

'You could say that. Isabel was traumatised. We'd only just learned that she had cancer. I appealed, but they dismissed the appeal as I knew they would. So, I opted to take it to an industrial tribunal. I engaged a QC, and his line was basically, how rich do you want to be? They've got this all wrong. Way over the top, etcetera, etcetera. But my union miscalculated the time limits within which I had to lodge an appeal to the tribunal, and I was out of time. I went to some adjudication panel to explain what had happened. But they dismissed my case. So, I sued the union, and got a chunk of compensation. But I would never work in local government, ever again.'

'After all those years.'

'Some say I deserved it. But, hey, it happened. I'm not a serial murderer. I just got my wires crossed a bit. There were some mitigating circumstances, but I won't bore you with the details. I suppose it didn't help that the principal witness against me was shagging – sorry, *engaging* in social interaction with the chairman of my employing committee. But he was never going to come down on my side of the fence, even though several of his political allies prompted him to do so. If he'd done so, it would have made his floozie out to be in the wrong. And that would've meant a total clampdown on his extramarital nooky.'

'Well, one day, you can tell me the gory details. What's past is past.'

Duncan nodded. 'That's generous of you.' He was relieved that she'd taken it so readily, and paused for a moment before going on hesitantly, 'It may seem presumptuous of me, but whatever you and I have between us…' he spoke with his hands, gesturing between them, '…whatever it is…friends, or whatever, I didn't want to go forward with this waiting to surface. No one else knows. I just didn't want, you know…whatever.'

'So, we're a couple of *"whatevers"*, then, are we?'

'If you like.'

Yet he knew that for some months he had been captured by feelings that ran much deeper than…a simple *whatever*.

'Okay,' Alice said with a smile on her lips. 'I can do *whatever*. Now get me another drink. Confessions always make me thirsty.'

'Just as well we're both on the bus.'

Chapter 41

May 1871

Eight months have passed since Mary Ellen's birthday, when she and Joseph, inebriated by their first taste of wine, had slept through the night in the woodman's hut. In the morning they had awakened fearfully to the reality of what had happened and raced back to the hall, hoping to slip in unnoticed before the household was awake.

Only twice since had they returned to the hut, both occasions leaving Mary Ellen with a sense of disappointment, their lovemaking failing to revisit the intense feelings they'd felt on that first occasion. From frenetic passion, it had distilled into perfunctory sex...not even making love, as Mary Ellen liked to think of it. On both occasions, once their intimacy was finished, impersonal, indifferent, as it had seemed to her, Joseph had made an excuse to return to the hall, leaving Mary Ellen to clean herself and tidy things away from any prying eyes that might chance on their love den.

Bewildered, and still with much to learn about the nature of relationships, Mary Ellen was starting to see that her *connection* with Joseph had altered but was unable to articulate the change. She *thought* she loved him, but was far from sure what love was, or how it was meant to feel. On a visit to the Ashton market just before Christmas, she had overheard an animated exchange between a man and a woman. 'I love you, but I'm not in love with you,' the woman had said. Mary Ellen had no understanding of the distinction. To her it seemed a cruel thing to say. Were the feelings she held for her sister Jane, love? And was it the same love her father had felt for her mother? Or his gun dogs, for that matter?

And how did Joseph feel? She remembered the intense and passionate feelings she had when they'd first had sex. Was that love? Or something else? Did Joseph love her? Or was it just about sex? Was that what love was? Was that all it was meant to be? Sex? Were you *in love* with someone only once you'd had sex? Or was that something else? Jane had had sex, and a baby, but there was no *love* involved because she'd no idea who the father was. So, Mary Ellen reasoned, sex and love are not the same.

So, was she just being used?

"I love you, but I'm not *in love* with you" didn't make any sense and playing back the overheard exchange in her head only served to confuse her more. Was it code for "The sex is what I want; nothing else?" Was that it? Was Joseph taking advantage of her? Using her for sex? That was all they seemed to do: kiss, grope, fondle, fuck.

Was that it?

Was her *relationship* with Joseph summed up in those four words?

How did she get from this to a home and family of her own? To stability and future security?

Chapter 42

At the hall, the Christmas and New Year festivities had seemed to drag on interminably into early summer almost, with an endless flow of guests coming and going, all making demands on the staff. She surprisingly found herself feeling sorry for Mouldy Martha and the rest of the kitchen staff who were forever on the go, wilting under the heat of the kitchen fire and the unceasing tirade that Cook fired at them.

On rare occasions when she did see Joseph, he spoke only to complain about how his workload had inexplicably increased. Since long before Christmas he had seemed to be on duty every hour of the day, taking on duties for which he had not previously been responsible, among which he was now called upon to assist the senior housemaid who tended to the Lady Makerfield. The housemaid was ageing, he knew that. But he was still a junior footman and puzzled that he should have been singled out for this change in circumstance. Moreover, it was unheard of for a footman to be called on to attend a lady.

Something, or someone, had altered the natural order of things.

Soon the family would be leaving Garston to spend summer on their Somerset estate. Many of the staff would go with them, and Mary Ellen wondered if she might be included. She had no idea where Somerset was, but it sounded exotic and far away – Summer Sett, she thought it was spelt, like a place where you found badgers.

As she climbed the stairs to her room, the intermediate landing door burst open, and Joseph appeared, his face a mask of panic.

'It's gone. It's gone,' is all he seemed capable of uttering.

'What's gone?' Mary Ellen said in an impatient tone. She had been unusually busy all day and felt weary.

'The hut. It's gone.'

'The 'ut? *Our* 'ut? Gone?'

'Yes. Gone. Completely disappeared.'

'How can a wooden 'ut disappear, stupid?'

'I don't fucking know. But it has. You can't even tell where it'd been.'

'Ah, you dozy bugger. You got lost in the woods, didn't you?' Mary Ellen was reaching the end of her tether.

'No, honestly. I know *exactly* where it was. But everything's gone. It's all just dead leaves and broken branches now. I've been out. To see for myself. I overheard someone talking about it. I nearly shit myself. I'd left that empty bottle of wine under the floorboards. And the blanket. They'll have found all that.'

'There's no way they could link you to the wine, silly man,' she said, trying to placate him, though she felt a tremor of concern herself. 'Anyone could have left it there. There's 'undreds o' people work on the estate, and another 'undred living not far away who wander about if they think they won't get caught. I used to do that myself. So, I know.'

'Well, I hope you're right. You've got family. I've not. If I lose my job, I'm homeless.'

'Stop worrying, and go to bed,' she tried a reassuring smile. Then asked as an afterthought, '*When* did they do this?'

'I'm not sure. It must have been a few months ago. We were there in April.'

'Well, there you go then. Ages ago. If anyone connected us to it, we'd 'ave 'eard by now.'

'I hope you're right.'

''Course I am. Stop worrying.'

But the news didn't settle Mary Ellen's unease, and she endured a restless night, in and out of confusing dreams. She couldn't afford to be out of a job any more than Joseph.

Chapter 43

They were once again in Alice's living room. Lyrical piano music which Duncan recognised as John Field's *Nocturnes* drifted from what he now noticed were tall and slim quadrophonic speaks at each corner of the room. A couple of mirrored hurricane candle lanterns burned side-by-side on the low table and the room lighting was dimmed perceptibly, between them giving the room a cosy, comforting ambiance. To Duncan, for so long adrift in an ocean of emotional in-determination and uncertainty, it felt like a safe haven, a place bolstered against the myriad trials that gathered in the outside world.

Wearing a cream floral midi-shirt dress that conflicted amusingly with the knitted sheep slippers on her feet, Alice, her hair uncharacteristically loose and tousled like a fiery red corona round her head, eased down beside him, gathering the folds of her skirt into her lap. Duncan, dressed simply in a shirt and blue jeans, was acutely conscious of her closeness, their upper arms and thighs touching, as if she'd placed herself against him with precise intent. Pleasantly comforted by her warmth, he pulled himself back into focus and tapped his finger on the family tree he'd prepared, and to which she could see he had added considerably more name boxes.

'There are a couple of anomalies it would be interesting to penetrate further,' he began.

'Mary Ellen and her two illegitimate children, for a start, I presume?'

'Correct. From what I've since unearthed, I think we can accept that whatever brought about the two illegitimate births, Mary Ellen later married Joseph Cunliffe, and bred half a football team with him before she succumbed to dementia at the age of eighty-four.' He tapped the names for John and Alice Liptrot.' Possibly brother and sister; possibly half-brother and sister. We don't know which.'

'Could we find out?' Alice wondered aloud.

'Never say never is my motto. We can make leaping suppositions, but they won't prove a thing. Assumptions don't count for anything in genealogy. There are no certainties, only outcomes. Joseph Cunliffe wasn't the father, or they would firstly have his surname, and secondly be listed along with the Cunliffe children in the 1891 census, when in fact they've kept the Liptrot surname.'

'Well, I think that's fairly conclusive. If Joseph Cunliffe was the father, there's no reason not to have them take his surname.'

'Exactly. So, they were fathered by someone else, who isn't, or didn't want to be, identified. What we do know is that in the 1881 census, Mary Ellen is recorded as a washerwoman, living in Arch Lane, not far from Garston Hall. Ten years later she's moved to Main Street in Billinge with Joseph and has already had four children by him. That made a total of eight in the household, and we can only assume they needed somewhere bigger. In all Mary Ellen had seven children. five with Joseph. There's no doubting her fertility.'

'Why would a birth certificate not show the father's identity?'

'Several reasons. But between 1837 and 1875, which covers the timescale we're looking at, if the mother informed the registrar of an illegitimate child's birth, and named the father, the registrar could and probably would have recorded the father's name. That invites us to speculate that Mary Ellen may not have known who the father was. That there were so many *possibilities* she simply couldn't remember. But there's a whole can of worms that ripples out from that idea, and it would be unbefitting of us to assume the worst.'

Alice affected indignation. 'I couldn't agree more. This is my relative we're talking about.'

'Well, needs must and all that in those days, I suppose. But, you're right. Let's not draw unfounded conclusions. Anyway, after 1875, a man could only be named as the father of an illegitimate child on the birth certificate if he consented and was also present when the birth was registered.'

'And one of them, John Liptrot, if I remember correctly, was before that 1875 date, and the other, Alice, was later.'

'Well, your memory's clearly better than mine,' Duncan said with a chuckle, 'I'd have had to look that up. But, if we're to get to the truth of the matter, we need to make assumptions.'

'I thought you didn't like assumptions,' Alice said reprovingly, poking him in the ribs.

'I don't, but they play a part. It's easier to get at the truth if you create a scenario based on assumptions, and then try to pull it apart. See if they break. Clearly, men unknown were involved since I very much doubt that John and Alice were immaculate conceptions. But the absence of evidence isn't synonymous with evidence of wrongdoing. Except when there ought to be evidence.'

'Isn't that a mangled version of one of the arguments for there not being a God.'

Duncan smiled, 'I believe so. But God or no God in this instance there ought to be evidence somewhere of the father.' He looked pensive for a moment. 'Well, I say *should be*, but of course there can be many reasons why there is no evidence. For a start, as I say, it presupposes that the woman *knew* who the father was. Certainly the parish clerks or Poor Law Guardians would want to know who the father was so that they could tackle him about the nineteenth-century version of maintenance payments. So, Mary Ellen must have had some over-riding reason for not disclosing the identity of the father.'

'And doing so twice,' Alice threw in.

Duncan nodded and sifted through his papers retrieving a printout of a census record. 'We know that in 1881, Alice was a washerwoman living in Arch Lane, in Ashton. Now, she could have been a washerwoman at her home base. But that, surely, would need a catchment of people living not too far away, to make it worthwhile. So, the other possibility was that she was a washerwoman at Garston Hall, where her father had worked until he died in February of that year. Ten years earlier, Mary Ellen is fifteen, and living at home. Is it possible that she was a washerwoman, or some other form of domestic servant, at the hall? Having had a father as a long-standing gamekeeper must have counted for something. Being at home doesn't mean she wasn't employed in some capacity at the hall. The census was always taken on a Sunday, and she would be recorded as living wherever she was on that day. So that points to her, on census day at least, not being other than living at home. Not that that gets us much further forward. She could have been employed at the hall, and Sunday was her day off. Would a washerwoman, assuming she *was* a washerwoman, be expected to work on a Sunday?'

'I think not. And I think I can see where you're going with this,' chipped in Alice. 'Could her employer at the hall, or his son, have taken advantage of her. Raped her, even?'

'You see correctly. Of course, it could just as easily have been one of the other servants who got her pregnant, but I would have thought she'd be less likely to protect their identity. This sort of thing happened a lot. They took a dim view of relationships between servants, but it still went on, although usually it was the woman who got thrown out of her job, by way of adding insult to injury. And yet Mary Ellen is still there.'

'So,' began Alice thoughtfully, 'if we surmise that Mary Ellen was in some form of domestic service at the hall, and that someone, the son, say, got her pregnant, then rather than throw her out on her ear, they kept her on as a washerwoman, out of...what? ...some form of loyalty, or obligation, to her father?'

'Or they wanted to keep her on a leash. Keep her in a position where her future welfare depended on her silence.'

'Well,' says Alice, 'you can see how that would work. Except...'

'Except, these were aristocrats, the landed gentry we're talking about. They'd dump Mary Ellen without a second's thought, gamekeeper father or not.' Duncan shook his head. 'No, there's more to this than meets the eye.'

Alice stood up from her chair. 'Fancy a cuppa? I'm parched.'

She headed off into the kitchen, from where Duncan could soon hear the homely sound of clattering mugs and a boiling kettle. He got up and walked into the kitchen, where Alice was preparing tea and had fished some scones from a cupboard.

'But it happened again. Six or seven years later. That's quite a time gap. What was going on in the meantime? I remember attending a lecture given by a member of the Genealogical Society about illegitimacy, and the impression they gave was that had the births been closer together might have suggested that Mary Ellen was a prostitute...something we were tiptoeing round a few minutes ago. But where she lived there were no sizeable towns. Ashton was the largest nearby, probably with a population less than fifteen thousand. If she *was* a prostitute surely, she'd need to travel further afield, to somewhere like Wigan, and that's quite a walk from where she lived. It must be at least six miles, even allowing for her knowledge of shortcuts.'

They returned to the living room, and Alice poured tea. Duncan looked pensive. 'I'm getting off track, here. I really don't think Mary Ellen was a prostitute. For one thing, since no one was going to describe themselves in the census records as a prostitute, they used a euphemism – *dressmaker* was a popular choice.'

'You're joking,' Alice gasps.

'Far from it. I wouldn't have believed it myself, but I collated employment statistics for my PhD research that showed a significant increase in the number of dressmakers in Ambleside and Grasmere that matched the growth in tourist numbers but more significantly the incidence of trades and craft people, builders, carpenters, masons and the like, who flooded into the area as development expanded. And, tourists aside, these for the most part where men who hadn't brought their wives with them or weren't married.'

'That's fascinating. Who would have believed it?'

'Of course, at the same time more and more industrialists from Lancashire and Yorkshire were setting up home in the Lake District, and there may indeed have been a genuine increase in demand for dressmakers and seamstresses. But the number of them was disproportionate, and concentrated in the central belt, between Windermere and Keswick. Call yourself a dressmaker and you're hidden in plain sight.'

Alice smiled. 'I wonder what Ann Summers' family tree looks like.'

Duncan looked puzzled. 'Who?'

Alice patted him on the shoulder. 'Don't worry about it. I was just being frivolous.'

Duncan sipped his tea and put the cup on the table. 'No, there's something about the timescale that doesn't sit well with me. What was Mary Ellen doing after John was born?'

'Being a mum, probably. Babies don't raise themselves.'

'Yes, quite, but how was she managing? Even if she *had* been working at the hall, she couldn't continue doing that *and* raise a child. So, what did she live on? I can't imagine her father's wages went very far.'

'Have a scone,' said Alice, now seated less close to him, and pushing the plate of jam-and-cream-covered cakes towards him. 'I can see why you're cut out for this sort of work.'

For a moment they ate in silence, and then Alice said, 'You said there were two anomalies. What was the other?'

'Mary Ellen's father. Gamekeeper John Liptrot. He was illegitimate, too.'

'Really?' chirped Alice, moving towards him so that their bodies touched once more.

'I haven't quite got to the bottom of it, but it seems that John Liptrot, as we now know him, was born John Waterworth, illegitimate son of Jane Waterworth. He was born in 1802, and then a year later, Jane married William Liptrot, after which John Waterworth appears in the records as John Liptrot.'

'I don't know how you remember all this,' Alice said with admiration, unexpectedly taking his hand in hers, smiling at him warmly, and giving his hand a reassuring squeeze.

'I'm impressed.' Alice, to her surprise, recognising the honesty in what she had said. Over the past months, she had come to realise that she was quite taken with this new man in her life. More than that. She was finally feeling comfortable around him, happy to be with him and have him there. And that counted for much in her semi-hermitically sequestered existence. When her marriage had ended, she'd sealed herself away from romantic intentions, male, and, she recalled with a wry smile, female. She became resigned to living alone and wholly self-reliant. For a time she had had friends in an around Liverpool, trustworthy friends who rallied around her after the divorce, supported her on the bad days without overtly intruding. She was good company; always had been. Sociable and reliable, *the* person to have at your dinner parties or social gathering. Without intending to, once she left Liverpool, she had become a loner.

But now all this was changing. Her life had acquired a new dimension, one that was deconstructing the barriers she'd built to protect her emotional self. Since that first encounter with this man whose hand she suddenly realised she was still holding, she saw that she was becoming a different woman, a modified version of a woman she once knew. One who no longer had historic records as the mainstay of her days because there wasn't anything else to occupy her time. Now barely a day went by when she didn't think of Duncan; rarely a week now when they didn't contrive to meet up for a pub lunch or glass of wine.

There had been no undue demands on either side, no tentative overtures to anything more…involved – though she idly wondered where they might be had she taken him to her bed when first she was tempted to, months ago. When work took Duncan away, or confined him to his office, they remained in casual contact because it was what they wanted. Yet, she realised, maintaining association with him had a satisfying glow about it, and that prolonged absence of communication left her feeling incomplete. They were, she found herself admitting, drifting together…in a satisfying, unhurried way, like continents but hopefully without the consequences…*or the inordinate length of time involved.*

'You can be impressed once I've worked it all out,' said Duncan, making no move to take his hand away from hers until he needed to, a moment that came all too soon. It was a hackneyed cliché, but when Alice had taken his hand it had been electrifying in its intensity. 'There's a long way to go, and just this one anomaly raises a shedload of other possibilities and, at this stage, more questions than answers.'

'So, is there anything I can do to help?'

'A glass of wine, perhaps,' Duncan suggested.

Chapter 44

June 1871

The household had been anticipating with little enthusiasm the return, for the first time in many months, of Lord Cavendish. From what Mary Ellen could glean, it was a prospect few were looking forward to, apparently, though no one would say why. Everyone was tight lipped and anxious as if his return was a doom-laden occasion.

She was making her way back from the garden with a basket of herbs cook had asked her to gather. Today, with new guests of Lady Garston arriving within hours for one of her dinner parties thrown to maintain the illusion that all was well with the Garston marriage. So, in the kitchen, it was all hands-on deck, and anyone not otherwise occupied was drafted in to help. Cook, Mary Ellen knew, would not forget the small favour; it suited Mary Ellen's purpose: she had finished her morning's chores early, and wanted an excuse to go outdoors for fresh air.

'Oi! Who the fuck are you?' a deep voice bellowed as she retraced her steps along the corridor, past Mrs Bonnivale's office.

Mary Ellen leapt with fright, startled, and turned to face the owner of the voice. Unkempt and sprawling across the table in Mrs Bonnivale's office she saw a man she didn't recognise clutching a bottle from which he was pouring white wine into a glass. An empty bottle lying on the floor suggested he'd been drinking for some time.

She curtsied as she has been taught and stepped into the room. 'I'm the second housemaid, sir,' she said in deference to the stranger, unsure of how to address him. She lifted the basket of herbs for him to see, 'I've been gathering herbs for Cook,' she said politely. She had no idea who the man was, but she had by now learned that subservience was the safest course in the first instance, until she knew otherwise.

'No, you bloody haven't,' he contradicted, less loudly, slurring his words. 'Second housemaids don't pick herbs. 'S a kitchen maid's job.' He leered at her and wagged a finger vaguely in her direction. 'Have you been doing naughties? Up to no good? Jigga-jigga with the gardener in the glasshouse, eh? You're all at it, I'll wager. Randy bastards, the lot of you.' This last he attempted to say as he drank from the glass, wine dribbling down his chin in consequence.

Mary Ellen stepped closer. 'No, sir. Cook asked me to 'elp. So, I did. It's busy in the kitchen today.'

A veneer of understanding slowly settled on his face and he nodded, 'Ah, yes, the money-grasping slugs are coming. Here for a freeloading weekend. Sycophantic bastards. Shoot the bloody lot. I would. Shoot 'em. Dead.'

For all his tousled appearance and slurred speech he was clearly not a servant or one of the tradespeople who called at the hall. He was wearing an immaculate dark blue checked jacket over matching trousers. Highly polished black leather shoes clad his feet. He was square-jawed, handsome in a rugged way and had an unruly shock of red hair that sprouted unmanageably from his head – like a scarecrow, Mary Ellen thought. His white shirt, partially unbuttoned, exposed another thatch of red hair across his chest.

Mary Ellen could recall Elizabeth talking about someone she called "Carrot Top", but at the time it meant nothing to her.

Now it did.

'Are you Lord Cavendish, sir?' she asked hesitantly, fearing she had already gone too far.

He beamed at her, his appraising eyes roving her body. 'Got it in one, you smart little thing.' He hiccoughed and held his hand palm outward towards Mary Ellen in an apologetic gesture before belching loudly.

'Sorry if I called you a randy bastard.'

Mary Ellen shrugged. 'There's no need to apologise, my Lord,' thankful to her sister for ensuring she understood the correct forms of address for aristocrats.

He looked at her as if he didn't understand what she'd said. 'Apologise? Oh, yes. Apologise.' He rose unsteadily to his feet and took a gulp of wine. 'What's your name, second housemaid? You're really quite pretty.'

'Miss Liptrot, sir.'

'No. What's your name? The one your parents gave you.' He was looking directly at Mary Ellen but listing to one side like a ship about to capsize and sink beneath the waves. 'Unless your first name really is *Miss*,' he chuckled at his own joke.

'Mary Ellen. Everyone calls me Mary Ellen, my Lord.' She was uncomfortable with that. First names are not used in Garston Hall.

He took two tentative steps towards her and extended a wavering hand in her direction. 'Mine's Cav...Ca...Caven...dish,' he stammered. 'Pl...Plea...sed to meet you, Mary...Ellen.'

Trembling with uncertainty she took the hand and curtsied again. 'Nice to meet you, my Lord,' she said timidly, releasing the hand quickly, bereft of any idea of what to do next. Hesitantly, she turned to leave, 'If you'll excuse me, my Lord, I'd better go. Cook will want these 'erbs.' She began to move towards the door.

Lord Cavendish remained standing, just, his legs buckling, leaning precariously, a hand grasping the back of chair. 'Of course. Mustn't keep Cookie waiting, must we?' he mumbled incoherently, taking another drink of wine. 'But,' he began, waving the wine glass at her and spilling most of its contents, 'will you do something for me first. Mary Ellen? Will you?'

Mary Ellen half turned to the door, not knowing what to expect, fearing the worst.

He belched again. 'Will you take me to my room. I'm buggered if I can remember where it is. There's so many fucking rooms in this God-awful pile.'

She was relieved and amused, and put the herb basket down on Mrs Bonnivale's desk, desperate to get back to her duties, but, she reasoned, her duties were to serve the household, to respond to their every request.

'And another thing,' Lord Cavendish added tangentially, 'When all this...' again he swings the wine glass in a sweeping arc, '...is mine, you'll be mine, too, Mary Ellen Liptrot. Would you like to be mine, Mary Ellen? Would you?'

Before she could reply, footsteps sounded behind her and she turned to face Mrs Bonnivale, open-mouthed, her jaw quivering with nascent rage as she took in the scene...a second housemaid *conversing* with Lord Cavendish. Such outrage!

'Miss Liptrot,' she croaked, unable to speak with any greater force, 'what on earth are you doing in here with Lord Cavendish?'

He sprang instantly to her rescue. ''S alright, Mrs B. 'S my fault. I saw Miss...Mary...pashing and called her in. I'm a bit...you know...pished, and Miss...was going to take me to my room. I know, I know, it's silly of me, but I can't remember, there's so many f…, so many rooms, I've forgotten.' He tapped the side of his nose with an extended forefinger. 'We wouldn't want to barge in on mummy with one of her…*friends*, by mistake, would we?'

Mrs Bonnivale turned to Mary Ellen and snapped. 'Get out. Go about your business.'

Mary Ellen picked up the basket and turned to leave the room, when Lord Cavendish lurching towards the door called after her. 'Nice to meet you, Mary…Ellen…Miss…er. Bugger. Time for bed, Mrs B.'

Chapter 45

As Mary Ellen finally ascended to her room at the end of the day, her spirits were buoyant following her encounter with Lord Cavendish, though she doubted he would remember any of it. Momentarily her mind slipped back into the adolescent fantasy she thought she'd left behind. But that was before she'd come face to face with the man. Marrying Lord Cavendish and becoming the head of the household had long been her dream, but she was no longer foolish enough to think of it as anything other than childish whimsy.

But now she had met him.

And she approved. He was quite a catch. *Or would be once he sobered up.*

She smiled inwardly at the thought but was brought back to the present by a muffled sound of banging, like a branch tapping against a window in a breeze; it came from Elizabeth's room. She had intended to drop in, as she usually did at this time of day, and wanted to ask if Elizabeth knew what a *sick ofantick* was.

Not knowing what the noises might be, she eased open the door to her friend's room. To her surprise, she saw Elizabeth on her bed on hands and widespread knees, her long black uniform skirt and pinafore top gathered loosely around her waist, her exposed breasts swinging backwards and forwards as a man between her legs, his back to the door, thrust into her. The old oak headboard rhythmically striking the wall was the source of the noise.

'Fuck,' Elizabeth said, sensing another presence and turning her head to look. She collapsed onto the bed, leaving the man's ejected cock pointing skywards. To Mary Ellen's horror she saw who the rapidly fading cock belonged to – Joseph.

She was dumbstruck, her mouth agape as realisation dawned on her. Harnessing a surging fury, she yelled, 'What the fuck? Beth, what the fuck are you doing?'

Elizabeth swung her legs round so that she sat perched on the edge of the bed and started to pull her clothes back around her. 'Oh, come on, Mary Ellen. It's only sex, for fuck's sake.'

'Only sex? Only sex?' she spat. 'So, if it's *only sex*, why 'im? Can't you get a man of your own?' Mary Ellen's legs started to tremble with rage. She steadied herself against the wall and hissed, 'You bastards. You fucking bastards...'

Elizabeth shrugged, but had the good grace to look contrite. It did little to soften Mary Ellen who continued fiercely, gesturing at Elizabeth with clenched fists, 'Anyway, I thought you had one of your own.'

'We had a row. We split up.'

'So, you thought you'd come and fuck mine...*'im*...Joseph.' She waved a hand in his direction, as if dismissing him from her thoughts.

Joseph turned to Mary Ellen, 'Sorry...' he began, struggling to make himself decent.

In unison the two girls turned on him. 'Shut up!'

Mary Ellen went on, her voice heavy with disappointment and betrayal. 'I thought you were my friend, Beth.'

'Oh, for fuck's sake, Mary Ellen,' she said again. 'It's only sex. It doesn't mean anything. I was just feeling horny, and he was passing. Anyone would have done, the way I was feeling. He was just in the wrong place at the wrong time. Well, the *right* place at the wrong time.'

Joseph was deflated in more ways than one. Mary Ellen ignoring Elizabeth's comment regarded him with a look of spiteful scorn. 'You're done,' she said firmly, pointing her finger at him. 'Don't ever come near me again, you cheating turd.'

Mary Ellen's inner self was a torment of rage she had no idea how to control. She had trusted this man...both of them. And they had let her down. Suddenly she felt as though her world was built on shifting sand.

As she turned to leave, Mary Ellen began to recover her composure, unwilling to let her anger erupt further, she paused and made a show of smoothing the front of her uniform as she stood before the pair.

'Carry on. Don't let me stop you.' She waved a dismissive hand as she left the room. 'Fuck yourselves silly.'

Up to that evening, Mary Ellen's notes in her diary had been of trivial, pleasant things: visits to her sister; time spent with Joseph; friendly chats with Elizabeth; walks in the estate grounds and woodland that reflected her general feeling of now being at ease with her place at Garston Hall. When she put pen to paper that night before giving in to despair and falling tearfully into her bed, it marked an unwelcome change of tone.

Caught Joseph fucking Elizabeth.
Bastards!!!!!

In the morning she awoke to a throbbing pain behind her eyes, and an unhappiness that weighed on her like a mantle of low pressure, which became easier to ignore once she began working. As the day went on, the fury within her subsided, but she remained weary and miserable. The shock of what had happened never far from her mind she found it difficult to harbour her thoughts, which hovered, unsecured and disjointed. She had looked on Joseph as a potential husband. Now it was clear he had manifestly proven himself unsuitable. She vowed never to forgive him. The experience served only to bolster the nagging doubts she had already been nursing about Joseph He was clearly far from the man she'd thought him to be.

Chapter 46

Returning from the kitchen clutching wine glasses and a bottle, Alice announced, 'It will have to be...' she inspected the bottle label, '...Domaine Faiveley Puligny-Montrachet Premier Cru Les Referts 2016,' she pronounced perfectly, down to the *deux mille seize*. 'Which judging by what I paid for it must have been a good year.'

'Goodness, don't open your best wines.'

'Oh, I'm not,' she smiled coquettishly at him. 'Our, er, relationship, our whatever, is nowhere near the level that accesses my *best* wines. You've years to go yet. You'll have to make do with this.' She laughed as she opened the bottle with a deftness that spoke of many bottle openings.

'So,' Duncan threw in, leaning back with an enquiring expression on his face, 'we have a *relationship*, do we? So what do I have to do to graduate to the *best* wines?'

'You'll have to wait and see.' Her eyes gazed directly into his, flirting, bright, sparkling, impish.

They touched glasses, 'Cheers. That's good to know.'

'What is?'

'That you're thinking we might have a relationship.'

Alice nudged him in the ribs, leaned across and kissed him on the cheek. 'Don't get ahead of yourself. Like the walrus, I think of many things... Of shoes and ships and sealing-wax. Of cabbages and kings – to paraphrase Lewis Carroll.'

For an instant, Duncan was nonplussed. The brief kiss was unexpected, but no less pleasant for the lack of foreknowledge. But, in spite of their playful banter, it was not something he was sure he could yet comfortably reciprocate, not without sailing into the uncharted, emotional waters that surrounded him. It certainly wouldn't be a spontaneous gesture, as Alice's had. Too late now, the moment had passed. So, he held the wine glass to his nose and inhaled. Then held it up to the light, taking in the rich colour.

'Beautiful just.'

'My, we *are* getting very literary. I wouldn't have had you down as a fan of Lilian Beckwith.'

'I wouldn't have described myself either as a cabbage or a king.' They laughed at that. 'And anyway…' he sipped his wine, and put the glass down, 'back to John Liptrot-Waterworth.'

'Back to John Liptrot-Waterworth,' Alice echoed. 'Probable, possible, father, William Liptrot. Mother, Jane Waterworth.'

'*Jane* Waterworth, sometime known as "Jenny", which confuses things for a while. Anyway, the puzzles are these: One, was William the biological father, who for reasons unknown refused to marry Jane at the time? Or declined not to be identified?'

'A blaggard, then?'

'Maybe. Maybe not. I can't say at this stage. Anyway, two, was William "bribed" to marry Jane to save them being a burden on the poor rate? That wasn't as uncommon as you might think, but it might suggest a loveless marriage, which nevertheless went on to produce a further six children. So, I think maybe not a bribe.'

'But like you say, not uncommon. I remember reading not that long ago about a Thai millionaire who was willing to pay a quarter of a million sterling to a man who would marry his daughter.'

'Yes, I read that, too, but it isn't quite the same, of course. We're looking at people who were intrinsically poor. For a father to need to bribe someone in the 1800s to save them being a burden on the rates, points to a huge dose of moral shame that would otherwise accrue. Imagine how it might have seemed if Jane's father had been a pillar of the local community, a justice of the peace, for example. Quite a lot of stigma would attach to having an unmarried daughter.'

'I can imagine. Father would not be a happy bunny.'

'Indeed not. But more likely it may have been a religious reason. Was one or other a Dissenter, a Presbyterian, perhaps? I know from research from a client in Bolton, that the Waterworth family have roots in the Forest of Bowland, and rural places like that were ripe for plundering by all manner of non-conformist religious beliefs. That's pretty much how the Society of Friends, the Quakers, began, with George Fox having a *vision* on Pendle Hill in the seventeenth century.'

'I think you're up to four now. Is there a four?'

'Four, was William a simple gallant soul, who married Jane, notwithstanding her 'baggage' ...love triumphs over all, etcetera, possibly even overriding his father's objection. Maybe that is why a whole year elapsed between birth and marriage. It wasn't uncommon for a man to wait before marrying someone to see if they could produce children, and then marry them after the first child was born. But here Jane already had given birth and a whole year then elapsed before William got his act together. He was around twenty-three when he and Jane married. So it wasn't a question of needing parental, or the bishop's consent. He was of full age, and Jane would have been seventeen at the time of their marriage, which if I remember rightly...' he consulted his notebook, '...was a marriage by banns. So, no seeming problem there.'

'Could there be any other interpretation?'

'I'm afraid so, one we've encountered before. Five, at the risk of offending any descendants alive today, Jane was a prostitute, and John the child of some illicit liaison with a person unknown. Well, perhaps not a prostitute, as such. Maybe she just got pregnant from a casual relationship, the proverbial one-night-stand.'

'Well,' Alice interjected, 'I suspect it was just as prevalent then as now.'

'Probably more so, though I doubt Jane was a prostitute for much the same reasoning I don't think Mary Ellen was. They were just too ...remote...from clients, customers, whatever you call them. It's just one of those several possibilities. And I'm getting a picture of the family, if not exactly God-fearing, then one with an intrinsic respectability.' He sighed heavily. 'I may just be overthinking this, but the Napoleonic Wars were just getting going around that time. In fact, as I recall, William and Jane married the day after the Napoleonic Wars started. But the question is, what was William doing in the year before the marriage that would stop them from marrying?'

He leaned back into the soft bagginess of the sofa and placed his hands behind his head. Alice spun round to face him, their knees touching.

'So, what's your money on?' Duncan asked, looking into her smiling eyes.

Alice thought for a moment. 'Well, given that John went through life using William's surname, the implied suggestion is that William was the biological father who for some reason waited almost a year before marrying Jane.'

187

'Agreed. The alternative being the gallant route. John with a father unknown, being adopted by William.'

'Was adoption a legal process in Georgian times?'

'No. Adoption as we know it is a product of the twentieth century. The closest concept to adoption was wardship, under which a guardian was given effective custody of a child by the Chancery Court, but this was little used and didn't give the guardian parental rights. I doubt if that was the case here. The issue would be far too costly and too insignificant to justify the rigmarole of formal proceedings. In any case, we're talking about fundamentally poor people. They surely couldn't afford to petition a court of law. And there was a kind of unofficial adoption, where a family simply took a child in and raised it as their own. By the end of the nineteenth century, some poor law authorities were calling it 'boarding out' and using it as an official alternative to putting neglected children in the workhouse or an orphanage. Obviously, we don't know if that is the case here. I doubt we'll ever find out.'

'So, have you a favourite theory?'

'Occam's razor. Simpler solutions are more likely to be correct than complex ones.'

'Which points to…?'

'One of two. Jane had John by an unknown father, and William agreed to marry her and give John his name. Or, William was the biological father, who eventually did the honourable thing.'

'But why wait almost a year?'

'It's hard to say. Maybe William wasn't around. At that time, he was a cotton weaver, but I can't see that occupation taking him away from home. And because he died in 1850, he doesn't appear in any census records after the 1841 census. So I guess we'll never know.'

Alice jabbed him playfully in the ribs and said, smiling, 'I thought you never said never.'

The rest of the evening passed in the wake of the delicious burgundy, and a thrown-together dish of curry.

'You like classical music?' asked Alice, picking her way through a drawer full of CDs.'

'I do. I learned to play the piano in my teens, but only to grade seven. I was rubbish. But Chopin was my favourite, piano music. In fact, I never listened to a symphony for years until one day I was watching something on television. The late Andre Previn was giving a masterclass with the LSO, which I took to mean the London Symphony Orchestra of which he was musical director at the time. But it turned out that it was the Leicester Schools Orchestra. Previn was taking them through the final movement of Beethoven's seventh symphony – the mad movement. I was gobsmacked and went into Manchester the same day to buy a recording of the symphony. I was converted to symphonies after that.'

'Favourite composer? Let me guess. You're a sensitive soul. Romantic music. Rachmaninov?'

'Got it in one.'

'Rachmaninov coming up.'

Duncan had not felt so at ease and contented in a long time, and it all came down to how he felt when in Alice's company. They seemed to harmonise so easily, to connect on several levels, and that comforted him immensely. It re-assured him, too, that *moving on* was a possibility, whether with Alice…or some other, as yet unknown. But like his research…his head was full of *as yet unknowns*. Where he *was* certain, was that Alice had been flirting with him all evening.

And he'd loved it.

Late into the evening, he put his notes away and prepared to leave. As they reached the door, Alice moved to stand in front of him and looked into his eyes, eyes that she knew had entrapped her from the first moment they met. She moved closer, and took his briefcase, putting it on a chair. Looking up at him, she stood on tiptoe, put her arms around his neck and pulled him towards her. Their bodies touched and he felt her breasts against his chest. She kissed him fully and passionately on the lips.

Holding her in his arms, touching her, kissing her, was electric. So many months had he wanted this without, until now, realising how desperately. And now her smell, her fragrant hair, her body pressed against his, familiar but unknown. Intimate. Glorious. Unsettling.

Alice was the one in the end who pulled back. Letting him go, she sank back onto her heels, took his face in her hands, stroked the line of his cheek with a finger, and said with a playful grin on her face, 'Now, go, before I forget I'm a lady.'

Chapter 47

August 1871

Lord and Lady Garston, along with Lady Makerfield, their two young children, and a galaxy of servants, had long since left for their Somerset estate. Elizabeth had gone, Joseph, too, but Mary Ellen was among the few left behind to serve Lord Cavendish and Lady Clarissa, neither of whom had any desire to spend what they looked on as boring weeks in the company of their parents and inevitable and tedious charade of balls, galas and events.

Over the ensuing weeks, Mary Ellen gradually came to understand why the domestic staff had collectively groaned when Lord Cavendish's return had been announced; why they might have regarded him as a disruption of their orderly routines. Servants were not meant to be seen by the family, but responsibility for servicing his rooms now fell to her, and that brought her into his capricious orbit on many occasions, from which privileged position she believed she saw cameos of a different man, not the man everyone spoke of, not the imperious, demanding extrovert everyone took him to be, but a man with a softer, kinder alter ego. For her part, she saw that when inebriated he was irrational and volatile, ate and slept whenever – and sometimes *wherever* – his unpredictable temperament dictated, surfacing in the most unexpected parts of the hall wandering aimlessly without apparent reason. At those times, she conceded, he could, as she'd overheard cook describing him, be a veritable '…*pain in the arse, a jumped up right royal Jack the Lad concerned with nothing and no one but himself.*' When sober, however, Mary Ellen saw that he was a charming, gracious and intelligent man who for reasons she had yet to fathom – and which alarmed her – treated her with a respect and kindness that was unheard of in aristocratic circles. His unexpected civility towards her puzzled her, worried her, in fact. It was so out of keeping with the norm she had come to expect of the household and been *told* to expect of Lord and Lady Garston, though she had yet to encounter either in person, or

190

probably never would. The lady's maids were frequently in attendance on their mistresses, and an arm's length friendship inevitably evolved between them. But Mary Ellen was a lowly housemaid in comparison, and not one who habitually *attended* Lord Cavendish or his sister other than to make up their rooms. When the bells rang, it was never her tasked to respond. So, his familiarity was disconcerting to her teenage mind, and left her grasping for understanding that eluded her. On one occasion, something she was never likely to forget and so grossly contrary to protocol his father would have groaned in despair, he had given her a gift, a silver locket on a chain.

She had been arranging the curtains of his room, when he had approached silently behind her and taken her by surprise.

'I have something you might like,' he said ambiguously.

When Mary Ellen turned to face him, a puzzled expression on her young face, not knowing what to expect, Lord Cavendish was dangling a silver locket and chain before her, a smile in his eyes.

'Do you like it? It's a pretty little thing. Like you.'

He was wearing a gold-coloured quilted floral floor-length housecoat, loosely tied at the waist and exposing glimpses of the calf-length white union suit he wore beneath. On his feet, he wore crimson heeled slippers with golden fastenings that looked incongruously vibrant against his pale, bare legs.

Worried about the ramifications of accepting a gift, her brow furrowed in bewilderment, Mary Ellen forced an uneasy smile, air escaping suddenly from her lips as she realised, she had been holding her breath. She felt herself trembling.

This was *so* not the order of things.

Lord Cavendish seemed oblivious to her consternation.

'Then you shall have it. Here, let me put it on for you.'

He moved behind her, and placed the locket and chain over her head, his breath light and warm on her neck, his hands soft as they brushed her skin. Mary Ellen unconsciously lifted her hand to her neck, touching the locket. It felt heavy as she started to tuck it inside her collar.

'Thank you, sir,' was all she could think to say. She had no way of knowing how to behave. Her legs quaked beneath her, her hands shook with a dizzying mix of excitement and trepidation. She could not know whether the flattery, and the gift, was premeditated, or that there might have been a hidden agenda she had yet to fathom.

'Don't hide it away.' His fingers brushed her hands as he took the locket, letting it fall onto the front of her uniform.

'We are not permitted to wear jewellery, sir. I'll get into trouble.'

He laughed theatrically. 'And who do you think you'll get into trouble with. Mary Ellen? Mrs Bonnivale? Oh, she's a dear; don't worry. Mr Grimes? Creepy little toe rag. You just let me know if they say anything to you. I'll deal with them.'

He paused for a moment, regarding Mary Ellen as she moved to leave the room. 'My father,' he said in a soft, clearly-spoken voice as if to better reinforce what he is saying, 'and that adulterous drama queen that, God forbid, is my mother, think servants are unimportant. An inconsequence; an irrelevance; a problem. Dispensable assets of little value.'

He looked into her eyes, Mary Ellen seeing an earnestness she did not expect. 'But where would they – all of us – be without you…and all the others…to make this shambolic pile a pleasant place to live, to bring our food, to make up their whoring beds, to be at their beck and call every hour of the day? Where would they be, eh? Tell me that, Mary Ellen. Tell me that.'

He paused for a moment, breathing deeply, smiled at her and rested his hands on her shoulders. 'No, I want you to know that while I can be a rat-arsed boor at times, I appreciate what you do, Mary Ellen Liptrott. I value that. I may not always show it. But I do.'

He smiled benevolently at her, her face a picture of puzzlement and dilemma. 'So, there.'

Mary Ellen was flummoxed, and not a little anxious; she was getting behind with her duties. 'I don't know what to say.'

'Take this…' he tapped the locket lightly with a finger, '…as a gift.'

'Thank you, sir,' was all Mary Ellen could muster. She was deeply worried by what had just happened, but, more than that, bewildered. And now she felt a growing need to pee.

'Keep it safe, it once belonged to a beautiful woman.' He stepped back appraising the locket. 'And now it does again.'

Chapter 48

'Well, well,' the voice sibilant, clearly enunciated but almost inaudible, 'what have we here?'

The pair spun to face the door. The woman Mary Ellen realised could only have been Lady Clarissa seemed to be flowing into the room, her feet barely moving, waves of diaphanous chiffon flowing in her wake, enfolding her elegant figure, yet doing little to conceal an evident nakedness beneath.

'Clarissa, darling. There you are.'

Lord Cavendish moved to his sister and held her close in his arms, as she rested her head casually on his shoulder. As they pulled apart, to Mary Ellen's surprise, he kissed her on the lips, lingering perhaps longer than a brother should before easing back and gazing into her eyes.

'How have you been, my sweetness?' Lord Cavendish enquired, but his sister ignored him and turned to face Mary Ellen. Unsteadily, she stepped towards her, placing slender hands on her shoulders, holding them lightly in place as she moved around her, circling like a predatory hawk. With unhurried movement, her hands slipped to Mary Ellen's waist, feeling its work-honed slimness, and then ran her fingers upwards across her stomach until she could cup her breasts. She squeezed gently. As if testing the ripeness of fruit.

'Nice tits, brother, dear. Firm, too. She'll be very popular with your sordid little band of perverts.' She stressed the word *sordid*, and Mary Ellen thought she detected scorn in her voice, but she by now too troubled by being in the presence of the pair of them to know anything with certainty.

Lady Clarissa circled Mary Ellen a second time, her fingers tracing lightly across her hands and buttocks, and then seeming satisfied, folded herself into a red velvet chair, causing her gown to fall revealingly open, sliding away to reveal shapely legs. That she was exposing herself seemed not to concern her. For her part, Mary Ellen strove to avert her gaze, but to her surprise found the image disconcertingly erotic, her eyes involuntarily drawn to the creamily smooth flesh, its firm elegance and the shadowy folds of darkness. Apart from her sister Jane, she had never seen a naked woman, and was alarmed to feel the vision arousing the same feminine-induced sensation she'd briefly experienced with Elizabeth.

In one smooth flourish of chiffon, Clarissa rose gracefully and moved to stand beside her brother, whispering in his ear. He nodded conspiratorially, and Mary Ellen thought she heard him say "Later". Clarissa turned to leave but paused to regard Mary Ellen with an enquiring look on her face.

'Has he bedded you yet?' she asked, her lips drawn into a smile not reflected in her eyes.

Mary Ellen, at a loss to know how to reply, dumbly shook her head, a concerned expression furrowing her brow.

'Oh, he will. He most certainly will, my dear.' She pointed to the locket around Mary Ellen's neck. 'He hasn't given you that without good reason. And if you believe all that tawdry guff about valuing your services, I heard him purring over you, you'll believe anything.'

And with that, she flowed away as quietly as she had entered, leaving Mary Ellen to wonder if she had been there at all.

Chapter 49

Mary Ellen, puzzlement fogging her mind, turned to face Lord Cavendish, gesturing to the door, indicating that she proposed to leave.

'Don't take any notice of Clarissa, Mary Ellen. She's…not…in the best of health,' he said, emphasising the words. 'I'm afraid she doesn't always know what she's saying much of the time.' He waved a hand in a circular motion at the side of his head.

Mary Ellen bowed her head, not knowing what to say.

'Do you believe in God?' he asked out of the blue.

The question caught Mary Ellen by surprise, embedded as it was with gravity and probing intent.

'I, er, yes. I suppose. Well, maybe not. I don't really know.'

'Do you go to church?'

'I have done. With my sister, and when my mother was alive. I still have her bible. But I don't go now. I…'

'Man's worst invention, if you ask me,' he voiced vitriolically. 'Bloody great confidence trick. Religion. Priests. Bloody leaches, parasites on humanity, the lot of them.' He mimed spitting on the floor.

Mary Ellen was taken aback, but a part of her was amused by his theatrics, and she wanted to smile, whether from relief or the drama of his outburst, she wasn't sure. She knew that unlike many country estates, religion was not a mainstay of Garston life. Daily prayers were not said. In generations gone by, this part of the country, and the Garstons had been strongly of the Catholic faith. Several of the family having been fined and imprisoned for recusancy, but Mary Ellen was not to know that.

'Are you a virgin?'

Again she was caught by surprise, and before she could respond he went on, quizzing her, all the while with a smile on his lips. 'Is there…someone? A husband in waiting, perhaps? A lover? You know you're not allowed to marry while in service,' he added with mock reproach. 'You'd have to leave, find another job.'

Mary Ellen, reeling with the discomfort that had befallen her, searched for the truth. 'There is...was. One of the footmen. We've been...seeing one another...for about a year. Only on our days off,' she added hurriedly as an afterthought. 'But I caught him sha–, in bed with someone else. So, I've dumped him.' Adding not altogether truthfully, 'I was never going to marry him. I only wanted him for sex.'

Lord Cavendish laughed lightly, a spark in his eye. 'I can see why a pretty little things like you might enjoy...*sex*, as you put it. Is he here? In the hall, at the moment? Or...?'

'They are both away. With the family, in Somerset. I hope I never see 'im, either of 'em, again.'

She turned to leave, conscious of an awkwardness, and an air charged with... what...? Things unsaid? Things wondered, undefined?

As she left, she felt annoyed with herself. In so many ways a maturing young woman; in others still with so much to learn about people. The encounter with Lord Cavendish had made her feel restless and was dismayed she hadn't felt able to deal with it better.

As if nothing had happened, Lord Cavendish turned back into his room and, filling a crystal tumbler with brandy, ambled lazily with it to the window where he stood motionless, arms akimbo, gazing proprietorially across the estate grounds.

Chapter 50

The estate was not the matter occupying Lord Cavendish's mind; it was the young housemaid who had just departed.

He closed his eyes, raising his shoulders to ease a tension. He could still smell the scent of her hair, still feel the soft, smooth alabaster sheen of her neck. She would be ideal, he thought, smiling inwardly at what he hoped might be to come. The gift of the locket, stolen from a London prostitute of his regular acquaintance, was merely the opening gambit in a game he hoped would not be too drawn out.

Meanwhile, he thought less dreamily, there was another he must attend. Turning slowly he crossed to his bed and opened an embroidered cloth valise that sat on it, taking from it a small leather pouch. Slipping it into the pocket of his housecoat he left his apartment.

Opening the door to his sister's rooms, he found her standing before the window, her weight supported by its frame, the sunlight giving her chemise a golden halo that framed the shadowy outline of her body beneath. The warmth of the sun had made her drowsy. Her eyes became heavy and fell shut as she slipped into the zone between sleep and wakefulness, where thoughts came randomly, confused and colourful. She saw herself walking through fields of golden corn, blue cloudless sky above, the sun warm to her skin.

Then, sensing another present, she turned to face him.

'You came.'

'Of course,' he said. 'I'll always come; you know that.'

Lady Clarissa turned to the window again, a shimmer of paranoia rising within her breast. 'They're watching. All of them. Dirty. Perverts. They watch me. All the time.'

Lord Cavendish moved to stand next to his sister and peered out of the window. Down below, gardeners were weeding an ornate section of the garden. 'Perhaps,' he said, putting his arms around her and turning her away from the window, 'if you didn't put yourself so openly on display, darling, they would have nothing to look at.'

'They shouldn't be looking. Perverts. Bastards.'

'Don't get distraught, sister, dear. I'm sure no one's looking at you. See…' he said, pulling the leather pouch from his pocket, '…I brought you a present.'

Clarissa's eyes brightened. She smiled and, back in the moment, poured wine into two goblets standing on a table beside her. Reaching into the pouch, Cavendish sprinkled a generous pinch of green herb into the wine, stirred it briefly with his finger, which he slipped playfully into Clarissa's mouth. She sucked his finger seductively, rolling her tongue around it before releasing it and raising the goblet to her mouth, gazing into her brother's eyes. She drank heavily, visibly relaxing in anticipation of the herbal mixture taking effect and crossed the room to a low and plush settee, beckoning her brother to follow.

Wrapping her chemise around her and tucking her slender legs beneath her she emptied the goblet, letting it fall to the floor, and lay against her brother's shoulder, her long hair cascading uncontrollably masking her face, her hand resting lightly on his chest. As the herbs took hold, bringing both a heady mix of confidence and waywardness she slowly untied his house coat, and with playful fingers loosened enough buttons on his union suit to slip her hand inside and ruffle his ginger-haired chest, teasing the hair into tight coils around her fingers. Tugging to further relax his clothing she slid her hand downwards, ran her hand along the insides of his thighs and felt his hardness.

She heard her brother sigh softly and knew what he was thinking.

Slowly she pulled herself upright, the room slowly spinning, golden sunlight illuminating the walls became multihued, shimmering rays of brightness interwoven with dark and sombre shadows. Unsteadily she rose to her feet, her chemise falling open, exposing her nakedness. With careful deliberation, she extended a hand towards her brother's smiling face and caressed it as she turned and walked towards her bedroom door. As she opened it, she turned back to her brother, and beckoned.

'Come,' she said.

Chapter 51

Duncan and Alice were relaxing in her garden, blue, cloud-dappled sky overhead, the air heady with the aniseed scent of sweet cicely, songbirds trilling from the hedgerows and among the trees that surround the small reservoir nearby. In the distance a dog was barking playfully. It had been only a few days since Alice had kissed him, on the occasion of his last visit. When he'd arrived today her kiss had been light and brief, before she led him through to the garden. He hadn't known what to expect, or how to greet her. So he was relieved when she took matters into her own hands.

A bottle of chilled sauvignon blanc sat open in an ice bucket, and two equally chilled glasses stood on a garden table, beads of condensation trickling down their sides. The hamlet was surprisingly quiet for a sunny summer day, albeit midweek. They were listening to Chopin *Nocturnes* on a small music box that Alice had "Bluetoothed" to her MP3 player, a feat Duncan regarded as borderline Satanism. For all his computer savvy, he had yet to understand Bluetooth.

His visit was on the pretext of bringing Alice up to date with his family history findings, and as the last chords of Chopin drift into the ether he produced several pages of notes, which he waved in the air saying, 'This is starting to become complicated, so I decided to prepare a timeline of what I'd found to date.'

Alice patted his arm, 'You didn't need to do that, Duncan. You've found what I asked you to find. That's as much as I expected.'

'Yes, I know. But…'

'But…?'

'I'm enjoying doing it, and I've nothing on just now. So, it gives me something to do. Keeps me keen, so to speak.' He smiled at her, knowing that the keenness had a sharper edge than family history. 'Anyway, it's probably simplest if you read through this. It won't take long, and it'll save me droning on. Oh, and I should say that these are just notes, not formatted as a professional report. I wouldn't want you to think my work was this sloppy.'

Alice laughed at him as she took the papers and read.

REPORT NOTES RELATING TO MARY ELLEN LIPTROT

BACKGROUND NOTES

Mary Ellen LIPTROT was born 2 October 1855, and baptised at St Aidan's church, Billinge on 6 October 1855. Her father is a gamekeeper, John Liptrot, and her mother is named as Alice.

Mary Ellen had several brothers and sisters:
1845: Thomas, born 18 August, baptised (St Aidan's) 17 September 1845. Died May 1867, aged 21.

1847: Jane, born 16 July, baptised (St Aidan's) 18 July 1847. Father still employed as gamekeeper.

1849: Mary Ellen, born 18 August, baptised (St Aidan's) 24 August 1849. Died March 1852, buried (St Aidan's) 21 March 1852, aged 2½ years. No grave record.

1851: Catharine, born 12 October, baptised (St Aidan's) 26 October 1851. Died January 1853 (? December 1852), aged 14 months, buried (St Aidan's) 9 January 1853. No grave record.

1853: Edward, born 4 November, baptised 6 November 1853 (St Aidan's). Died – not known.

1855: Mary Ellen, as above.

1858: Henry, born 14 April, baptised 25 April 1858 (St Aidan's) – father's occupation given simply as 'Keeper' (not thought to be significant). Died 3 October 1914, aged 56. No burial details.

1861: George, born 5 November 1861, baptised 11 November 1861 (St Aidan's). Died – not known.

CENSUS DATA

1861: John and Alice Liptrot are recorded living at Penny Hall, Ashton-in-Makerfield. Also present are Thomas, aged 15 (coal mine labourer); Jane, aged 13 (scholar); Edward, aged 7 (scholar); Ellen Mary (sic), aged 5 (scholar), and Henry, aged 2.

[NOTES: The gap between Jane aged 13, and Edward aged 7 is an indicator of "missing" children. Confirmed by the records for Mary Ellen and Catharine, see above.]

1871: No address is given for the family other than Arch Lane. John Liptrot is now aged 68, but his wife, Alice, is absent (presumed deceased). Edward is still at the family home, aged 17 (coal mine labourer). Mary Ellen is now 15, Henry aged 12; George, aged 9, is still at school.

1871-1881: Undated/unexplained entry in the records for Wakefield Prison (i.e. West Riding House of Correction) showing Mary Ellen Liptrot from Wigan. There is no indication of what the misdemeanour might have been, or the length of the sentence. She does not appear in the Quarter Session indictment books, and so she must have been tried through the Petty Sessions. However, there are no Petty Session records for Halifax Borough Court or West Morley Division that cover the year 1878-1881. Why Wakefield? No women's prisons in Lancashire??? Was ME tried in Wigan but imprisoned in Wakefield. If so, why?

[NOTE: Wigan Borough Gaol used only as a lock-up and demolished in 1868 when the police station was moved to the town hall. [Ref: https://www.prisonhistory.org/wp-content/uploads/2018/06/Guide-to-the-Criminal-Prisons-of-Nineteenth-Century-England-R1.pdf].

Mary Ellen's second illegitimate child was born in 1880, so the period 1871–1881 cannot relate to the entire period of incarceration. More likely it relates to the period covered by the particular prison ledger. The numbering in the ledger – 22/52 – suggests a sentence of 22 weeks.

1881: The family are still living in Arch Lane, but now Mary Ellen is the head of the household, aged 24, and employed as a washerwoman. Also present are brothers Henry, aged 21 (coal miner), and George, aged 19 (coal miner). Their former residence, Penny Hall, is occupied by the new gamekeeper, indicating that John Liptrot has either retired, or died.

1881, 16 May: Mary Ellen, marries Joseph Cunliffe (coal miner), at Holy Trinity church, Ashton-in-Makerfield.

1891: At this date, Mary Ellen Liptrot is no longer present in Arch Lane. Through her children, John, aged 17, and Alice, aged 11, she is found, aged 35, as the wife of Joseph Cunliffe, aged 35 (coal miner) living at 118 Main Street, Billinge. Joseph and Mary Ellen have 4 children: James, aged 9; Margaret, aged 6; Mary Ellen, aged 3, and Henry, aged 1.

1901: Joseph and Mary Ellen are living at 139 Main Street, Billinge, and they now have another son, Samuel, aged 8.

1911: Joseph and Mary Ellen are living in Winstanley (address unknown, although this may be a loose reference to Billinge, since the two areas are contiguous and referred to as 'Billinge and Winstanley' in some records), along with Margaret, aged 26 (single), James, aged 20 (widower), Henry, aged 21 (single) and Samuel, aged 18 (single). Also present Joseph Cunliffe, nephew, aged 7 (?possibly son of James and his deceased wife).

1921, 21 December: Joseph Cunliffe dies, aged 66.

1939, 26 May: Mary Ellen Cunliffe née Liptrot dies, aged 83. Place of death is given as 154 Upholland Road, Billinge. Cause of death: senile decay. The informant is her son Henry Cunliffe, living at 122 Upholland Road, Billinge and Winstanley. Under "Occupation" on the death certificate ME is recorded as the widow of Joseph Cunliffe, coal miner. An address is given there – 64 Wigan Road, Ashton-in-Makerfield. This is at variance with the place of death but is not thought to be relevant.

[NOTE: ME is the last survivor of her family. All her brothers and sisters died before she did – see separate note.]

Duncan sipped his wine and watched Alice as she read. His eyes scanned her face, the soft roundedness of her cheeks, her brow lightly furrowed in concentration, the neat trim of her hair gathering in light curls at the back of her neck, the small ear lobes which, for the first time, he noticed contained a small diamond stud. Her eyebrows moved up and down slightly as she read, her eyes catching the sunlight. It was an image he could sketch with perfect accuracy, but right now it's not a sketch he longed for, but the real thing.

Unseen by either of them, a passing neighbour paused at the garden gate and nodded approvingly. 'It's a hard life, for some,' she called out, walking away.

Alice looked up with a start and called after her. 'The wine won't drink itself, Mary. Someone has to step up and be counted.'

She turned to Duncan, and said, 'Well, that does what I asked you to do, as I've said before. Job done.'

'Well, job done. Yes, but…'

'But?'

'I'm intrigued to know more about those two illegitimate children. And while I've found out who the girl in the picture is, I'd ideally like to prove the descending line to you. To firm up the relationship.'

'I thought you'd done that. She's my great, great grandmother.'

'Yes, that's what Ancestry and the paperwork tells us. But I'd like to confirm the line with a bit more certainty. It's not knowing who the father of John and Alice were…or maybe even fathers, plural. It will only annoy me if I don't tie up that lose end.'

'But if the father's, or fathers', names are not recorded, how can you do that?'

'I'm thinking it will come down to DNA profiling, which won't be easy because we need something that carries the DNA down across the years.'

'But *you* can't do the profiling. Can you?'

'No,' Duncan said, 'but I know someone who can. If I say "Pretty, please", or beg.'

'Who might that be.?'

'Sandy Glen. Someone I know through the genealogical forums.'

'He sounds like a holiday resort.'

Duncan laughed. 'Yes, I suppose so. But it's a *she* not a *he*. Lives in Blackpool and works for the DNA lab that does some of the testing for Ancestry.'

'Won't she get in trouble for doing that?'

'I doubt it. She's a part-time tutor at Lancaster University, so she could use our case as a demo for her students. In fact, it's probably better for her, because messing up our samples would be of little consequence. We'd just have to repeat the process. It doesn't have to be evidential standard. Just enough to establish the link will do.'

'And I remember you saying something about Mary Ellen's sister being married to two men on the same day. Is that possible? Surely not?'

'Well, that was more easily cleared up,' he said leaning back and draining his wine glass. 'I traced one of your DNA links to someone living in Texas, of all places. She's a descendant of Mary Ellen's sister, Jane, although I've not checked to see which of Jane's children moved to America. Anyway, her ancestry records show two marriages one to a Thomas Mousdell, the other to a Thomas Hiddin.'

'On the same day?'

'Same day. Same church.'

'St Aidan's in Billinge.'

'You'd think so. But no, this time it was the parish church in Ashton, Holy Trinity, I think, which given that Jane was still living in Arch Lane makes sense. It turns out that the man she married was in fact Thomas Eden Mousdell. The name Hiddin being an early spelling of Eden, which was also his mother's maiden name.'

'And no one noticed?'

'Let me show you something.' He sifted through his papers and produces a copy of a marriage certificate. 'Tell me if you notice anything about these that is unusual.'

Alice studied the papers, then said, 'Ah, yes. Groom given as Hiddin, groom's father as Mousdell. That's odd by any standards.'

'And not only that. Everyone except Jane has signed the certificate with a mark, indicating that they couldn't read or write. So, no one would notice the wrong name.'

'What about Jane? Wouldn't she have noticed?'

'Possibly, but if you take into account that she was literally within days of giving birth, her mind was likely on other things. She'd just sign on the dotted line and not read the certificate. Maybe afterwards she noticed, and the mistake was corrected. That would explain why your Texan cousin would have two records.'

Duncan looked pensive for a moment as a thought bubbled to the surface of this thoughts. 'And I've just realised that if Jane could read and write, isn't it likely, maybe, that Mary Ellen could, too? Maybe, once the two sisters had gone their separate ways, they wrote to one another. That could prove enlightening.'

'Well, I can see you're an optimist. What are the chances of finding letters between these two from, what, nearly a hundred-and-fifty years ago?'

'Slim would give us something to cling to.'

'Well, I agree with you. It's all very intriguing.'

Duncan nodded, and was suddenly aware that he had spent more time talking to Alice than he'd talked to anyone for months. It made him feel good. The chance to communicate. It seemed such a simple thing. But when you live on your own, you might go for days and not speak to anyone; not even say a word, unless you talked to yourself. It wasn't something you realised, until you started talking again. Yes, it made him feel very good, almost as good as sitting in this lovely garden with Alice drinking wine.

Alice refilled his glass and got up. 'Back in a mo.'

When she returned, she said, 'Change of subject,' and placed an envelope on the table in front of him.

'What's this?' he asked.

'Tickets.'

'Tickets? For what?'

'Open the envelope. See for yourself,' she said playfully. 'Do I have to do everything?'

He opened the envelope and two tickets fell out. They were for a concert at Manchester's Bridgewater Hall.

'I hope you don't think I'm being presumptuous. But I thought you might like the programme. Rachmaninov. An early evening concert by the Camerata. They started doing post-office concerts at six. Just for an hour. Catches folk before they head home. Let's the traffic die down.'

'That's a lovely idea,' Duncan admitted. 'The tickets, not the concert idea. Well, both actually. When is it?' He studied the tickets, but before he said anything Alice went on, 'It's on your birthday. I can't believe we were good friends the whole of last year, and you never mentioned your birthday. Not once. I had to drag it out of Nellie. I hope you're free on that day.'

'Well, I can't think of anything that would mean more to me. So, it's a date. Thank you.'

This time he leaned across and kissed her. 'Thank you.'

Chapter 52

Sunday, 22 October 1871

'So, did you have a nice birthday t'other week?' Jane asked as she poured tea into two mugs. Mary Ellen had finally got round to calling on her sister, who for her part wasn't for once labouring beneath a mound of household chores.

'Well, I suppose the highlight was emptying Lord Cavendish's slop pot.'

'As good as that, eh?'

'Even better. This time he'd shit in it, and then been sick all over the carpet.'

'How the other half live, eh?'

Mary Ellen laughed at the memory as she spooned sugar into her tea and sipped it appreciatively.

Jane enjoyed having time with her sister, who was maturing rapidly; for an hour or so she was able to relax in her company and not be fretting about what the boys were up to or what she'd be preparing for their next meal.

'You'd think 'e could manage to find the bog; it's only through a door. But no. Drunk again. Or drugged up.' Mary Ellen laughed again. 'But 'e's cute, in a helpless kind of way.'

'*Cute*? I wouldn't have said Lord Cavendish was *cute*. Not from what I've heard. Folk say he's a self-serving bastard. Only interested in himself.'

'Well, 'e may be a bastard; I don't know. But 'e's all'us good wi' me – when he's sober enough to remember who I am.'

'What do you mean...*good* with you? You're not supposed to be anywhere near him. Aren't you supposed to swan around, up and down the back stairs, out of sight? Do your jobs, then disappear?'

'Well, I'm supposed to do 'is rooms while 'e's having breakfast with the family. But 'e doesn't always bother. Can't stand 'is parents, 'e says. Says they're a boring lot of morons – whatever they are. I thought morons were mushrooms.'

'But if he's still in his rooms when you go to make them up, aren't you supposed to leave them and go back later?'

'Yeah. We are. But a few times 'e's insisted I do the rooms while 'e's there, reading the newspaper or summat. And then 'e talks to me. Like I'm a 'uman bein' and says 'e doesn't care about rules.'

'Does Mrs Bonnivale know?'

'Dunno. I've noticed 'er give me a funny look a few times, if I'm getting behind with my work. But she's never said nowt.'

'A *few* times! How often do you have your little *talks* with him?'

'Two or three times a week; 'e's very nice to me. Says 'e likes me. Give me a present, 'e did.'

'What!' Jane exploded, concern spreading across her face. '*What*?'

'He give me a locket. As a gift. Said it used to belong to a lovely lady and now 'e wanted me to 'ave it.'

'Oh, for fuck's sake, Mary Ellen. What have you done?'

'I've done nuffin. Just accepted a gift. See,' she said, producing the locket from beneath the collar of her blouse.

'For Christ's sake. And have you thought what might happen if he accuses you of stealing it?'

Mary Ellen tried to affect indignation, and sat upright in her chair, her chin in the air. 'Lady Clarissa saw him give it to me. And she didn't say nuffin.'

'Well, she wouldn't, would she; not if they were in it together.' Jane sighed heavily. 'This just gets better, Mary Ellen. Not only are you messing around with Lord Cavendish, but in front of his sister. Have you any idea how much trouble they could land you in. You could go the prison for stealing. And there's no prisons for women round here. You'd end up in Strangeways, or somewhere else, miles away. How would that suit? You'd never get a job again, even if they let you out. Bugger it; they've sent people halfway round the world just for stealing a loaf of bread, and here you are with a bloody locket. Silver, looking at it.'

Jane picked up the locket and examined it, slipping a catch to open it.

'Oh, no,' she said as she saw what was inside. 'What's this?'

Mary Ellen bridled. 'It's just hair. The red 'air's 'is; t'other's mine. I got 'is from an 'airbrush in 'is bathroom. I just thought…'

Jane snapped at her, wagging a finger in her face. 'No, Mary Ellen, you *didn't* think. That's the trouble. This is madness. You could be sacked. Father could be sacked, and we'd all be out of a home. Did you *think* of that?'

Mary Ellen looked crestfallen. 'No, s'pose not. But it's only a locket, Jane. It's not valuable, 'cos 'e wouldn't 'ave give it me if it was, would 'e?'

'It might *only* be a locket. But it's silver, so it *is* valuable. Jesus. What would Mother say, God rest her soul? What would Father say? Oh, God, we can't tell him. He'll take his belt to you. You'll have to give it back.'

Mary Ellen sat up defiantly. 'I'm not giving it back. It was a gift, and I'm keeping it.' With that she took it from Jane's hand and slipped it into a pocket.

Jane refilled their mugs, a look of dismay settling on her face. 'Well, you can't carry it around with you. That's just asking for trouble. And you can't wear it. So, you'd better leave it here. For safe keeping until we figure out what to do. Whether his lordship says anything about a missing locket. You might be able to slip it back into his room, somewhere, out of sight, like as if he'd dropped it.'

Mary Ellen's shoulders dropped in resignation. 'S'pose,' she accepted reluctantly and returned the locket to her sister.

'I'll put it in your box in our bedroom. No one will find it there. Does Joseph know?'

'Fuck, Joseph.'

'What?'

''E's done. We're done. Caught 'im rutting Elizabeth. Two-timing bastard. I 'ope his cock rots.'

It was Jane's turn to be deflated. She reached out and took Mary Ellen's hand. 'Oh, I'm so sorry. I thought he loved you. Or at least was heading that way.'

'So did I. But Elizabeth waggled 'er tits at 'im, and 'e was on 'er like a rabbit on 'eat. She said it was 'er fault; said she was feeling randy.' She paused momentarily, adding, 'I can understand that. But did she 'ave to grab Joseph? There's plenty of gardeners 'anging around the place. And anyway, it was Joseph what 'ad to decide to stick 'is cock up 'er. If 'e loved me, 'e wouldn't 'ave done that. Would 'e?'

'You wouldn't think so. But that's men for you. Can't keep it in their kecks. What's it like at the hall. You must still see him every day.'

'Oh, no, they're all away in Somerset, except Lord Cavendish and his sister. I didn't get to go, which is fine by me. And they say they might stay away for Christmas and not come back until early next year, or even later.'

'Ah. Well that explains something.'

Jane got up and delved into a kitchen drawer, handing Mary Ellen a bundle of letters, each bearing a red stamp.

'These have been coming for you for a few weeks. Someone's written Bath on one of them. That's Somerset, I think. They must be letters from Joseph.'

Mary Ellen pushed them away. 'Throw 'em away. I don't want 'em. Chuck 'em on t'fire.'

'Don't' you just want to read them first? See what he has to say? Anyway, it might not be Joseph who's written them.'

'Couldn't care less.'

'They might be from Elizabeth.'

'She can't write. She told me. She just fucks.'

'You might be cutting off your nose to spite your face.'

'It's my face; I'll do what I like with it.'

Jane sighed and put the letters to one side. Later she'll put them in Mary Ellen's box, in case of a change of heart.

Finally she said: 'So, it must be fairly quiet with most of the household away.'

'Quiet enough. We still 'ave to do all the rooms even though nobody's used 'em, but, yeah, it's a bit easier. At least Greasy Grimes isn't there, and those two toe rags, John and Henry 'ave gone, too.'

'Well, that's good. Won't be quite so much like hard work all the time.'

Mary Ellen rinsed the mugs in a bowl of tepid water as Jane got up and went to the window. May Ellen joined her and slipped her arm around her waist, pulling her to her in a sisterly hug. The trees in the lane had shed most of their leaves, and broken twigs and branches brought down by last night's wind lay strewn about. For the moment, the sun was shining through the swaying trees, dappling the cottage in a weak autumnal light.

Jane turned back into the room and started peeling a few potatoes from a sack beneath the sink. Mary Ellen found a large pot in a cupboard and half filled it with water into which Jane dropped the peeled potatoes ready to start on making a stew.

'Papa says it's going to be a cold winter,' Jane said reflectively. 'I'd best get the lads stocking up with logs.'

'Well, they may as well do something to earn their keep. Time they did. Anyway, 'Enry can go labouring in t'mines soon, can't 'e?'

'Says he doesn't want to. But he might have to, whether he likes it or not. Unless he gets something better.'

The quarrel over the locket having passed, Mary Ellen relaxed and smiled at her sister. 'So, anyway, what about your love life. How's it going?'

'It's going…okay.' For a brief moment a distant look came into her eyes as if she was drawing on memories. Then laughingly, she said, 'Not that it's any of your business.'

'Tommie Mousdale, is it?'

'Still Tommie.'

'Going to get wed?'

'Maybe. Not yet. He's still living with his parents, and there's no room for me. Shares a bedroom with two of his brothers, and I don't fancy taking on all three of them.'

'Well, you've got enough 'oles for three, if you change your mind.'

'Mary Ellen,' Jane gasped, 'you're disgusting sometimes. I don't know where you get it from.'

They both laughed at the idea.

'And, anyway, we don't know what's going to happen with this place when Papa retires. We'll have to find somewhere else. Or pray for a miracle.'

'So,' Mary Ellen continued, a wicked smile lighting up her face, unwilling to let the subject go, 'what do you do about sex?'

Jane affected outrage. 'Mary Ellen! You don't expect me to answer that.' But she was amused all the same. 'We manage.'

Mary Ellen is still feeling mischievous. 'Is 'e any good? At sex? In the sack, like?'

Jane playfully wagged her finger at her. 'Now, that's going too far. Now shut up and come and help me make a stew.'

Chapter 53

Duncan had been looking forward to his birthday since Alice had produced the tickets for the Camerata concert. From lunchtime meetings, geocaching walks and discussions about family history to an evening at a concert in the company of a beautiful woman, he was acutely conscious of travelling a road not journeyed for some time. They were openly demonstrating to the casual eye that they were together, a couple…an item, and he was pointedly visited by the realisation that, for him at least, it was a certain and demonstrative step forward.

Isabel had been the only woman in Duncan's life, from their days at school and university through into adulthood and, as everyone who knew them had predicted, a happy marriage. Many were surprised, some – his parents especially – disappointed that they had had no children. That had been not so much a conscious decision as simply an aspect of the evolution of their loving relationship that had never arisen, as if the intensity of the love they felt for each other was something they wished not to share with a family. They had never, he realised, discussed the question of having a family. The joys, and tribulations, of parenthood were simply not for them. That's all there was to it.

So, his progression into a relationship with Alice was taking him into untested territory. His life with Isabel had grown organically, nurtured by a constant repertoire of loving touches, friendship, mutual respect, companionship and tenderness.

And now, he saw, it was happening again. The same touching familiarity; the same gradual drift into togetherness.

When he arrived at White Coppice to pick Alice up, she was looking radiant, and Duncan caught his breath. She was wearing a white short-sleeved, knee-length wrap-around dress embellished with stylised flowers over which she wore a chiffon scarf that encircled her neck and fell to her waist.

She beamed at him. 'You look as though you've seen a ghost.'

'I'm not sure what I've seen, but it's beautiful.'

Alice reached up and kissed him. 'I hope you don't think me presumptuous – again, but since the concert finishes quite early, I've taken the liberty of reserving a table for dinner. At Adam Reid's restaurant in the Midland Hotel.'

'Well, if that's your idea of presumption, be my guest. I'm salivating already. Wow, thank you.'

'It is your birthday, after all.' And with that she kissed him again. 'Happy birthday, Duncan.'

By no stretch of imagination could the thirty-mile drive into Manchester be considered as spectacular, or even moderately attractive. The M61 motorway was a racetrack, and the circuitous route Duncan took to the NCP car park off Deansgate simply one grim urban vista after another. It was not a journey he had made for some time; he and Isabel had joked among friends that when Harry Ramsden's fish and chip restaurant had closed, there was no earthly reason for visiting Manchester. That wasn't true, of course. There were many good reasons to visit the city, and the two of them had enjoyed years of Hallé concerts at the old Free Trade Hall under several musical directors – Loughran, Skrowaczewski and Nagano. Now a Radisson hotel, the hall was built on the site of the Peterloo Massacre in 1819, when cavalry charged into a crowd of 60,000–80,000 who had gathered to demand the reform of parliamentary representation. More recently, Charles Dickens had performed there in the summer of 1857 in Wilkie Collins's play *The Frozen Deep*. In 1872, Benjamin Disraeli gave his paternalistic *One Nation* speech, and in 1904, Winston Churchill had delivered a speech at the hall defending Britain's policy of free trade.

Today's concert was at the replacement venue, the Bridgewater Hall, named after the Third Duke of Bridgewater, who commissioned the eponymous Bridgewater Canal that crossed Manchester. Concert goers were milling around as Duncan and Alice walked the short distance from the car park to the hall. As they approached, coaches were disgorging more concert goers, and so they passed through the glass doors into the tiled lobby as part of a tsunami of animated, voluble people. There was a scrum at the bar, but Duncan somehow contrived to find himself directly in front of a waitress who had developed the knack of not noticing impatiently gesticulating arms and hands ostentatiously waving money in the vain hope of attracting her attention. She promptly and efficiently provided him with two glasses of white wine, with which he retreated to find that Alice had found a seat at a table.

The various parts of the auditorium were reached by flights of stairs and lifts, the latter made inadequate for the purpose once the five-minute bell rang by the press of people. Alice found her way to the door marked "Dress circle", and to his delight, Duncan found that she had bought tickets in the centre of Row A, looking down on the stalls, acoustically the most perfect place in the entire hall. They settled themselves in the plush seats and looked on as the orchestra filed onto the stage, the focal point of which was the magnificent Marcussen organ, which covered the entire rear wall with wood and burnished metal.

The concert began with Rachmaninov's *Scherzo in D minor* a short piece, his earliest surviving composition for orchestra, composed when he was a student at the Moscow Conservatory. Another early composition, *Prince Rostislav*, a symphonic tone poem followed, rarely heard in concert halls. In a performance nothing less than breathtaking by the previous year's winner of the Leeds International Piano Competition, the rest of the concert was consumed by Rachmaninov's ever-popular second piano concerto that had many of the audience, Alice and Duncan included, on their feet in rapturous applause.

'Well,' said Duncan, drawing knowledge from the depths of his memory, 'if that's how Rachmaninov coped with depression and writer's block, I can't wait to be depressed.'

Alice laughed lightly at him as they got up to make their way out. 'I'm not sure all that makes sense, but I know what you mean. I remember a young girl from Chetham's, Anna Markland, playing that in the early 1980s, when she won the BBC Young Musician of the Year. It's such a moving piece.'

Duncan looked at Alice in a way she didn't understand. Then, as they reached the foyer, he turned to her and said, 'You won't believe this, and I confess I'd almost forgotten it until you mentioned her name, but years ago I was given permission to organise concerts in and around Wigan for pupils at Chets. I can fairly truthfully claim to have given Anna Markland her first public recital outside the college, when pupils came to give a "Young Musician's Recital". "Old wine in new bottles", we called them.'

'Well,' Alice said, stepping back and regarding him with a look of admiration, 'now I *am* impressed. You an impresario.'

'I was hardly that, and she was such a delight to know. I wonder where she is now.'

They were now outside the concert hall and threading a way through the crowds as they raced off to find coaches, trams, buses and cars. Alice slipped her arm through Duncan's as they strolled the short distance to the Midland Hotel, a splendid railway hotel built at the northern terminus of the Midland Railway's service from London. The hotel restaurant had been known as Trafford in the days when Queen Elizabeth, the Queen Mother had dined there in the late 1950s. Now, after several incarnations, the restaurant was under the control of a young and highly renowned chef-patron, Adam Reid.

Once inside, they headed for the restaurant bar, where they ordered kir cassis while they studied the menus. Before the drinks came, Alice excused herself, returning a few minutes later, seating herself close to Duncan, to his eyes the most beautiful woman in the room. He inhaled her now familiar fragrance and felt the warmth of her body against him.

They agreed to have the chef's signature menu, central to which was grilled Cornish turbot with apple and watercress, followed by lamb from the Rhug Estate in Denbighshire. There are two desserts, Duncan noticed, and said 'I'm not sure I can manage two desserts. But I'll give it a go.'

As the waiter retrieved the menus and left, Alice eased the chiffon scarf from around her shoulders, and Duncan was certain she was not wearing underclothes, at least not a bra. Was she aware that her dress was revealing more than intended! He wondered.

The thought brought back a flush of memory. It was a tease in which Isabel excelled: to casually drop into conversation, in a restaurant or at a social gathering when he could do nothing about it, that she wasn't wearing underwear. To intensify the sensation, it was during the 1980s revivalist heyday of silk stockings and suspender belts. That alone was enough to arouse him; the fleeting glimpse of bare skin above the top of a stocking as she crossed her legs, usually deliberately and provocatively.

Was Alice playing the same game?

Briefly he thought about Isabel – his guilty conscience calling him? His mind teasing him. He tried to imagine it was Isabel sitting across from him. But he saw only Alice, and in that moment felt a hunger and longing he had not experienced for many years. And he silently wondered what else she might not be wearing.

They spoke of many things as they worked their way through the dishes placed before them. Duncan's eyes rarely leaving Alice's, and his inner self filling with a confidence long since lost. He wanted nothing more now than to take this woman home, and to take the one bold step he had shied away from almost since the first time they met. Yet even now, with the evidence before him that any other man would recognise in an instant, he quaked at the thought that he may have misread Alice.

She had a mischievous grin on her face when she said, 'You've had far too much to drink to drive. Just as well I've arranged for us to stay the night here. I hope you don't mind.'

'To stay…here?' For the first time he gave the room and its magnificent chandelier more than a cursory glance.

'Seems silly to go trawling around Manchester looking for another hotel when we have a perfectly good one right here. Don't you think?'

'I do. Think. That is…'

'Excellent. So, how about a cognac. Purely as a digestif, you understand.'

Duncan's mind was a fever of imagination, myriad competing and confused thoughts colliding in a turmoil of longing, urgency and intense desire. When Alice made the first move, and rose to leave the table, he followed hazily, wishing they could spend more of the evening together.

As they left the lift on the second floor, Alice stopped outside Room 204. 'There's only one problem,' she said, smiling at him, her eyes sparkling with innocent mischief. 'I only booked the one room and checked-in earlier. What do you suggest?'

Duncan was speechless, an inane grin spreading across his face, as Alice inserted the key and entered the room, her smile beckoning him to follow. None of the splendour of the luxurious suite registered with Duncan. He had eyes only for Alice, who draped her scarf across a chair and turned her back to him momentarily. When she turned round, she had unfastened the wrap-round dress, holding it open before letting it fall to the floor.

Nothing of what Duncan saw ever came from Marks and Spencer.

Alice smiled at him playfully.

'Could you manage just a little more dessert? While it's your birthday.'

Chapter 54
April 1872

Christmas had passed, the new year, a leap year, arrived dismally in a fizzle of dank, miserable days when rain clouds gathered low and menacing, turning the world monochrome. Lord Cavendish had been absent since early November, spending time and money among the glitterati of London, the young aristocratic Lords of the Manor in-waiting, the heirs apparent, unthinkingly smoking, gambling, whoring, drinking away their inheritance. None overtly acknowledged it, but all passed their days waiting for their fathers to die, some more in distant hope than imminent expectation.

In the cold embrace of a bitter winter, Lady Clarissa had determined on self-imposed confinement and spent the whole festive period warmly cocooned in her rooms, captive of drug-induced temperaments and wiles, longing only for the return of her brother, reluctant even to patrol the corridors of the hall. In her suite, she stared for hours with glazed, unseeing eyes into the swirling gloom beyond the greying, rain-streaked windows. Under the gravity of desolation her thoughts tumbled and collided in a chaotic randomness that left her worn out and despondent, devoid of motivation.

As a confident and beautiful young child in the care of a stern, unloving, grey-haired governess yet carefree and given to mischief, she often made drawings and paintings of herself in a wedding dress, a handsome and successful husband by her side, all of which the governess took delight in tearing apart and throwing onto the fire until, with the passage of time, Clarissa had stopped crying as she did so, and simply sat sullen, tight-lipped, no longer willing to expose her anguish to the woman.

Children, too, were part of her plan, along with a fine, many-roomed mansion in verdant grounds with a river running through it, stables for thoroughbred horses, a walled garden overflowing with floral colour, and a household of obedient servants to respond to her every wish. But she had fallen under her brother's wayward adolescent influence when still in her teens and seeing her dreams vaporise had by tiny, uncertain steps yielded to the deviations of the narcotics he persuaded her to try, sending her swinging unpredictably and violently from euphoria to anxiety to incoherent distress.

Once the delight of her parents, even as their own marriage broke apart on the rocks of mutual infidelity leaving them to drift into parallel, disconnected worlds, she found herself, like her brother, completely without affection, adrift on a loveless ocean bounded by danger and deceit: a sociopath in the making. The mourning state of the Royal Court throughout much of her young life was a condition she came to hate, oppressed, until she no longer cared, by its unending persistence. Though removed from its epicentre, her parents' need to be seen in public to share the grief of their queen became increasingly unbearable for the young girl. In the wider world, many saw the queen's mourning as obsessive, generating public unease, but by then Lady Clarissa had closeted herself in her apartment, her lack of direction an anchor that fixed her in mounting despair…a condition she sought to neutralise in the solace among the herbs and opiate tinctures her sibling brought.

And yet she loved him; the very man who had destroyed her dreams, changed her life irrevocably, but who remained the only source of affection in her fatigued life. Whether knowingly and intentionally no one could say, but he had manipulated her into a domestic exile that underpinned her cruel abandonment.

Before her brother's will took hold of her spirit, she had had several suitors – mostly kind, gentle, generous, good-looking, courteous and fun-loving – and dallied with them for so long as it took to decide they weren't of the cloth from which a husband could be made. But long periods when she was on her own remained, days extending into weeks and weeks into months. She had coped with them by resorting to drink, but when wine ceased to blur the edges she turned to her brother for aid.

Lady Clarissa's maids grew ever more concerned for her well-being. They lost count of the days when they'd found her collapsed on the floor, comatose, oblivious, her clothes torn and hanging in shreds where she had rent them from her body to escape their cloying hold, or in a struggle with inner demons. A doctor, an elderly specialist in psychotic episodes, was called and travelled what for an ageing man were many painful miles on horseback from Liverpool.

Clarissa in an outburst of base profanity refused to admit him to her chambers, hurling an ornate vase at the housemaid who had presumed to call him.

Before dressing, she frequently stood at the windows of her room, naked but for the flimsy sheen of a nightdress, often with its hem raised as she pleasured herself, knowing in more lucid moments that to do so taunted the men working below, dared them to turn their heads upwards towards her. But none ever did, though they had long become adept at regarding her with averted gaze. Broodingly she would stand above them, gazing down as she aroused herself in a crescendo of violent trembling as she fantasised about those hardened, calloused men defiling her. But that would never happen, however much she thought she craved it. Only one could satisfy her quest for inner serenity and rescue from torment, and her heart had quickened at the news that he would soon be back.

On the morning of his return, she stood again before the windows, anticipation coursing through her veins. The sky slowly brightening, no longer the bland greyness that seemed to have remained unchanging for months. The dark form of a bird flew by, a blur mocking the woman by the window, mocking the bent forms of the gardeners below, mocking their different forms of imprisonment, crowing its own freedom.

Lord Cavendish returned in a flurry of hail two weeks after Easter having travelled by rail from London, and then by pony and trap. In a tiresome mood, drained by the long journey and ignoring all who welcomed him home, he headed straight for his sister's rooms, and was not seen again for several days.

Mary Ellen, in spite of unbecoming ambition, had no cause to suppose that Lord Cavendish might feel the need to seek her out, noting only that his bed had not been slept in since his arrival. On that circumstance, none felt the need to speculate. Everyone knew where he was.

On the fourth day, dishevelled and unshaven, wearing only a short-sleeved undergarment, his hair grown long and tangled during his absence, he appeared at the door of his sister's apartment as Mary Ellen passed silently by. A smile lit up her face and joy briefly fired her heart, doomed in an instant when, seeming unaware of who she was, he yelled in his rich aristocratic baritone voice, 'You there. Send food. Now, God damn you. And wine. Lots of fucking wine.'

Chapter 55

In half an hour, Mary Ellen would complete her duties for the day, much reduced while the family remained away. Taking advantage of the more easy-going atmosphere in the household she was bound for the family home on Arch Lane where she planned to spend the night with her sister and brothers.

For now, she worked silently in the corridor outside Lord Cavendish's apartment, lightly dusting gilt-framed paintings of stern-faced family ancestors in sombre clothes, a suit, bow tie, waistcoat decorated with a gold watchchain posed stiffly as they were painstakingly recorded for posterity. The women, their dress styles dictated by propriety, were for their part enveloped lavishly in copious folds of fabric that revealed nothing of the woman beneath. Mary Ellen was thankful she didn't have to wear such extravagant and weighty fashions; her housemaid's uniform was bad enough.

Lost in thought, she failed to hear Lord Cavendish's door opening, but some sense alerted her to his presence behind her. It had to be him. No one else would be in this corridor at this hour. She paused in her task, her body tensing, a tingling sensation coursing down her spine. And then he was there, filling her space with his manly frame, though yet to notice her as he studied a sheaf of notes he was holding in his hand. She tried to skip out of his way but failed.

'Christ. Fuck. Sorry – *sorry*.' He was as equally shocked as she as they collided, his penetrating eyes startled above prominent cheekbones as he grabbed her arms to steady himself as much as she. Mary Ellen, long since divested of her childish fantasy of marrying this man, nevertheless felt her heart thumping in her chest, fear blended with adrenalin and a sharp tang of something else…something arousing…*sensual*. Something, for a fleeting moment, underpinned by…*lust*. Just for a moment she allowed herself to dwell on the impossible. To imagine some other circumstance. She blinked, and the thought was gone.

'Oh, bugger, it's you.' His face betrayed a mind searching for a name. 'Mary Ellen, isn't it? I'd forgotten...*almost*...forgotten. About you.'

He looked contrite, and gave her a reassuring smile, exuding a charm to which she had not hitherto been privy, but for just an instant his mind seemingly on other things, as if trying to grasp an elusive thought. Then, still holding her by the arms, he rallied. 'Actually...*actually*...come in. For a moment.' He was more self-assured now, his breath heavy with brandy and cigar smoke and he swayed, just a little, as he stepped back to usher her into his apartment. Unsteady on his feet, one hand placed firmly in the centre of her back, pressing gently as much it seemed for his own steadiness as to shepherd her into his room.

What must it be like to be so supremely confident, she thought; for charm to be so natural, so overcoming that you know it can be trusted even when the worse for alcohol? At that moment, as he closed the door behind them, she was in his thrall. Yet without fear, without anxiety. He was her master; she his servant. And, anyway, she thought, *What could she do?*

More to the point, what could he do that she would be able to prevent?

That was an altogether different matter.

'My,' he sighed, placing the papers he'd been carrying onto a small table, and regarding her as if for the first time, 'you're such a pretty thing, Mary Ellen, and more...grown up than I recall,' he said, approvingly, taking her hands in his and holding her arms away from her body, openly admiring her and what little womanly shape displayed through the layers of her uniform. Releasing one hand, he placed his fingers beneath her chin and tipped it upwards so that he was looking directly into her eyes.

She laughed lightly, trying not to betray the unease she felt. This...familiarity...was so removed from the proper order of things, but she had long since learned that Lord Cavendish, the umpteenth Earl of Garston, was cut of a different cloth from those who decreed *the way things should be.*

'Not really,' she said, her cheeks burning as she tried to look down. But he raised her chin again, drawing her eyes back to his.

'Yes, really,' he said. 'A very pretty young woman.'

She flushed again not knowing how to respond. Sensing her discomfort, he forestalled her.

'Do you still have that locket I gave you?' he asked conspiratorially, his voice low.

'Of course, sir. I treasure it, although I fear to wear it openly.'

221

He nodded reflectively. 'I can understand why. There are rogues and vagabonds without.'

She didn't know what the mysterious rogue and vagabonds to which he referred might have been without, but as he crossed the room to refill his glass with brandy, she followed him, placing the duster she was still clutching into a deep pocket beneath her apron.

He drank from the crystal glass he held, savouring the warmth of the brandy, then placed the glass on a low table, moved closer to her, a smile in his eyes. Mary Ellen could not have anticipated his next words, but they brought back of memories of the time she had playfully said the very same thing to Joseph, so long ago now, it seemed.

'Would you like to kiss me?'

He held his arms wide, inviting her into his embrace. Her thoughts sparked into sudden and chaotic commotion.

What was he saying?
What was he asking?
Where was this leading?

Seeing disquiet in her eyes, he moved slowly towards her, one hand circling to hold the back of her neck. Her body trembled as he fingered the soft down beneath her crown of hair pulled taught beneath her housemaid's bonnet. Briefly she closed her eyes as much to savour the moment as to imagine she was someone else observing what was happening: two young would-be lovers caught in the moment before their first embrace. For, she knew with certainty, *that* was what was happening now. Not *lovers*, no, not lovers. But young loves, caught in a fantasy. And though there was tension in the air, and a lack of conviction that this wasn't some elaborate joke, the instant was laden with an exquisite certainty that, though capable of evaporating in an instant, was far more likely to become the kiss he was inviting. This, she knew, was no love story, no coming together, falling into each other's arms, captivated by passion, no parted lips, no teasing tongues, no eyes closed in expectation, no being lifted from her feet and carried to a bed. And yet, as she saw him staring at her, a reassuring half smile on his lips, she closed her eyes. His fingers caressed her cheek, and she felt him lean towards her.

For his part, he knew he was taking advantage of his position, as he had done countless times in his reckless life; he knew his attraction to women…of all walks of life. He could…and *did*…take whomsoever he wanted, when he wanted. Yet with this vulnerable young waif, a servant in his employ, someone whose life he could destroy in an instant, the authoritarian sense of possession, of proprietorial ownership, was less prevailing. To his surprise, he realised that far from wanting to *take*, he wanted to *give*…no, not give exactly, just not be accepted dutifully or obediently, to be *received*. He wanted his kiss to be welcomed, to be received with pleasure. It was the difference between kissing her because he *could* and kissing her because he *wanted to*.

His lips, still moist with brandy, were soft, far from what she had anticipated. This was Heaven, this was bliss, an experience beyond all her dreaming. She opened her eyes as he pulled gently away, and she searched his eyes for a betraying flicker of mockery and disdain. But she saw none, just a smile as he leaned towards her again, arms circling her body, pulling her close to him. The taste of brandy was warm on her lips as she breathed him in, his tongue parting her lips, firing bolts of delight through her young body.

Once more observing as from afar, she was held spell bound. His passion, swelling against her stomach was real, exciting and determined. His lips hardened, his tongue filling her mouth, teasing. His force caught her up, pushing her to his desire as much as satisfying her own, heedless of the consequences, regardless of whether she could handle the drama.

Pulling away, she found herself placing her hands against his chest. 'Perhaps I should go,' she began hesitantly, not knowing where she might go that he wouldn't find her again; or even certain as she mouthed the words that she meant them. She still feared mockery and the raillery that would inevitably follow for as long as she remained at Garston. But she felt sure that he wanted her as much as she had always wanted him, even before she had ever met him, lost in her childish world. For now, she needed to take stock, to slow things down. This could never be more than what it was at this very moment. He held her in his arms as she turned slowly, her back now to him, gently pulling against his taut frame. Briefly, she leaned into him, his hands exploring ways of breaching her uniform – one cupping her breast through its unyielding fabric, finding and fingering the aroused nipple, the other vainly trying to reach the hem of her skirt, failing and resorting instead to reaching into her groin, and again she felt him hard against her lower back.

'Really? You want to go?'

She turned to face him again, her face one of pleading despair. His eyes beseeching, uncomprehending. 'Really. I still have work to do,' she said with little commitment, a placatory smile forming on her lips, hoping he would release her.

'Really?' he repeated. 'I think not,' his voice deeper now, sterner, ringing with the aristocratic stature. 'I don't think you really want to go at all; I think you want…*more.*'

And with a swiftness that left her defenceless he kissed her again, more savagely, more laden with lust and intent, her lips burning from the forcefulness. Sensing that events were moving beyond her control she leaned away from him.

'Really. Please,' she implored, pushing away from him.

In an instant, his eyes lost their steeliness and softened, and she found herself longing for that first kiss, that first tender, heart-warming thrill, teasing, exploring, hesitant. Could he, *would* he, ever kiss her like that again?

To her relief, he eased away, placing his hands on her shoulders. Leaning forward he kissed her forehead.

'Better?' he asked.

'Better. Yes,' she said, happy that he didn't appear angry. But nor did he yet seem ready to let her go. His fingers again stroked her neck, and he leaned against her, his lips lightly tapping their way up her neck and resting once more, gently on her lips.

'But,' he began, his thoughts suddenly elsewhere, 'before you go. I have a request. You can't deny me that, surely.' The smile had returned to his face, and he turned to a leather case on his desk. 'Look at these,' he said, showing her a selection of photographs of women, several in stages of undress, others fully nude. 'Don't you think they're beautiful?'

Mary Ellen took the photographs in her hands and stared at them. The women were all artfully posed, slender scarves of chiffon draped across their laps, jewels in their hair, small, firm breasts exposed not unlike several of the figures in the hall's art gallery. She had never taken offence at the artwork. She took no offence now. She saw no reason to. They were photographs of beautiful women, very beautiful women. And who wouldn't want to gaze on such beauty?

But she could not have anticipated his next request.

'Would you let me take photographs, like that, of you?' Seeing her querying look, he went on, 'Pictures like this are popular in London; they're all the rage.

My friends can't see enough of them. It's all, as you can see, very tasteful, nothing…saucy. That would never do.'

Mary Ellen was speechless, flattered and embarrassed in equal measure. Why would he want photographs of her to sport around his friends? How would they see her? Something to be mocked? Laughed over as they pulled on their Havanas, swilled champagne and told risqué jokes? Perhaps not. If they were laughing at her, they would be laughing at him. And she felt certain they would not dare to laugh at him.

'I…I…' she started, a piercing sense that something she didn't understand was going on and that she was being pitifully naive. 'I don't know.' Then, with growing confidence, added, 'I'd 'ave to think about it.'

He nodded and smiled; his eyes bright with sincerity. 'Of course you would. And, because I like you, and because you're such a sweet little beauty…,' he again placed his index finger under her chin and raised her head so that she was gazing directly into his eyes, '…I'll be honest with you. I can sell photographs like these; lots of them. And so, I'll pay you.'

In that one short sentence, Mary Ellen's resolve moved closer to his request. Money, when there was so little of it, was ever an incentive. She'd heard tell of the things some women did for money. She would never stoop to that, no matter how desperate she became. This wasn't like that, she reasoned. This was vastly different. He was talking about artful pictures; tasteful, pleasing pictures – and, she had to admit, they *were* pleasing. She was drawn to them herself. Flattered that he might see her as an equal of those beauties. But it was something she would need to discuss with her sister.

'Five pounds,' he said. 'Every time we take photographs, I'll pay you five pounds.' He laughed: 'I'll even pay you in pennies and farthings, in case people think you've stolen the fiver.'

She giggled at that, and he laughed with her. Once more she was feeling his confident charm, his certainty that she would acquiesce, if not today, then later.

'I don't even know 'ow many pennies there are in five pounds,' she said, aware that his offer of money, so much money, in fact, would bring new optimism to her family.

'More than a thousand,' he said, and laughed aloud. 'I don't even know myself. Maybe I'd better offer to pay in sixpences. There wouldn't be quite so many of those to carry around.'

Chapter 56
Late May 1872

The strong rain-laden south-westerly that had battered the cottage throughout the night had eased, although, she could see by the light of a fitful moon forcing its way through the shredded clouds, its passage was marked by a lane scattered with broken branches. In the middle darkness of night, Mary Ellen had been awakened by its relentless howl, and lay tucked in her bed, clutching the bedsheets to her chest, watching rain lashing at the window, and regarding her sister who slept soundly through it all. This had always been their room, since they had moved from the smaller cottage now occupied by one of her brothers. Her view of the world shaped by the windows from which on sleepless nights she gazed at the starry heavens, comforted and secured by the knowledge that her parents slept in the next room and that there was never anything to fear from the fury of the elements that beat at the dark, gritstone walls at times as if intent on wiping them all from the face of the earth.

Now in the growing stillness, unable to regain sleep, she thought again of the proposition Lord Cavendish had put to her…and of what had passed between them.

Had it really happened? she wondered in a haze of recollection.

How could it have happened?

In a moment of self-awareness she was surprised by the idea that she could have had such an effect on a man like him; that he could actually *desire* her. That she could *arouse* him.

He was a lord. How could he be aroused by a housemaid?

But the moment passed, and she fell again to thinking it was all some elaborate hoax leaving her with no idea where it might lead. It was one thing to know that she could arouse the likes of Joseph; quite another that she could enflame an aristocrat. Perhaps in this one respect all men were the same, but with little experience on which to base a judgement she was drawn again to the conclusion that Lord Cavendish was playing her for a fool; that he was toying with her.

The night before, relaxing in a rare night away from the hall, she had confided Lord Cavendish's proposal to her sister, but nothing of what had physically passed between them. That much she didn't want to share; not yet, at least. If all else failed her, she would still have the memory of those tender lips on hers; something that in the hours that had followed had assumed an importance tethered in childhood dreams. For now, she wanted to keep it that way.

Jane had been distracted, lost in her own thoughts too much to dwell on Mary Ellen's plight.

'So,' Jane began, 'let me get this right. Lord Cavendish, who by the way you shouldn't even be talking to, wants you to get your clothes off and pose in the nude while he takes photographs of you that he's then going to sell to his friends.'

'That's what 'e said. And 'e said 'e'll pay me. And we can use the money.'

'Well, assuming he's for real, how do you feel about it?'

Mary Ellen had a worried look, 'I'm not sure. I've been thinking about it, and what bothers me most is that I don't know if 'e's joshing with me or being serious. What if I go back and say I'll pose for the pictures, and 'e just laughs at me?'

Jane looked pensive for a moment. 'If he's messing with you, then it'll all come out in the wash, he'll have a good laugh at your expense, you'll be embarrassed, but, if you're lucky, it'll be forgotten in no time. And anyway, let's face it, he could do pretty much whatever he likes with you, at any time, and there's sod all you can do about it. He doesn't need to dress it up, taking photographs, or whatever. If all he wanted was to tup you, believe me, he'd do it. You wouldn't be able to stop him.'

Mary Ellen shrugged. 'S'pose not.'

'On the other hand, if he's serious then you'll get paid for taking your clothes off.' Jane again looked thoughtful, then said, 'but what if he tries to tup you as well as take pictures?'

'What do you mean?'

'Well, if he pays you for taking the pictures, that's just business. But if he pays you for sex, that's illegal and you could get a month's hard labour for that.'

'Ah. In that case, I'd better ask him for the money first, then it'll be for taking pictures.' Mary Ellen chortled, 'And anyway, what makes you think he might want to sex me?'

'I don't, but he might. How would you feel about that?'

It didn't show on her face, but Mary Ellen smiled at the thought. 'I'm not bothered about taking my clothes off for pictures, the walls are full of paintings of naked women. Nowt wrong with them. It's art, and he said there wouldn't be anything saucy. If he wanted to 'ave me afterwards… I dunno. I'd have to see how I feel at the time. Would it be wrong? Would I be a bad person? I've fucked Joseph. Lord Cavendish would be just like any other man when 'e's got nowt on. They're all the same; aren't they?'

Jane sighed heavily. 'If that's how you want to see it, it's your decision, Mary Ellen,' she'd said a little too dismissively, regretting it as she spoke. She placed her hand on her sister's in a conciliatory gesture. 'Only you can decide, lass. There comes a time when you have to leave childish ways behind and make a woman's choices. Though you're right, we could certainly use the cash.'

For a moment Jane's eyes wrinkled into a smile that lit her face, 'You never know. You could get a rogering you'll never forget.'

'Well, in that case…'

Chapter 57
June 1872

There were many rooms in Garston Hall Mary Ellen had never entered or knew anything about; rooms in parts of the hall from which the lower staff were prohibited. In any case, her duties and her daily round were governed by a routine that left no time for exploration, had she even dared to open closed doors to rooms she was forbidden to enter. God alone knew what might lie beyond.

In Lord Cavendish's room, one she'd been trusted to enter on her own for some months, she felt comfortable; this was *his* room, but, for her, it was also a haven. In her sometime naivety she had once thought this might become *her* room, but that was a long time ago. She knew where everything was, and where everything belonged, which was a blessing when one of Lord Cavendish's more restless episodes scattered them about the room. Having finished preparing his bed, she turned to dusting the several ornaments that decorated the mantle, the tables and the windowsills. All was quiet; an unseasonal storm that had raged for the past few days had abated and left an unearthly silence in its wake. So, she was surprised not to have heard him when Lord Cavendish approached her. He had a knack of moving quietly about the place that she found disconcerting.

'Mary Ellen,' he boomed, smiling encouragingly as he came to her and kissed her lightly on the cheek, his lips lingering longer than was necessary, as if he was tasting her, as Elizabeth had done. 'You look as radiant as ever.'

His words and composure reassured Mary Ellen, and she curtsied and smiled at him: 'Thank you, my lord.' He studied her face intently, and briefly she felt overcome by the sense that he was penetrating her soul.

He took her by the hand and led her to a chaise longue at the foot of his bed. 'There's no need to curtsy. Or call me "Lord". Not when it's just the two of us.'

'Sorry.'

'No need to apologise either.'

'Sorry… I mean…yes, sir.'

He stood and gazed down at her. 'Now,' he said, 'I can't help noticing that you're a little behind in your daily routine. Were you waiting for me to return from breakfast, by any chance?'

Mary Ellen flushed at having been read so easily. She clasped her hands in front of her and began twiddling her thumbs in nervous agitation.

'Is there something you want to tell me. About my proposition, perhaps.'

Mary Ellen harnessed her courage. 'Yes, sir. I've decided that if you want to take pictures of me, that's alright.' She hesitated before going on, 'If you pay me like you said you would. It's just that, well, we need the money. We'll need to find another place to live when Papa retires. And he's already stayed on longer than he should. He was supposed to retire last year.'

Lord Cavendish beamed at her, reaching out to touch her shoulder. 'That's splendid news, Mary Ellen, splendid. And, of course, I'll pay you. In fact,' he said, looking around the room for a small leather pouch that sat on the table beside his bed, 'I'll give you half a crown now, as a gesture of my good faith.'

Mary Ellen took the silver coin in her hands. She had no recollection of having seen one before, and it represented several days' work in the household. Now she had it, and more to come, simply for posing for photographs.

'Now,' Lord Cavendish went on, his hand holding his chin, 'if I remember correctly, your day off is Sunday. Right?'

'Yes, sir.'

'Good. Well, if you're happy to do so, we can begin this very next Sunday. The family won't be back for a few weeks, which means that it's lighter duties for you at present, but I still wouldn't want to disrupt the house routines needlessly. If we do this on your days off, you won't be missed.' He tapped the side of his nose with a forefinger, 'and nosey people won't ask questions.'

Mary Ellen looked up at him, this handsome-faced young man, so full of certainty, confidence…and charm. So virile, so masculine, so strong and yet so…rebellious. Just his very presence set her pulse racing, that and the increasing certainty that this was not a hoax.

And he'd said *days*, plural. Did he intend more than one day to take his photographs? There was no way of knowing, but the prospect of earning even more money for her family filled her with joy. Likewise the possibility that he might kiss her again as passionately as he had done when first he propositioned her.

Chapter 58

Sunday, 9 June 1872

Mary Ellen, her duties for the day finished, raced to her room and changed hurriedly out of her uniform, leaving it where it fell. Naked and shivering in a breeze coming through the window, she washed quickly in the cold water from the basin on its stand. Swiftly, hands tugging at thin metal hair clips she unfastened her long hair, pulling a brush through it as it fell about her bare shoulders before putting on a grey dress decorated with small red flowers and running her hands down it to smooth away creases.

Promptly at two she found herself outside Lord Cavendish's room. Tentatively she knocked on the door, lightly. When there was no answer, she knocked again, more firmly. She was free to enter the room at any time, but this was different. This was not part of her domestic duties. So, she waited for the door to be answered.

Suddenly, he was there, his coloured face betraying that he had already been drinking, but instead of inviting her in, he came out and put his arm around her shoulder. He wore an eight-buttoned double-breasted waistcoat of rough beige material over a white shirt with ruffed collar and cuffs. Matching trousers covered his legs; red and gold leather shoes covered his feet. Ruggedly handsome, his cheeks betraying a light growth of ginger hair that had not been present when last they met. Mary Ellen wasn't sure whether she liked that, though it leant gravitas to his face.

'Mary Ellen. Come this way,' he said, smiling encouragement and shepherding her along a corridor into a part of the hall she did not frequent. Beside an ornate double door he stopped and led her inside. The room was small and gloomy, two walls being consumed by dark-wood book-laden shelves, floor to ceiling, the remaining two wood panelled but covered with paintings, some of them as erotic as the pictures he had shown her. Perhaps this was where he intended to take his photographs, though there was little room, and the dark wood seemed to absorb the light. A desk stood central to the room covered with books, some lying open as if their reader had only recently departed. A large globe of the world, the like of which Mary Ellen had never seen, stood by the fireplace beside a high-backed chair. A low circular table held several pipes and a jar of what Mary Ellen assumed must be tobacco. She was not aware that Lord Cavendish smoked a pipe, so she wondered if this was perhaps Lord Garston's room. It was luxurious but with the emphasis on cosy comfort rather than extravagant opulence.

No sooner had Mary Ellen taken in the room than Lord Cavendish led her through another door and along a narrow passage, stopping in front of yet one more door that gave into a large parlour. It was the most beautiful room Mary Ellen had ever seen, hung with tapestries of hunting scenes and images of what she took to be angels, though these angels were not beyond exposing their bodies in an erotic manner. Central to the room was a salon suite sofa, flanked by two armchairs, four side chairs and two footstools all in deep red velvet emblazoned with the Garston coat of arms. Behind the sofa a large painting of a naked man hung on the wall, and on either side paintings of semi-naked women disporting themselves by a languid pool around which cherubs lounged. Against one wall stood a decoratively carved coffer on which a glass bowl filled with fresh flowers had been placed, and beside it a small hexagonal table bearing several leatherbound books.

Lord Cavendish led Mary Ellen through into the next room, a bedroom, a huge room in which the main item of furniture, a canopied and curtained four-poster bed, seemed lost. It was hung with gold and silver drapes and had a counterpane over bright silken sheets. Another green velvet chaise longue stood at the foot of the bed, and in front of that a strange boxlike structure on three legs. Mary Ellen audibly gasped with excitement; there was so much about this mansion of which she knew nothing. Candlesticks held burning candles, their shimmering light giving movement to the room. More candlesticks stood on chests of drawers and two on high wrought iron stands similar to those she had seen in the parish church. The candles were unnecessary. Two large, floor-to-ceiling windows, their curtains drawn back allowed the afternoon sun to flood in. Unlike elsewhere in the mansion, these windows were recessed to allow a benchlike seat to occupy the window space. Smoke spiralled from what Mary Ellen knew from her occasional visits to church was an incense burner. It was a magnificent room, and Mary Ellen realised that this was where Lord Cavendish intended to take his photographs, and that the boxlike structure was the camera.

Reading her thoughts he said, 'I hope you like the room. No one uses it these days. We keep it for visiting guests; the more important ones, that is.'

'It's beautiful. I could spend all day in here.'

'Well, for a few hours anyway.'

She pointed at the incense burner. 'What's that smell? It's beautiful.'

'It's called Byakudan; it's from Japan. We call it sandalwood.'

'It's very relaxing,' Mary Ellen said, breathing in the fragrance.

'It's meant to be. Now,' he said turning away and crossing the room to the camera, 'this is my camera. Weird little thing, don't you agree?'

Mary Ellen inspected it. It was a large wooden box with bellows, like the squeezebox her father sometimes played. A circular brass device with a glass centre was at the front of it, and a large black shroud draped over the back.

'How does it take photographs?'

Lord Cavendish shrugged his shoulders. 'Buggered if I know,' he said. 'I just have to put some special plates into the back of it and press this little rubber bulb, and that takes the picture. Then I take the plates away to a lady photographer of my acquaintance, and she makes the prints you saw. I'm not clever enough to do the tricky bit, which she tells me has to be done in complete darkness. Seems odd to me, but it works.'

'So, what do you want me to do?'

'I want you to pose on this chaise longue, just like the ladies you saw in those photographs I showed you. I'll take some pictures, then you're free to go.' He turned round to locate a leather holdall that had been lying beside the bed. Opening it he took out a small leather pouch, held it by the leather laces and shook it up and down, setting its contents jingling.

'As promised, your payment. Put it somewhere safe.'

Mary Ellen burst out laughing. 'I'm only wearing this dress. I 'aven't got anything to put money in.'

Lord Cavendish smiled at that and put the pouch on a chest of drawers. 'Let's put it here for now, then.'

Turning to face Mary Ellen he placed his hands on her shoulders and looked into her eyes, one eyebrow raised in a question. 'You are happy to do this for me, Mary Ellen? I want you to be sure.'

Charmed by his honesty, complicit in his plans, Mary Ellen could only nod.

'Excellent. Now, while I prepare the camera, you can use the next room,' he pointed to another door, 'to…divest yourself of your very pretty dress. And in there, you'll find a few chiffon shawls and scarves and wotnots that are my sister's but which she's happy for you to use. So, choose whichever you like, and come back when you're ready. Oh, and would you like a glass of wine?' he asked, turning to a decanter of red wine. 'I'm having one. Do you like wine?'

Mary Ellen nodded, at which Lord Cavendish beamed roguishly. 'And where did a second housemaid learn to like wine?'

She flushed, embarrassment suddenly filling her cheeks with colour. 'I… I… er…'

Lord Cavendish laughed and held up his hand to stop her. 'Don't worry. We know the odd bottle goes missing, and no one's blaming you. With what my sister drinks it's a wonder there's any left.'

Mary Ellen drank from the proffered glass, placed it back on the chest of drawers and went into the adjacent room. When she returned, Lord Cavendish had his head covered in the drape that hung from the camera. Wearing nothing but the most luxurious, long chiffon wrap she had ever touched, Mary Ellen sat on the chaise longue, leaned back against the raised rest and lifted her legs, stretching them down the length of the seat and arranging the wrap around her.

When Lord Cavendish re-appeared, he gazed at her. 'Beautiful. Absolutely beautiful.'

The next hour passed in a glorious daze for Mary Ellen, during which Lord Cavendish repositioned her, re-arranged the chiffon progressively until it hung seductively from one shoulder, its translucency allowing her large areola and dark nipples to be tantalisingly glimpsed through its flimsiness. Each time, he disappeared under the camera drape and took another picture, re-emerging to make more adjustments to her chiffon, none that fully exposed her breasts or the lower part of her body. All carefully posed so that Mary Ellen's young body lay temptingly on display but never nakedly revealed.

Once they had used up Lord Cavendish's stock of film plates, he held his hands out and taking hers raised her from the chaise longue.

'Mary Ellen, you've been wonderful. I'm so pleased with what we've done. I hope you like the pictures when you see them.'

'I'm sure I will, sir,' she said, smiling up into his face, inviting the kiss that came a moment later and tasted of wine.

'If you're happy, we can do this again,' he suggested.

Not caring whether he meant the kiss or the photography, she said demurely, 'I'll be more than 'appy.'

Back in her room, Mary Ellen gazed out of the window. It was midsummer; the nights were light for many more hours yet, light cloud floated across a still blue sky, and she thought of visiting her sister to pass on her new earnings for safe keeping. But something held her back. She was vibrating with excitement, her body trembling with the memory of her time with Lord Cavendish, his lips on hers, her body so yearningly close to his. She longed to feel his arms surround her once more, to taste him, to inhale his manliness, to feel his arousal pressing against her. She herself was intensely aroused, and she understood why Elizabeth might have felt that way the night she took Joseph to her bed. She longed for that now, not with Joseph, for she swore she would never forgive his betrayal. But two could play at that game, and there were ruggedly handsome gardeners out there who would willingly meet her needs. She was eyeing one now.

But that was not what she wanted; *he* was not what she wanted. Her mother had always told her that two wrongs don't make a right. So, she slipped into the bathroom she shared with Elizabeth, took off her dress, filled a bowl with cold water, lifted the tin bath from the wall and sat in it…and poured the cold water over her head.

Chapter 59

June 1872

Perched on the rock by the lake edge where she had first kissed Joseph, Mary Ellen was in a reflective mood, soaking up the sun's warmth.

She was in a quandary.

As she watched a pair of great crested grebe and a small family of chicks dipping in and out of the reeds along the lakeshore, she fell to contemplation. So much seemed to have befallen her in recent months that she'd had little time to take in: the gift of a locket from Lord Cavendish, the betrayal of Joseph and Elizabeth, the proposal of Lord Cavendish, the hours she spent with him while he took photographs, and the sudden increase in wealth. And there was, too, something she couldn't fathom about the affection that clearly flowed between Lord Cavendish and his sister. She had witnessed him kissing her fully on the lips; not lightly, which she could accept, but passionately. And Clarissa had held his head in her hands as he'd kissed. She couldn't imagine herself doing that with any of her own brothers, even though she might begrudgingly admit her older siblings were tolerably handsome in a rugged way.

And there had been the days Lord Cavendish spent alone with his sister, in her apartment rooms. Mary Ellen knew there was only one bed in there. So, where did he sleep? And why had the housemaids who served Lady Clarissa been told to leave them unattended until summoned?

Mary Ellen could rationalise none of what was making her uneasy; her lack of comprehension serving only to render matters yet more disquieting.

What disconcerted her most, alarmingly so, however, was the easy familiarity Lord Cavendish affected towards her. She *knew* this was not the correct order of things; he'd acknowledged as much. She knew that many would be annoyed or disappointed in her had they been aware; some would be outraged. It hadn't occurred to her until that moment that she could be dismissed for even being alone with him in his apartment. And yet he was freely pleasant, agreeable and open with her. Nor, when he was alone with her, did he make any pretence of concealing the fact that he found her physically attractive. He had kissed her – something she wanted him to repeat; she had felt his arousal.

But…a lord should not behave in such a manner with a housemaid, with any servant for that matter.

And yet he had singled her out and treated her if not as an equal then as a someone he could converse with, someone he was willing to relate to when in all honesty he could, and probably should, ignore her completely. Moving on to taking her photograph had taken their relationship to a singularly more advanced level; one that was personal and intimate. She was going naked in his presence, though he hadn't taken advantage of that condition. Perhaps his confidence in his charm gave him the certainty that he could do whatever he wished with this young woman, whenever he wanted.

Just because he could didn't mean he would.
Or that he was going to.
Did it?

Mary Ellen turned to wondering if he'd decided to be friendly with her as the first move in a ploy to develop her trust and, in due course, accept his advances. Better a compliant partner than one who might cause problems. But she reminded herself, he didn't need to do that. He was the one in control; he was the one with the power over her. He could simply have ordered her to have sex with him, or to pose for his photographs.
Couldn't he?
And if she'd refused, what then for her and her family?
Exactly. That was the point. He held the power; she held nothing; she was nothing. Yet he wasn't being dominant; he was treating her with respect; well, she smiled inwardly, with a little roguishness thrown in. But that was alright. Wasn't it? If he wanted to have her, was she going to resist?
The more Mary Ellen thought about it, the more confused she became. She wanted to understand but was struggling. She recalled that her mother had a

saying: *If summat looks too good to be true, 'appen it is.* Her father was more prosaic: *If tha's lookin' a gift 'orse in t'gob, mek sure it's not a donkey.*

She wasn't entirely sure what her father had meant. So, for now, all she could do was go along with Lord Cavendish's bidding; that seemed the safest course. And one she was about to follow again. If he was leading her up the garden path, so be it. But he *had* paid her for their first photographic session. If he'd intended anything else, he wouldn't have done that.

Would he?

Chapter 60

The weeks following their night at the Midland Hotel had been every bit as loving as the night itself. Days spent together, Skyping or FaceTiming when they were apart, flowed seamlessly into one another in what to Duncan felt like a daydream from which he would soon awaken to find it had all been a figment of his imagination. Days out geocaching, some with Nellie, who had beamed in a self-congratulatory way at their evident togetherness, were interspersed with short breaks the like of which neither had experienced for some time: a couple of nights at the Samling in Ambleside; a few days in Edinburgh, and, most romantic of all, a week at the secluded Knockinaam Lodge near Portpatrick in Galloway, where Churchill and Eisenhower had met to plan the D-Day landings. If this was how a new, loving relationship was fashioned, he didn't want it to end.

But his past was never far away, and on a warm and sunny day, in a relaxed frame of mind, he had decided to visit Isabel's grave. To his surprise, given the lateness of the season, he found that it was overflowing with self-seeded lily of the valley, a bell-shaped flower long associated in folklore with romance. As he saw the display and remembered the flower's significance the hairs on his neck began to rise as if an electric shock had passed through him. He and Isabel had been in France one year at the beginning of May to find that the hotel where they were staying made a point of giving lily of the valley to their guests as a token of welcome. Over a glass of wine in the hotel garden Isabel had presciently told him that if anything happened to her, he must move on, find someone else to love; not spend his life grieving or moping around.

And now here he was, with a new love in his life, seemingly blessed by the only other woman he'd ever loved. So, when, after nights sleeping with Alice at White Coppice, he finally brought her to Brimstone Cottage to stay for a few days, taking her to what had been Isabel's bed seemed the most natural thing to do, free of lingering associations.

On a visit to York, where Duncan needed to check some ecclesiastical records in the Minster, they noted that a collector's fair was being staged at the racecourse. It was intended mainly for philatelists, but there were other collections there, too, and, he thought, it may be possible to get some idea of the worth of Isabel's stamp collection, not that he was yet contemplating its sale.

As Duncan passed through the hall looking for a specialist dealing in British stamps, Alice dropped behind at a stand selling postcards, most of which he was certain would be of interest to philatelists. She was picking her way through boxes of postcards when she paused and pulled out a number of them held together by an elastic band. Slowly, she flicked through them, and Duncan watched as she haggled with the dealer before agreeing a price.

'What have you got there?' Duncan asked.

Alice was unforthcoming. 'Let's get a coffee, and I'll show you. I think you'll need to be seated.'

Puzzled Duncan did as Alice suggested, and they wandered through to an anteroom where food and drink was being served. With coffees in front of them, Alice produced the postcards she'd bought, and picking through them took out one in particular, placing it in front of Duncan.

'Anyone you know?' she asked with a smile on her lips.

The picture was of a beautiful woman, naked, posed in front of a mirror. Soft shadowy light accented her features while simultaneously highlighting her eyes.'

'Victorian erotica,' Duncan mustered. 'All the rage in the late nineteenth century. Arguably the closest you could get to pornography.'

'And...' Alice went on.

'And...judging by the text at the bottom, a "Cavendish Beauty".'

'And...' Alice persisted.

Duncan wasn't sure what she was getting at. Then he saw what it was.

'Bloody. Hell. Sorry. Bloody hell.'

'Exactly. If that's not Mary Ellen, I'm Charlie's aunt.'

'You are so not wrong about this. Her hair is down, unlike in your picture, but that is definitely Mary Ellen, you can see the distinctive mole on her cheek, and she's very...'

'Careful what you say next, darling,' Alice chortled.

'Well, I mean, she is...amazing.' He held the picture at arm's length, studying it. 'You know,' he said, 'she was a stunningly beautiful young woman.'

Alice placed the rest of the postcards on the table. They showed the same woman, but in different poses, some more revealing than others.

'What are the odds on our finding these so far from where they must have been taken?' Duncan pondered.

'What are the odds on our finding them at all, let alone it being the very person central to everything we've been doing over the last couple of years?'

'Well, not quite *everything*,' Duncan chimed.

'Don't be smutty.'

Duncan laughed. 'That's amazing, absolutely amazing. I'm not sure what it tells us, but when I can get my brain in gear it must tell us something.'

'Well, for starters, it suggests she'd found a way of making money, because I can't see her posing for these pictures so naturally if she was being coerced, don't you think? She's smiling happily in every one of them.'

Duncan held a finger in the air. 'Ah…just a minute.'

He reached into the briefcase he never went anywhere without and pulled out his iPad. Once it had fired up, he scrolled through several pages until he found what he was searching for.

'Got it. I thought the name rang a bell. I've got the 1861 census for Garston Hall. Check out the names.' He handed the iPad to Alice, who ran her finger down the list of names.'

'Cavendish. That's the name of the son of the household. Cavendish Garston. How close to home is that?'

'My thoughts exactly. Was Mary Ellen posing for Lord Cavendish? And had he forced her? Or had she gone along with it, possibly in return for payment.'

'Can we find out?'

'I've no idea, but I'm going to give it my best shot. If only because it would go some way to explaining why in your picture Mary Ellen is so expensively dressed. Clothes like that were not cheap. She had to have found the money from somewhere to pay for them.'

Duncan took Alice's hand in his and kissed it. 'Well done you, well spotted. What a find.' He sat up and shivered theatrically. 'Spooky. I feel quite energised by that.'

Alice smiled and gazed into his eyes, raising a quizzical eyebrow; it was an expression he was coming to know. Standing slowly and picking up the postcards she said, 'Then let's see if we can think of something to do with all that energy.'

Chapter 61

'Mary Ellen, you're as beautiful as ever. And you've been out in the sun, I see, I notice the colour in your cheeks.'

Standing at his door, she made to curtsy, but remembered what he'd told her, so simply smiled at him as they set off along the corridors to the guest rooms.

'And you're wearing such a lovely new dress.'

Really?

The dress was nothing of the sort: a plain, unfussy hand-me-down made years ago by her mother from a pedlar's remnant of grey-blue-purple linen, coloured using a natural damson dye, in much the same way her father dyed the now off-white bedroom walls in Penny Lodge. Made originally for Jane; on Mary Ellen, now grown taller than her sister, the dress exposed her ankles and flat-soled, black leather shoes that had also once been her sister's. Several head-to-toe-clad biddies in the village would think her brazen to dress in such a revealing manner. But she wasn't wearing the dress for the villagers; she was wearing it because it's simple line and white ribbon belt at the waist accentuated her figure, making her feel more shapely, more feminine. To her curious delight, she found the sensation of the material caressing her bare skin stimulating, exciting her, making her aware more than ever of her growing body. If her *relationship* – however it might be described, whatever it might be – with Lord Cavendish had given her anything, it was a welcome boost to her womanly self-confidence.

And apart from anything else, she thought wryly, *I would soon be exposing more than bare ankles.*

Her only regret in matters of dress was that she couldn't afford the vivid yellow, magenta and electric blue material, coloured with the new artificial dyes, that had been sweeping the country in recent years. From a covert vantage point overlooking the Great Hall, she'd envied the bright colours worn by several daring ladies attending Lady Garston's *soirées* – radically, given that the Court was still officially in mourning.

But she longed for colourful dresses and the confidence to wear them.

Maybe, with Lord Cavendish's help, her day would come.

So, for now, when Lord Cavendish paid her a compliment, even when she knew he was just being agreeable, she accepted it with good grace, as she did the glass of wine, he poured her when they reached their inner sanctum. The room was warm, a fire burning dully in the grate and incense again drifting on the air alongside motes of dust caught in the light movement of air caused by the circulating heat from the fire.

Placing his wine glass on a table, Lord Cavendish picked up a small box. 'I have the first photographs now. Do you want to see?'

Mary Ellen was excited. 'Are they what you wanted?'

'See for yourself. They're beautiful.'

He handed her the box, from which she took two or three of the photographs, regarding them as if she couldn't bring herself to believe *she* was the attractive young woman posing in the picture.

'I can't believe that's me,' she said handing the photographs back. 'She looks so…beautiful, a real woman, but…oh, look my 'air's a mess. Look see.'

'Actually,' he said in his distinctive deep tone, tapping his forefinger on the picture she was referring to. 'I rather like that. It makes you seem…a little more waif-like, someone in need of comforting. Just the sort of nuance that will appeal to my friends. Very much so, I'm hoping.'

'Won't they want to know who I…*she* is?' she asked, unsure what he meant by *nuance*.

'Bloody damn sure of it. But I won't be telling.'

'No?'

'God, no. They'd be charging up here and queuing to have their way with you. And believe me, you wouldn't want that.'

'No?' She fleetingly imagined the prospect, so it came out as a question. A queue of men wanting her. Jane had said men would be queuing up for her hand in marriage, but then she realised that wasn't what Lord Cavendish had meant.

'No,' he said emphatically, as if reading her mind and replacing the box of photographs on the table. 'You're my little secret, Mary Ellen. I hope you don't mind. You, me…oh, and my sister, when she's not away with her fairies and demons. You haven't told anyone else, have you?'

Mary Ellen looked fearful. 'No, I 'aven't *told* anyone I was letting you take photographs of me. She stressed the word "told" because then what she was saying would be true. 'But I did talk to my sister about it, first. She won't' say nuffin. But she'd've wondered where the money come from, if I didn't say sumamt. She'd think I'd filched it.'

He nodded. 'No, that's fine. Of course, you have to tell your sister. I quite understand. But no one else. Agreed?'

She nodded her agreement as he turned towards her, moving to stand closely in front of her, until their bodies were touching. She could feel a comforting warmth radiating from him, solid strength in his torso, muscles in his arms as they encircled her and pulled her against him. And she felt an arousing sensation exciting her own body, weakening her legs.

'No, most definitely not.'

As she'd hoped he would, he leaned forward and kissed her lightly, running his tongue along her lips in a way that increased the surge of excitement she was feeling. But abruptly, he pulled away.

'Today, my dear sweet Mary Ellen, I'd like to try something different. But only if you're willing. And, oh…' he went on, turning back to the table to retrieve a small leather pouch, handing it to her, 'here is your payment. Five pounds, as agreed.'

She took it in her hands, and smiled at him, her eyes twinkling amusement as she made a show of pretending to look for a pocket in her dress. 'I still don't 'ave anywhere safe to put it.'

He laughed with her. 'Then let me put it here, for the moment,' he offered, replacing it on the table. 'Now, while I prepare this box of tricks,' he said, pointing to the camera, 'you'll find whatever you want to wear in the next room, as before.'

When she returned, Lord Cavendish had moved the camera so that it now pointed towards one of the windows, at the bottom of which a velvet seat was plump with gold-tasselled cushions.

She had draped a long chiffon shawl around her shoulders, letting it fall to the floor, and holding it in her hands below her waist. She felt more confident than during their first photographic session; the pictures he'd shown her had done much to support her, to re-assure her, so she was less self-conscious as she moved towards the window, allowing the shawl to fall open.

'Let your hair down,' he suggested. 'It's beautiful hair. We can arrange it artistically, to give my wayward friends something to dwell on.'

She did as he had said, but after taking a few pictures in which her hair cascaded to cover her breasts in what she thought was an artistic pose and attempting to create images more alluring by using a handheld mirror to reflect her face, he decided to adjust the tresses so that while the chiffon shawl continued to lie across her lap, her breasts lay fully exposed.

That, she came to realise, was the picture he'd hoped for all along.

So, why didn't he just say so?

I'm being paid for sticking out my tits, she thought. *Fuck it, if that's what he wants…*

And with that she pulled herself into a more upright pose, thrusting her chest forward in a gesture that seemed to please Lord Cavendish, his manhood increasingly evident within the tight fabric of the lightweight trousers he was wearing.

An hour later, as he started to put away the camera plates he'd used, Mary Ellen recalled Lady Clarissa's assurance that her brother would seek to *bed* her, as she'd put it. She wondered if this was to be the moment. Already she'd decided it was a prospect she would not resist. She knew she would never have this man as a husband, but, if only on one occasion, she could *have* him; she *would* have him, and if it called for feminine wiles, so be it.

As she moved towards the door, gathering the chiffon shawl around her nakedness, more for what little warmth it gave than to protect her modesty that was no longer in the purely artistic domain, she felt him approach her from behind. Gently, he slipped his arms around her, clasping his hands under her breasts so that the outside of his thumbs and wrists supported their firmness. She leaned back against him, his manhood unavoidably pressing against her arse cheeks, the manly smell of him filling her nostrils sending her thoughts spiralling in expectation.

'We must do this again, Mary Ellen. Perhaps one more time. If you're happy with that.'

Deflated she spun round to face him, tilting her face upwards, inviting the kiss.

'I'm yours to command, kind sir,' she said teasingly.

He smiled and nodded. 'Then let it be,' he said.

Chapter 62

In her disappointment, as she lay on her bed at the day's end, Mary Ellen realised that images such as they had taken that day were not the complete picture. Lord Cavendish, she began to understand, ultimately wanted to capture her fully naked. The more she dwelt on that, the more she saw his plan, that he was leading her gradually towards that goal. If she was right, it was an idea she decided to put to the test. What Lord Cavendish could not have known, she reflected, was that for Mary Ellen, while the money he gave her was a huge incentive, she truly wanted to be with the man, to feel him against her, to feel him *inside* her. Having come this far, she would do anything for him. Posing naked was as far as they could progress photographically; after that she would return to the daily routines of second housemaid.

In the meantime, she would make the most of every moment in what she came to see as the *privileged* company of Lord Cavendish. The privilege was, she knew, destined to end sooner or later. It wouldn't last.

A week later, the prospect to see if she was right presented itself as she responded to Lord Cavendish's request to take more photographs and walked the corridors and rooms to what he now with tongue-in-the-cheek humour described as his "Studio". Before entering, she turned into what she amusingly thought of as her "dressing room".

A grey, windy day swirled outside, thunder rumbled in the distance, but in the "studio" a fire brought comforting warmth, wall-bracketed gas lamps – a new introduction at Garston – gave off a low light; incense and the smell of polished oak panelling perfumed the air. The *chaise longue* she immediately noticed had been moved from the foot of the four-poster bed and for the first time she saw a large, freestanding oval mirror skewed at an angle in front of the window. The most profound change, however, was Lord Cavendish himself. Instead of the casual shirt and fabric trousers he had previously worn, he now sported what Mary Ellen took to be a dress, a full-length multi-coloured robe with short sleeves, a form of dress unlike any she had seen before. The sort of dress a woman would wear. *So, why would a man wear women's clothing?* she pondered.

'It's a kaftan,' he told her, seeing her interest in his garment, adding vaguely, 'a gift from an admirer. In eastern countries, these are worn by men of wealth and rank. It's made from silk.' He lifted it away from his body, 'Here, feel.'

Mary Ellen did as she was bid. 'It feels wonderful. Soft to touch.'

'And you,' he exclaimed pleasantly, spreading his arms to frame her body. 'You're wearing something different, too.' He smiled knowingly as he inspected it. 'It looks not unlike a…nightdress. Surely, not something for outdoor wear, I would say. Something to relax in, perhaps. I've never seen anything quite like this, it opens down the front, held in place by…' he tugged lightly at a chiffon scarf that she'd tied around her middle, '…this flimsy attachment. It reminds me of something my sister…'

'It *is* your sister's,' Mary Ellen admitted. 'You said she didn't mind if I used 'er things. So, I borrowed it. I 'ope I didn't do no wrong. I've not been in 'er room; 'onest. It was with the things she left for me to wear. I came this morning to try it on. I 'oped you'd like it. Seein' as 'ow it's your sister's.'

A wave of panic overwhelmed her briefly, wondering if the last remark had been ill-judged, alluding as it did to a relationship the precise nature of which was rooted in nothing more than speculation and tittle-tattle. But Lord Cavendish smiled reassuringly, resting his hands lightly on her shoulders, and leaned forward to kiss her forehead.

'You did no wrong, Mary Ellen. On you, it looks splendid. I'm sure my sister won't mind.'

She thanked him and hesitantly waited for him to prompt her to ready herself to take photographs.

'Now,' he began easily, as questioning smile on his face, 'what shall we do today?'

Silently, Mary Ellen turned to face him and with slow, measured movements, an impish smile shaping on lips lightly touched with coralline salve found among Lady Clarissa's possessions, released the scarf, allowing it and the delicate material it was holding in place to fall loose about her body. Outwardly affecting innocence, she let the flimsy material slip from her shoulders with a provocative purpose she had not known she owned, halting its fall to the floor to hold it briefly, tantalisingly across her breasts before allowing it to cascade to the floor.

248

Her body trembling with exquisite daring, she stooped to gather the fallen chemise and scarf, turning casually to place them on the bed.

She stood naked before him.

'Perhaps I should just wear this,' she said, tilting her head downwards to present him with her naked form. He had seen her naked form before, but this…staging…had nuances of deliberation, a sense of purpose, an intent.

Lord Cavendish felt his manhood stir at this vision of the young woman, thankfully an arousal concealed by his kaftan. It was not the first time he'd seen her naked, but this was subtly different. She was playing him, he realised. She's quite a tease. He liked this young woman. She was…fun. Of the many woman he'd taken over the years, she inspired a less cavalier sentiment in him, one he couldn't convincingly explain. His sister certainly took the view he was toying with Mary Ellen, and he thought he'd discerned a note of disapproval from her. But his sister's pronouncements were never clear at best, rarely rooted in reality and not known for their sentiment. For himself he nurtured an inexplicable protectiveness towards Mary Ellen, a sentiment he had previously only directed to his sister. His pleasure at being in Mary Ellen's company was acute, and here she stood before him, naked as the day she was born.

'Well,' he said, 'it's certainly very…natural. Wouldn't you say, my pretty one?'

'As God intended.'

'So, where should we pose you today?'

For the first time, Mary Ellen took the initiative, moving to stand in front of the oval mirror, which she repositioned. She was facing out into greyness beyond the window, the sky intermittently slashed by bolts of lightning, but her frontal self was reflected in the mirror.

'Best of both worlds,' Mary Ellen suggested. 'You see my ti–, breasts, my front, in the mirror, and my arse, for good measure. That way you get all of me in one picture. Front and back. You can charge double for that,' she laughed.

Lord Cavendish hadn't thought of that, but as he began to visualise the outcome, he knew he would have a stunning picture to hawk around his friends. So, he was especially careful when it came to positioning the camera, placing it and Mary Ellen, so that what shadows were formed by the light from outside were artistically strategic. To be certain of capturing the image he wanted, he took several of the same position, each time making small timing adjustments to the camera exposure and to the way Mary Ellen was posing.

Several more images were made without the mirror, but none quite matched the naked double image of Mary Ellen. In that regard, she had proven a more instinctive photographer than him, and that might have irked him. But he was outwardly relaxed and happy to fuss over Mary Ellen, checking that she was warm enough, replenishing the fire when it burned low, keeping her glass of wine topped up. For her part, Mary Ellen revelled in the attention, uncaring of her nakedness, and found she was enjoying the wine, certain she could never afford a bottle for herself. At times during the afternoon she saw the funny side of the scene and couldn't help smiling to herself as an aristocratic young man of considerable wealth and influence, clothed in a flamboyant dress, fussed attentively around her, a completely naked young woman. It was not a situation anyone would have believed; had they been told. Nor would they have understood the sexual restraint.

But unlike the two previous occasions, once the photography was finished that was to change. Mary Ellen had twice willed Lord Cavendish to take her, but as she had dressed, he had made no move to do so, allowing her to return to her room. Today, however, as she turned to gather up the chemise from where she had placed it, Lord Cavendish stepped before her, took her face in his hands, and kissed her gently on the lips.

'Mary Ellen,' he said, stepping back and regarding her nudity as if for the first time, 'here you are, naked as the day you were born. And here...' he stretched his arms outwards, the kaftan radiating colour, 'I stand clothed. That doesn't seem fair, wouldn't you say?'

Before she could reply, he pulled his arms into the baggy sleeves of the robe, and freeing it from his shoulders allowed it to drop to the floor. He, too, was naked; his revealed manhood pointing stiffly skywards from a thatch of red hair.

'Is that better?' he asked.

Mary Ellen, suddenly wide-eyed, unable to frame words to respond, simply nodded mutely as he took her effortlessly into his arms and carried her to his bed.

Chapter 63

Lord Cavendish's sexual prowess was borne of many and varied encounters. For Mary Ellen, sensing such might be the case, but far from caring, it meant that instead of the rough, self-satisfying thrusting she'd come to know was Joseph's *modus operandi*, she understood for the first time that sex could be a mutually pleasurable experience. Lord Cavendish had been gentle, considerate and encouraging, when he could so easily have taken her brutally and left her in pain, bruised and, as Joseph had made her feel, cast aside like an old dish rag. But he hadn't; he'd been caring and patient, and stimulated Mary Ellen in ways she was too inexperienced ever to have imagined, raising her to intense heights of pleasure. For her it was a new and exquisite encounter with sex, one that demonstrated that all men were not created equal either in proficiency or size. Nor in the aftermath did Lord Cavendish leave her to her own devices as Joseph had become wont to do. Instead, after the first vibrant explosion had ceased careering through her body and her pounding heart returned to normal, he held her in his arms, turned sideways and kissed her with gentle passion. In no hurry to depart.

She burrowed herself into his embrace, wishing the moment would last forever, but knowing in her heart *forever* was beyond hope's reach.

When, still simmering with pleasure, she finally returned to her room, a room bathed in the warm glow of the lowering sun, she lay prone on her bed and relived every moment, fingers lightly touching every part of her body Lord Cavendish had visited, recalling his touch, believing she could still feel his caressing hands. When, finally, she fell asleep, it was into a deep and satisfying slumber laden with dreams of palaces and princes.

In the morning, her dreams washed away by the murky waters of reality, a pale, unpromising day served only to raise her disappointment in Joseph to new heights, and she was thankful he was no longer part of her life, not least because the family would return from Somerset a few days hence.

Until that day, she performed her duties with the memory of Lord Cavendish foremost in her thoughts but dismayed to find his bed unused for several days and Lady Clarissa once again forbidding all visitations from the household. On the fourth day, she finally caught sight of him as he clambered unsteadily into a pony and trap and left the estate, bound, she later learned, for the train to Liverpool and then onward to London.

Mary Ellen, intent on doing the week's washing and ironing to help her sister, returned to Penny Lodge on her next Sunday afternoon off, a muggy day, bright but with banks of purple rain clouds threatening, to find her sister distraught and angry, storming round the kitchen, unable to settle.

'Those little brats,' she screeched un-Jane-like to make sure that wherever they were hiding, they would hear her, 'I'll swing for them. I'll fucking kill 'em.'

Normally in control of her emotions, it wasn't like Jane to swear or lose her temper. So, Mary Ellen wrapped her arms round her, holding her close and asked, 'What's 'appened? What 'ave they done?'

'What have they done? *What have they done?* What *haven't* they done, the little snot rags?'

'Sit down and tell me,' Mary Ellen prompted, ushering her fretful sister to the kitchen table. 'I'll make a brew. And then *I'll* kill 'em, so's you don't 'ave to.'

'I don't know what's got into them. Constant bloody mithering; they get my goat. I turned my back for half an hour while I did some shopping, when I come back the place has been ransacked, turned upside down, clothes thrown everywhere, chairs tipped over, one of the curtains has been ripped and pulled down, and it looks like one of them's pissed on the kitchen floor. All because I said they couldn't go to Billinge Fair.'

'No, surely not,' Mary Ellen began, but as she rounded the kitchen table, saw what she meant. 'The little rats. Why do something like that; what's got into 'em?'

'Buggered if *I* know,' Jane said, pulling up a chair and sitting at the table, as Mary Ellen made a pot of tea.

'Are you sure it's George and Henry we're talking about. It can't be them, surely? Maybe some toe rag broke in. Everyone round 'ere knows we don't lock the doors. You'd only 'ave to get someb'dy gobbin' off in t'pub, and some scrote at t'bar, waggin' 'is ears.'

Jane seemed mollified and reached out to touch her sister's shoulder in appeasement, her shoulders sagging. 'You may be right. It doesn't sound like something the boys would do. But I won't know until they come back for food. And then I'll have it out of them, if I have to take the strap to them.'

'Well, 'appen.'

'Luckily whoever it was didn't find your box. The one with the locket in it, thank God, otherwise all that would have gone. They'd've got a penny or two for that locket. Maybe you should think of hiding it somewhere else. If the buggers come back, they'll try harder next time. I wasn't gone all that long. Maybe they heard me coming back and scarpered.' She sighed heavily as her anger began to dissipate, 'As if we don't have enough to worry about.'

Mary Ellen sat up, suddenly remembering the other reason she'd returned to the family home. 'Well, this should help.' She pulled a leather pouch from a pocket and poured its contents onto the table where they clattered and spun noisily. 'Another ten pounds, plus my wages for last month.'

'Where...? Oh, yes...' a smile coming to her eyes, '...posing for mucky pictures.'

Mary Ellen protested, 'They *weren't* no mucky pictures. They were lovely, I've seen 'em. Really...artistic. Didn't realise as it was me for a minute, when I saw 'em. And now 'is lordship's buggered off to London to sell 'em. But,' she went on, gesturing to the coins on the table, ''e paid me, like 'e said 'e would.'

'Well,' Jane went on. 'So long as it was just pictures and nothing else.'

'It *was* just pictures,' Mary Ellen lied, 'nuffin else,' and for once her sister failed to detect the lie, a skill at which she was normally adept.

As Jane, in a more relaxed state, started peeling potatoes for corned beef hash, Mary Ellen began the laborious process of heating buckets of water to fill the dolly tub in the outhouse. Once all the dirty clothes were in the tub, she left them to soak for a short while and escaped the steamy atmosphere to head up Arch Lane in search of early blackberries or wild garlic. The air was moist and warm following an earlier rain shower, steam rising from the lane and hedgerows. It was probably too early for the blackberries, she realised, but she detected the lovely aromatic smell of the ransoms long before she saw them. They always made a tasty addition to a stew.

On the way she passed neighbouring Torpen Lodge, a substantial grey-brick house recently built as a residence for the line inspector employed by Liverpool

Waterworks to work on the nearby service reservoir and pipeline that distributed water around southern Lancashire.

Drawing level with the garden gate a voice rang out.

'Mary Ellen. Prynhawn da, cariad.'

The incumbent line inspector was Welsh, his family raised in the parish of Llangadwaladr on the island of Anglesey. So, it was not surprising to hear Welsh ringing out along the lanes for the entire family, young and old alike, had good voices, and on a warm summer's evening it was not unusual to hear their collective dulcet tones singing across the hedgerows. It was one of the joys of living in Arch Lane.

'Morgan. 'Ello. Not seen you in a while,' she said as she spotted her friend attacking a hedgerow with a pair of shears. ''Ow are you?'

Morgan Jones was several years older than Mary Ellen, the third child of the family, and worked with his father inspecting the water pipeline, many miles of which they had to check for leaks on a daily basis by horse, on foot or by rail. He had two older sisters, married and living farther down the lane – one having married Mary Ellen's oldest brother – and two young brothers like herself, the four of whom were endlessly up to mischief, one moment the tightest of friends, the next the fiercest of enemies. But Mary Ellen and Morgan had always got on. For a time, she'd wondered whether the two of them might one day have become a couple, but it had never happened, destiny seeming always to contrive to keep them at romantic arm's length, adolescent hormones champing at the bit, but never quite given full rein. And now he had a girlfriend just a few weeks from giving birth to their child.

Instead, they'd become good friends, and it was on that friendship she was suddenly thought to call.

'Busy getting ready for the brat we're about to 'ave come and ruin my beauty sleep.'

Mary Ellen beamed at him, a twinkle in her eye. 'You must know what caused it. It wasn't the fairies, you know. Find out what is was and tie a knot in it before it 'appens again. Better still, chop it off, would be my advice.'

'A bit drastic, Mary Ellen. No, it was that Welsh witch indoors. Seduced me, she did. Slipped something into my tea, I wouldn't think. 'Ad 'er evil way with me when I was under the influence, and now look, see. Up the duff.'

'Ah, but you know you love 'er.'

'Course I do,' he chuckled. 'Only jokin'. Any'ow, what's 'appening with you. All hoity-toity, isn't it, working up at th'all.'

''Ardly. It's 'ard graft. Some days I don't know my arse from my elbow and can't feel either.'

'Well, it's better than going 'ungry, being in t'work'ouse. Anyhow, what's going on at yours. I could 'ear Jane yelling blue murder from 'ere.'

'Well, someone's been in and thrown stuff about and pissed on the kitchen floor. Jane though it might have been the lads, but I'm not so sure, and I can see 'em now coming down t'lane wi' your two. So, I doubt it were them.'

'Well, look at 'em, butter wouldn't melt and all that, but you're right. They wouldn't mess their own 'ome.'

'Well, I 'ope not for their sake. Jane's quite 'andy wi' a strap when she puts 'er mind to it. Wouldn't want to be in their shoes if it were them.'

She watched as the four boys came down the lane. 'Anyway,' she said to Morgan, 'can I ask you to do summat for me?'

'Course, as long as it's not illegal.'

'No, I just want you to look after summat for me. It's a box I keep my things in, bits of cheap jewellery, mam's bible, a couple of diaries, sort o' thing. There's nowhere safe in our 'ouse, and there's loads o' time when there's nob'dy at home. So, I wondered if you could look after it for me, for a while. Won't be forever.'

'Course I will. I've a secret hidey-hole in one o't'walls. Nob'dy knows about it. Just me and Megan. It'll be safe there.'

'Thanks Morgan, I'll get it now,' she said, turning away. 'And then you can get back to your beauty sleep. Christ knows you need it,' she laughed loudly as Morgan made a rude gesture with his fingers.

An hour later, calm has returned to Penny Lodge. The boys had been aghast at what had happened, George affecting what indignation he could muster at the very idea that his sister would think them capable of such a travesty. Jane, seeing that she'd wronged them, accepted their innocence and promised to make them a blancmange.

Mary Ellen had long since tackled the tub of washing, wrung it out on their ancient mangle and hung it out to dry in the early evening sun. If it dried quickly enough, she'd take an iron to the items of clothing that would be on display but ignore anything that would be out of sight.

She found the circumstance to her amusement. She spent all day skivvying for the aristocracy, and then came home to do more. Had Mary Ellen understood the concept of irony, she would have seen it for what it was. But unlike the chores she carried out at the hall, Mary Ellen enjoyed washing and ironing. There was something soothing about the process; something she enjoyed. And this was something she was doing for *her* family. She didn't need more reason than that.

Chapter 64

Duncan and Alice having set off from White Coppice in plenty of time were taking a roundabout route through Woodplumpton and Inskip to a country pub near St Michael's on Wyre to meet up with Sandy Glen. Hopefully she could tell them what chance there might be of DNA having travelled down the years that could positively link Alice back to Mary Ellen. As Duncan knew only too well, it was one thing to trace a family member on paper, but quite another to be able to prove it scientifically; that was proof positive, although the reverse methodology – DNA to paper – could be an equally difficult task: Duncan knew of several people, including one in his own family, where there was a proven DNA link, for which a connection could not be made using extant records.

Alice had long since succumbed to Duncan's tenacity in pursuing her familial connection, to see if he could move them closer to identifying her unknown great, great grandfather, the father of Mary Ellen's firstborn. It was one of the qualities she had come to love about him. The dead end they faced, she'd come to understand, was par for the course in genealogical research. Finding a route through the several mazes to an answer came only with application, technique and a measure of bloody-mindedness. Duncan had all three skills.

Sunlight dappling through roadside trees, they had driven in companionable silence since leaving the motorway north of Preston. They were in Alice's car, which, Duncan registered, she drove supremely well, proactively rather than re-actively, as Isabel had often done with hair-raising consequences.

Out of the blue, Duncan said, 'I think we need to ramp up our research into life at Garston Hall. See if we can't positively confirm Mary Ellen was working there. We know her father was; so there's a reasonable degree of probability that she did, too.'

Alice said, 'If you remind me when we get back home, I'll check the library's online catalogue. I'm sure I found a reference to a book about Garston Hall in among all the stuff I've been wading through. But hasn't the hall been demolished?'

'From what I discovered in the National Archives, it was demolished in the nineteen-twenties, but I seem to recall it had been sold some years earlier. So if we can trace the records of sale, we may pick up on something useful. It's worth a try, anyway. And I can make a better job of analysing the census records and rating and valuation books.'

'Well, it can't do anything but help us, to see the bigger picture.'

'Quite. I've just been following a conventional paper trail until now. That will only go so far. Time to be professional.'

Alice turned briefly and smiled at him. 'You can be a little terrier at times, can't you?'

He jokingly barked like a dog, making Alice laugh aloud.

Chapter 65

Sandy Glen had arrived before them, and sat nursing a half empty glass of wine as they walked in. Fair-haired, blue-eyed and arrestingly eye-catching they found her in a corner of the country pub studying a menu, her shoulder length hair falling forward, framing her face. Her poise exuded the air of a person self-confident and assured, a commanding presence.

'Duncan,' she exclaimed as they approached, beaming at him and rising to kiss him on the cheek, 'so nice to see you again. I'd quite forgotten how tall you are.'

'Likewise, Sandy, nice to see you, too. It's been a while.' He turned to introduce Alice.

'So, this is the lady you've spoken so fondly of, is it? Please to meet you, Alice.'

Alice took her proffered hand. 'I hope he hasn't been speaking out of turn.'

'Far from it; nothing but the nicest. Made you out to be quite an angel.'

'I'm hardly that, he is prone to exaggerate, but it'll do for now.' Alice laughed, regarding this smartly dressed, attractive woman with feminine curiosity, and to her surprise found herself wondering if her evident familiarity with Duncan had ever progressed beyond genealogy and DNA. Thankfully, she knew Duncan well enough to recognise the implausibility of such an idea. She herself had needed the best part of two years to move her own relationship with him to the bedroom. Yet to her chagrin, the thought had briefly crossed her mind, and she scolded herself irritably for its unworthiness.

Duncan jovially gestured to Sandy's glass of wine as he moved towards the bar. 'Can I get you another? I'm getting wine for Alice; she's graciously allowing me to drive her precious Mini on the way back.'

Sandy nodded. 'Don't mind if I do. Jim, my husband, brought me and went off to pregnancy test some sheep at one of the farms over Knott End way. He's a vet, I assume you'll gather from that. He'll come back for me, when I call.

Meanwhile I'll just sit here enjoying this rather agreeable pinot grigio and what I'm sure will be your scintillating company.'

Duncan returned with drinks and they ordered food.

Sandy regarded them both quizzically, raising a well-groomed eyebrow in unspoken question, as if waiting for them to begin. When they didn't immediately respond, she said, 'Well, your story all sounds a bit mysterious. Trying to pin down one of your relatives, I gather,' she asked, turning to Alice.

Alice nodded. 'My…what was she? Great-great-grandmother had two illegitimate children, from one of whom I'm descended. On paper, at least. Duncan, being Duncan, wanted to see if he could fathom who the mystery father was. Using DNA, he said, would give us something more tangible than census records to work from.'

Sandy laughed lightly. 'I well remember Duncan's steadfastness from the courses we were on. Talk about a dog with a bone.'

Duncan chipped in. 'Well, you know what I'm like with loose ends. I like to pull them and see what unravels.'

'So, what do you want my help with?'

Duncan framed his thoughts before saying, 'We were wondering to what extent, and in what form, DNA that could be used to prove family lineage might travel down through time. I'm always reading about archaeologists digging up dinosaur bones and getting DNA from them. A bit like they are supposed to have done in that dinosaur film *Jurassic Park*. So, I figured that if there was any basis for retrieving DNA that far back, the late nineteenth century should be a doddle.'

'Well, that's not quite the same thing,' Sandy explained, smiling genially at them both. 'But while we're waiting for our food let me knock the *Jurassic Park* idea on the head.'

Alice shivered as if she felt cold. 'The very thought that the things they did in that film might be possible rather spooks me. Please tell me they can't do it.'

'Well,' Sandy began, 'if you remember, the film story involved a mosquito that they said contained dinosaur DNA being preserved in amber, and for the purposes of the film, they recovered the ancient DNA and used it as a genetic blueprint for recreating the dinosaurs. The only thing is, debunking the whole idea, that when amber preserves things, it only preserves the husk, not the soft tissues. And that rules out the idea of blood being preserved inside a mosquito in amber.'

'So, a myth?' Duncan suggested.

'Well, that particular aspect was. But it doesn't end there.'

'No?'

'No. I read a paper a few months ago about a scientist's finding a mosquito preserved in lake sediments from around forty-five million years ago. Apparently, it had red pigment in its abdomen, and when they tested the pigment chemically, they discovered haemoglobin-derived porphyrins.' Seeing their puzzled faces, she added: 'They're the breakdown products of haemoglobin, the red protein that carries oxygen around the body in the blood of almost all vertebrates.'

Sandy sat back in her seat. 'None of which is especially germane to your situation, I suspect. At least, I don't think you want me to go so far back.'

Alice and Duncan laughed. 'Not quite. Just over a hundred years should do fine,' Duncan said. 'We just want to know whether DNA could travel to the present day in a form that would enable someone like yourself to establish a fairly basic family connection. Whether Alice is DNA-related to the woman we believe to be her great-great-grandmother.'

'Well, without boring you with too much jargon…and stop me if you know all this. Every cell in our body contains DNA, and about ninety-nine-point nine percent of the DNA between two humans is the same; it's the remaining point one percent that makes us unique. And while that may seem a very small amount, it represents around three million what we call base pairs – two bases on opposite strands of a DNA molecule held together by weak chemical bonds – that are different between two people. We compare these differences using what is known as polymerase chain reaction technology to determine generic family relationships.'

Sandy paused to let them take that in, and took a mouthful of wine, but was sure they'd both understood what she was telling them. So, she went on, 'Each person's DNA contains two markers, one inherited from the father, the other from the mother. At each stage of development, all our cells contain the same DNA, and this allows us to home in fairly accurately on relationships. Even so, evidential sources of DNA,' Sandy explained, 'are variable at best. What you're looking at almost certainly won't give you evidential standards. It wouldn't stack up in a court of law, for example. But at your level of enquiry it *will* show family ties. Blood is good, because the white cells are a rich source of DNA. Sweat stains, too, something we all produce no matter how much we might try to cover it up with perfume or aftershave, provide skin cells that are also rich in DNA. "No contact is without trace", as my professor used to insist.'

'So, we're looking for something sweaty or bloody, basically,' Duncan said. 'What about hair follicles? I thought you could get DNA from hair, so long as the root was intact.'

'Yes, that's true. But you're going back well over a hundred years, and the best chance of getting DNA from hair so old would entirely depend on it having been kept in airtight conditions. Locked away, somewhere. And the fewer people to have handled it, the better. The more degraded a sample is, the more difficult it will be to attribute it correctly. I'm afraid that, like *Jurassic Park*, what you see on television these days, where they pull up the profile of a suspect in a matter of minutes is a load of bunkum.'

'Well,' Duncan said. 'I'm sure you know me well enough to realise I'm not likely to fall for that scenario. But assuming we do find something useful, are you okay with doing this for us? It's not going to cause problems for you, is it?'

Sandy took another mouthful of wine and shook her head. 'I'll enter an official record of it, of course, and then I'll pass it on to some of my better students as a practical exercise. But I *will* make sure my bosses are aware of what I'm doing. So there's no comeback. Some might argue that we shouldn't be doing this. But I take the view that we have to teach the new generations how to discover the old generations.'

Their food arrived, as Alice said, 'We'd appreciate anything you can do. But I guess it's down to us to find some DNA samples, and I've no idea how we're going to do that.'

'We just wanted to be sure,' Duncan added, sipping his ginger beer, 'that it was possible, before we got bogged down looking for ancient blood traces, or whatever.'

'It is. And when you find something, give me a call, and I'll come to you, and use the opportunity to take a new sample of Alice's DNA to compare with.'

As they started on their food, Alice suddenly paused, her knife raised in an exclamation mark. 'I've just had a thought.'

Duncan chuckled softly, 'And I thought it was a low-flying jet.'

Alice nudged him in the ribs. 'I have a picture at home of my great grandfather, wearing a flat cap. And I think I've got the cap. I've a box of stuff that was my dad's, and I'm sure there's a flat cap in there. It's not something my dad ever wore. He told me it belonged to his grandfather.'

Sandy nodded her agreement. 'It would certainly be worth testing. There'll be sweat, hair and dandruff in there. All grist to the mill. Let me know how you get on,' adding as an afterthought, 'oh, and if you do find anything, use forensic gloves to handle it. It'll make my students' job easier if they don't have to eliminate you from the process. You can get gloves on Amazon. Or I can send you a few pairs.'

Chapter 66

The long-anticipated return of the Garston household from their extended sojourn in Somerset happened on a warm, sunny Sunday afternoon, sparse, wispy clouds streaking a cerulean sky, a gentle breeze holding flying insects at bay from the gardeners for whom they were a torment, an occupational hazard. It was one of the gardeners who saw the approaching cavalcade of horse-drawn coaches first, rushing to the hall to alert the housekeeper.

Mary Ellen, on her Sunday afternoon off, was in no hurry to find herself confronted by either Elizabeth or Joseph or to be drawn into hours of unpacking and the chaos that followed the family's return. So, she remained perched on "her" rock by the lake, taking a leisurely, circuitous route to the family home, and watched the return with mixed feelings; the obsequious fussing of the footmen and valets – she spotted Joseph and was pleased to see he looked stooped and worn out – and a curious sense of the contentment that the household would be complete once more in spite of the heavier workload that would ensue.

For months, throughout the dark winter, there had been whisperings among the remnants of the domestic brigade left behind at Garston that the family would move permanently to Somerset and sell the hall and its estate. The mere fact of the length of their stay away from Garston gave rise to uneasy speculation among the staff now isolated in the north of England. For the moment, however, it seemed Garston was once more the place of family residence.

From a distance, Lord Garston, dressed in a needlessly heavy overcoat given the warmth of the day, looked overweight and unsteady on his feet, stumbling as he alighted from the carriage. Lady Garston, in contrast, holding a fringed, floral parasol over her head, looked frail, as beautiful as ever, but slender and fragile as her husband escorted her through the magnificent entrance and into the hall. From a second carriage, Lady Makerfield emerged, her maid beside her. Both looked, Mary Ellen thought, as if they were bound for a funeral, dressed as they were in head-to-toe black save for a white cotton coif that her ladyship secured with a bandeau to which a black veil was attached.

Sour. Bitter. Twisted. Menacing, were the words that sprang to Mary Ellen's mind as she watched the two elderly women tottering into the hall, both supporting themselves on insubstantial canes.

Conspicuous by their absence were the two footmen, John and Henry, and Mary Ellen silently hoped they were no longer part of the household. But the sight of the butler, Grimes, was not a pleasant one.

From among the returning company, only Lord Cavendish was missing, and as Mary Ellen gathered her things and resumed her journey to Penny Lodge she wondered if she would ever see him again.

It was dark by the time Mary Ellen returned to Garston, the sky bright with stars and a slender crescent moon. As she gazed heavenward, a streak of light shot across the sky; a shooting star, a bringer of good fortune she believed. Or, as her mother would say, the spirit of a new baby falling to Earth, ready to begin its new life. Either way, it was a good omen.

Once in her room, warm night air wafting through the window she had left open, her thoughts turned to Elizabeth. She could hear her in the next room unpacking her belongings and sorting them into her small wardrobe and chest of drawers to the accompaniment of the occasional expletive. Mary Ellen smiled to herself; Elizabeth was neither the tidiest nor most patient of souls and set little store in the ordered placement of clothes she'd noticed in Mary Ellen's room. That aside, she had befriended Mary Ellen, brought her under her wing, shared intimate moments with her, taught her much over the years, more than enough – was it? – to compensate for the betrayal of their friendship by having sex with Joseph, someone who in surrendering to Elizabeth's demands had openly demonstrated he didn't have the makings of the man she wanted to spend the rest of her life with. Maybe, on reflection, Elizabeth had done her a favour.

As she started to unbutton her dress, she hesitated, recalling something her sister had once told her: forgiveness doesn't excuse someone's behaviour, it prevents their behaviour from destroying your heart.

When someone does something wrong, don't forget all the things they did right.

Mary Ellen refastened her dress, coming to a decision.

Outside Elizabeth's door she paused, listening for the sounds of more than one person. But all she could hear was Elizabeth, who seemed to be humming softly to herself. She sounded contented, and that brought a comforting warmth to Mary Ellen's heart.

Elizabeth looked up as the door opened, an uncertain smile on her lips.

'Fuck. Mary Ellen, you give me a fright.' She started to move towards her, arms outstretched in welcome, then hesitated, remembering the atmosphere that had settled over them before the family had departed for Somerset. 'Mary Ellen, how are you?' she asked with restraint.

Mary Ellen, for her part, forgave her in an instant. How could she not? In recent times, she had come to understand…what was it she'd called it…? *Lust.* It counted for little but explained a lot. She wasn't about to let what had happened destroy her heart, her friendship…and so she rushed into her embrace.

'Fuck, I missed you, Beth,' she said, holding her friend firmly to her breast, squeezing the breath from her.

Releasing her, Elizabeth stepped back and appraised Mary Ellen. 'Me, too, it was so bloody tedious without you around, so…*desperately*…boring. Dragged on worse than a month of Sundays.'

She regarded Mary Ellen again.

'You've come on, girl, bloody hell.'

She moved towards her again, her arms outstretched, caressing Mary Ellen's cheek with the back of her hand – it reminded Mary Ellen of how Lord Cavendish had done the same – touching her beauty spot – that, too – resting her hands on her shoulders, slipping downwards to cup her breasts, measure the shape of her waist and hips. 'Bloody hell, have you come on. What a stunning bitch you are, Mary Ellen. You look so happy, so…womanly. You haven't half grown up. Something's happened to you while I've been away. Something really good, I can tell. Something that most definitely suits you.'

They both laughed, Mary Ellen uneasily, but thankful that their friendship had been restored. Suddenly, Elizabeth's eyes lit up.

'You've got a man! Bugger, you've got yourself a man. Who is he? Come on. How did you manage that?'

May Ellen protested. 'No, there's no one. 'onest. There's been no one,' she lied, a half lie, perhaps, but a lie, nonetheless. She wasn't about to let Elizabeth know the truth. No one must know the truth. Yes, something had indeed happened to her, but no one must ever find out. It had to remain her secret. There would be no notes in her diary about that.

'What? All those randy gardeners and foresters, and you didn't cop off with any of them?'

Mary Ellen laughed and shook her head. 'I kept well out of their dirty clutches, but 'ad more than enough offers to last a lifetime, believe me. Randy gits.'

Elizabeth turned to her; her face suddenly solemn. 'Listen, Mary Ellen, I'm sorry about…you know…with …'

Mary Ellen held out her hand. 'Forget it. It's in the past. *He's* in the past.'

'Well, that's going to knock him for six. He's been sending you letters most bloody weeks, begging forgiveness, telling you how sorry he was. Bugger, he even had the nerve to come and tell me what he was doing. Wanted to read the letters to me.'

'Never read 'em. Burned the lot. I knew they were from 'im.'

'He's come back hoping you'd forgive him.'

Mary Ellen shrugged. 'Fish'll talk first.'

'Well, I suppose I'm to blame for the letters. I put him up to sending them. Well, sending one, not the millions he seems to have sent. It must have cost him a fortune, buying stamps and paper and envelopes.'

'More fool 'im.'

'Yeah,' she nodded her agreement, 'and it was all a bit weird when we got to Somerset.'

'What d'you mean?'

And she told her: how Joseph deluded himself into thinking that one unfulfilled night of sex with Elizabeth meant more than it did, had tried to repeat the experience, and might have succeeded, Elizabeth feeling needy at the time, had he not failed to "get wood", as she put it.

'Poor bastard, just drooped, like wilted rhubarb. Not a pretty sight.'

Mary Ellen chortled. 'So, after limping out with you, 'e decided 'e'd try an' make it up with me? Cheeky bastard.'

'Well, you can't blame the man for trying. So, you'd better make sure he gets the message soon, or he's going to be hounding you like a lovesick puppy. He's knackered, poor lad. That witch, the old woman, ran him ragged. Bring me, fetch me, carry me. As if that crone she has as a maid couldn't do everything for her.'

Casting her mind back to the picture of the family returning, she remembered who had been missing from the entourage. 'And what's happened with the two Jack the Lads? John and Henry.'

'Well you might ask. They've been sacked for indecent behaviour in public. The good people of Bath are not minded to put up with what they did. Got into a fight, and ended up getting a right kicking, the pair of them. If the rossers hadn't turned up, they'd be dead.'

'What on earth were the dozy bastards doing?'

'Trying to tup a couple of young girls. Behind a pub, in an alleyway. They were drunk. Not that that's any excuse. But their girls' brothers turned up looking for them, and took the matter into their own hands. Luckily, for them, they managed to get away from the rossers, or they'd have been in the lock up, and on trial for assault.'

'Well, I can't say I'm sorry to see the back of 'em. All'us thought they were dodgy.'

Mary Ellen sighed, wrapped her arms around Elizabeth, and held her tightly, lightly kissing her cheek, breathing in the smell of her hair.

'I've missed you,' she said. And meant it. 'Can I sleep with you tonight? You know…just…sleep. Like we used to?'

Chapter 67

When Joseph did encounter Mary Ellen, his hope for a joyous reunion was dashed in a few choice words.

How could he have been so stupid as to expect anything other?

'Mary Ellen, please. I'm sorry. How many times do you want me to say it?'

They had bumped into one another on the servants' stairs, both taken momentarily by surprise. But Mary Ellen had known they would inevitably meet before long, and was prepared. She was not in a forgiving mood.

'You can repeat yourself 'til the cows come 'ome, for all I care. Makes no diff'rence to me.'

Joseph pleaded with her. 'I sent you letters. I wrote to you. I said I was sorry. Did you not read them?'

'No,' she replied emphatically. 'I *didn't* read them. I chucked them on the fire.' She was lying about that, but Joseph would never know; not that she cared.

She started walking away from him, climbing the stairs to her room.

'I... I...' Joseph spluttered as Mary Ellen rounded on him, turning to face him and stepping down towards him, but not so far that she didn't still dominate him from two steps above.

She pointed a menacing finger at him. 'You tried it on again, with Beth. Don't deny it. And you want me to take you back? Forget it, Joe. And...and, if you keep pestering me, I'll resign. I'll leave Garston. How do you expect me to trust you again? You're sick in th'ead. You're twisted. So, bugger off, and leave me alone.'

Instead of continuing to her room, Mary Ellen took one of the intermediate landing doors that gave on to the hall's central staircase intent on remaining in the body of the hall rather than in her room, where Joseph could corner her. She was fuming; indignation as much as anything else bubbling inside her. She had no doubt that she could deal with Joseph, but he was clearly shaken by their exchange and might not heed her warning to leave her be. Keeping out of his way was the immediate solution, but her thoughts on how to accomplish that in the confines of the hall were disturbed as she caught sight of the dark-clad figure of Lady Makerfield's maid shakily descending the staircase and disappearing in the direction of her ladyship's rooms.

Why on earth would she be in this part of the hall? She was rarely seen outside her ladyship's wing of the house. She could barely walk fifty paces without help. So, why was she on completely the wrong side of the hall?

The answer, when it came a few hours later in the form of a summons to attend Mrs Bonnivale in her room, left Mary Ellen astounded.

'Miss Liptrot,' Mrs Bonnivale began using her family name, a sign that all was not well, 'can you explain why this,' she turned to pick something up from the table behind her, 'pair of silver sugar tongues should be found in your room?'

'Wha…? I …I…' she stammered, much as Joseph had done only a short while earlier, unable to venture an explanation. 'I don't know nuffin about no sugar tongues, Mrs Bonnivale. 'onest. I ain't never seen 'em before.' She was trying to think quickly in an effort to explain herself. But she didn't know what it was she was trying to explain. 'There must be a mistake.'

'Don't make matters worse for yourself, Miss Liptrot. This is a very serious matter. These…' she waved the offending sugar tongues at Mary Ellen, 'these were found under the pillow on your bed.'

'Someone's having a josh,' she ventured, more in hope than expectation. 'I 'aven't been to my room since I left it this morning. Ask anyone.'

'I don't need to ask anyone, Miss Liptrot. You were *seen* leaving your room only a few hours ago.'

'I never,' she protested feebly. 'Who says they saw me? Who found them? They're lying.'

'Mind your place. Don't be insolent, Miss Liptrot. Please stop lying; it will do you no good, mark my words. You were seen by Lady Makerfield's maid, leaving your room – when, by the way, you should have been about your duties elsewhere – just a few hours ago. And these…' again she waved the sugar tongues in Mary Ellen's face, '…are Lady Makerfield's personal sugar tongues. They are of great sentimental value to her ladyship and belonged to her mother.'

A look of profound disbelief settled on Mary Ellen's face. It was unfathomable. Her eyes began to fill with tears. *She* knew she hadn't taken the tongues but would anyone believe her. How could she possibly prove her innocence?

She took a deep breath, and looked Mrs Bonnivale steadily in the eye, holding back her tears and spoke softly in an effort to sound as honest as she knew she was, her lips quivering as she fought to control her emotions. 'I swear on my brothers' lives, Mrs Bonnivale, I don't know nuffin about this. I ain't stole nuffin. There must be a mistake. I saw Joseph, Joseph Cunliffe, on the stairs. 'e'll tell you. I never went to my room.'

Mrs Bonnivale turned to replace the tongues on the table and turning to face Mary Ellen again took a deep breath, swelling her bosom across which she folded her arms. 'It was Joseph Cunliffe who found them,' she said. 'He said he'd gone to your room to leave you a message, which he intended to place under your pillow. That was when and where he found the tongues, and promptly came to me with the revelation. And quite rightly, too.'

The slimy rat, she thought. *How could he? How could he? The bastard.* So, this was the man who wanted her love. Wanted her to take him back. *Well,* she thought venomously, *I'll be spinning in my grave before I'll take him back.* It was all so very clear now. This was his way of repaying her for rejecting him. *What a shitty way of behaving*, she thought malevolently.

The cold realisation of her predicament and its implications for her future at Garston struck to her heart, a surge of dismay swelling inside her.

Mary Ellen's time in the aristocratic world of Garston Hall was at an end.

Resignedly, she said, 'I'll collect my things and leave. But I ain't done nuffin wrong. It shouldn't be me wot's leaving.'

'I'll remind you again, Miss Liptrot, to mind your place. And mind how you speak to me. You are dismissed, yes, but her ladyship intends to press charges against you for theft. You'll go to prison for this. The constable is already on his way. You are to remain in my custody, until he arrives.'

She regarded here sternly, taking her by the arm and escorting her brusquely from the room.

'Now, upstairs and out of the uniform you've disgraced.'

Chapter 68

A visit to Arch Lane, in search of Penny Lodge, had been Alice's idea. For some months, she had tussled with her conscience, concerned that the drive to unravel Mary Ellen's secrets – assuming there were any – was encroaching on time Duncan ought to be turning to more remunerative activity. She said as much over dinner one evening, but he had insisted that their search for Mary Ellen's past was not a distraction; it was, he assured her, taking her hand in his, a labour of love, with very little labour and heaps of love. She had murmured her appreciation, 'If you're sure.'

Neither anticipated much to come of the visit, there was no certainty that Penny Lodge would still be there. If it was, there was the slender chance the present incumbents knew something of the history of the family that had lived there before them. A remote prospect, but on such slender pickings, Duncan knew, many a breakthrough was founded. There was nothing to lose, and a hearty lunch at a country pub in the offing.

Of late Duncan had lavished his attention on Alice and rejoiced in his rediscovery of the joy a responsive and intimate loving relationship brought. But even she had been prompting him not to neglect his work, conscious that he seemed loathe to return to the genealogical fray. Making love and drinking wine at every ends' turn didn't put money in the bank. Alice had a secure job, a steady income, but Duncan was dependent on gaining a portfolio of clients, and for that he needed a higher profile than the one he was presently projecting. Or, more to the point, *wasn't* projecting. She needed to redirect his frame of mind along avenues of application to something other than hedonism.

*The honeymoon was over...*but Alice could feel herself making light of her concerns and chose to forestall any uneasiness by suggesting an exploratory visit to where Mary Ellen had been born and lived for much of her life. A compromise, she thought, that would in all probability add nothing to their knowledge, and that would give her a pretext for drawing the search to a close.

Arch Lane, the road signs proclaimed, was a "No Through Road" and Duncan silently hoped that it wouldn't be the sort of dead end that was all too familiar. As they drove slowly along the hedge-rowed lane, he was aware of many gaps between the cottages that remained in comparison with his recollection of census records. A couple of cottages to the south, neither of which bore the name 'Penny Lodge'; a farm to the north, and then nothing other than a pleasant country lane until they arrived outside a large, walled house. With no name in evidence to identify it by, he circled into its drive entrance to consult his map. As they ticked off the cottages they had passed, another car, turning into the house, pulled in beside them.

Duncan wound down his window and asked, 'Is this Penny Lodge?'

The woman driver shook her head. 'No, it's Torpen Lodge. I'm going in. If you like, I'll ask if they know where it is.'

'That's kind of you,' Duncan thanked her, getting out of the car and following her along the driveway. As he caught up with her, she was talking to a man in the doorway, and turned towards Duncan as he approached.

'No one seems to know about Penny Lodge,' she told him.

The man in the doorway shook his head. 'I've been here some years, and I've never heard of Penny Lodge,' he said. 'Maybe they'll know at the library in Wigan. Is it important?'

'Only to the extent that I'm a genealogist, and my friend –' he turned to gesture towards the unseen car at the entrance, 'is related to someone who lived there. We were just tracing what lineage we could. Apart from anything else, even if we can't find an actual property, it seems to help just being in the area they lived,' He paused, and smiled, 'I'm sorry, I must sound a bit weird.'

The man shook his head. 'Not so weird as you think. I spent years working as a line inspector for Liverpool Waterworks, checking the pipeline from the reservoir in the fields behind us,' he gestured over his shoulder with a thumb, 'all the way through to Liverpool. I was spooked more than once, getting a chilling sense that someone had been there before me, doing exactly the same thing and was looking over my shoulder to check I was doing my job right. And I know for a fact, that the last line inspector to live here at Torpen, was from North Wales, Anglesey, I think. Probably a Jones, I wouldn't doubt.'

'Well, that would be easy enough to check in the records.'

'If you do find out, I'd appreciate knowing. I've often wondered who came before me, but never knew how to find out.'

'That's not a problem, I'll let you know as soon as I find anything. What's your name?'

'Geoff. Geoff Parry. What's your friend's name?'

'Alice. Alice Marsh, but the person we're looking for is her great-great-grandmother on the maternal branch of her tree: Mary Ellen Liptrot.'

Geoff Parry's face was suddenly aghast, expressing astonishment. 'I think you'd better get your friend and come in for a cup of tea,' he said enigmatically.

Duncan registered the surprised tone but nodded and trotted off to bring Alice to the house. Some premonition prompted him to collect his briefcase from the boot of the car; it contained all the documents that related to Alice's family tree.

Seated at the kitchen table sipping tea, Geoff regarded the pair of them. 'It may seem an odd thing to ask – you'll understand why I'm asking, in a moment – but can you prove the relationship to this Mary Ellen Liptrot?'

'Not yet by DNA; that's not so straightforward. But,' Duncan said, opening his briefcase and extracting a large file of documents, 'on paper, most definitely.'

Spreading copies of birth and marriage certificates on the table before them, Duncan demonstrated Alice's family lineage back through her father, maternal grandmother, great grandfather to Mary Ellen herself. He then produced a hand-drawn sketch of the tree on which he'd highlighted the blood lines in red ink.

'Okay,' Geoff said. 'I accept that. Now, hold your breath. I have something I'm sure you'll find fascinating.' He stood up and left the room, returning a moment later carrying a tall and substantial cardboard box and placed it on the table. He tapped the box, 'This is one I've bought, but it's what's inside that will amaze you.'

He looked at the pair of them, questioningly. 'Are you prepared to be amazed?'

Alice nodded eager to discover the contents of the box. Duncan said, 'Amaze away.'

Geoff open the box; inside they saw a black book they could see was a bible. Beside it, radiating quality, was a rosewood box with a brass inlay.

Duncan was the first to speak. 'Wow, that is beautiful.'

Alice reached out to pick up the bible, but Duncan touched her hand and said, 'Wait; if this is what I think it could be, we don't want to touch it with our bare hands.'

'Ah, yes,' Alice agreed, picking up on what was in his mind.

Geoff looked shamefaced. 'Bugger. I've touched the Bible and tried to get into the box. But it's locked, and there's no key.'

'Not to worry. I just don't want to complicate things any further if it can be avoided. I'm getting a tingling sensation about this, and if it turns out to be what I think it might be, we'll be forever in your debt. Alice, what do you think?'

Alice leaned forward and studied the brass inlay. She pointed to an inscription on it. 'I think that says it all.'

Duncan spun the box and read the inscription.

A gift, with deepest affection, to Mary Ellen Liptrot
Lord Cavendish Garston.

'Oh, my goodness,' Duncan went on, turning to speak to Geoff. 'You can't imagine how much that simple inscription tells me. This could be a major piece in our puzzle.' He turned to face Alice, 'If this belonged to Mary Ellen, I can't wait to discover what's inside.'

'Take it,' Geoff said. 'Take it. I'm satisfied that it rightly belongs to Alice. I've had it all these years and not known what to do about it. I'd have to break the box to get inside it, and I wasn't about to do that. You've solved my problem. Take it, with my blessing. I hope it tells you what you want to know. Come back and tell me what you find. But you'll need to find a key. I can't imagine you're going to force open such a lovely thing.'

'Certainly not. It a Coromandel writing box, probably not in itself of great worth these days, but there's provenance and, hopefully, contents that will raise its value for us. I can't thank you enough. How did you come by this?'

'It was in a concealed cupboard. Come through, I'll show you.'

They stood up and followed him through the house into an annex that had been built on at the rear.

'When we were building this, we had to demolish some of the walls, one of which had been papered over. When it all came away, it exposed a cupboard. Must have been a small larder, or something for storing food. But the box and the bible were in there. The bible was wrapped in old newspaper. I'm sorry, it was dry and crumbling, and I threw it away. I can see now that it might have had a date that could have been useful. I should have kept it.'

'You weren't to know. In any case, I expect it's going to be what's in the box that will carry more meaning for us.'

'Well,' Geoff went on, 'it seems this was your lucky day. Blimey! What are the odds on the rightful owner of something I've had for years and known nothing about turning up on my doorstep, out of the blue?'

'For us, this is better than winning the lottery, I can tell you, and I feel just as excited. I'm positively buzzing.'

Alice laughed, and turned to Geoff. 'He does a lot of that. Buzzing. Every time some obscure person pops out of the ancestral woodwork, he's like a child at Christmas. Easily pleased and very excitable.'

'And like a dog with a bone, I daresay.'

Alice chuckled, and patted Duncan on the shoulder, 'And then some,' she said. 'Come on, Christmas boy. Time to see what present you've been given.'

As they took their leave and drove back along Arch Lane, Duncan half turned to Alice and said, 'Humour me. I know we want to see what's in the box, but as we're in the neighbourhood, there's somewhere I think we should visit.'

Alice said nothing as Duncan turned off the road they'd used earlier in the day and took the narrow road that led to the village of Billinge.

'Isn't this where Mary Ellen's son, John, is buried?'

'It is, and I'm hoping there may be someone in the church who can let me see the burial registers. It would be nice to find where he was buried. I seem to remember you telling me you'd been with your father some years ago.'

'Yes, but I couldn't find the grave. I'd got it into my head it was in one particular place, but when I searched there years later, I couldn't find it. I probably didn't try hard enough.'

'Well, let's see if we find anything today. If not, there's a couple of nice pubs in Billinge serving local ales.'

Their good fortune was still in the ascendency. Not only was the church open to visitors, but the verger was present and had access to the burial records for the early part of the twentieth century. When they explained what they wanted to find, he showed them into the vestry and set the register on the table before them. The entries were in date order but ordered by the date of the first interment. There was no name index. So, it took half an hour or more of careful checking to find what they were looking for, and more beside.

From a graveyard layout plan, they were able to locate the grave of Alice's great grandfather, the illegitimate John Liptrot. What they also found, to their surprise and delight was not only John Liptrot, but his mother.

This was so unreal.

They had found Mary Ellen.

Silently the pair stood before the grave; Duncan the first to break the silence. He stepped forward and touched the headstone, and said quietly, 'Mary Ellen. We have your box. Thank you.'

Alice was bemused, but when she turned to Duncan, she saw his eyes were brimming with tears. There was a depth of emotion to this man she had not appreciated but was coming to understand was profound.

They had found Mary Ellen, and on the very day something of hers had passed by chance into their hands. They would have traced Mary Ellen at some stage, anyway, doing so was easily within Duncan's capabilities; it was just serendipity's blessing that had turned them this way today.

Chapter 69

Hell had opened its doors and taken Mary Ellen to its bosom.

In a fury of aristocratic outrage, she had been taken unceremoniously from Garston Hall in the back of a horse-drawn cart, ignominiously handcuffed to a burly, bearded constable, casting her innocence onto unhearing ears. Incarcerated in the lock-up in the new town hall in Wigan, in a tiny cell shared with a shrivelled old woman who smelt of urine and shit, she sank into despair, unable to comprehend what had happened.

Unfed, unwashed, and uncared for, Mary Ellen found herself the next day facing three stern-faced magistrates, who paid only perfunctory attention to her case before sentencing her to twenty-two weeks' imprisonment. The only witness for the prosecution, Joseph, who had had the decency to look downcast and shame-faced and avoided Mary Ellen's hardened gaze.

She would do for him, when she was free!

He lied. She knew he had lied. He knew he had lied. And to his shame, he knew that Mary Ellen knew he had lied.

'Liptrot!' a voice barked loudly.

Another night in the lock-up had passed in a fitful sleep, leaning uncomfortably against iron bars with only an unclean, thread-bare, flea-infested blanket for warmth. Thankfully the smelly old woman had gone, and she had the chill lock-up to herself. The harsh voice roused her sharply, and she opened her eyes to see an obese uniformed constable unlocking the iron-barred cell door. Silently, he entered and brusquely grabbed one of her wrists, fixing it with the ratcheted clasp of a pair of steel handcuffs. Then fastened her other hand, grasping the linking chain and hauling her from the cell.

'I need to piss,' she complained.

The constable grunted. 'You'm 'ave plenty o' time for pissin' on the way to where you'm goin'.'

'What about summat to eat?' she asked pleadingly.

'B'ain't no money fer feedin' thieves. Not now, or where you'm goin', like as not.'

'Where am I going?' she asked.

'No concern o' yers.'

'But it *is* my concern,' she protested. 'I'm the one's wot's going.'

The constable hauled her closer, his fetid breath rank, and slapped her in the face, a blow so forceful she would have struck her head on the doorframe had not his grasp on the handcuffs kept her on her staggering on feet.

'An' I'm the one wot's to tek yer. Now shut the fuck up, or you'm get more o' the same.'

He dragged her into a courtyard at the back of the town hall, where she became conscious of disapproving faces gazing down from office windows. A horse and cart awaited, into which he lifted her bodily, throwing her into the cart, grasping a breast with one hand and thrusting the other between her buttocks as he did so. She landed heavily; the breath knocked from her, a stab of pain searing her stomach and a sliver of wood tearing her skirt.

The constable clambered up beside her, and passed a heavy chain anchored to the sides of the cart through the handcuffs around her wrists.

'Mek yersel' comf'table,' he laughed. 'It's a long day.'

'Where are we going?' she asked again.

The constable smirked. 'To Wakefield,' he sneered, 'that's where. Fuckin' Wakefield. An' it's goin' to tek all fuckin' day.'

Wakefield?

Where on God's earth was Wakefield?

Mary Ellen sat uncomfortably in the back of the cart, resting against the headboard, the cart open to the elements.

'Wot if it rains?'

'Thar'll geet wet, 'appen.' But as he clambered down from the back of the cart, he grasped his groin, exposing himself and giving his manhood a meaningful hoik. 'Course, once we'm out o' town, yer can allus earn a rug to keep you'm warm an' dry. Mebbe a crust, too.'

'I'd rather fuck a pig than touch that pathetic excuse for a cock,' she hissed.

He snarled viciously. 'Suit yersel', yer thieving bitch. But yer won't do yersel' no favours wi' that attitude. You'm ain't wi' th' hobnobs now. It was them 'as dobbed yer in, don't forget.' He climbed up onto the driving seat, and picked up the reins, turning to sneer at her again. 'Yer'll be meetin' a diff'rent class o' friends where you'm goin'.'

As they pulled out of the courtyard and set off along the track leading to Hindley, it started to rain.

Mary Ellen was numb with disbelief, bitterly cold and sodden.

She had endured the sixty-mile journey hunched morosely in the back of the cart against the rain that had persisted for most of the journey and soaked her raggedy clothing. At the three horse changes that had been necessary along the way, here custodian had left her trussed in chains in the cart, as he went into the warmth of the coaching inns for ale and food. After their initial exchange of insults, he had ignored her, providing neither water nor bread throughout the long hours. *Try not to let him see how wretched I feel*, she reminded herself as he clambered back behind the horses. Still unable to grasp how she found herself in this predicament, she wiped her nose on her sleeve and sank slowly into despondency, long since devoid even of the ability to cry, powerless in the face of overwhelming adversity.

She must have dozed off. When she awoke, they were passing an area of three-storey, bay-fronted houses each with a small front garden from one of which a dog barked aggressively as they passed. Surely this must be Wakefield, the end of her journey, and in confirmation a shop sign proclaimed, "J Bastions and Sons, Master Butchers, Wakefield". With her only experience of imprisonment the temporary confinement of the lock-up she had left that morning, she had no notion of life behind bars, no acquaintance with anyone who had spent time in prison. But she had no grounds for optimism, and the sight of the gaunt four-storeyed building that confronted her as they turned in through forbiddingly high iron gates raised little enthusiasm beyond the expectation that she would soon be out of the rain. There, however, the positives ended.

Once inside the prison, she was brusquely handed into the custody of a taciturn jailer, a small, scrawny man wearing a dirty, collarless shirt and a grubby waistcoat, who unfastened her handcuffs, spoke only to confirm her name, took her tightly by the elbow and led her along a pale-green painted corridor lined with iron doors to a cell, thrusting her inside and pulling the door shut behind her. She stood mutely in gathering darkness, shivering uncontrollably in her damp clothing, and listened as she heard the man turn the key to her door.

The cell smelt stale, its walls stained and damp with condensation, the only illumination, a weak pale light that eked from a small window high on the wall and fitted with glass as stained and grimy as the rest of the cell. A grey hair flock mattress lay on wooden planks raised from the floor on horizontal piles, on which were placed two blankets, a bar of carbolic soap and a towel. A small cabinet in one corner supported an enamel bowl beside which stood a pitcher of cold water. Inside the cabinet she found what she took to be a piss pot; larger than the chamber pots they had at home, smaller than a bucket. Barely twelve feet by six, this stark room she coldly realised was now her domain, all that she would know in the coming months. She could only hope that the silence pressing down on her at this moment would be shredded in the morning by her encounters with other inmates.

Still shivering, she sat on the edge of the bed, drew her knees up towards her chest and wrapped her arms around them, resting her chin on her knees.

And waited in the gathering darkness.

She must have dozed again because the sharp sound of a grill in the doorway being opened awoke her with a start. It was snapped shut again almost immediately, and it was another five minutes before she heard activity outside her cell. A key rattled in the doorway, which was flung open to reveal a buxom, fleshy woman, dressed in heavy woollen clothing over which she wore a black apron; a female jailer, carrying a lamp in one hand, a tray in the other and a bundle of material tucked under her arms.

'Fucking good-for-nothing idiot,' the woman swore harshly, which Mary Ellen took to be her new visitor's appraisal of her, until, placing the lamp on the cabinet top, she went on, 'What kind of a moron leaves yer sitting around soaked to the skin?' She gestured over her shoulder with a thumb, 'That kind of good-for-nothing idiot. If he had a brain, he'd be dangerous.'

Placing the tray and the bundle of clothing on the bed, she gestured to Mary Ellen to stand up. 'Get out of those clothes; you'll be dead of a chill before we even get to know you.'

Mary Ellen thought she detected a note of humour in what she'd said, but it failed to register on the woman's careworn face which spoke only of concern. She did as she was bade and stripped naked, slipping the coarse woollen shift the woman was holding out to her, over her head.

The woman nodded towards the tray. 'Bread and a bowl o' stirabout. Tastes like shit, but it's 'ot. Get it down you. Pinch your nose if you can't stand the smell. You were later than we expected, so there's nowt else 'til mornin'.'

Mary Ellen nodded her understanding.

The woman regarded her sternly, folding her arms across her ample bosom. She shook her head slowly and spoke words that shook Mary Ellen to the core. 'Don't know much about what you've done, but we've orders to keep you in solitary. No visitors, no mixing with the other bad bastards in this place, though you might come to think that's no bad thing, 'cept you won't get the chance to find out. Bloody 'arsh if you ask me. Someb'dy, somewhere's taken a real dislike to you. Solitary's s'posed to give you time to be penitent, to seek redemption, but I'm buggered if I've ever seen anything good come from solitary. Then again,' she went on, 'you have a choice. You can go mad in here, on your own, with your own thoughts, or you can go mad picking oakum with a room full of society's dregs. Either way yer end up mad. An' yer don't want that. Whatever yer've done to get yersel' in 'ere's none o' my business, I don't care, meaning it does me no good to know, but you seem a decent enough lass. Six months'll be gone in no time. Just won't bloody seem it.'

She flapped podgy hands as if washing them of her disapproval. 'Anyway, like I'm sayin', b'ain't none 'o my business. Cross me, and I'll give you bother. Be'ave yersel' and we'll get on fine. I've a job to do, and that's to keep yer in 'er Majesty's custody fer six months, but there's nowt says I can't be half-way civil. Guvnor's a Christian man, believes you can all be saved from yersel's wi' a bit of civility…and the words o' the "Good Book".' She paused for breath, 'Anyway I'm not 'ere all day. Watch yersel'…' she gestured with her head towards the cell door, '…when that bastard's on duty, afternoons mostly, he likes to watch the ladies pissing. Gets off on it. So, if it ain't dark when yer need to piss, move the pot close to the door so's 'e' can't see yer. Now, eat that shit, 'fore it goes cold,' she said, pointing to the bowl of gruel.

And with that she picked up the lamp, turned and left, slamming the cell door shut, and closing the hatch.

Mary Ellen picked up one of the blankets and wrapped it round her for warmth, then turned to the bowl of stirabout, the light now almost gone from the cell. The woman was right; it tasted gruesome, but slowly it brought warmth to her. When she finished, she lay on the hard bed. So, this was it. Twenty-two weeks, one hundred and fifty-four days, locked away in a cell barely bigger than a coffin.

She might as well be dead. She couldn't survive this, the monotony, the tedium, the endless days ticking slowly by. What had she done to deserve this? She hadn't stolen the sugar tongues. So, why was she here? She was innocent.

Not guilty.

It had all happened so quickly. She had no use for silver bloody sugar tongues and didn't know anyone who would have wanted to buy them from her when it would have been obvious where they came from; they probably had the Garston crest on them. In any case, what she'd earned from Lord Cavendish and his photography meant she was, compared to many, well off. It didn't make sense. Why would she want to steal a stupid pair of sugar tongues and put everything in jeopardy?

More to the point, why would Joseph betray her as he seemed to have done?

No answers to her questions filtered into her dismal cell, and as the little window turned black, she fell into a restless sleep, bone weary from the arduous journey and the cold soaking.

In the morning, she awoke feeling sweaty and nauseous, swung her legs from the bed and vomited into the chamber pot she now had to use to piss in. She had never been sick in her life before. Ever. It was not an experience she wished to repeat, the acrid stench filling her cell.

She lay back on the bed, and moaned, clasping her hands to her stomach, and gazing with unseeing eyes at the cobwebbed ceiling. Why keep her in a cell on her own, for six months? It was inhuman. The woman was right; she would go mad. And, she was lucid enough to realise, her experience wasn't going to be that of six months of living in confinement, but one day – the same day – a hundred and fifty-four times.

Deprived of the oxygen of contact, the busy-ness of the daily Garston round, the sense of purpose it gave, she must surely die.

The days passed slowly and monotonously, the only routine – beyond the visits of the jailer she now knew to be called Mrs Murcheson and the accompanied visits to the jakes where she emptied her pot – was that she imposed on herself. She had no way of measuring time, and knew only dawn and dusk, but she fortified herself with an iron determination not to give in to her plight, and had taken to pacing her cell, resolved not to let her body become crooked and bent through inactivity. So, ten times each day, she rose from her bed, and walked up and down the tiny room, counting to one hundred and then repeating the process another four times. Then she would rest until she was ready to start again.

It was all she had to do.

That and worry. But worry would get her nowhere.

As she prepared to get up and start once more, she became aware that something was happening inside her body, she was sure of it. She swung her legs to the floor, and placed her hands on her stomach, realising to her discomfort that in the eight weeks she had calculated it had been since Lord Cavendish had had sex with her, she had twice missed her periods. The first time, she put down to the drama of the change in her circumstances, but after missing her period for a second time she knew she was pregnant. She had thrown caution to the wind when Lord Cavendish had taken her to his bed, and now his seed had sprouted inside her. She was having his baby; a new life was forming inside her. There was little evidence yet – her stomach didn't dome – but there was the nausea that had plagued her first weeks in prison. And the missed flowerings. And while her breasts were no larger. They had become tender to the touch.

She didn't know for sure; nor was there anyone she could ask, but, if she was right, it would only be a matter of time before she was showing.

She was having a baby.

In prison.

The only saving grace, she thought optimistically, was that she would be released by the time the child was born.

Wouldn't she?

Quickly she calculated the months, deciding, as much by guesswork and reasoning as anything else that, yes, she would be free.

But she was in Wakefield.

Wherever Wakefield was. A day's long journey in a horse and cart; an impossible trek on foot, and with no idea of where she would be heading.

How would she be able to journey back to her family, heavily pregnant, and undernourished from the poor prison food?

The answer when it came, took her by surprise.

The door to her cell clanged open, a fresh-faced Mrs Murcheson beckoned her to leave.

She smiled at her, placing a hand on her shoulder. 'You 'ave a guardian angel, my dear. You're free to go; you've been pardoned.'

'But...' Mary Ellen began in amazement, hastily stepping clear of her cell against the temptation that it might still claw her back.

''Ow? What?'

Mrs Murcheson put a finger to her lips, then pointed to the huge wooden door, inset with a smaller wooden door, that marked the exit to the outside world.

'Bugger off, afore they change their mind.'

As she walked away from the prison, turning to Mrs Murcheson briefly and thanking her for her unwarranted kindness, she saw a familiar figure; the last person Mary Ellen expected to see standing before her.

'Mary Ellen,' Lord Cavendish said, hurrying towards her, arms outstretched, 'I'm so sorry about all this. I had no idea.'

Mary Ellen felt faint and thought she was about to collapse. Gently he took her by the arm and wrapped a heavy cloak he'd brought around her as he led her to a waiting horse-drawn hackney cab, a far cry from the carriage that had brought her to this dismal place.

As they journeyed to the railway station for the train that would take them to Leeds and on to Manchester and Wigan, he explained, 'I only found out what had happened two days ago when I returned from London.' His face screwed into one of distaste, 'It was all the doing of that godforsaken grandmother of mine. She got her maid to plant the sugar tongues in your room and then coerced your Joseph into finding them and reporting the so-called theft to Mrs Bonnivale. Then they prevailed on the magistrates' court – father being the most recent chairman, not that he really knew what was going on, his head's all over the place with business matters – to ensure you were sent as far away as possible, and, I gather, placed in solitary confinement. That couldn't have been very pleasant.'

Mary Ellen took his hand in hers. 'None of it was pleasant, but you saved me. It's over now, isn't it? You came to rescue me.'

'When I explained to Father what had happened, he was outraged. Said he'd been hoodwinked, and immediately ordered your release. I got here as quickly as I could. I'm only sorry that it took so long, but I've been away. Oh, yes, selling your photographs, and getting you fifteen proposals of marriage.' He laughed to lighten the moment. 'All of which I rejected, of course. On your behalf.'

'Oh,' she began, more light-hearted than she had felt for some weeks, 'couldn't you not 'ave accepted just one?' Finally, she was starting to accept that her release was for real.

'You only need one,' Lord Cavendish went on, 'and that's your Joseph. He took a great risk in coming to tell me what had happened and confessed to being forced to commit perjury in court against you. Perhaps, when you're back home, you can look on him in a more favourable light.'

'Maybe,' she said hesitantly.

'Well, if I've remembered what you told me, you fell out because he'd had sex with your friend.'

Mary Ellen nodded mutely.

'Well, these things happen. I've had sex with lots of people, and you still love me,' he said playfully, nudging her in the ribs, and laughing lightly to pass off the pleasantry.

Mary Ellen bridled theatrically, and smiled at him, meeting his eyes. 'What makes you think I love you?' When he failed to respond, she went on, 'Anyway, I have good reason to.' She patted her stomach. 'I'm having your baby.'

Chapter 70

Duncan and Alice could scarcely believe their good fortune not only in finding Mary Ellen's decorated box, but at the prospect of discovering what lay within it.

'Whatever's in there,' Duncan said, tapping the box, 'this calls for a celebration. I don't know about you, but I'm almost too afraid to open it, in case we're disappointed.'

Alice smiled at him lovingly. 'Well, you're the one who hugs prehistoric rocks to commune with the past.'

Duncan started to protest, but Alice went on, 'This actually belonged to Mary Ellen; she touched it; she held it; put in it whatever was important to her. This is not a connection with some arbitrary, unknown group of prehistoric people, but of one, very specific individual…to whom I'm related. It's a bit like coming across a book signed by the author.'

'How so?'

'Well, unlike all the other books – printed in some factory in China most likely – you *know* the author has actually handled the books that are signed. Mary Ellen has touched this box, caressed it I wouldn't doubt, it's such a lovely thing. In a way, I don't care if we never open it. Just knowing that it's travelled safely through a hundred-and-fifty years to be here, now, is amazing.'

'But you do want to know what's inside, don't you.'

Alice rubber her hands together excitedly. 'Can't wait.'

Duncan produced a grubby cardboard box filled with a random assortment of items from broken pens, bundles of wire and string, paper clips, electrical gadgets she had no idea about, and a small, red, tin Oxo box, which he opened to reveal a collection of keys.

Alice leaned forward and kissed him. 'You find a key; I'll find a bottle of something fizzy.'

They had returned to Brimstone Cottage, to which Alice was now a regular visitor as much as Duncan was to White Coppice, the pair having decided that two idyllic cottages in lovely settings was better than one…for now and moved unpredictably between living in one and then the other, whichever was most convenient.

Duncan, before Alice had first stayed at the cottage, in a defining expression of self-intent had redecorated what had been his and Isabel's bedroom, and even bought a new mattress and sheets for the bed. He wasn't sure what had prompted the action. It certainly wasn't rooted in a desire to erase Isabel's presence from the cottage; in fact, Alice insisted that he did no such thing. So, he didn't tell her what he'd done, but when they first made love there – *after* they'd made love – he had found a sense of comfort in the notion that he hadn't betrayed Isabel by taking another woman to *her* bed. A psychiatrist, he'd reflected obliquely, would probably have found something disturbingly profound in his motives, such as they were. But he felt it was the right thing to do, and, though it wasn't the case, Alice had not seemed disturbed by the idea that she might be sleeping in another woman's bed, making love in *her* bed. During the denouement of her own marriage, she had been tormented by the idea that her own husband might have slept with…*her*…in their bed. But he'd assured her they hadn't. And she chose to believe him. For her own peace of mind.

'Veuve Clicquot will have to do,' Alice announced cheerfully, returning from the kitchen clutching a bottle and two champagne flutes. 'You don't seem to have anything better.' She sighed theatrically as she sat beside him, 'I can't keep slumming it like this, you know. What's wrong with Moët?'

'You mean, as enjoyed by Scarlet Johansson? Sadly, I don't have her money. So, you'll have to make do with Veuve Clicquot until I become rich…which isn't going to happen any time soon.'

Alice laughed sweetly. 'Well, at least I've got something Scarlet Johansson doesn't have.'

Duncan looked up puzzled.

'You.'

They both laughed. 'Sadly,' Duncan began, 'I can't help feeling she'd prefer the champagne.'

'Her loss,' Alice chimed. 'Now, what's in this box?'

Duncan returned his attention to the box, and rummaged through his assortment of keys, rejecting several before finding one that fitted. Holding his breath, he turned the key, meeting resistance, moving the key slightly and suddenly feeling it engage the mechanism, which, with a muffled click, sprung open.

'Wait,' Alice said, getting to her feet. 'Sandy said not to touch anything with our hands. We need those gloves we bought.'

Be-gloved, Duncan lifted the lid and peered at its contents: a collection of letters, a small prayer book and a silver locket on a chain. He inspected the letters, passing each in turn to Alice.

'These are all postmarked "Bath Somerset" and addressed to Mary Ellen at Penny Lodge.'

'None of them is open. They've never been read,' Alice said. 'Why on earth would she not read so many – how many? Twenty – letters spanning, what,' she checked through the postmark dates, 'almost a year?'

'We'll never know, without opening at least one of them.'

'Let's do that,' Alice ventured.

Duncan hesitated.

'Is something the matter?'

Duncan sat back and sipped champagne. 'I'm not sure. I need to think for a moment.' He leaned forward again, placing the champagne flute out of harm's way, and tapped the letters with a gloved finger. 'There's a story in there; inside those letters. It must be part of Mary Ellen's story. Do *we* have the right to open them?'

'Well, it's not like opening a pharaoh's tomb, is it? And if we do open them, are we not keeping Mary Ellen's story alive? I know it was serendipity, but that box has found its way to us for a reason.' She paused. 'But I know what you mean.'

'It isn't only that,' Duncan went on. 'With my not-very-experienced philatelist's head on, I can't help feeling they'll have more value unopened. Keeps an air of mystery.'

Alice nudged him in the ribs. 'That's never stopped you opening a vintage bottle of wine.'

'No, but I've never had to face this kind of dilemma until now. And I don't know what's right; what a historian or archivist might say.'

'Well, I'm a historian, of sorts, and an archivist. Also of sorts.'

'And what do you think? Should we open them?'

'Well,' she began thoughtfully, 'we've gone much deeper into the life of Mary Ellen than I originally intended. Certainly much further than I thought possible. I just wanted to know who she was. You've already unearthed quite a bit about her and her family. So, from that point of view, it seems reasonable to continue trying to learn about her.'

'And if we did open them, do we open all of them?'

'There's no need to do that,' Alice airily suggested. 'If, as you suggest, they contain elements of Mary Ellen's story, then by opening the chronologically first dated of them we discover the start of that story.'

'And then open the last in the sequence, to see how the story panned out.'

'Exactly.'

Duncan sipped his champagne again and held out his glass to be filled again. 'Even so, can I suggest that, for a moment, we do nothing with them? I need my mind to settle on a course of action that I'm easy with. Trust me on this; it's a genealogist's thing. If we just leave them, maybe only for half an hour, we might have a better sense of the right thing to do. Once we open them, the damage is done.'

'Agreed,' Alice said, reaching into the box and extracting the locket. She was by now well accustomed to Duncan's unusual take on things. It was what made him good at what he did. 'And this seems equally fascinating.'

'Open it,' Duncan said. 'I don't feel quite so bad about opening a locket. We know they had photography in those days, so it's probably just a couple of pictures, and that could help fill gaps in our knowledge.'

Alice examined the locket carefully, and teased open the catch, placing the opened locket on the table in front of them. Inside lay two tiny scrolls of paper each tied with a thread of cotton, one pink, one blue. From the ends of each protruded strands of hair, one dark brown, the other unmistakably ginger. As they turned the scrolls in their fingers, they saw that the one tied with pink cotton, contained the brown hair, and the letters 'ME' had been written in now faded pencil on it. The other, its solitary letter even more faded, "C", contained the ginger hair.

'Well,' Duncan began, picking up the scroll with the ginger hair, 'it may be a long shot, but I'm starting to see where your red hair came from.'

'Oh, my goodness,' Alice said, holding a hand to her mouth as a thought crossed her mind, and tentatively looking towards the bookcase in Duncan's living room. 'Do you have that book I found a few weeks ago about the history of Garston Hall?'

'Yes. Why?' he asked getting to his feet to go in search of the book.

'Everything in the book was in black and white, except for one picture that had been tinted,' Alice said to his retreating figure. 'If I'm not mistaken, one person in a family group photograph had ginger hair. I just can't remember who it was.'

Duncan returned with the book and flipped through the pages. 'Easy enough to find out.' He stopped at a page towards the end of the book. 'Here it is. Bloody hell. Sorry.'

Alice looked at the picture and ran her finger along the caption beneath it. 'Lord Cavendish Garston. He's our ginger nut, isn't he?'

'It certainly looks that way. But why...?'

'Why would his hair be found in a locket among Mary Ellen's belongings, along with strands of hair rolled up in paper with her initials on it?'

'Good question.' Duncan suddenly became business-like. 'Well, we know from those postcards you found that Mary Ellen was portrayed as a "Cavendish Beauty" and here we have what we can reasonably assume are locks of her hair and, possibly, if it's not stretching credibility too far, locks of Lord Cavendish's hair, too. Why that should be? I've no idea, but these need to go into sealable packets, and we need to get them to Sandy as soon as we can.'

'And what about the letters?'

'Yes, I still can't make my mind up about those.'

'I suppose it comes down to value versus intrigue.'

'That's my take on it, too. But bear with me...' He picked up his mobile phone and scrolled through the contacts, explaining, 'I've been contemplating selling Isabel's stamp collection. I don't 'do' stamps myself, and I've been in touch with a couple of dealers to get some idea of the worth of the collection. Maybe this one...' he punched "Dial", 'can persuade us one way or another.'

In the event, the outcome was inconclusive. The letters, the dealer had told him, had value opened or unopened. If they were opened and gave some insight into the culture of the time, that was one thing. There was always a market for social history. If they were simply love letters, they said much less. The fact that they went from Somerset to Lancashire had a certain intrinsic value to a collector of postal history; not many letters flowed between those two counties. But that didn't make them rare enough to command high values. What did, thought

Duncan getting to his feet and leaving the room, was something altogether different; something only a philatelist would know, or someone who'd taken an interest in the collection of an enthusiastic philatelist.

When he returned, he held a small Lupe magnifying glass, and with it inspected each of the letters in turn. They all bore red-orange stamps of the era with perforated edges and letters of the alphabet in each of the four corners. As he checked each of them, he put one to the side, and continued with the others. Then he returned to the one he'd put aside, and checked it again, walking to the window to get better light.

'Is something the matter?' Alice asked.

'I'm not well up on philately, but this...' he waved the letter in the air, 'is getting me just a little bit excited. In fact, I can feel the hairs on the back of my neck standing up.'

'What's so special about that one? They all look the same to me.'

His hand trembling, he handed the letter to Alice, suddenly thankful that they were still wearing gloves, and pointed to the stamp on the letter.

'Stamps like these – Penny Reds, they're called – were generally mass produced, but never in huge quantities. So, there were many printings. To indicate which printing was used, numbers were inscribed into the design of the stamps, hidden inside the wavy lines in the margin. I won't say what the numbers might be, because I don't want to influence you. But use this...' he handed her the Lupe, 'and tell me what number you see on this particular stamp. It will be in both margins. Sideways on.'

Alice took the letter and the magnifying glass and walked to the window. When she returned, she said, 'To my eyes, the numbers look like seventy-seven.'

'To my eyes, too.'

'And that's significant because...?'

'Well, I know this much, because that particular plate number is missing from Isabel's collection, and I asked her why.' He took the letter up again and checked the stamp a further time.

'This stamp comes from printing seventy-seven, or plate seventy-seven, as they're called. This plate was never meant to exist. The stamps were created, but never sold by post offices because they were not thought to be of good enough quality. The original printing plate was destroyed, but a few stamps found their way into circulation, and this...' he pointed to the letter, 'is a plate seventy-seven penny red.'

'So, I'm guessing by the animated state of your face – you've gone bright red, by the way – that this is valuable.'

'Let me show you.' He left the room again, and returned a moment later carrying a book. He flipped through the book until he found the page he wanted and showed it to Alice. 'The figure against plate seventy-seven is Stanley Gibbon's valuation of one of these stamps. This catalogue is a bit out of date, but you'll get the idea.'

Alice's face turned white, and for the first time in a long time her ladylike demeanour slipped, and she swore aloud. 'Fuck me.'

Duncan smiled at her and patted her arm. 'Later, darling, be patient.'

'Six hundred thousand pounds? For one grubby little stamp?'

'One sold about ten years ago to an Australian collector, for over half a million sterling, and another more recently for just under that. You've got yourself a pot of money there, sweetheart.'

Alice smiled broadly and theatrically placed a hand on her heart and looked coy, 'Oh, I could never part with it. It has such sentimental value; it's part of my family's heritage. It has far more than monetary value.'

'Bollocks.'

'Quite. How do we sell it?'

Chapter 71

Slowly, she opened her eyes to a darkened room and a pair of hands bright with blood. Filled with the sound of a high-pitched squeal, the room was revolving. She could not explain the blood and the piercing noise, or the dimly lit room. Then through the pain of blood pounding in her head, she realised the noise was herself, screaming as her body struggled to eject the child that had grown inside her.

The feeling was like nothing she'd ever experienced; a tensing of muscles, a curious pulsing and then a surging throb of intense pain. She was distantly aware of something dry and cool being placed on her forehead; of a voice murmuring words that failed to register their meaning; of shadowy figures moving to and fro in solemn silence.

Pain. Intense pain. Surging, easing, surging again.

She spat an obscenity at whoever, or whatever, was causing the pain, thinking, *I must be dying. Is this what it is like to die? Am I already dead?*

Forgive me, Father, for I have sinned.

The room continued to revolve, but a transient burst of comprehension, a flash of clarity, muscled through her confusion, made sense of the dark, spinning room and the bloodied hands.

I'm having a baby; I am giving birth to my child.

To his *child.* Our *child.*

But what is wrong? Why is there so much pain?

And blood?

The pain crashed over her in waves, growing more intense; she felt she was being torn apart. The room toppled, righted itself, then slipped sideways again; the atmosphere swithering from chill blast to airless heat. She felt tears rolling down her face, her lips quivered uncontrollably for it was suddenly too much, the pain, the fear…the sensation of Nature taking its burning course.

Murmuring voices again; comforting, reassuring, confident. 'When you feel the urge to push, you just do so.'

She felt warm hands between her legs, dry cloth stroking her thighs, and then another surge of pain.

A quiet voice: 'It's crowning. Won't be long now.'

With a prolonged flourish of pain she finally felt something slither between her legs: wet, hot, slippery. Then a dark head of hair, plastered in cream-grey slime, a confusion of tiny, curled limbs.

And silence. And a relaxing slide back into the comfort of oblivion.

'Where's my baby?' she demanded plaintively, regaining awareness. 'Give me my baby.' She could hear the blurred words hovering above her but failed to locate their source.

A man dressed in black appeared above her weary form, a crucifix of gold hanging at his chest, a black book in his hands. His face brooding, his brow furrowed, his eyes dark…and disapproving, devoid of light and compassion. His lips were moving as he read from the book, the words coming and going: 'Trusting in Jesus, the loving Saviour, who gathered children…we now commend this infant… May the…saints lead him to the place of light and peace… *In nomine Patris, et Filii, et Spiritus sancti.*'

She slipped briefly once more into an empty darkness. And awoke again to a gentle, soothing voice.

'I'm sorry. We did all we could. I'm so sorry.'

Beyond the immediate circle of light, a man wearing a gown stained with blood grimaced awkwardly. A pinch-faced woman dressed in black, leaning on a cane, looked on from the shadows by the doorway silently cursing the abomination against God that had almost entered the world.

Mercifully, *God has worked his ways*, she thought sourly, her expression a shrivelled prune of distaste and disapproval. *A blessing in disguise.*

The voice went on. 'We need to retrieve your placenta. We must get it out soon. I'm so sorry…about your son. We did everything we could to save him.'

In a glowing moment of lucidity, realisation dawned, and she heard herself howl her grief at the ceiling. A long and terrible wail rooted in despair and the pulses of pain that still agitated her drained body.

How could this be?
Where was he *when she needed him?*

295

As they fussed between her legs, she screamed her misery again, long and despairingly loud, into the room where the child she had borne for nine months had come lifeless into the world.

Weighed down by remorse she segued into nothingness, into a dark, welcoming void impervious to pain. She surfaced at intervals from her darkness to see sunlight and then moonlight filtering through the curtained windows, the room dark, lit by candles, perfumed with incense. Dark figures hovered around her, flitted about the room, cooling her brow, soothing, calming.

For three days she endured the agonies of her desolation, waking only to sip the broth someone brought, too weakened to resist.

On the fourth day, she awoke as if from a dream, awareness more profound than she had known since childhood. The events of the recent days slowly assembled themselves in her mind and fashioned a realisation too miserable to accept, too powerful to resist.

She screamed.

And screamed.

And screamed.

In howls of pain-wracked hopelessness, she screamed her remorse…until she died.

Chapter 72

When Alice and Duncan next met Sandy Glen – a meeting they'd anticipated with a mix of trepidation and relish – it was to hand over the items they hoped would allow enough DNA to be gathered to establish Alice's familial link to Mary Ellen. They were confident of the relationship, on paper, but DNA had a way of forestalling all argument.

Mary Ellen's locket had been sealed in a bag, along with a flat cap Alice knew had belonged to her great grandfather – Mary Ellen's fatherless son – and had somehow survived intact. The bible, which they deduced had belonged to Mary Ellen's mother went in there, too. In the box of items passed to Alice from her father following his death, she found a pipe, one she knew he loved to puff away at, clouds of pale blue smoke filling the room whenever he did. All that remained was for Sandy to take a swab of Alice's DNA, for which she had come prepared.

'I can't make any promises,' Sandy said, packing the items in her briefcase, 'but I'll get my best pupil on to it. She's so punctilious it makes me wince with pride. Just wish she could do things a bit more quickly. But I'd rather have things done right than rushed.'

'I couldn't agree more,' Alice said mischievously, patting Duncan's arm affectionately, the oblique inference of Alice's remark not registering in Duncan's mind until they were well on their way home.

'So,' he began, realising what she'd been alluding to, 'you're not into spontaneity, then.'

'Penny dropped, has it?' Alice teased. 'You know the answer to that perfectly well. Now drive faster.'

'But that's not spontaneous.'

'Maybe not, but there's a lot to be said for anticipation, too.'

They never got to find out. As they drove, Duncan's phone pinged, and Alice read a text message from Geoff Parry:

Found something else you will want to see. Home all afternoon.

Their plans swerved as they changed course and headed for Arch Lane.

'It looks like it's a collection of diaries.' Geoff Parry had been waiting for them and opened the door as they approached. 'I found them even deeper in that hiding place than I'd looked previously. It had a false bottom. They seem to relate to Mary Ellen's time as a housemaid at Garston Hall, though from what I could see, they are not continuous. There are several gaps between the entries, and one whole volume, for want of a better description, is missing. But, even so, I'm guessing what remains will be rather germane to your research.'

Duncan took the diaries, homemade, loosely bound into book form with sewing thread, scrappy sheafs of paper, old menu sheets by the look of them. 'You have no idea how invaluable these could be. Even if there are gaps, there'll be plenty to tell us that we would otherwise have no way of knowing. These are priceless. I can't thank you enough.'

As they drove home, Duncan said, 'Have you any idea how often documents like this, relating to the lives of *ordinary* people, ever make it to the present day?'

'From your question, I'm guessing it's not often.'

'You are *so* right. Big country estates like Garston have registers, accounts ledgers, Steward's records, even mentions in newspapers. Farmers, the landed gentry, too. But the ordinary person...well, for a start, a lot of them couldn't write. Clearly there's more to Mary Ellen than I'd imagined.'

Until they were safely home, and wearing gloves, the diaries had been placed in a plastic bag, which Alice now nursed on her knee.

They spread the diaries on Alice's dining table and examined their contents.

'They begin in eighteen-seventy, when Mary Ellen had been working as a housemaid at Garston for some time, a few months, anyway.' Duncan was turning the pages slowly, but speed reading their contents.

Alice worked her way through them more methodically, placing them in chronological order. 'She had a remarkably neat hand for someone who was...what? Just fifteen at the time. Her spelling and grammar would be the envy of many much older than her.'

'You can't imagine how exciting it is to read such clear handwriting. In my business, I can waste days just trying to decipher the script of the day. It was my weakest subject when I was studying at Strathclyde. This is such a joy.'

'But it just seems to be a record of the work she'd done each day, or fairly inconsequential events about the family. Nothing that tells us much,' Alice suggested.

Duncan nodded his agreement. 'What they *do* tell us is firstly that she worked at Garston Hall from the beginning of eighteen-seventy or thereabouts; that she lived in at the hall, but seems to have had Sunday afternoons off, when she usually,' he flipped through several pages, checking the entries, 'but not always went to the family home in Arch Lane.'

Alice chuckled. 'She didn't spend all her free time with her family.' She, too, turning backwards and forward through several pages. 'She seems to have had a boyfriend called Joseph, because here...' she pointed to Mary Ellen's entry for the day which showed a large heart shaped outline in the centre of which she'd written "Fucked Joseph" and below which she'd neatly penned "No longer a virgin".

'Well,' Duncan chuckled, 'she's clearly not one for mincing her words. But she could never have imagined that anyone would ever read her notes. But what do you make of these hieroglyphics?' pointing to the seemingly random appearances of a cross within a circle. 'Was she religious, do you think? Although a cross within a circle is a bit pagan.'

Alice flipped through the pages again, a few times, and said, 'Not in the sense you mean. If I had to suggest something, I'd say they marked the start of her monthly cycle, her periods. Clever girl.'

'Why would she need to do that?' Duncan asked, aware that he could be venturing into an aspect of femininity the details of which he preferred not to know anything about.

'Well, I'm guessing she'd want to be prepared. To know in advance when she was...you know...coming on. There were none of the solutions to the monthly issue women take for granted these days.'

'As you say, clever girl.'

Alice looked contemplative for a moment, then went back to the entry about losing her virginity, and ticked days off on her fingers. 'There's another interpretation, and if I'm right, then Mary Ellen was an exceptionally clever young lady. It may be coincidence, but somehow, she seems to have known that having sex was safer at certain times of the month than others. She hasn't recorded that she was sexually active with this Joseph, or anyone else, during the part of the month when she would have been ovulating. Shame on me for thinking she might have been promiscuous. But there are several entries where she clearly has been with Joseph.'

'We've no way of knowing what went on at Garston, of course, but I know from background reading I did for my PhD that domestic staff in households often formed liaisons, even though they were forbidden. This could well have been the case at Garston. Certainly she got it together with this Joseph. So, I wonder if he's the one who sent her all those letters. Maybe it's time we got round to taking a look.'

Alice and Duncan had decided on a course of inaction with regard to whether or not to open Mary Ellen's letters, acknowledging that once they did open them, there was no going back. But as Alice scanned the pages of the diaries, she found another entry that caught her attention.'

'Ah,' she said. 'I wonder if this might prompt us to reconsider our decision to leave the letters unopened for the time being?'

She had found the entry that related to Mary Ellen finding Joseph having sex with someone – another maid, presumably – by the name of Elizabeth. And another that spoke of 'the bastards' having left with the family for Somerset.

Duncan hugged Alice and cleared his throat. 'I think maybe it's time to have a peak into one or two of those letters, don't you think?'

Their self-imposed dilemma over the wisdom of opening and reading the letters in the end was assuaged by what they found in just two: the first and the last. In the first, Joseph was ardently pleading for forgiveness, his untidy, almost juvenile, looping handwriting filling the sheets of paper, so obviously begging Mary Ellen to take him back, to forgive what he'd done. In the last, the theme was the same, and from that Duncan and Alice deduced that nothing had changed, presumably because, from the evidence before them, Mary Ellen had not read the letters. The lad had been begging forgiveness for more than a year. Unanswered. Unforgiven.

With a pasta bake they worked their way through a bottle of Puligny Montrachet, later opening a second – for good measure – as they curled up in front of the fire.

Duncan was reflective, mellow and deeply in love with the woman in his arms. 'Those diaries,' he said, 'tell us so much. But there's a couple of omissions, as I see it.'

'That and the fact we're no nearer knowing who the mysterious father was.'

'True, but I am starting to get a feel for that, and I'm hoping Sandy's DNA profiling will provide the answer. But, no, there's the question of the photographs of Mary Ellen and the "Six Honest Serving Men".

Alice sat up. 'The six what?'

Duncan smiled, and kissed her. 'Ironically, given what I do for a living, it's the only bit of history I remember from my school days. It was a saying written on the wall in the history classroom: 'I keep six honest serving men; they taught me all I knew; their names are what? And why? And when? And how? And where? And who?'

'And that helps us how?'

'We need to answer those six questions, if we can, about Mary Ellen and the photographs. We need to see if there's anything in the diaries that gives us a clue.'

'And we need to see if we can find anything that tells us why Mary Ellen was in prison. You said you found an unhelpful entry for Wakefield prison, but maybe the diaries will shed light on that.'

Alice stood up.

Duncan looked up at her, a questioning expression on his face. 'You want to do that now?'

Alice beamed at him mischievously. Slowly, she unzipped her skirt, letting it fall to the floor, and started to unfasten the blouse she'd been wearing. 'No,' she said, 'I want to do something else. Time to be spontaneous; it's taken us all day.'

Chapter 73

She opened her eyes to a world she did not recognise and rough hands streaked with blood, a circle of women and shadows. The sound of a high-pitched scream filled the room. She could not explain the blood or the piercing noise – or for the moment the dimly lit room, although its features she was slowly beginning to recognise: the four-poster bed, the ornate fireplace, the window seats glimpsed through half-closed heavy and ornate brocade curtains. Then through the ache pulsating in her head, she realised the screaming was coming from herself, her body forcibly ejecting the child within her.

Something dry and cool touched her forehead, someone murmured words of encouragement, shadowy figures moved to and fro.

Pain. Searing pain. Surging, easing, rising again.

She mouthed an obscenity at whatever, whoever was causing the pain, as an outburst of lucidity brought realisation to bear.

I'm having a baby. Fuck. I am giving birth…to my child.

To his *child.*

Our *child.*

So, why does it feel like I'm being ripped apart?

Who are these people? What am I doing in *this* room?

Beyond the theatre of light, a figure, dressed in black, stood in the shadows, watching as the midwives did their work. She rested gnarled, arthritic hands on a walking stick, her walnut face a mask of revulsion and hatred.

'Won't be long now. It's on its way. Keen to get into the world, this one.'

A cool hand on her brow; warm hands between her thighs, and one long hard push that spat a new life into the world in a surge of relief.

'A boy,' someone whispered.

'Hissht, ye,' a voice remonstrated harshly.

'His name is John,' she said pleadingly. 'Let me hold him.'

A firm voice: 'We need to help him to breathe a little better. Just relax.'

Unable, unwilling to fight the fatigue, she lapsed into a fitful sleep, lost in the comfort of rich sheets of Egyptian cotton, a warming blanket of wool, a familiar, lingering smell of sandalwood, and filtering sunlight.

She was a mother now.

Time passed. Then, sombrely they returned, carrying the swaddled child to its mother. Raised now on pillows, she peeled away the layers of clothing and took her baby to her breast, which he nuzzled and sucked instinctively, greedily slurping, his mother's milk trickling chin-wards. It was like nothing she'd imagined, this first cradling of a child that had grown inside her, kicking, tumbling, restless in her womb, impatient to be born. He was brightly pink, his red hair unmistakable, his skin wrinkled, crumpled, and he was hungry. She lightly stroked his head, brushing strands of greasy, unmistakeably red hair from his eyes – a shock; she thought babies were born bald – tracing the line of golden eyebrows and marvelling at the distinctiveness of his blond eyelashes. She smelt his new-born baby smell, breathing in the iron-sharp smell of drying blood and the lingering scent of a cleansing lotion used to remove the worst of the goo that had enveloped him. His nose wrinkled as he fed, a tiny hand with miniscule fingers clasping her breast possessively; his eyes tightly clenched; his brow furrowed in concentration.

'Hello, you,' she said softly, touching the tip of his nose with her finger.

He was so small, yet so perfect; beautiful. She couldn't get enough of this tiny, scrunched up scrap of vulnerable humanity. She leaned down to kiss his forehead, causing her nipple to slip from his mouth.

'Waaaaaa-ah,' he wailed his instant disapproval until she cradled his head and returned him gently to her breast.

'Is he alright?' she heard herself ask, a worried tone catching her voice.

A soothing response confirmed that he was, and two women dressed in grey smocks over which they wore white aprons brought a cradle to the side of her bed.

As the feeding slowed and then stopped, the child slipped from her breast, milky residue lingering in the corners of his mouth, and fell into an instant and contented asleep. His breath settled into a steady rhythm, tiny snuffles, as if he was learning the scent of her so that he'd know her again, as dogs learn the scent of humans. She traced the curve of his tiny face, touched the fledgling eyebrows lightly afraid that she might wake him. Tentatively, she stroked the top of his head, soft and unformed, and, her eyes starting to close, suddenly became aware of how tired she was feeling. Taking the sleeping child from her, one of the birthing women placed him gently to rest in the cot beside her.

'Get some peace,' one of them murmured, a gentle hand on her brow, helpful hands re-arranging the birthing gown she had worn. 'Try to sleep.'

When she awoke, her child mewling in his cradle, *he* was there, perched beside her on the bed, holding her hand, a look of mild surprise on his face.

She started as uncertainly she took in the stern face of aristocracy, relaxing only as the face erupted into a wide smile and a countenance she had come to know.

'There you are,' he said softly. 'And there *he* is. You did well, they told me. Like shelling peas, they said. A natural mother.'

She smiled at him. 'I don't understand. They took him from me. Said he wasn't breathing.'

He stood abruptly to his feet and briefly turned to the window in an effort to conceal the anger swelling in his eyes. 'Don't dwell on that now. You need to rebuild your strength.'

'I need to know what happened. I thought he was dead.'

He was yet to be drawn. 'As you can see, he's far from dead. Quite a lively little beast, in fact.'

'But why would they take him away?'

Lord Cavendish squirmed uncomfortably; she was not going to relent.

'They lied,' he conceded reluctantly. 'The conniving bastards lied, and they'll rue the day. Mark my words; mark my words. I'll piss on that witch's grave.'

'But I don't understand.'

'I'm not sure you'll want to understand,' he said evasively.

But he told her, nonetheless, of what he'd discovered; of the macabre twist of fate Providence had woven. How, given the proximity of birth dates, the horrified Lady Makerfield had realised they could foist off Clarissa's incestuous, *damned-for-all-eternity* child onto Mary Ellen, and give her child in its place. That there was no evident father for either child other than Lady Clarissa's brother seemed not at first to have crossed her ladyship's mind, so concerned was she at the stigma of an incest-born child, if that was what *it* was, finding a place in the Garston household.

The midwives, sworn to secrecy on pain of dismissal, were unenthusiastic if not wholly innocent accomplices. Mercifully, Clarissa's child lived only briefly, just long enough to be baptised and named Edward. And yet they decided to adhere to the plan; to give Mary Ellen's child to Clarissa, to lie to its mother that it had died. Most families faced with a similar predicament – unique as it was – would have cast both children adrift, into adoption by locals willing to give them a home, few as they were likely to be, in return for paid, benevolent silence; or a foundling hospital at best, the crowded and unsanitary conditions of the workhouse at worst.

Lady Makerfield, he told her, had long ago observed Joseph and herself returning to the hall early one morning and, deducing what they'd been up to, had taken exception to the liaison, vowing to break the pair apart, a ploy that was brought into play when Joseph was sent with the family when they left for Somerset, and Mary Ellen left at Garston. When, to her horror, Lady Makerfield learned that Mary Ellen was pregnant with Lord Cavendish's child, she further swore on all that she held sacred that she would not be allowed to keep such a scandalous creature, a future, grasping hostage to fortune.

If necessary, she would end its life.

'She's a bitter and twisted old witch,' Lord Cavendish hissed. 'Thankfully, the Almighty had other ideas. There was no place in Heaven for Edward, or, I confess I'm greatly saddened to say, for the mother that bore him.'

'He died?' she asked, slowly grasping what he was saying.

He nodded grimly; his lips pursed. 'Not only that. When you were giving birth a few days later, Clarissa awoke to the reality of what had happened. It was too much for her. She died; she just screamed and screamed until her heart exploded. *Fatigue* they said. Lying rogues, the lot of them.'

Understanding settled uneasily in Mary Ellen's mind, leaving her gasping with incredulity. 'So, they were still going to give my baby to Lady Clarissa, and – what – tell me mine had died?'

He nodded his confirmation, his face a mask of distaste. 'Well, first they were going to pass off Clarissa's baby as yours. Swap the two, and leaving you to bring up a baby that, as it turned out, was deformed.'

'Fuck,' she spat, turning to the cradle, anxiously regarding the sleeping child. 'He is mine, isn't he?'

'And mine,' he nodded. 'Poor little sod having me as a father.'

Mary Ellen looked up at him, a speculative glint in her eye. 'You'll make a wonderful father,' she ventured warily.

Lord Cavendish detected her unasked question. 'No, Mary Ellen. I'm sure you must realise that I can never be acknowledged as the father…it wouldn't be…'

Her face was ashen, suddenly downcast. 'You're going to abandon me? And our baby?' she asked, sudden fear and trepidation raising the pitch of her voice.

'No, no, Mary Ellen,' he soothed. 'I'll not abandon. Well, not exactly. You'll be taken care of, Mary Ellen. You and *our* baby. I won't abandon you. But you must understand that *we* could never be parents to – John, you named him? – outside these walls. Not in the conventional sense. I will provide for you both, generously, of course, until such time as you marry someone who can care for you fittingly. I've already made it clear that you and your family are to stay in one of the cottages for as long as you need to, without the need to pay a rent, and you won't ever want for anything, ever again…or go to prison, again.'

They both laughed at that, but Mary Ellen was at a loss for words. It was too much to take in. Too much to contemplate. But relieved that for the family, at least, there was the continued certainty of a roof over their heads.

'Oh,' he went on, 'anyone you do decide to marry, must meet with my approval. I won't have my child, *our* child descending into poverty.'

Mary Ellen was still far too fatigued to grasp the import of what he was saying. She had long known that her childhood dream of marrying this man and living in the luxury of Garston Hall was just that, a dream, a fantasy. But given the way their relationship had altered over the last year, a part of her had optimistically hoped that the fact of carrying and giving birth to his child might in some way alter that.

But, of course, it never could. She saw that now.

Worn out from her exertions, she leaned wearily back against her pillows and half raised a hand as if trying to grasp something she knew to be beyond her reach. Lord Cavendish stood to leave, pulling the bedsheets over her body. Turning, he stooped to pick up a package he'd placed on a bedside table and presented it to her.

'This is for you. I'll have it engraved for you.'

He was holding a beautiful rose wood casket with ornate inlays in gold. It was the most beautifully crafted object Mary Ellen had ever seen. Her mouth gaped in silence.

'It was my sister's, Clarissa's,' Lord Cavendish explained. 'She told me several months ago that she wanted you to have it. You must have…connected with her in some way. I think she knew that you and she were both carrying…you know…my…'

'Child? Children.'

'Yes. I suppose it was her way of reinforcing the connection between you.' He shrugged apologetically, 'I confess, I've never understood my sister. I loved her, of course, but she was rarely in the same realm as the rest of the world. So, who am I to judge her? I'm just sorry that I…'

He never finished his sentence. Instead, he took his leave, kissing Mary Ellen's forehead, as he had done so many times before.

'Get some rest. And don't be afraid. I'm away to put plans in place for your future, but I'll return shortly.'

As Mary Ellen drifted into a weary slumber, she thought, *That's twice now he'd come to her aid.*

Chapter 74

Alice was in contemplative mood, Ashkenazy tinkling his way through Bach's *French Suites* in the background, the volume at a level that prevented the music from intruding into her thoughts. She was thinking of Duncan, of how she'd come to love him, and how, once she was certain of that, she'd had to manoeuvre him to the relationship they now so enthusiastically enjoyed. They still lived in separate cottages, for now, but were rarely apart, and seldom wanted to be. It meant two toothbrushes, two of everything in fact, but that was small consequence, of little importance. She always felt she was with him, even when they were inevitably apart, that he was always there, part of her being. It was an exquisite feeling, a loving, sharing companionship in which they both moved in unison, in harmony, in understanding one another without the need to articulate thoughts and feelings. With Duncan, she felt whole. When they made love, it was always tender, sensitive and caring, though not without passion when passion was called for. He was a considerate lover, not given to routine, no stranger to impromptu sex in the most unlikely places. No, she wouldn't go there, not now; just remembering some of the moments, the places they had made love was inconveniently arousing an appetite he had revitalised. Yet, she reflected, he was in many ways repressed, and she had several times shown him ways of pleasing her she was sure were new to him. It was hardly surprising, she knew. He and Isabel had been together since school days; they'd known no one else, so it was understandable that there would be aspects of lovemaking that had eluded them. Of course, she could be wrong, but without imposing a sexual routine, void of the thrill of spontaneity, she had helped him to a better understanding certainly of what she needed, and, she was sure, of what he needed too.

As she thought of him, she became emotional as the magnitude of the change to her life bore down on her. She was so happy, contented, wholly at ease, the memories of her former life like ripples in the sand, washed away into oblivion by the tide.

The music came to an end, and she stood up to turn off the player, heading into her bedroom to prepare for the day. Today, they were returning to meet Sandy Glen, to see what magic she had performed with the DNA samples they'd provided. The idea tingled her spine, causing the fine hairs on her neck to rise. Today would be confirmed what she, in herself, already knew. She couldn't wait.

Dressed in a soft, flowing, low-cut dress accentuating her figure and falling to just above her knees, Alice headed for the door as she heard Duncan's car pull up.

He kissed her gently and stood back to admire at her. Only one thought crossed his mind.

'No,' Alice said, placing her index finger on his lips, 'we don't have time.'

'Well,' Sandy began, opening her briefcase and extracting a sheaf of papers along with the several plastic bags in which Duncan and Alice had supplied her with items for testing, 'this proved rather interesting. My pupil loved the challenge, and, as I think I mentioned, she is OTT painstaking.'

'I would have thought a pre-requisite in your profession,' Duncan ventured affably.

'Indeed it is, and I shouldn't really moan about her taking her time. You can't rush these things; she's just methodically slow in everything she does.' Sandy laughed lightly and pulled a face, 'and watching her eat a pie is not a thing of beauty, I have to say.'

Alice chuckled, 'Is there a beautiful way to eat a pie?'

'No, I think not,' Sandy went on. 'Anyway...what we've found. Where shall I begin.'

'At the end,' suggested Alice. 'Is Mary Ellen my great, great grandmother?'

Turning to Duncan, Sandy smiled openly, 'Keen one you've got here, Duncan.'

It was Duncan's turn to smile. 'You don't know the half of it. But I wouldn't have her any other way.'

Sandy picked up her notes. 'Yes,' she said emphatically. 'We got what we needed from the strands of hair in the locket to get a match with your DNA. Mary Ellen is...was...your great-great-grandmother.'

She turned to another sheet of paper, 'and from a hair we found in the cap you gave me, we found the same DNA profile. The pipe was less forthcoming; all rather dried up, I'm afraid. But, unless there's been an imposter in your life all these years, masquerading as your father, then it's a reasonable conclusion that the man you knew as your father was indeed your biological father. For it to have been otherwise requires a genealogical sleuth, and I've no idea where you'd get one of those.'

They all laughed, and Alice said, 'On eBay, do you think? Maybe not.'

They were amused by the idea, but Alice was shaking. The link had been proven, and that was more than she'd hoped for, much more. That's what happens, she thought happily, when you surround yourself with clever people. She regarded both of them in silent admiration.

'Did you have any joy with the red hair?' Duncan asked. 'I'm expecting that to prove interesting, if you did.'

Sandy beamed at him. 'You're not wrong there, Duncan. There is a clear DNA link from your "red-haired man" to Alice, "Ginger Tom" as my student took to calling him. Whoever he was, he was definitely your great-great-grandfather. But I've no way of knowing who he was.'

Duncan visibly relaxed. 'We have our own theory on that.' And he explained about the inscription on Mary Ellen's box, the tinted photograph of Lord Cavendish, the photographs they'd found of Mary Ellen depicted as a "Cavendish Beauty" and the letter "C" written on the paper wrapped around the hair.

Sandy sat upright. 'A scallywag, eh? So, I could be in the presence of nobility. I'm honoured.'

'I can't see it myself,' Alice commented, 'but I suppose you must be right. If Lord Cavendish really was the biological father of my great grandfather, the child in the picture, then, yes, I suppose I am.'

'Blue blood, eh?' quipped Duncan.

Alice shook her head. 'I can assure you my blood is quite red. But I'm guessing all this is what they call circumstantial.'

Duncan and Sandy both agreed. 'Strongly circumstantial, but circumstantial, nonetheless.'

As they drove home in brilliant sunshine, Alice said, 'I suppose that's as far as we can go. We might *think* Lord Cavendish fathered Mary Ellen's child, but we've no way of proving it.'

'And if we could prove it, we'd only be tempted to do it all again, with Mary Ellen's second illegitimate child, Alice, born seven years later.'

Duncan nodded. 'I doubt very much that we'd get the same good fortune a second time as we did this. Just imagine the odds against finding those pictures when we went to York, then being handed Mary Ellen's own box and diaries.'

'Did you finish reading the diaries?' Alice wondered. 'It would be nice to think that if Lord Cavendish was responsible for that erotica, that Mary Ellen was not coerced into it, or the apparent sexual encounter that seems to have followed.'

'Yes, I did finish the diaries, and now you mention it, you've reminded me of something. Do you mind if we head for my place?'

'Not if you're cooking dinner. But why? Not that I mind, of course.'

Once back at Brimstone Cottage, Duncan opened up his laptop and scanned through his notes. Then he retrieved Mary Ellen's diaries and turned the pages. Towards the end he pointed to an entry.

'I thought this was a bit cryptic, so I did some digging. It wasn't conclusive, and I'd forgotten it until now. Towards the end of the diaries, the entries are fewer and chronologically spaced.'

Alice studied the entry Duncan was referring to. It was dated 1873 but without a day or month. In fact, there were two entries, written on separate pages. The first read:

C's baby died

The second,

C passed away.

Duncan scrolled through his laptop notes until he found the page he was looking for.

'We don't know who "C" is. It could, of course, be Lord Cavendish, but he had a sister, younger than himself, Lady Clarissa.'

'Or it could be someone completely unrelated.'

'Exactly. But I did some more digging. Both entries seem to date from around the time Mary Ellen was giving birth to your great grandfather. Sometime in eighteen seventy-three. In fact, there seems to have been a plethora of Garston deaths around then: Lady Garston died in the same year, followed only a month later by the so-called Lady Makerfield, though I've never been able to confirm that there was such a legitimate title. There's nothing in *Burke' Peerage*. On top of that, I found a record indicating that Lord Cavendish died in eighteen-ninety-one, in Somerset. So, C, whoever C is, wasn't Lord Cavendish. If Lady Clarissa died in the same year as her mother and grandmother, that would have been quite a bad year for the family.'

'Understatement of the year I would say,' Alice interjected.

'Quite. I found death records for all three, though I haven't bothered getting copies of the death certificates. We don't need to know what they died of, do we?'

'I wouldn't have thought so. But we could always go back to that if we needed to, can't we?'

'Of course, but...' again he scrolled through his digital files, 'I found that someone else had written an account of the history of Garston Hall in which there are some curious references. One was a reference to the fact that the family abandoned Garston and moved to live in Somerset, though by then there were precious few of the family left, just his Lordship and his son. So, Garston would have been far too big for them. I also found a reference to the contents of the hall being auctioned off in eighteen ninety for around nine thousand pounds, although I can only find specific reference to two items: A Stoke Minton table service that went for fifteen guineas, and a Copeland China breakfast service that sold for just a little more. If those were typical, then to get up to nine thousand pounds in all, the hall must have been stuffed with antiques, paintings and the like.'

'And where are they all now?'

'A fair point. There was a note that when the hall was demolished, they found a muniment chest in one of the outbuildings and this was mentioned in the journals of one of the archaeological associations. There is an index card in what was Garston library, thankfully now all digitised, but there's no indication where the chest is now.'

Alice stood up and kissed him lightly on the forehead. 'Let me make some coffee. Your poor little brain must be working overtime.'

'I just don't like it when I can't square off the ends.'

When Alice re-appeared clutching mugs of coffee he went on, 'I also found a mention, which...' he tutted, tapping at his laptop, 'I can't find now. It implied that the daughter of the household, Lady Clarissa, was something of a recluse. Never left her rooms; never entertained once she was beyond her teenage years. Several of the family appeared in photographs in newspapers opening some fair or other, standing with preening politicians, but never Lady Clarissa.'

'So, how did she become pregnant?' Alice paused in her train of thought. 'You don't think...?'

'I don't know what to think. But what was it, Sherlock Holmes said?'

'When you rule out the impossible, then what remains, however improbable, must be the truth, or words to that effect.'

Duncan sipped his coffee. 'Oh, I don't like the sound of this.'

'But, if what we're thinking *was* true, that might explain a stillborn child. I don't know. I'm not up on these things.'

'If what we're thinking was true, then something very tragic happened to that entire family in eighteen seventy-three. Something they never got over. Shame probably being the least of it.'

Alice sat beside him and took his hand. 'I'm almost sorry I started this, now. We should have let sleeping dogs lie.'

'You weren't to know. *I* wasn't to now. That's the thing about genealogy, it often uncovers unpalatable truths and realities.'

'And some of that tragedy lives on in me, I suppose. And I'm the end of the line. That's a sobering thought I'd prefer not to dwell on.'

'Indeed you are, my love, so I think we owe it to Mary Ellen to keep that line going as long as we can.'

Alice looked startled. 'Woah…you're not thinking babies, I hope.'

'Not at all. I was just thinking I need to take very great care of you.'

'Well, you're doing okay so far. And, by the way, there was some post I picked up when we came in. You never know, you may have a long-lost aunt who's left you a fortune in her will.'

Duncan collected the post, putting aside the obvious bank statements and rubbish, opening only a single envelope.'

'Bloody hell,' he said loudly, and showed Alice the letter, who turned to the bookcases where rows of albums had once stood. Now, she noticed, the space was filled with historical books.

'You sold Isabel's stamp collection.'

'I did. I knew she'd bought well, the auctioneer said as much, but this…' he took the letter from Alice's hands '…this was far more than I imaged.'

'What was it?' Alice asked, looking at the letter again. 'Ninety-seven thousand, three hundred and fifty pounds.'

Duncan was already on his feet, opening a bank statement he'd put aside. 'And it's already in the bank.'

'Not exactly a long-lost aunt, eh? More a long-lost love. I think we should drink to Isabel. I never met her, but I'm sure I'd have got on with her.'

'Oh, I can tell you,' Duncan said ruefully, 'the two of you would have been as thick as thieves. I wouldn't have stood a chance.'

Chapter 75

Lord Cavendish rarely saw his father; such had been the story of his childhood, his adolescence and early years of maturity. To the young man his father was some vague personage who provided a home and wealth for them but having sired two children saw no need for familial involvement with them. When he *was* present, on rare occasions, he was a formidable figure both physically and, in his demeanour, yet he had always managed to stay aloof of the mechanics of family life, even when cloistered in the smaller family home in Somerset the family gathered in for several months of the year.

Cavendish had never seen his parents in other than the most fleeting of intimate moments, an occasional peck on the cheek or an almost symbolic embrace as if to re-affirm their relationship. When he himself was coming to terms with the sexual side of his adolescence, frequently using his innate charm to beguile servants into submission, he wondered if his parents ever had intercourse. It was not a vision he found appealing; it was not a vision he could even imagine. That it had happened at least twice was evident from the presence of himself and his sister, but that it was an ongoing activity he found hard to believe, not least because only a few months after Clarissa was born, they took to separate rooms. In darker moments he wondered if he might have been adopted, a circumstance fuelled by his shock of red hair that by all accounts was not a family trait for as many generations as anyone could recall. Increasingly, as his mother spent less time with his father and more with visiting gentry who found her beauty irresistible, it only served to undermine his confidence because he grew ever more certain that his genetic relationship to his father was tenuous, if it existed at all.

That his father might not be the man who had raised him required that he believed that the infidelity his mother had openly displayed during the last ten years of his life had been a feature of it before his birth. He didn't want to believe that and chose to doubt it. He loved his mother, passionately at times. She aroused in him an affection that was at odds with the scant love she had shown him, and which became less over the years, both parents leaving him to fend for himself once he had outgrown his guardians and tutors. The absence of overt affection had made him insular and self-determined, and created a Narcissistic, dispassionate world in which he was at the centre. He often pondered whether his mother had distanced herself from him, leaving him to be raised by nurses and governesses, because she was trying to make him find his own way in life, because she wanted him away from his father's influence. But, if that was true, then *why*? His father was not an intolerant man, neither cruel nor impatient with either of his children. On the contrary, he had long been supportive of Cavendish, gave him a generous monthly allowance, paid the rent on an apartment in London for him in the belief that the capital was the place for a young man of aristocratic standing. Yet in recent years things changed. His mother's love was unconditional if not demonstrable, but his father came to see in him only disappointment.

So, it was with anxiety to the forefront of his mind that Cavendish responded to the butler's message that his father wanted to see him in his study. As Mr Grimes showed him in, Cavendish asked for a glass of brandy. He returned with it at the same moment his father entered from an adjacent room.

A tall and broad man, Lord Garston was never anything less than imposing in stature, though Cavendish knew nothing of his business acumen. His shock of grey hair flew back from his forehead in exuberant, natural waves, a marked contrast to the straight and often unmanageable hair of Cavendish, colour notwithstanding. As he approached his son, Lord Garston checked the time on a pocket watch secured to his waistcoat by a gold chain and without acknowledging his son's presence sat down in high-back leather chair. When, finally, he did look up, he motioned Cavendish to sit opposite him.

'Cavendish, how are you?'

'Fine,' he began uncertainly. 'I've been...' He was going to tell his father about the success of his photographic enterprise, but a hand raised sternly in front of him, cut short his response. There was a pause as his father rescued his coat tails from beneath him and looked to be determining how to reveal the reason, he had summoned his son, it wasn't to enquire about his health. His father had always been plainspoken, not given to beating around the bush, a characteristic not inherited by his son. Whatever purpose brought Cavendish here, it would be explained quickly, clearly and directly to the point.

It was, a moment later.

'Your mother's dying,' he said. 'It won't be long. Leukaemia. Had it for some time apparently.' He shifted in his chair. 'Not that I knew until recently. Too late to do anything about it. Doubt you *can* do anything, anyway.'

It was the longest speech Cavendish had heard his father give, and it was not what he'd expected. He had been apprehensive and prepared to tell lies if it had been necessary. Now he was having to process a truth that was dreadful to take in.

And it was coming so soon after his beloved sister's death.

Why could it not have been that witch of a grandmother? He comforted himself in the knowledge that her day, too, would come. Soon, if there was any justice in Heaven.

'What?' Cavendish remarked inanely. His father wasn't given to repeating himself.

'She didn't want me to tell you. But with...Clarissa...well, I felt you should know.' 'Why didn't she want you to tell me?'

His father looked pensive for a moment. His thoughts in turmoil. It was one thing to live separate lives, to acknowledge the loss of some of the love he once shared with a young and very desirable woman; quite another to realise that the object of that affection was slipping away.

'She has been dogged by illness for some time. She didn't want you dogged by it too.'

'I must go to see her.'

'I'm not sure she'll appreciate that. But you're right. You must go. But just now the nurse is with her. She'll be asleep.'

'When then?' he asked, enveloped in a wave of conflicting emotions that threatened his well-being.

'Leave it for an hour or so. I'd better go, as soon as she's awake, and tell her that I've informed you. I'll get Grimes to come and find you. Stay in your rooms.'

Cavendish nodded mutely and drank from the glass of brandy Grimes had brought earlier.

As his father rose to leave, he turned to his son. 'What happened...about...that...unfortunate...that...' he waved his arms as if floundering in a tidal wave, trying to fish the words he wanted from fresh air, 'that...child. *Clarissa's* child.'

Cavendish couldn't help noticing the stress his father had placed on the child being that of his sister, and a vagueness about what had actually happened.

Even though he was the father.
Nor did he seem to be aware of Mary Ellen's child.

Cavendish pondered the truth, the whole truth and nothing but the truth. Instead, he told a blatant lie, 'We found a wet nurse for him. Some...unfortunate, whose own child was stillborn.'

His father seemed appeased at that. 'Be sure to provide for them. Properly, I say.'

Cavendish, on the other hand, regretted having told the lie. There'd been no need for it, except, perhaps, to save his father further grief, and he wasn't even sure why he'd done that.

Turning again to leave, Lord Garston stopped, and gestured with his arms at the room. 'Too large for those of us that are left. If...when...your mother dies, we'll close this place. Sell it. Move to Bath.'

Job done, Lord Garston harrumphed loudly as he left; Cavendish stood silently, taking in that parting shot. He lifted his drink with trembling hands, his legs straining to support him. With rising despair he drained the brandy and threw the empty glass into the fireplace, where it shattered loudly.

Chapter 76

Some months later…

Duncan had been away in London for more than two weeks, crossing swords with the National Archive receptionist and eating too much unhealthy food. He was desperate to see Alice, but for the past few days his mobile calls had been going to voicemail. Still weary from travelling, he drove to White Coppice and let himself in. The cottage felt cold, and silent. Alice was not there, and he started to panic. Where could she be? He tried her phone again. More voicemail.

A knock at the door.

'Duncan,' a voice called, 'is that you?'

He opened the door to see Alice's neighbour, Mary.

'I saw the light come on, and thought I'd check.'

'I've been away. I can't contact Alice. I'm worried for her.'

'She's fine. She's gone away. Insisted I didn't tell you. Said she wanted it to be a surprise.'

'Where? What? Surprise?'

'She told me if you turned up to tell you to go back to your cottage. She'd be in touch.'

'But…'

'I promised I wouldn't say anything, and I won't. There's nothing for you to worry about.'

It was a puzzled and even more weary Duncan that let himself back into Brimstone Cottage. He gathered up the mail he'd ignored earlier and placed it on the table. Out of habit, he fired up his desktop; it always took a while to update itself when he'd been away for any length of time.

He filled the kettle and rummaged in a cupboard for the emergency supply of Long Life Milk.

Coffee.

319

As he sat down, waiting for the heating to come on, his computer pinged. Incoming mail.

There was an email from Alice. It contained only a string of numbers, and had an attachment, which he opened. It was a photograph of Alice standing, if he wasn't mistaken – though he found it hard to image – in Alice Springs. In Australia. Not the town, Alice Springs, but the actual location, Alice Spring, close by the telegraph station. A message had been printed over the image:

Wish you were here. Love you, always. Alice.

She was dressed in an open-topped T-shirt and pale blue cotton shorts into the pockets of which she'd thrust her hands. A pair of sunglasses had been pushed up onto her head.

He went back to the email and studied the figures:

9781521010068-189

It took a moment for the penny to drop, but then he recognised an ISBN number, the numeric commercial book identifier. He had no way of knowing which book it was, so he logged into Amazon and entered the ISBN, minus the last three digits, which he realised were not part of the ISBN.

Down under Dreaming: Travels in Australia

He knew he had the book somewhere. It took a minute to find.

Eagerly, he turned to page 189 and found a slim envelope, and read the first sentence: *I'm standing in Alice Springs …*

Is that where Alice was?

Really?

Really?

He opened the envelope to find two airline wallets. Inside the first was an open-ended First-Class ticket with Singapore Airlines from Manchester to Perth in Western Australia, on a flight leaving two days hence. In the second envelope was a digital ticket for an onward flight with Qantas from Perth to Alice Springs.

Duncan sat at his computer and sent a reply to the email; it would be midmorning in Australia:

I love you, too. On my way.

He drained his coffee and set off to find a suitcase. He had some packing to do.

Later, gathering his thoughts as he luxuriated in his love for Alice, he leafed through the unopened mail. Among the letters was the latest copy of Gibbons *Stamp Monthly* a philatelic magazine to which Isabel subscribed, and which he had yet to cancel. The cover said it all:

Plate 77 Penny Red on Cover sells for a record price.

Epilogue

Lord Cavendish was true to his word, although Mary Ellen, her sisters and brothers had to leave Penny Lodge to make way for the new gamekeeper, he installed them in another cottage nearby. With a child to raise, she could not return to her duties as a housemaid, but he fabricated a position of "Washerwoman", and paid her a wage for that, more in fact, than he needed to. She never carried out any work as a washerwoman; it was simply his way of ensuring that the estate provided her with an income, as his father had unwittingly instructed him to do.

He also ensured that their child, John, wanted for nothing and visited his son frequently, always bearing gifts.

Shortly after the birth of John, Lord Cavendish decided to try his hand at the more complex aspect of photography, developing the film plates, and printing the images. In that he was not successful, but he was the one who had taken the badly-developed picture of Mary Ellen and John that had started Duncan and Alice's quest.

Lord Cavendish did, however, take more photographs of Mary Ellen to add to the collection he sold to acquaintances in London. It had been one of the later images that Alice had found at the York Collector's Fair, by the time the picture had been taken, his "Cavendish Beauty" business was flourishing, giving him, for the first time in his life, an independent wealth.

From a small advertisement in the *Ashton Advertiser*, Duncan saw that "Proprietor: Mary Ellen Liptrot" had set up a small laundry and washing business, which she called "Hey Presto".

Lady Garston and Lady Makerfield both died within a month of one another, in 1873, only months after Clarissa had died, and John Liptrot had been born. It was an eventful year at Garston Hall. Lord Garston, on his own save for a son who seldom seemed to be at the family home, sold Garston in 1889 and moved to Bath in Somerset, taking only a small group of household retainers. Two years later, Lord Cavendish died from an overdose of drugs, although the death certificate simply said "Exhaustion".

In 1881, Mary Ellen finally married Joseph Cunliffe, with whom she had five children. Mary Ellen's brothers, Henry and George, were both employed as coal miners in pits that had originally formed part of the Garston estate.

The father of John Liptrot's half sister, Alice, is still unknown. It could have been Lord Cavendish.

CPSIA information can be obtained
at www.ICGtesting.com
Printed in the USA
LVHW010103070721
692013LV00008B/420